Barefoot Season

SUSAN MALLERY

Barefoot Season

MIRA®

MIRA®

ISBN-13: 978-1-61793-912-9

BAREFOOT SEASON

Printed in U.S.A.

To the women who serve, leaving behind
home and hearth, friends and family.
This is for you, with gratitude, love and respect.

A special thank you to SGT Betty Thurman,
who willingly offered personal stories about
what it was like. Any mistakes in this novel are mine.

And to SPC Jeanette Blanco who read the book
for a "gut check." Many thanks for your comments
and insights. A Fool's Gold cheerleader high five!
You're the best.

One

"I'm going off to war tomorrow. I might not make it back."

Michelle Sanderson slowly pulled her attention from the five-year-old truck she was thinking of buying and focused it on the guy standing next to her.

He was a kid—maybe eighteen or nineteen, with red hair and freckles. Cute enough but way too young. Still stuck with too-long arms and legs and a chest that had yet to fill out. More man than boy, she supposed, but not yet done with the transition.

"I'm sorry," she said, sure she must have misunderstood. "What did you say?"

He gave her a wide grin and a wink. "I may not have long in this life. After you buy the truck, we could go get a drink or something. Celebrate me going into the army."

"It's two in the afternoon."

"Then we could head back to my place."

Michelle didn't know whether she should start laughing or tell him he was an idiot in terms that would make him cry like a little girl. The latter would be easy enough. She'd served ten years in the army, nearly half of them in either Iraq or Afghanistan. She'd had to deal with more than her share of horny young guys who assumed they were irresistible. She'd gotten really good at showing them they were wrong.

Laughing would be a bit tougher. Mostly because every part of her hurt. Not just her hip, which had the excuse of a recent run-in with a couple of bullets from armed insurgents, followed by a partial joint replacement, but the rest of her. She'd spent more time than she even wanted to think about in the hospital. Healing happened in its own time, her physical therapist had told her. She'd tried to beat the odds, which had netted her nothing more than an extra three nights in the hospital before she'd finally been released.

"Aren't I a little old for you?" she asked.

He gave her a wink. "Experienced."

Despite the pain, she managed a chuckle. "Yeah, right. Looking to have your fantasies fulfilled?"

"You know it."

He was so eager, she thought, feeling more weary by the second. And obviously he hadn't passed the vision test yet. She knew she wasn't at her best. Her pale, too-thin body gave away the length of time she'd been in a hospital bed. Her eyes were hollow, her color too gray to be considered normal. She had a cane to help her walk. Which just went to show how powerful a young man's hormones could be.

Before she could figure out how to pass on his invitation, a yellow Lab came bounding around the side of the house. The animal raced up to her and jumped. Michelle took a quick step back to avoid being knocked over. The movement put pressure on her hip and fiery pain shot through her.

For a second, the world spun. She felt herself starting

to black out. Nausea threatened. One or the other, she thought desperately, fighting to stay present. Not both. A surprisingly strong arm wrapped around her body, holding her in place.

"Buster, get down."

She blinked and the cool, damp afternoon returned to focus. The fire in her hip banked enough to allow her to breathe. The kid stood so close she could see the freckles across his nose and a small scar on his right cheek.

"You okay?" he asked.

She nodded.

He stepped back and studied her. The dog stayed back, his eyes dark with worry, a low whine indicating his concern.

She held out her hand to the dog. "It's okay, Buster. I'm fine."

The dog stepped forward and sniffed her fingers before giving them a quick lick.

"Hey, I wanted to do that," the kid said, managing a shaky laugh.

Michelle smiled. "Sorry. He's more my type."

"You're hurt."

She raised the cane slightly. "Did you think this was a fashion accessory?"

"I didn't notice it, really."

Which proved her theory about his poor vision. "Just a flesh wound." Actually flesh, bone and a few tendons, but why get into the details?

He looked from her to the army-issue duffels on the sidewalk, to the cane and then back into her eyes. "Were you there?" he asked.

"There" could have been a hundred places, but she knew what he meant. She nodded.

"Sweet. What was it like? Were you scared? Do you

think…?" He swallowed, then flushed. "Can I make it, you think?"

She wanted to tell him no. That staying home, being with his friends, going to college, would be so much easier. Safer. More comfortable. But the easy way often wasn't the best way, and for some, being a part of something meaningful was worth any price.

Her reasons for joining had been far less altruistic, but over time she'd been molded into a soldier. The trick was going to be figuring out how to find her way back.

"You'll be fine," she said, hoping she was telling the truth.

"A hero?" he asked with a grin, then slapped his hand against the truck. "Okay, you've done your best to confuse me by being sexy *and* a war vet. But I'm not going to be distracted. I want ten thousand. Not a penny less."

Sexy? That *did* make her laugh. At this stage in her life she would have trouble qualifying as a trophy girlfriend for a man pushing ninety. But hey, a compliment was always nice to hear.

She turned her attention to the truck. It was in decent shape, with relatively new tires and only a few dents. The mileage was low enough to allow her to get a few years out of the thing before she would have to start replacing parts.

"Ten's crazy high," she said. "I'm paying cash. I'm thinking closer to eight."

"Eight?" He clutched his hands to his chest. "You're killin' me. You really going to do that to a future hero?"

She chuckled. "Come on, kid. We'll take her for a drive and swing by a mechanic friend of mine. If he says the truck is good, I'll give you nine-five and you can call it a win."

"You've got a deal."

* * *

Two hours later, Michelle let the guy—Brandon—off at his place. A mechanic she knew on the base had given her the thumbs-up on the truck and she'd handed over an ordered stack of crisp bills. In return she'd collected paperwork and keys.

Now, as she pulled away from Brandon's house, she eyed the gray sky. She was back in western Washington state, where rain was so prevalent that a day of sunshine was the lead story on the local news. Leaving luggage in the open was taking a risk and she'd dropped her two duffels in the back. She decided the clouds looked more lazy than ominous. Her duffels should be safe enough on the drive home.

Home. It was a long way from where she'd spent the past ten years. Blackberry Island, an actual island in Puget Sound, connected to the mainland by a long bridge, might technically be within commuting distance of Seattle, but it was a world away. The single town on the island billed itself as the "New England of the West Coast." A selling point she'd never understood.

Quiet, touristy, with quaint stores and a slower pace of life, the island celebrated all things blackberry. There were silly traditions and a rhythm to the seasons that had always seemed annoyingly out of step. At least before. But what she once hadn't appreciated now seemed appealing to her.

She shifted on her seat, the pain in her hip as constant as ever. The physical therapists had sworn it would get better, that she was healing quicker than they'd expected. She was already bored with the recovery process—it took too damn long. But there was no rushing her body along.

She found her way to the main road, then onto the

freeway. She headed north, merging with the traffic. The number of cars surprised her. Their orderly progress. She was used to Hummers and assault vehicles, not SUVs and sports cars. The damp, cool air was also something she'd forgotten. She switched on the heater and wished she'd thought to pull out a jacket. It didn't matter that it was May. Seasons were for sissies. Summer came late to this part of the country. Fortunately, the tourists came early.

She knew what to expect over the next four months. Starting with Memorial Day and going through Labor Day, the island would be crawling with visitors. They came for the boating, the famous Puget Sound cranes and for the blackberries. Blackberry Island was the you-know-what capital of, well, the West Coast. Vacationers would crowd the restaurants, buying all sorts of knick-knacks and handmade items. And they would eat blackberries.

They would put fresh blackberries on their pancakes, in salads, on or in nearly every type of food known to man. They would purchase blackberry ice cream from vendors and blackberry cookies from kiosks. They would buy tea towels and mugs with blackberry motifs and taste the dubious results of the annual blackberry-chili cook-off. Best of all, they would fill every room in a fifty-mile radius. Including the rooms at the Blackberry Island Inn.

Michelle could practically hear the happy hum of the inn's bank balance filling. Like most businesses on the island, the inn made most of its annual income during those precious four months. The days would be long, the hours endless, the work backbreaking, but after being gone for so long, she was eager to dive back in. To return to the one place she could count on never to change.

* * *

"Is she here yet?"

Damaris asked the question from the doorway to Carly Williams's office.

Carly looked up from the welcome card she'd been making. Part of what the Blackberry Island Inn offered guests was personalized service. She found out about her guests before they arrived, then put a handmade welcome card in their room. The Banners, an older couple who had come to bird-watch and do some wine tasting, had mentioned how much they loved the water. Carly had made sure they were in a west-facing room and was creating a card that featured a photo of Blackberry Bay at sunset.

Bits of ribbon and lace were spread across her blotter. A glue stick sat upright, next to her battered tweezers. She absently rubbed at a tiny square of glitter on the back of her hand.

"She's not here," she told Damaris, then gave her a smile. "I said I'd let you know when she arrived."

Damaris sighed. Her glasses had drifted down her nose, giving her an absent air. More than one newly hired server had assumed her slightly scattered appearance meant that she wouldn't notice if an employee was late or didn't offer more coffee the second a sip was taken. All mistakes that were later regretted.

"I thought she'd be here by now," Damaris admitted. "I've missed her so much. It's been too long."

"It has," Carly murmured, not wanting to think about how her life would be altered when Michelle returned. Reminding herself that *she'd* been the injured party didn't stop her stomach from churning.

Everything was different now, she told herself. She was capable, and for the past three months she'd been the one running the inn. She was a valued asset to the inn. If only Michelle would see it that way.

Damaris moved into her office and took the chair on the other side of the desk.

"I still remember when she hired me," the fiftysomething cook said with a sigh. "She was what? Sixteen? I had children older than her. She sat right where you are. So scared. I could see she was shaking." Her lined mouth turned up in a smile. "She'd checked a book on interviewing out of the library. She'd tried to hide it under some papers, but I saw it."

The smile faded as the dark eyes narrowed. "Her mother should have been the one taking care of things, but it was never like that. Michelle loved this place."

Carly drew in a breath. She and Damaris had argued plenty of times about mother and daughter. Carly was willing to admit Brenda had her flaws, but she'd been the one who had rescued Carly. Given her a job and purpose. Carly owed her. As for Michelle...

"I hope she's happy with the changes," Carly said, by way of distraction. The band of tension around her chest was already tight enough that she had to consciously relax in order to draw in a full breath. She didn't need more stress in her life right now. "You've told her what we've done, haven't you?"

"I write her every month," Damaris said with a sniff. "Not that her mother ever did."

So much for diverting anyone, Carly thought. But she wasn't going to give up. "Your blackberry scones are so popular with the guests. I've been wondering about offering packages of them for sale on Sunday morning. So our guests could take some home with them. What do you think? Would it be too much work?"

Damaris relaxed in her chair. "I could bake more. It wouldn't be difficult."

"We could sell them in packages of four and eight. Use some of that decorative plastic wrap we bought."

Damaris already knew the cost of each scone, so calculating a price was easy enough. Carly wanted to include a recipe card with the scones, but knew better than to ask. Damaris protected her recipes the way tiger moms protected their cubs—with teeth, claws and intimidation.

"I'm going to check to see if she's here," Damaris said as she rose.

Carly nodded, then reluctantly followed her out of the office. Little about the inn would stay the same now—there was no way to deny it, although she'd give it her best effort. Brenda was gone and Michelle was back. That was enough to shift the dynamics, but there were also complications. Ten years away would change anyone, so Carly knew Michelle would be different. The question was, how different? People didn't always evolve in a positive way.

She paused in the hallway. Evolve in a positive way? Maybe she should stop checking self-help books out of the library for a few weeks and relax with a nice romance instead.

She walked to the front room and stepped behind the dark, raised, hand-carved desk that served as a reception area. Touching the familiar, worn surface relaxed her. She knew every scar, every stain. She knew the bottom left drawer got stuck when it rained and that the knob on the top right drawer was loose. She knew where the cleaning staff hid extra towels and which rooms were more likely to have plumbing problems. She could be blindfolded and walk into any room. Standing there in total darkness, she would be able to say where she was based on the scent, the feel of the light switch, the way the floor creaked when walked on.

For ten years, this inn had been her home and her refuge. The fact that Michelle could take it away from her with a flick of her wrist was beyond terrifying. That it would also be wrong didn't seem to matter. In the world of moral high ground, Carly feared she'd wandered into quicksand.

"There!" Damaris yelled, pointing out the window.

Carly glanced toward the freshly washed panes, seeing the sparkling glass and the white trim rather than the truck pulling up beyond. She focused on green grass and the explosion of daisies.

The flowers were her hobby, her passion. Where others noticed little beyond a variation on a theme, she saw Shasta daisies and gerberas. Broadway Lights, Gold Rush, daisy Golden Sundrops and, of course, the unique blackberry daisy. Daisies were a part of the very essence of the inn. They were featured in vases at the restaurant table. They danced across wallpaper, colored the murals and were embossed on the inn's notepaper. She'd kept the bright colors of her garden in mind when helping Brenda choose the new roof. Now the dark green composite shingles were the perfect backdrop, the color repeating in the shutters and the front door.

Damaris raced across the lawn, her white apron flapping like butterfly wings. The older woman held open her arms and embraced a woman much taller and thinner than Carly remembered. She watched, even though she didn't want to, listened, even though she couldn't hear.

Michelle straightened, grinned, then hugged the other woman again. Her hair was longer now. A dark tangle of waves and almost-curls. Her face had more angles, her eyes more shadows. She looked as if she'd been sick. Carly knew that she had, in fact, been injured. Michelle looked fragile, although Carly knew better than to trust appearances. Michelle wasn't the type to give in to weakness. She was more like the scary alien from the movies—the one that would never give up.

She and Michelle were practically the same age—Michelle older by only a couple of months. Back before anything had changed, Carly had known Michelle's face better than her own. She could account for every scar, telling the story of how it came to be.

There were three defining moments in her life—the day Carly's mother had left, the night she found out her best friend had slept with her fiancé and the morning Brenda had discovered her crying in the grocery store, unable to afford the quart of milk her obstetrician insisted she drink each day.

Separately, each of those moments barely added up to a quarter hour. A minute here, two minutes there. Yet each of them had shifted her life, rotating it and tossing it on the floor, breaking that which was precious and leaving her gasping for breath. Michelle had been a part of the fabric of her world—ripping it apart until there were only shreds left.

Carly drew in a breath and looked at the woman walking toward the inn. Once again she was dangling by a thread. Once again, Michelle would define her future and there wasn't a damn thing she could do about it. Unfairness caused her chest to tighten, but she consciously relaxed, telling herself she had survived worse. She would survive this.

The phone rang. Carly returned to the front desk to answer it.

"Blackberry Island Inn," she said in a clear, confident voice.

"Let me check that date," she continued, tapping on the computer keyboard. "Yes, we have rooms available."

As she took information, confirmed the arrival time and credit-card number, she was aware of Michelle moving closer. The hunter returned. Which left Carly wondering if she was going to be part of the celebration or simply her next prey.

Two

Knowing and seeing were not the same thing. Michelle stared at the front of the inn and knew the hits were going to keep on coming.

"It's so good to have you back," Damaris said, giving her another bone-crushing hug.

At least that was familiar, as was the other woman's scent of cinnamon and vanilla from the pastries she made each morning. But everything else was wrong. From the roof—a hideous green color—to the matching shutters. Even the shape of the structure had changed. The lines of the building where she'd grown up had shifted, growing out in a way that made the inn look stubby. As if it had a muffin top and needed to lay off the blackberry scones and go find a Zumba class.

To the left, where the restaurant had been, an extra room jutted out, slicing through the side lawn and razing the slope she'd rolled down as a kid. To the right, a garish, wartlike growth was stuck on the side—all bright colors and windows displaying the usual island crap. Dolls and lighthouses, wind chimes and dangling stained glass.

"There's a gift shop?" she asked, her voice more growl than question.

Damaris rolled her eyes. "Your mother's idea. Or maybe Carly's. I never listened when the two of them talked. They're like the birds. Making noise and not saying much."

Damaris's small, strong hands gripped her arms. "Don't worry about them. You're home now and that's all that matters." Her mouth tightened in concern. "You're too thin. Look at you. All bones."

"From being in the hospital," Michelle admitted. There was nothing like a painful rifle shot to kill the appetite.

Out of the corner of her eye, she caught the flutter of wings. They were there—the ever-present Puget Sound cranes circling the gray water of the Sound. The birds brought visitors and scientists. For some reason people found them interesting. Michelle had never been a fan. When she'd been eight, she'd spent a whole summer getting pooped on by the cranes. She wasn't sure if it was just bad luck or an avian conspiracy. Either way, she'd gone from a fairly neutral opinion to hating them. Time away hadn't lessened her desire to have them gone.

She returned her gaze to the inn and felt her gut lurch with disappointment. How could anyone have done this to the once-beautiful building? Even her mother should have known better.

She probably had, Michelle told herself. This was Carly's doing, she was sure of it.

"Come inside," Damaris said, moving toward the porch. "It's going to rain and I want to feed you."

The unrelated thoughts made Michelle slightly less uneasy. At least Damaris was the same—welcoming and loving, always needing to feed those around her. Michelle would hang on to that.

She walked haltingly next to the much shorter woman, knowing she should probably be using her cane but refusing to show weakness. Not when the situation felt so strange. And in her world, not knowing what came next meant she was in danger.

One of the thrilling results of multiple posts in Iraq and Afghanistan, she thought grimly. Along with nightmares, a hair-trigger temper and an attractive little tic that showed up under her left eye from time to time.

She'd foolishly allowed herself to believe that the second she saw the inn, she would be okay. That being home was enough. She'd known better, but still, the hope had lived. Now it shriveled up and died, leaving her with little more than the pain in her hip and a desperate longing to be ten years old again. Back when crawling onto her dad's lap and feeling his strong arms holding her tight made everything all right.

"Michelle?" Damaris's voice held concern.

"I'm okay," she lied, then smiled at the other woman. "Or if you don't believe that, how about I plan to be okay eventually? Can you live with that?"

"Only if you promise to eat."

"Until I burst."

Damaris's hair had gone a little gray and there were more wrinkles around her eyes, but other than that, she was as she had been. At least that was something. Michelle was still searching for a piece of her home that was recognizable. Even the gardens were different, she thought as she stopped to look at the yards of happy daisies waving in the slight breeze.

Their color exploded in a cheerful pattern, edging the lawn, creeping up toward the main building, sliding

around the side. They were all different, as if someone
had sought out the obscure, the most bold. Their bright-
ness seemed like a scream to her bruised senses and she
wanted to shield both her ears and her eyes.

The front-porch stairs brought her attention back to
the inn. She braced herself for the fire that would sear
her and the subsequent nausea and sweat.

She put her right foot on the first stair, then lifted her
left. Preparing for the flames didn't make them any less
hot. Pain tore through her, making her want to beg for
mercy or, at the very least, stop. With all the changes
they couldn't have put in a ramp?

By the time she made it to the top, she was coated
in cold, clammy sweat and her legs trembled. If she'd
eaten that morning, she would have vomited—an ele-
gant homecoming. Damaris watched her surreptitiously,
worry darkening her brown eyes.

"Is it your mother?" she asked, her voice quiet, as if
she didn't want to hear the answer. "I know the two of
you never got along, but still, she's dead. You can't blame
yourself for not making it back to the funeral."

"I don't," Michelle managed, the words forced out
through clenched teeth. Being shot was one of the best
excuses around.

A few more breaths and the pain faded enough to be
bearable. She was able to straighten without gasping.
Which allowed her to notice that the furniture on the
porch was new, as was the railing. Her mother had certainly been free with whatever profits the inn brought in.

"Hello, Michelle. Welcome home."

She swung her gaze to the wide double doors and saw
Carly standing on the threshold.

There were changes there, too. Short hair instead of
long. The same color of blond, the same dark blue eyes,

but now they were edged in subtle makeup. Less Goth, more ladies-who-lunch.

The simple black skirt and flats, the long-sleeved, pink shirt with a tiny ruffle on the cuffs, were perfectly professional for the inn. They made Michelle feel rough by comparison. She was aware of her baggy cargo pants—still the easiest things to pull on that weren't sweats. Her long-sleeved T-shirt had been to war and back and looked like it. She couldn't remember the last time she'd used mascara or moisturizer. Or had her hair cut by someone who'd actually studied to be a stylist.

By contrast Carly was pretty. Prettier than she remembered. Feminine.

Growing up, Michelle had been the beauty—with her long dark hair and big green eyes. Carly had been cute. The sidekick in the "who has the best smile" contest. Resentful of yet another change, Michelle wanted to turn away. To go back to…

Which was the issue. The inn was all she had and leaving wasn't an option.

Carly continued to smile, looking calm and in control. "We're so excited you're back." The smile faded. "I'm sorry about Brenda. She was a wonderful woman."

Michelle raised her eyebrows. There were many words to describe her late mother. *Wonderful* wasn't one of them.

More worrying, however, was the other woman's attitude. As if it were her place to welcome anyone. As if she belonged here.

"It's been a long time," Carly added. "I haven't seen you since…" She paused. "It's been a long time," she repeated.

The words, possibly impulsive, possibly planned, reminded Michelle of her last hours in this place. She supposed she should be embarrassed or guilty, that Carly expected an apology. Yet despite what she had done, Michelle found herself wanting Carly to apologize. As if Carly was the one who had done wrong.

They stared at each other for a long minute. Michelle fought memories. Good ones, she thought resentfully. She and Carly had spent thousands of hours together, had grown up together.

Screw that, she thought, pushing them away. She walked purposefully toward the door. As expected, Carly stepped aside to let her pass.

The inside was as changed as the outside. The cheerful curtains were new, as was the fireplace surround. The hardwood floor had been refinished, the walls painted, and there was a god-awful daisy mural in the hallway leading to the restaurant.

But the reception desk was the same, and that was what Michelle hung on to, mentally if not physically. As the room seemed to dip and swirl and shift, she understood that expecting nothing to change had been foolish. She had thought she would return to exactly what she'd left—minus her mother. That when she stepped into her home, it would be as if she'd never left. Never been to war.

"Are you all right?"

Carly reached for her as she spoke. As her arm moved, the light caught the gold charm bracelet on her wrist.

Michelle knew it intimately. As a child, she'd been mesmerized by the sparkly, moving bits of gold. As she grew, she'd learned the history behind each charm, had made up stories about the delicate starfish, the tiny high heel. The bracelet had been her mother's and it was one of the few good memories she had about the woman.

Now Carly wore it.

Michelle didn't want it but she sure as hell didn't want Carly to have it.

Anger bubbled and boiled like water spilled into a hot skillet. She wanted to grab Carly's delicate arm and rip off the chains of gold. She wanted to smash and take and hurt.

She drew in a breath like she'd been taught. While she wasn't a big believer in PTSD, she'd been told she suffered from it. So she'd listened to the counselors when they'd talked about avoiding stress and staying rested and eating well. She'd listened, then she'd picked and chosen what she thought would work for her.

She did the breathing because she couldn't pick an action and every part of her hurt. Then she limped away, each step burning, the soft tissue weeping in protest.

She went down the shorter hall on the right, turned a corner and stopped in front of an unmarked door. At last something that hadn't changed, she thought, touching the frame where small cuts marked how she'd grown. The cuts ended abruptly, not so much because she'd stopped getting taller, but because the man who had cared so much, the father who had loved her, had left.

She turned the door handle, needing to be inside. Needing to be where she could retreat and lick her wounds.

The door was locked. She tried again, then pounded her fist against the wood—the thuds sharp and determined.

The door opened, exposing a wide-eyed teenage girl.

"Oh, hi," the girl said, her freckled nose wrinkling slightly. "Sorry. The guest rooms are all upstairs. This is private."

"I know what this is," Michelle said, speaking for the first time since entering the inn.

"Who is it, Brittany?" a young girl called from the back of the apartment.

"I don't know." The teen turned back to the door, looking expectant, as if waiting for Michelle to leave.

Michelle wanted to make her way to her room, to fall on her bed and sleep. Because sleep, when she could find it, healed.

She pushed past the teen and stepped through the looking glass.

Nothing was as it was supposed to be. Not the walls or the rugs on the floor or the furniture. The tattered plaid sofa was gone and in its place was a tightly slipcovered couch in shades of blue. Daises were everywhere—in vases, on pillows and pictures. Even the curtains were a testament to the mocking flowers. Where there weren't daisies, there were blackberries.

She stared at the new chairs, the kitchen table she didn't recognize and the toys. A dollhouse in the corner. Stuffed animals and a stack of games on the wide windowsill.

A girl, maybe ten, stepped in front of Michelle. Her eyes were big and dark blue, her expression fearful. She had an iPod in her hand.

"Who are you?" she asked, then those big eyes widened. "I know," she breathed, and took a step away, nearly flinching as she moved. "You need to leave. You need to leave now!"

"Gabby!" the teen said, sounding shocked.

Michelle moved quickly, backing out of the room, ignoring the protesting agony wrapping itself around her hips and making her stumble. Everything was wrong. There was too much pain and the room was tilting. She couldn't breathe, didn't know where she was. It was as if she'd stepped on what she thought was solid ground and instead found herself falling.

She went as fast as she could, feeling the damage, knowing she would pay later and not caring. Back the way she'd come. In the entryway, Carly waited. Still perfect in her girly clothes and Brenda's bracelet. Michelle stopped in front of her.

"You're fired," she said, speaking clearly, despite the burning sensation in her hip.

Carly went pale. "What? You can't do that."

"I can. This inn is mine, remember? You're fired. Pack up and get out. I never want to see you again."

She passed Damaris, stumbled more than walked down the stairs and made her way to her truck. She nearly passed out from the pain of dragging her left leg inside, but made it, then started the engine and drove away.

Two sharp right turns later, she pulled to the side of the road and put the truck in Park. Harsh sobs squeezed out of her throat. Her hands shook and cold invaded down to her bones.

There were no tears—only the sounds and knowledge that just because she'd come home didn't mean she had anywhere to go.

Three

"The special tonight is a variation on chicken Marsala," Carly said, smiling at the older couple sitting by the window. "Mushrooms, fresh herbs and a Marsala cream sauce with rigatoni. It's one of my favorites."

The woman, her white hair piled on her head, smiled. "I'm not sure my waistline can handle that, but it sounds delicious."

Her husband nodded. "We brought our own wine. That's okay, isn't it?"

Carly looked at the bottle. A blackberry sticker sat on the top left corner of the label, which meant the bottle had been purchased in town.

"Of course," she told them. "There's no corkage fee. Would you like me to open your wine now and let it breathe?"

The husband grinned. "I don't know. That sounds pretty fancy."

"You're the one who picked the great wine. Why don't you let me open it? While you're deciding on dinner, I'll get the wineglasses and you can have a taste."

"Thank you." The woman patted her husband's hand.

"We're having a lovely time. This is our third visit here. We haven't been in a few years. You've made some wonderful changes."

"Thank you. I hope we won't have to wait so long for the pleasure of your company again."

She excused herself and retreated to the butler's pantry off to the side. After collecting wineglasses and an opener, she returned to the table and took care of the guests. Next she checked on the other three tables before heading for the kitchen to pick up salads.

So far no one had noticed anything was wrong. Or if they had, they hadn't commented, which was nearly as good. If she kept busy, she couldn't think, couldn't worry, couldn't panic.

She stepped into the bright, hot kitchen and found her salads were ready. She grabbed them and returned to the dining room.

The motions were easy, for which she was grateful. *Scattered* didn't begin to describe how she felt. *Terrified* was probably closer.

Fired. She couldn't be fired. This was home. She'd lived here for nearly ten years. She'd put her heart and soul into this place. She loved it. That had to count, right? Possession was nine-tenths of the law. Would gathering clichés help? Something had to. Michelle couldn't simply walk back in and fire her.

Only she could.

Fighting tears, Carly ducked back into the butler's pantry. The marble countertop was cool against her fingers. Marble she'd chosen, along with the cabinets, even the tables and chairs in the expanded restaurant.

She'd promised, Carly thought, hanging her head as her eyes burned. Brenda had promised that she would give Carly a share of the inn. Two percent a year until she owned half and they were equal partners. By rights Carly should now own nearly twenty percent of it. Only the inn hadn't been Brenda's to give.

All those years ago when Michelle had claimed her daddy had left the inn to her, Carly had assumed her friend was just saying what kids say. "This will be mine." Because Michelle lived there and worked there. But Michelle had been telling the truth and Brenda had lied and Carly had nowhere else to go.

She wiped her face and forced a smile before returning to her customers.

It was nearly seven-thirty by the time she escaped back to the owner's suite of the inn—the rooms where she and her daughter had lived since Gabby's birth. Rooms she'd made her own, rooms with memories.

Gabby was watching TV, but looked up and smiled when Carly entered. Brittany, her regular babysitter, quickly set down her iPhone. Gabby scrambled off the sofa and rushed to her.

"Mom."

She didn't say anything else, just hung on.

Carly hugged her back, knowing that like nearly every other mother on the planet, she would do anything for her child. Including protecting her from the truth—that they might be evicted from their home.

"How was your evening?" she asked, smoothing Gabby's blond hair off her face and staring into her blue eyes.

"Good. I beat Brittany on two puzzles on *Wheel of Fortune.*"

The teenager grinned. "See. All that spelling homework is helping."

Gabby wrinkled her nose. "I'd rather do math."

"Dinner was great," Brittany said, coming to her feet. "Thanks."

Carly had delivered the chicken Marsala pasta for them at five-thirty. She worked in the restaurant two nights a week, but at least was able to bring home dinner during her shift.

"I'm glad you enjoyed it."

"We did," Gabby said.

Brittany had already shrugged into her coat.

"Meeting Michael?" Carly asked, standing before walking the teen to the door.

The teenager smiled. "Yes. We're going bowling with friends."

"I should hear on the summer camp in the next couple of weeks," Carly said, catching her daughter's soft snort. Gabby wasn't a fan of summer camp, mostly because it involved getting outside and doing things like hiking and kayaking. Her daughter preferred to read or play on her computer.

"My summer classes are from eight to twelve." Brittany pulled her long, red braid out from her jacket. "So afternoons are good." She hesitated, then lowered her voice. "That was her? Michelle?"

Carly nodded.

"She's nothing like I expected. I didn't think she would be scary. Not that she did anything. It's just, I don't know…"

Carly's first instinct was to defend, which only went to prove one never outgrew being an idiot.

"She's not so bad," she said by way of compromise. Which was pretty big of her, considering she'd been fired.

"Okay. Have a good night."

Brittany left and Carly settled on the sofa. Her daughter curled up next to her, her head on Carly's shoulder.

"I don't like her," Gabby whispered. "Does she have to stay?"

Carly wanted to say she didn't like Michelle, either, but knew that would be a mistake. Doing the right thing was a pain in the ass, she thought, stroking her daughter's hair.

"Let's see how it goes before we make any judgments," she said lightly, ignoring a sense of impending doom.

"You always do that, Mom," Gabby said with a sigh. "Look at both sides. Sometimes don't you want to just be mad?"

"More than you'd think."

The reality was Michelle needed her. At least in the short term. Someone had to run the inn and, with Brenda gone, that left Carly. Michelle would need time to recover, to remember what it was like to work here. The firing had been impulsive. Words, not intentions.

It was like whistling in the dark, she thought, pulling her daughter close. Or not believing in ghosts, evidence be damned.

An hour and a half later, Carly kissed her daughter's forehead. "Sleep well," she murmured. "I love you."

"I love you, too, Mom."

The words were spoken in a sleepy tone. Gabby's eyes were already drifting closed. Even though her daughter had stopped asking for a good-night story years ago, she still liked being tucked in. She was nine, would be ten in the fall. How much longer until she started thinking of her mother as more of an annoyance than a friend?

Carly couldn't remember the age when she'd found everything her parents did either foolish or embarrassing.

At seventeen, she'd been desperate to be free of them. Funny how it had taken her mother running off for her to realize how much she needed her around. But it had been too late to say that, to find out the rest of what she needed to grow to be a woman.

She kissed Gabby again, silently promising never to abandon her child, no matter what, then stood. A night-light guided her along the familiar steps. For all Gabby's claims of growing independence, her daughter still preferred the soft glow while she slept.

At the doorway, Carly paused and looked back at the now-sleeping child, then at her room. She'd made the curtains herself and put up the shelves. Paint was cheap and she haunted the Blackberry Island Thrift Store for bargains, like the cheerful quilt still in its store plastic wrap. She kept a big jar at the bottom of her closet and put all her loose change into it. That was the fund for her daughter's birthday and Christmas. Despite the lack of money, they'd made it.

All that would change if she got fired. She wouldn't just lose her job; she would lose her home.

For a moment, she stood in the half darkness and remembered when this room had belonged to Michelle. Most weekends they spent their nights together, usually here, because it was better. Safer. When they'd been Gabby's age, they'd made daisy chains to wear and offer to guests. They'd run down to the beach and thrown rocks into the Sound. Michelle would wade into the cold water, but Carly kept to the shore. She'd always been afraid of the water. She had no explanation, no early trauma. The phobia simply existed. Unfortunately, she'd passed it on to her daughter.

On her good days, she told herself she'd more than made up for that with love and caring and a stable home life. Their world was orderly and predictable. They were happy. No matter what it took, Carly had to make sure that didn't change.

The motel room could have been on any one of a thousand roadsides. The bed was small and hard, the sheets rough, the carpet stained. The dark drapes didn't quite meet in the middle. Car lights swept across the window, creating a pattern on the opposite wall. There was a steady drip from the faucet in the bathroom.

Michelle supposed she could have found a nicer place, but she hadn't had enough interest. This place would do for the night. It had the added advantage of being close to the main highway into town and a favorite stop for truckers. She was unlikely to run into anyone she knew. Right now being anonymous was a win.

She ran water in the shower until steam filled the small bathroom. After stripping down, she stepped into the spray and let the hot water wash over her. She used the soap, rubbing the tiny bar into her hair, then rinsing.

Despite the heat, she shivered, eventually turning the taps off and drying with the small, thin towel provided. She couldn't see herself in the mirror, which was fine. It wasn't as if she was going to put on makeup. Her lone concession to her skin while deployed had been sunscreen. Now that she was back in the Northwest, she didn't even have to bother with that.

As she dressed, she avoided looking at the still-healing scars on her hip. She was sure the surgeon had done his best to tidy up the injury, to mitigate the blast marks from the gunshot, but he hadn't had much to work with.

In her head she knew she was lucky. She was all in one piece. A partial hip replacement was barely a footnote compared to what others had suffered. She'd survived, meeting every soldier's goal of not getting dead. The rest would take care of itself.

She left the small bathroom. A stack of take-out menus sat on the narrow desk in the corner. Food was probably a good idea. She was still on antibiotics and pain meds. Having something in her stomach would make them go down easier. Or she could avoid them completely, solving the problem in another way.

The paper bag stood on the nightstand. She crossed to it and removed the bottle of vodka.

"Hello, you," she murmured, undoing the top. "I'm not looking for anything long term. How about just spending the night together?"

The counselor at the hospital had warned her that using humor as a defense mechanism would get in the way of her healing fully. She'd told him she could live with the flaw.

The night was quiet. The steady rumble of cars was practically a lullaby compared to what she'd heard just a few months ago. There was no threat of explosions, no roar of heavy equipment, no jets overhead. The night was cool instead of warm, the sky cloudy instead of clear.

Decisions would have to be made. She couldn't avoid the inn. She belonged there, or she had. There was also the issue of Carly. Saying she was fired had felt good. Maybe she should keep her around so she could fire her over and over again. A little gift to herself.

"That's bad, even for you," she told herself, still staring at the vodka.

Exhaustion pulled at her, making her want to lie down, to close her eyes. She resisted, despite the need to heal. Because sleep came at a price. Sleep brought dreams and the dreams were a new level of hell.

"Not with you," she said, lifting the bottle. "With you, there's just a real good time."

She drank deeply, letting the liquor burn down her throat and swirl into her empty belly. She drank until she was sure there wouldn't be dreams, until she was sure that for one more night she got to forget.

Four

The knock on the back door of the kitchen had Gabby scrambling out of her chair and racing toward the sound.

"I'll get it! I'll get it!" she yelled.

There was no point in telling her to be quiet, Carly thought. Gabby was a morning person. Most days Carly didn't mind, but after a night of tossing and turning, her daughter's high-pitched voice pierced her brain like glass.

Gabby fumbled with the lock, then threw open the door.

"Uncle Robert!"

She flung herself toward the man in the doorway, arms open, her entire being expectant. Robert caught her and swung her high in the air.

"How's my best girl?" he asked before kissing her cheek.

"Good. We're having blackberries on our pancakes."

Robert chuckled. "And that's news why?"

They laughed together, then he lowered her to the ground. Gabby returned to the table and Robert closed the door.

"How was it?" he asked, walking into the kitchen.

Carly knew what he meant and didn't know how to answer. She shrugged, then busied herself getting him coffee. Robert took his usual seat—he was a regular at their breakfast table, joining them a couple of times a week.

"Thanks," he said, taking the cup of coffee. He turned to Gabby. "Ready for school?"

She nodded eagerly, her blond hair bouncing with the movement. Gabby adored school, both the classes and her friends. At least there she was happily social.

"So what are you studying this week?" he asked. "Calculus? You're in college, right?"

Gabby giggled. "Uncle Robert, I'm nine."

"Really? You look older. I would have thought you were twenty."

The conversation was familiar. Gabby adored her uncle and the feelings between them ran deep. Family was good, Carly told herself. Although it had taken having Gabby to convince herself of that. Her daughter was a blessing she wasn't sure she deserved, but the rest of the familial relationships were iffy at best.

Robert had been more than kind, more than giving with his time and attention. Some of his actions were fueled by guilt, she knew. Robert was a good man, someone who took commitments seriously. Someone who expected the same of others. His brother, Allen, hadn't shared Robert's sense of obligation, walking out on Carly long before Gabby was born.

The leaving had been shocking enough, but having him clean out her bank account, taking every penny she had, had been worse.

Robert had stepped in, offering to let Carly live with him. She'd refused and instead had come to work at the inn. Robert had tracked his brother down, but Allen had refused to return and he'd already blown all the money. Their divorce had followed. He'd never paid child support, but he'd signed away his rights to his daughter. While Carly could use the money, she figured having him gone was a good exchange. He was one of those men who created trouble, then walked away without bothering to think about the shattered lives in his wake.

Gabby finished her breakfast and carried her bowl to the counter. She set it in place.

"I'm going to brush my teeth," she announced before dashing from the room.

Robert's gaze followed her. "I can't believe how big she's getting."

"She'll be ten soon." Collecting her own coffee, Carly sat at the table.

"You saw her yesterday?" he asked.

There was no reason to ask who "she" was. Carly had confessed her concerns about Michelle's return to Robert. He'd also been witness to the trouble between them ten years ago.

"Yes," she admitted. "Briefly. She's…different. Thinner. She walks with a limp, which isn't a surprise."

"She was shot in the hip, right? That's what I heard."

Carly nodded.

"Did you talk?" he asked.

"Not really. She was tired."

Or so Carly had assumed. She wasn't going to admit what Michelle had said. Wasn't even going to think about it until she had to. Then she would make plans.

The panic returned, but she ignored it. Time enough to lose it later, she told herself. When she was alone. To give in to the fear now, to worry in front of Robert, was to invite something she didn't want.

He looked enough like Allen to be both intriguing and to make her want to bolt. Medium height, dark hair and eyes, with broad shoulders. Allen, younger by nearly six years, had the allure and easy smile of a man who lived on charm. Him leaving was as inevitable as the tide that lapped against the rocky shore of the island.

Robert was nearly as good-looking, but without the destructive bent. He owned an auto shop on the far edge of town. He was a good man who wanted to take care of her and Gabby, and she'd let him. Because it was easy. Because he didn't demand a real relationship and she didn't want one.

But she was starting to wonder if easy had a higher price than she'd realized. If they were using each other to avoid having to find what they really wanted with someone else. Of course, if Michelle really did fire her, it would be less of an issue. She had a feeling that being homeless would make her less attractive on the dating scene.

"Are you okay?" he asked.

"I knew she was coming, but it was still a shock to see her."

"I'm sorry. About all of this."

"Stop saying that. It was never your fault."

"He's my brother."

"I'm the one who married him. I knew what he was and I married him, anyway."

Married him after finding him with her best friend two days before the wedding. It didn't matter that Allen had blamed Michelle, had claimed she'd seduced him and it wasn't his fault.

Carly remembered everything about the moment. She'd finally bought a topper for the cake. She'd found it in an antiques store in Aberdeen. The porcelain was delicate, the couple a little old-fashioned. But there had been something about the way they'd faced each other, the tiny hands clasping, that had called out to her. She'd bought it and brought it to her small house and had cleaned it so carefully. Then she'd taken it over to show Michelle.

There were so many things she remembered about that afternoon. The cranes had been everywhere. They were loudest in spring, no doubt dealing with bird hormones and nest-building. She remembered it had been sunny— a rare event in the Pacific Northwest.

She'd walked into the inn, still feeling strange about being there. She and Michelle had only recently reconciled. Their friendship, solid for so many years, had been tentative. She'd walked into the owner's apartment, her eyes slow to adjust to the sudden shadows, and she'd stumbled as she'd made her way through the living room and into Michelle's bedroom. She'd entered without thinking, without knocking. They'd still been in bed, both naked, in a tangle of arms and legs.

At first she hadn't believed what she was seeing. She'd stood there, holding the cake topper in her hands, feeling as if something was terribly wrong but unable to figure out what. Like a dream, where chairs were on the ceiling.

The out-of-focus blurring had sharpened as she'd realized what had happened. That the person she should have been able to trust more than anyone had betrayed her. With Michelle—the woman already responsible for destroying most of what she had.

Allen had jumped to his feet and run to her. He was still hard from the lovemaking, his penis damp, his hair mussed.

"Carly, please. It was an accident."

She was sure he'd said more, pleaded, begged. Blamed

Michelle, who had sat in the bed, her eyes as blank as her
face. Carly had waited—not for Allen to convince her
but for Michelle to say something. Eventually she had.

"You should go now."

That was it. Four words. No explanation, no apology.
Just "you should go now."

Carly had run.

Two days later, she'd walked down the aisle and married Allen. Because it had been easier than facing the
truth. Because she'd been afraid of being alone. Funny
how she'd ended up alone, anyway.

"You'll figure it out," Robert told her. "You and Michelle were friends. Once you talk, you'll be friends
again."

She nodded because it was easier than telling the
truth. That while Carly was the injured party, Michelle
seemed to be the one who had come home looking for
revenge.

Michelle stepped into the kitchen at the inn and
breathed deeply. The fragrance of cinnamon mingled
with bacon and coffee. Her mouth watered and for the
first time in months she was hungry.

The room was different—bigger, with longer counters
and more windows, but the heart was the same. Damaris
still ruled from her eight-burner stove, and servers and
helpers jumped when she barked their names.

Michelle watched as the cook flavored eggs with her
secret spices and flipped pancakes. Diced vegetables and
cheese were added to omelets, blackberries added as a
side to everything. Toast popped, the juicer whirred and
the ever-present slap of plates was accompanied by the
call of "order up."

Her head hurt nearly as much as her hip. A testament

to the aftereffects of too much vodka and too little food. But as she watched Damaris, the pain faded to the background. Here, in the chaos, she was finally home.

"Last order," Damaris called, slapping down another plate.

Michelle glanced at the clock. It was nearly nine. This time of year the breakfast crowd faded early with most of the customers heading off to work. Midweek inn visitors were usually purposeful, with plans and itineraries to be followed.

"Morning," she said as Damaris turned off burners.

The cook spun and pressed a hand to her heart. "When did you get here?"

"A few minutes ago."

Damaris hurried toward her, wiping her hands on her white apron. "It's so good to see you," she said, pulling Michelle close and hugging her. "You're hungry." Damaris released her. "You must be. I'll make your favorite."

"You don't have to."

Dark eyebrows rose over the frame of her glasses. "You think I don't know that? Sit."

Michelle limped over to the stools by the counter and sat. Damaris poured her coffee and passed it over, then studied the ingredients on the counter.

"You didn't stay here last night," she said, slicing cinnamon bread. "I asked."

"I didn't want to." An almost-truth. "It's strange being back."

"That's because you waited too long. What were you thinking? Ten years? In all that time you couldn't come back once to see me?"

Michelle didn't answer. Her reasons for not visiting had nothing to do with Damaris and everything to do with Carly and Brenda.

"What do you think of the changes?" Damaris kept her attention on the eggs she whipped.

"That they're more than you said. The whole inn is different."

"I didn't want to upset you. Carly suggested the remodel, but then your mother ran with it. The contractor was from Seattle. God forbid Brenda should hire local. I think she was sleeping with him."

"My mother?"

"He took advantage of her, if you ask me. The new roof and kitchen remodel became what you see. I almost felt sorry for her. He left when he was done and never came back. Such bad luck with men." She looked over her glasses. "Like I said, I almost felt sorry for her."

Michelle couldn't summon even that much compassion. "She should have known better. The inn didn't need to be different. It wasn't hers. She didn't have the right."

"Did you think that would have stopped her?"

"No."

The pounding was back in her head. The hip ache had never gone away. She supposed she could take one of the pain pills the doctors had given her but she didn't like how they made her feel. Loopy.

Talk about irony. She had no problem washing away her life with vodka but resisted pain medication. Of course, in the scheme of things, that contradiction wasn't even a footnote when compared with the rest of the jumble in her head. She had a feeling she was one step away from being a case study in some medical magazine. Or maybe she was giving herself too much credit.

Damaris set a plate in front of her. Cinnamon French toast with sausage. And blackberries on the side.

"Really?" she asked, nudging one of the berries until it threatened to roll off her plate. "Even with me?"

Damaris grinned. "Habit."

Because all food was served with blackberries here on Blackberry Island. When she was little, her dad had teased that they should be grateful they didn't live on Broccoli Island or Spinach Inlet. She remembered laughing and laughing, then drew in a breath and tried to remember the last time she'd found anything remotely funny.

She sliced off a small piece of the French toast. The edges were crispy, the cinnamon visible through the layer of egg. Once on her tongue, the flavors mingled, sweetened by the maple syrup. The bread itself, light yet substantial, had what those in the business called "mouth feel."

Most people believed that scent memory was the most powerful but for Michelle it was taste. She could remember this breakfast from what felt like a thousand years ago. Could remember where she'd been sitting, what the conversation had been about. Damaris had made this exact meal for her on her first morning working for the inn.

"God, you're good."

Damaris laughed. "At least that's the same."

She poured herself coffee and pulled up a stool, watching as Michelle devoured the food.

Michelle finished the French toast, then went to work on the sausage. It was exactly as she recalled, made locally by organic farmers at the north end of the island. She ended with the blackberries.

"Are they from Chile?" she asked. It was way too early in the season for them to be local.

Damaris's eyes widened. "Shhh. That's practically blasphemy. Everything we serve is local."

"You're such a liar. Is that what we're saying now?"

"No, but people assume."

"It's fifty degrees outside and the first week of May. No one thinks these are local."

Damaris sniffed. "There's a greenhouse on the far side of the island."

"It's the size of a toaster. They could plant maybe two bushes in there."

"Still." Damaris reached for her own cup of coffee. "What happens now?"

Michelle had a feeling the cook wasn't asking if she planned to take her plate over to the sink or not. The question, and answer, was more complicated than that.

"I return to my regularly scheduled life. Run the inn, like I did before."

"You can't do it by yourself."

Michelle glanced at her, wondering if she'd heard about what had happened with Carly the previous night.

"It's bigger now," the cook continued. "Thirty rooms. The summer's coming. You know what that means."

Crowds, tourists and a houseful of guests.

I fired Carly.

Michelle thought the words, testing them, enjoying the sense of satisfaction they produced.

Reality would be different, she thought, gripping her coffee. Reality was hard work and long hours. With her hip and the physical therapy that would require, not to mention the fact that stairs were going to be a nightmare, Damaris was right. She couldn't do it on her own.

This close to the summer season, finding a replacement for someone who knew the inn would be difficult. While the words had come from her heart, she knew letting Carly go would be stupid.

"You're saying I have to keep her."

No need to say who "she" was.

Damaris shrugged. "For now. She won't want to go. She has her daughter. Gabby. A sweet girl, considering."

Damaris had always been an ally. Impulsively, Michelle stretched her arm across the stainless counter and squeezed her friend's hand.

"I missed you."

"I missed you, too."

The door to the dining room swung open and a dark-haired woman a little younger than Michelle entered. She wore a pink blouse tucked into black trousers. Her hair had been pulled back into a ponytail.

"Isabella, come. This is Michelle. Michelle, my daughter-in-law. Isabella is married to Eric."

Michelle smiled. "I can't believe he finally got married."

"Four years ago," Isabella said.

Michelle remembered Eric being the kind who didn't see the point in having a girlfriend. Why limit yourself to just one? He'd hit on her a couple of times, once even flashing her his penis. It was the first one she'd ever seen and her unplanned "Really? Is that what all the fuss is about?" had not only deflated him but insured he didn't bother her again.

"Congratulations," she now told Isabella, hoping Eric was a better husband than his past behavior implied.

"Thank you."

"They have a baby. A little girl."

"That's nice."

An awkward silence filled the room.

"Okay. Well, it was lovely to meet you." Isabella turned to her mother-in-law. "The last of the customers left. I'm closing up the dining room. I'll be back at eleven-fifteen."

"See you then."

"Bye," Isabella said, and left.

"She's a hostess here. She works breakfast and lunch," Damaris said. "The schedule is convenient for her. She can make some money and be home with the baby."

"Good."

Michelle knew she should ask more questions, get involved. She was back now. But dealing with people, the easiest part of the job, suddenly seemed impossible. She wanted to retreat to a small space where she would feel safe. Somewhere familiar.

She rose and reached for her dishes.

"Leave those," Damaris told her. "I'll take care of them."

Michelle walked around the table and embraced the woman who had always taken care of her.

"Thank you," she whispered, kissing Damaris on the top of the head.

"Welcome home, Michelle. I'm glad you're back."

"Me, too." Sort of.

She limped to the door leading to the dining room. From there she would enter the inn and figure out what was next.

"Michelle?"

She paused and glanced back.

Damaris smiled. "I'm proud of you."

Michelle felt her throat tighten. "Thank you."

Five

Her mother's office, *her* office now, was one of the few places that wasn't different. Michelle settled on the old wooden chair and grinned when she heard the familiar squeal of protest. The chair was older than her, dug up from some office furniture sale years and years ago. Like the desk, it was scarred and old-fashioned, but serviceable.

The computer had been replaced, probably more than once in the past ten years, she thought as she pushed the power button on the tower. Although it wasn't as new as the one she'd used in Afghanistan.

Behind her, built-in bookcases covered the wall from floor to ceiling. Old ledgers dating back decades gathered dust. The smell of aging leather and musty pages comforted her. Here, with a watercolor of the inn as it used to be, with the familiar fading braided rug underfoot, she at last felt at home.

In the 1950s her newly married grandparents had inherited an unexpected windfall and had impulsively purchased the inn. Michelle's father had been born and raised here, as had she. Three generations of Sandersons had left their mark on the halls and floors of the old building. Michelle had never imagined living anywhere else.

Ten years ago circumstances—okay, guilt—had caused her to join the army. Within eleven months she'd been sent overseas, eventually ending up in Iraq. Working in the supply office had kept her busy. Knowing that she was making a difference had caused her to request two more deployments.

She'd spent her leave time in Europe, had wandered through Australia for nearly three weeks, had seen the Great Wall. As far as she was concerned, she was ready for the Been There, Done That T-shirt. If she had her way, she would never leave the island again.

She turned her attention to the screen and clicked on the icon for the inn. A box came up, demanding a password. The computer might be new, but the software had obviously been transferred from the one before. She entered her old password and screens flashed in front of her. She navigated easily through reservations, then to the computer version of a check register.

The dates there made her frown. All the entries abruptly ended three months ago. What had—?

Her mother's death, she realized. Brenda had taken care of the bookkeeping for the inn. She would have been the one using the computer. Carly hadn't, which meant what? That none of the bills had been paid? She remembered Carly having many flaws, but being irresponsible wasn't one of them.

She turned her attention to the paperwork stacked on the desk. She looked for a pile of bills but instead found a pad of paper with a neat, handwritten list.

"April 17. Blackberry Island Water. $237.18."

The entries went back the three months and included two mortgage payments each month for different amounts. Michelle studied the list, recognizing the writing as Carly's. So she *had* been paying bills, but by hand. She wasn't sure if the other woman hadn't used the computer because she didn't know how or didn't think she was supposed to.

Michelle dug in the drawers and found the checkbook. Her mother's writing jumped out at her, a rambling scrawl that contrasted with Carly's smaller, neater entries. Michelle stared at the numbers, seeing the actual form of them rather than the amounts. She drew in a breath and braced herself for the inevitable.

Inhale, exhale, and there it was.

The subtle slam of a car hitting the side of a mountain. Guilt. It hit her from every direction, making her writhe in her seat as her breakfast turned from comfort food to something heavy in her stomach.

Self-reproach mingled with shame, but the emotions were elusive. Because she and her mother hadn't gotten along, because the other woman had blamed her for things that a teenager could never be responsible for, Michelle knew deep down inside she'd been glad she hadn't been here at the end. And that being glad was wrong.

It wasn't that Brenda had been alone. Carly had been there, or as Brenda had referred to her in her infrequent emails, "the true daughter of my heart." But Carly wasn't family.

Knowing in her head that ambivalence was the cause of the guilt didn't make it any easier to endure.

"Focus," she told herself. The hangover had faded enough that the headache was nothing more than dull background noise. After ten years, who knew what kind of financial turmoil the inn had experienced. She would dig into the numbers and come up with a plan. The army had taught her to excel at logistics.

She reached for the mouse, only to have the phone ring. The sharp sound cutting through silence caused her to jump. Her heart raced and a cold sweat instantly coated her body. Fear joined the ache in her hip and made her want to duck under the desk. Instead, she picked up the receiver.

"Sanderson," she said from long habit, then unclenched her teeth.

"There's a call for you on line one. Ellen Snow from Island Savings and Loan."

Carly's voice was calm. Had Michelle only imagined the thrill of firing her the previous night?

"You're still here?"

"So it seems. Did you want to take the call?"

By way of answering, Michelle pushed the flashing button, disconnecting Carly and connecting the other call.

"This is Michelle Sanderson. How can I help you?"

"Michelle, how great to talk to you. I'm Ellen Snow from the bank. I don't know if you remember me."

Michelle leaned back in her chair. "We went to school together."

Ellen laughed. "That's right. I was a year behind you and my brother, Miles, was a year ahead."

The images were vague. Blond, she thought. Nordic. Miles had been popular, Ellen less so.

"I remember," Michelle said, going for polite rather than accurate.

"I just want to say I think what you did is wonderful. Serving our country that way. This probably sounds strange, but thank you."

Michelle opened her mouth, then closed it.

What was she supposed to say in return? Her reasons for joining had been far from altruistic, and now that she was back she wanted to slip into normal, to pretend it had never happened. Hardly actions worthy of thanks.

"Ah, you're welcome."

"Now that you're home, I'm assuming you're going to be taking over the inn?"

"Yes."

"Good. As you may know, the bank has two notes on the property. A first and a second mortgage." Ellen's tone had shifted from friendly to business. "We should talk about them as soon as possible. Is ten-thirty good for you?"

A second mortgage? When had that happened? At least it explained the second monthly payment, but why?

She closed her eyes and saw the new roof, the larger restaurant, then swore silently. Her mother had been in charge—it was the gift that kept on giving.

"Ten-thirty this morning?"

"Yes. I have some time then."

It wasn't as if Michelle had anything else to do. "I'll be there."

"I look forward to it."

Island Savings and Loan stood in the center of town. The once-thriving business district had been taken over by stores and restaurants that catered to tourists rather than locals. Most of the companies that served locals had been eased toward the outskirts of town, but the Savings and Loan stood where it had for nearly a hundred years.

Michelle parked in front, then walked through the glass doors—one of the few concessions to modern times. The rest of the building was brick, with hardwood floors and a mural completed in the 1940s.

There was no security guard, and if she ignored the high-tech cameras mounted on the walls, she could almost pretend she was a kid again, going to the bank with her dad.

An older woman stood in front of a lone teller. Otherwise, there didn't seem to be any other customers. Michelle glanced around at the offices lining the walls, then walked toward the one with Ellen's name stenciled on a wood-and-glass door.

She knocked on the open door.

Ellen looked up, then smiled and stood. "Michelle, thanks so much for coming in. How are you?"

"Fine, thanks."

She did her best not to limp as she entered the small space. Her T-shirt and cargo pants had seemed fine back at the inn, but here, with Ellen, she felt underdressed and grubby.

The other woman was as thin as she'd been back in high school. Long blond hair hung past her shoulders. Hazel eyes were framed with discreet makeup. Pearls, probably real, sat on top of a light green twin set. Low heels and a black knee-length pencil skirt completely Ellen's "I'm a banker, trust me" look.

As Michelle took the offered seat, she tried to remember if she'd bothered to comb her hair that morning. She'd showered, so she was clean, but her lone concession to grooming had been to brush her teeth.

"I was so sorry to hear about your mother," Ellen said gently, waiting until Michelle sat before resuming her place behind her desk and leaning forward. "It must have been difficult for you. I heard you'd been injured around the same time. It's not fair, is it?"

"No, it's not."

Ellen sighed. "The loss and being hurt. Now this." She motioned to the slim file on her desk.

Michelle stared at the closed folder. "What do you mean?"

The other woman pressed her lips together, as if considering her words. "Have you had a chance to go through the finances of the inn?"

Michelle regretted leaving the vodka bottle in her motel room. Right now a drink seemed like a smart move. "No. I'd only been in a few minutes when you called."

"Then let me bring you up to speed." She opened the file. "I really hate to be the one to tell you about this. I wish it could wait." She paused.

Michelle felt the familiar sensation of something crawling on her skin. "Just say whatever it is."

"The inn is in trouble. If it were up to me, we wouldn't be having this conversation. I know you just got home and need time to readjust, but we have a loan advisory board. The new regulations are so strict. Back in the day I'd have more control. I'm so sorry."

Maybe it was a lack of sleep, but Michelle would swear the other woman had just given an explanation that hadn't made anything more clear.

"What are you talking about?"

"The loans on the inn. There are two mortgages, both delinquent. I'm afraid we're talking about foreclosure."

Michelle shot to her feet, ignored the stabbing agony in her hips. "What? That's not possible. How can you say that?"

"I'm afraid I can say it because it's the truth. The last three payments were made on time, but they were only for current amounts. There are months of back payments on both mortgages. With penalties and interest."

Michelle sank back into the chair. The pain in her hip radiated out like light from the sun. It burned through her, making it difficult to concentrate.

"We own the inn outright. Maybe my mom took out a loan to pay for the renovations, but how much can it be?"

Ellen handed her a single sheet of paper with two loan balances. They totaled nearly half a million dollars. The amount in arrears was nearly thirty thousand.

Michelle dropped the paper on the desk and sucked in air. This wasn't happening. It couldn't be. Not even her mother would be so irresponsible.

"I think most of the money went into renovations," Ellen said gently. "Not to speak ill of the dead, but Brenda spent money more easily than she should have. The first mortgage payments were often late. When she approached me about a second mortgage, I wasn't sure I could get it through the committee. I really had to convince them to give her the loan." She sighed. "Which makes this mess partially my fault. From your reaction, I'm guessing you didn't know."

"No. She never said anything. The inn was held in trust until I was twenty-five. By then, I was gone and she continued to run things." Into the ground, she thought bitterly, wondering how much of the money she'd blown on things for herself. Clothes and jewelry. New cars.

She couldn't believe it, couldn't take it all in. Once she'd seen the renovations, she'd thought there might be a few bills to deal with, but nothing like this.

"What happens now?" she asked.

"That depends on you. This business has been in your family for a long time. Letting it go will be difficult."

"I'm not selling."

"You don't have a choice," Ellen said, her voice sympathetic. "The back payments are problematic. I know Brenda kept up the insurance, but there may also be back taxes. Even with the summer tourists coming, you won't make a dent in what's owed. If you funnel all the money into what's overdue, how will you survive the winter? It's prime property. I've been approached by several interested parties. You could walk away with a lot of money, Michelle. Start over somewhere else."

"No." The word came instinctively. "No, I won't sell. There has to be another way. I have money."

"Half a million dollars?"

"Of course not, but don't I just have to get the loan current and then keep making payments? I have savings. I didn't spend much of my salary and there are bonuses for overseas deployments."

Her instinct was to offer all that she had, but she held back. After all, there might be other pressing bills. The income or property taxes Ellen had mentioned or vendors who couldn't be put off.

She started to stand, but forced herself to stay seated. She knew that once she stood she would bolt, running until all this was behind her. And then what? She would have to come back. Better to just get it over with.

"I can pay at least half the back mortgages amounts by tomorrow. Maybe more. I have to figure things out." She scooted to the front of her chair and stared at the other woman. "Come on. You said it yourself. I've been off protecting our country. That has to count for something." Complete crap, she thought. But possibly useful crap.

Ellen sighed. "I would love to say yes. I'm on your side, Michelle. You have to believe me. These new rules are so frustrating. I know what you're capable of. But it's not just about the money."

"What else is there?"

"Management of the inn."

"I'll be running things."

"That's what the committee is afraid of."

"What? I know what I'm doing. I've worked there for years. In high school, I took care of everything. You know that. I never went out with my friends or played sports or anything. After high school I worked full-time at the inn." Unfairness made her want to throw something. "Dammit, I got my degree in hotel management while I was gone. I know how to manage the inn."

Ellen nodded. "I know. I agree completely. I remember how you'd always be working during school." Her mouth twisted into a smile. "My mother used you as an example for Miles and me. How you were so responsible and we weren't. It was a little annoying."

"So why doesn't that count?"

"It does, with me. Not with the committee. Brenda was required to come in for quarterly meetings. She talked about Carly. How Carly took care of things. How the inn wouldn't survive without Carly. Unfortunately, they believed her. Since your mother passed, Carly's been paying the bills."

The hits kept on coming, Michelle thought bitterly. "You're saying they would trust Carly over me? She can't even use the computer. She's—" Michelle swallowed the rest of what she wanted to say. Ranting wouldn't help her case.

"I know you and Carly have a difficult past."

Difficult didn't begin to describe it. "So the committee, whoever they are, doesn't trust me, but if Carly runs things, then I have a shot at keeping the inn?"

Ellen nodded. "Unfortunately, yes. I had a feeling you wouldn't want to sell. They didn't believe me, but then they're not one of us. I consider you a friend. The last thing I want is another local business shut down. I'm tired of outsiders running things around here. I pleaded your case last week and they've agreed to the following concessions."

She handed Michelle another piece of paper.

The list was short. The back payments had to be made within sixty days. All accounts with vendors had to be current by the end of the month. The inn had to maintain an eighty-five-percent occupancy rate through the summer, pass all inspections and stay current on the mortgage payments. The last item on the list was the one that made her hip ache the worst.

Carly Williams was to agree to stay on for at least two years.

"I'm sorry," Ellen said. "It's the best I could do. I know how you feel about her. I have to admit, I'm not her biggest fan, either. She took advantage of you being gone and she used your mom. She's even wearing her jewelry. It's awful."

Ten years in the army had taught her to follow orders, whether or not they made sense or she wanted to. She could argue, she could scream, but unless there was a winning lottery ticket worth half a million dollars in a drawer in her desk back in her office at the inn, she was screwed.

"I'm not losing the inn," she said. "My dad might have been a first-class bastard, but he left it to me and I'm going to keep it. I'll do what I have to."

"You can have a couple of days to think about it," Ellen told her. "There's still the interested buyer."

"I don't have to think about it. I'll do it. I'll do all of it."

"Even work with Carly?"

"Sure."

"It'll be difficult."

"You have no idea."

Six

The Shop at Blackberry Island Inn was one of Carly's favorite places. The space had been added nearly two years ago and was slowly building a loyal customer base. Big windows allowed in light, even on the gloomiest days, while the custom shelves and racks provided plenty of display space.

The store sold the usual kitschy island mementos—magnets, mugs and key chains done in both blackberry and daisy motifs. But there was also a section devoted to local artists and a display of unique china. Brenda had insisted on a doll collection, which Carly didn't love. They'd both chosen the books of island history and pictures.

Mornings were often slow at the shop, but the lunch crowd at the restaurant brought in customers. Carly used the quiet time to dust, check inventory and organize invoices. After getting Gabby off to school, she manned the front desk of the inn, checking out guests and making sure the cleaning staff was ready to go. In the late morning, she would return to the front desk to check in those arriving, handle correspondence and talk to vendors. The couple of hours she spent in the store a few times a week were as close to "me time" as she ever got.

Today she walked through the store, stopping to touch her favorite pieces, aware she was telling them she might be gone soon. As if the carving of an orca breaching and surrounded by spray would miss her.

The front door opened and the attached bell tinkled. She turned and saw Leonard Daniels walking toward her.

"Hi, Carly."

"Morning, Leonard."

Leonard was their resident ornithologist, specializing in the Puget Sound crane. He was here on a grant that paid for his room at the inn. They generally had two or three scientists at any one time.

Tall and thin, with dark-rimmed glasses and pale skin, despite his time outdoors, Leonard personified the phrase "geeky scientist." He favored plaid and khakis, inevitably had binoculars around his neck and a small netbook computer under one arm.

He crossed to her, his gait more energetic than usual. "We have eggs."

She knew enough to understand he didn't mean the breakfast variety. "Already?"

He nodded. "Two in the first nest I found and one in the other. Within a week I'll have enough data to determine a potential chick population." His dark eyes brightened with excitement. "I'm hoping this is the third growth year. If it is, then we can finally look at taking the cranes off the endangered list."

He paused, as if expecting her to share his joy.

"That's great, Leonard."

"I know. We should celebrate."

"It's kind of early in the day."

He pushed up his glasses, then looked at his watch. "Oh, right. Okay. I'm going back to work."

He left the store.

She watched him go, hoping he wasn't going to try to change the nature of their relationship. He was a paying guest and she'd always been friendly to him but the last thing she wanted in her life was a man. Men were trouble. It had taken her a while to figure that out but she wasn't going to forget the lesson now.

There hadn't been anyone in her life since Allen had abandoned her. Over ten years. Sure, it would be great to have hot sex with a guy, but aside from that, she didn't need the aggravation.

She turned back to mental inventory, only to have Wendy, one of the servers, come in. Wendy worked the breakfast shift at the restaurant. She had three kids and a husband who worked nights. He got the kids off to school when he got home from his job and she took over until he got up in the late afternoon. They spent their evenings together, before he left and she went to bed.

Wendy was reliable and the guests liked her—which made her someone Carly didn't want to lose.

"What's up?" she asked.

Wendy wrinkled her nose. "Damaris got in my face this morning, which I can handle, but she came out and yelled at one of the customers, which I didn't like. Jeez, what's up with her? She gets in these moods. The guy wanted an egg-white omelet. She told him no special orders. When he said it was for his heart, she told him that his being fat wasn't her fault."

Carly felt her mouth drop open. "Please say you're kidding."

"I wish I were. Most of the time she's fine, but every

now and then she gets in a mood and takes it out on customers. You'll talk to her?"

Carly wanted to say no. This was the sort of thing Brenda handled. The other woman had actually enjoyed taking Damaris on. If it had been up to Carly, Damaris would have been let go years ago. Firing the temperamental cook had been on her to-do list, just as soon as she got her shares of the inn. Now she wasn't sure if she had a job, let alone the authority to fire anyone.

"I'll talk to her," she said, knowing she owed that to Wendy.

"Thanks. I'm heading home. Have a good one."

"You, too."

Carly had nearly an hour to fume and worry before Ann showed up to work in the gift shop. Not sure what she was going to say, she walked through the inn to the restaurant kitchen. Damaris sat on a stool, her cell phone to her ear. When she saw Carly, she frowned before saying she had to hang up.

"You know he was a big, fat guy. Do you think one egg-white omelet is going to make a difference?"

So much for idle chitchat, Carly thought. "He's a customer."

"The customer isn't always right. Most of the time the customer doesn't know what he's talking about. I made the omelet. I didn't want to, but I did."

"Your job is to cook their food. Being rude and critical doesn't help our business."

"Our business?" Damaris raised her eyebrows. "It's Michelle's business, not yours."

"I'm speaking as an employee. We have a responsibility to do our best. That's what we're paid to do." Carly could feel her face heating. She'd never been very good at hiding when she was upset. "Do you think Michelle would have been proud of your actions? That she would be happy about what happened?"

Damaris stood and crossed to Carly. The cook was about five inches shorter, but much broader and more willing to be aggressive.

"Don't you tell me my job, missy. I was cooking before you were born. She's back now. How long do you think before she fires you?"

Less time than Damaris knew, Carly thought, knowing she had no power, no position of strength.

"You were wrong and you know you were wrong. Not just because it's bad customer service, but because it was rude. Whatever you think of me, saying things like that won't help the business. You claim to care about Michelle but your actions are hurting her."

Damaris smiled. "Uh-huh? And who do you think is going to be here at the end of the day? Me or you?"

A question Carly didn't want to answer. She turned and left the kitchen.

Frustration gnawed at her. Anger made her want to lash out. Maybe she should go ahead and leave. Start over somewhere else. Have a real life that wasn't dependent on forces she couldn't control and people who lied. People like Brenda.

She stopped in the hallway, needing a second to get control of herself and calm down.

"Why did you do this?" she asked out loud, knowing there wasn't going to be an answer. Carly wasn't a big believer in the dead coming back and having a conversation, and even if they could, she doubted Brenda would bother.

She'd been used by Brenda. At times the other woman had been sympathetic, even kind. But in the end, she'd only cared about herself. Now Carly had nothing. Her

carefully hoarded emergency fund held all of sixteen
hundred dollars. Barely enough to cover a deposit on a
small apartment, let alone rent. Not to mention living
expenses while she looked for work. She doubted Michelle would fire her and then give her a recommendation, which meant getting a decent job would be beyond
difficult.

Which left what? Being homeless? Public assistance?

Her eyes burned. She sucked in a breath and told herself she wasn't going to give in to tears. Not yet. Not
when there could be a bigger crisis brewing.

She squared her shoulders; she would get through this.
She'd gotten through plenty. She was strong and a hard
worker and she had Gabby. Besides, ice cream had been
on sale so she'd bought a quart. If necessary, she could
have a sugar-based pity party later.

She walked into the main room of the inn and found
an older couple standing by the window. They weren't
guests, so she wondered if they were hoping to get a
room. She had three available, at least for tonight. The
biggest of them had a balcony and a view.

"Hello," she said, smiling automatically. "Can I help
you?"

The couple was casually but expensively dressed.
More island chic than big-city vacationers. He was tall,
she shorter, both fit with blond hair and tans.

They turned to her.

"Seth Farley," the man said. "This is my wife, Pauline. Do you have a moment? Could we talk somewhere
private?"

They didn't look like salespeople or vendors. She'd
been careful to pay all the inn's bills, so they weren't
after money. Lawyers seemed unlikely.

"Sure. Let's go in here."

The "here" was a small conference room set aside for business guests.

When they were seated around the large table, she offered them coffee.

"No, thanks," Seth told her. "I'll get right to the point. My wife and I are psychologists. We've been in practice together for nearly twenty-five years. We have a program for married couples interested in working on their relationships. I won't go into all the details, but we get together with two or three couples at a time for three days. We've been holding our retreats in Seattle, but we think that getting out of the city might help couples more fully immerse in their therapy. We've investigated several places and are interested in your inn."

"Oh." Carly brightened. Returning guests were always welcome. "This is our only meeting room, though. We don't have conference rooms like traditional hotels."

"We don't need a space for the seminars themselves," Pauline told her. "We have that taken care of. We're looking for housing for our clients. Three rooms Tuesday through Thursday from the middle of May through late September."

Summer was their busiest time, she thought. While the weekends were always full, there were usually rooms available midweek. Having guaranteed bookings for that many weeks would be great.

"I would have to check our availability," she said, then remembered there was more. "And talk to the owner."

Seth drew his eyebrows together. "I thought you were one of them."

So did I.

"No," she said brightly. "But I've worked here for ten years, so I'm confident your clients would enjoy their stay. Let me get the dates from you along with your card.

I'll check the reservations and speak with the owner, then get back to you by the end of the week. How's that?"

"Perfect."

Seven

Michelle sat with her fingers on the keyboard. It wasn't that she didn't know how to open the programs; it was that she didn't want to.

Reality was damned unpleasant. Sometimes she wondered what it would be like to be one of those people who could simply drift away. To be on another mental plane and not care about this world. Only not caring wouldn't fix the problem. This was her inn. The one thing that had kept her going while she'd been away. The thought of coming home. If home was fucked-up, she was going to have to fix it herself.

She typed purposefully, focusing only on gathering information. She was used to spreadsheets and charts and graphs. Her time in the army had been spent in and around supplies. Deciding what to order. Getting them where they needed to go. Getting the inn back on its financial feet was nothing compared with the logistics of housing, feeding and caring for thousands of soldiers on the other side of the world.

She quickly sorted through the previous year's tax returns, wincing when she saw the loss. Sure, avoiding taxes in every legal way possible was great fun, but seeing the amount of money the inn had lost made her heart sink. The only bright spot was that losses meant there weren't overdue taxes.

She printed out the tax return, then started printing out other reports. The checkbook register. Accounts Receivable and Accounts Payable. She found that her mother had purchased not one, not two, but three new cars in the ten years Michelle had been gone. The last one, a BMW convertible with the price tag well over $70,000, had been repossessed.

She sorted through desk drawers and found unpaid bills under boxes of paper clips and staples. Then she added Carly's neat list of deposits and bills paid.

After opening a new spreadsheet, she began to enter the information. What came in and what went out. She balanced the checkbook, then did it again because the number couldn't be right. She looked at reservations and saw there were many weeks when they weren't even close to the number required by the bank.

Two hours later, she stood and limped slowly around the room. Blood circulated, pouring into her hip and causing pain. She was stiff and sore. But the worst of it was on the inside.

Growing up, she'd always been her father's favorite. Even as a little kid, she'd known her dad preferred her to Brenda. She'd accepted his love, his devotion, and had known that he was the one who stood between her and her mother. Brenda had been indifferent at best, and critical and hurtful at worst.

Sometimes she wondered if her father's favoritism had hurt Brenda. If, in return, Brenda had taken that out on her daughter. There was no way to know how much of her mother's actions were the result of circumstance and how many came from a sucky personality.

Michelle couldn't remember when she first learned that her parents had "had" to get married. She'd been born seven months after the wedding. While Michelle and her father had loved the inn, loved the island, Brenda had resented being trapped here. There were no trips to Europe—the inn couldn't be left for that long. No summer vacations—that was the busiest time. No weekends anywhere. The inn came first.

Michelle remembered her mother screaming that she and her father were so selfish. At seven, Michelle had been a small but determined opponent. "If we're so selfish, why do you always get your way?"

A question for which her mother never had an answer.

Brenda had resented her husband's abandonment more than she had mourned his absence. He'd left them both—devastating Michelle. The desertion had not only proved he didn't love her best, it had left her at the mercy of her mother.

At the time, Michelle had wondered if she would leave, too, but Brenda didn't. Instead, Michelle had been the one to go away. Looking now at the financial math that was her family's legacy, she thought that Brenda had won in subtle ways. A bad decision here, a foolish purchase there. Individually they were inconsequential. Taken in total, they were a disaster.

She studied the payroll reports. Boeing didn't need this many people working for them. The inn only had thirty rooms, but seven maids. And what the hell was a reception greeter? Just as confusing, some people seemed overpaid while others didn't make enough. Damaris hadn't had a raise in six years. That was bad enough, but Carly's financial situation was worse.

Michelle stared at the biweekly paycheck amount. Even taking into consideration the fact that she got free living quarters and a couple of meals a day, she wasn't making close to minimum wage. She had a kid. The medical insurance sucked. There had to be out-of-pocket expenses for that, not to mention clothes and shoes and whatever else children needed.

While she was aware she should probably be happy that the other woman was practically living in poverty, she mostly felt embarrassed and maybe a little guilty.

Michelle wanted to put all the blame on her mother. The inn had been left to her in trust. She was supposed to take care of it. But Michelle knew she was the one responsible. She'd been the one to leave, the one who hadn't come back, the one who had never asked. Now she had two mortgages, a pending foreclosure and a list of rules and demands that made her skin crawl.

Someone knocked on the door.

"Come in," she barked without looking up.

"You sound like you're still in the army."

She saw Damaris step into the office. The cook had a tray in one hand.

"I brought you lunch. I didn't think you'd eat on your own."

Michelle glanced at the clock and was surprised to see it was nearly three. "Do you always work this late?"

"Sometimes yes. Sometimes no." The cook put the tray on the desk, then sat in the empty chair. "I had to order my meat and produce."

"What time do you usually get out of here?"

Damaris shrugged. "Two. Two-thirty."

Michelle did the math in her head. She knew Damaris got to the restaurant sometime around six. They opened at seven and she worked through lunch.

"You haven't had a raise since I left."

"Tell me something I don't know."

Michelle wanted to ask if her mother had been doing this on purpose. If her goal had been to destroy the inn. She doubted her friend would have an answer.

"I'm giving you a raise now. Retroactive three months." She named an hourly salary. "Better?"

Damaris nodded. "You've always been a good girl. None of this is your fault."

"What have you figured out? About the inn?"

"I hear things. People don't get paid. Checks bounce. No one blames you."

Michelle glanced at the tray. Damaris had made her a roast-beef sandwich. Her favorite. There were chips and a small salad and a chocolate milk shake.

She reached for the glass and scooped out a spoonful of whipped cream. "Thanks."

"Someone has to take care of you. You're too skinny. How will you ever get a man?"

For the first time since arriving home, Michelle laughed. "I don't think getting a man is my biggest problem right now."

"A man would help."

Michelle thought getting through the night without having nightmares and waking up in a cold sweat was probably a better first step, but she didn't say that. The information would only frighten Damaris.

The other woman poked at the papers on the desk. "Is it bad?"

"I haven't figured that out yet." She stuck a straw in the milk shake. "Do you think my mother screwed up on purpose?"

"I don't know. She wasn't the type to have a plan. I think maybe it just happened."

"What about Carly? Did she help or hurt the inn?"

Damaris shrugged. "I don't like her very much, but I don't think she did anything wrong."

Not exactly what Michelle wanted to hear. Carly's low salary made her suspicious and their past made her want to show her the door. The deal with the bank was a problem, but more than that was the fact that Carly didn't even know how to work the computer system. Her carefully handwritten notes proved that.

If Carly wasn't stealing, then it was all Brenda.

"How long has Carly worked here?" Michelle asked.

"Practically since you left. One day she was here. Pregnant. Brenda gave her one of the rooms. After Gabby was born, she moved into the owner's suite and Brenda took the two bedrooms on the second floor."

Michelle wanted to ask what had happened to Allen. If Carly had been alone and pregnant, he'd obviously left. But why?

"The customers like her," Damaris said grudgingly. "She's good with them, but she's not the boss of me."

That made Michelle grin. "What are you? Five?"

Damaris chuckled. Then her humor faded. "Are you going to fire her?"

If wishes were horses, Michelle thought. "Not today."

"Soon?"

"That eager for her to be gone?"

"It goes back to the 'boss of me' thing."

"I'm the boss of you now."

"Good. I like that." Damaris stood and walked around the desk. "Give me a hug. I'm going home."

Michelle stood, then winced as the fire surged through her and she nearly lost her balance.

"What's wrong?"

"Nothing. My hip."

"Don't you have something you can take?"

"I'd rather not." She'd rather drink.

Damaris put her hands on her hips. "You were always stubborn. You must get that from your dad. Take something. I'll wait."

Determination gleamed from behind her glasses, telling Michelle this wasn't a battle of wills she was going to win. Besides, by the time she got back to her motel room, the pill would have worn off and she would be able to drink as much as she wanted.

"Fine," she grumbled, then reached for her backpack. She fished out the prescription bottle and swallowed a pill. "Happy?"

"Always."

Michelle kept Carly waiting for two days. Despite the fact that they were spending their workdays in the same building, they seemed to be skilled at avoiding each other.

Carly spent her time alternating between wondering if she should start packing up and praying she didn't have to go. She was able to fake it enough with Gabby that her daughter didn't seem to notice anything was wrong.

Ann had asked to come in late, so Carly was in the gift shop at lunch on Thursday. Several customers were browsing the book section while a teenage girl and her mother sighed over the dolls. Carly rang up a teapot, then wrapped it.

"I hope your friend loves it," she said as she handed over the package. "It's beautiful."

"I think so, too," the middle-aged tourist said. "Have a nice day."

Carly gave her a friendly wave, then turned and nearly ran into Michelle, who had apparently crept silently into the store. Carly had to jump back and steady herself on the counter.

"You have a minute?" Michelle asked.

Carly glanced toward the customers. "I shouldn't leave them."

Michelle eyed the few people looking around. She pointed to the alcove by the rear storage room. "What about there?"

Carly nodded. She could see the cash register and know if anyone was ready to check out.

She crossed to the doorway. Michelle followed more slowly, her gait uneven, her hip obviously troubling her. Carly wanted to ask how she was, but held the words inside. For all she knew, she was about to be fired. Again. Showing compassion in the face of that seemed to be giving away the grain of power she had left.

She hadn't decided if she was going to plead her case or accept her fate with dignity. Two nights of sweating her bank balance had done nothing to improve her lack of a bottom line and going through the Seattle paper hadn't given her much in the way of job options.

As Carly leaned against the door frame, she saw that Michelle looked more tired than she had when she'd first arrived. Lines of weariness and pain pulled at her mouth. Dark smudges shadowed her eyes and there was a gray cast to her skin. Her long hair hung limp, and if she lost any more weight, her cargo pants were going to slip off her skinny hips.

Michelle braced herself against the wall.

"Do you need to sit?" Carly asked, then wanted to smack herself for asking.

Michelle shook her head. "I'm fine."

She was a lot of things, but fine wasn't one of them. Carly told herself this wasn't the time to remember that, years ago, Michelle had been her best friend in the world. That they'd grown up together until ugliness had ripped them apart. Still, she wanted to connect with her former friend, to talk about all that had happened, to find a common middle ground. To heal, she thought wistfully. Closure and something positive out of this mess would be nice.

"You're not stealing."

Michelle made the pronouncement with the ease of someone sharing facts about the weather. Carly's head jerked, as if she'd been slapped. All the warm, gooey feelings evaporated until she was left with anger and the knowledge that she was a down-to-the-bone idiot for expecting anything close to friendship from the woman in front of her.

"I thought maybe you were, but you're not," Michelle continued. "I've been over the bank statements and books for the past three years and I can't find where you've done anything wrong."

If Carly thought she had a hope of surviving without her job, she would have walked away. Simply turned and disappeared into the afternoon, maybe after giving Michelle a well-deserved kick in the teeth.

"How disappointing," Carly snapped. "I'm sure finding out I'm the bad guy in this would be a highlight in your day."

"I'm due a few highlights, and you're right. I'm disappointed. I would love to fire you."

"You did fire me."

"You didn't leave."

"I wasn't sure you meant it." Carly hated to admit the truth.

"I did," Michelle told her flatly. "But it's not a luxury I can afford."

"What does that mean?"

Michelle studied her. "You have to keep this to yourself."

"All right."

"I don't know why I'm about to trust you."

"If it's about the inn, then you can trust me. I've worked here nearly ten years. I care about this place. If that's not enough, then hey, I don't steal. That has to be worth something."

Michelle's left eyebrow rose. "Attitude?"

"I've earned it."

Michelle closed her eyes for a second, then opened them. Emotions swirled through her green irises. Whatever she was thinking, the thoughts weren't happy.

"The inn is in trouble. Financially, we're sinking. I was at the bank a couple of days ago and it's bad."

Carly considered the information. "I don't understand. We had a pretty decent winter. Lots of guests, considering the season. When I paid the bills, there was money in the bank."

"Not enough. Two mortgages were taken out on the property. Ten years ago, there wasn't one." Accusation sharpened the words until they were a knife.

"The renovations," Carly breathed, knowing they had to have cost a fortune.

"Something you pushed my mother to do."

"What? No. They were her idea. We had to get the roof repaired and things sort of spiraled from there." Mostly because Brenda had gotten involved with the contractor. Getting him to do more work had kept him around.

"Sure. Blame the dead woman."

Carly straightened. "You can rewrite history all you want, but that won't change the facts," she said, crossing her arms over her chest. "The renovations were your mother's idea. She's the one who wanted to build this gift shop and expand the restaurant. If you need proof, I can show you the files. She did the drawings, made notes. This was her vision. I wanted to spend the money on remodeling the bathrooms."

Aware of the customers close by, she consciously lowered her voice. "If you'd bothered to come back even once, you'd know that."

"Don't make this about me," Michelle told her. "Trust me, you don't want to fight with me. I'm not who you remember. I can take you down."

Despite the tension between them and the seriousness of the moment, Carly laughed. "Seriously? You're threatening me physically? You were in the army, not the CIA. You can't kill me with a matchbook cover, so get over yourself. You're moving about as fast as a woman in her late nineties and you're obviously in pain. But this is so like you. Reacting without thinking. You're still impulsive."

"You're still annoying."

"Bitch."

"Double bitch." One corner of Michelle's mouth twitched as if she were about to smile.

In that nanosecond, Carly felt the connection that had always been there. Then Michelle's expression turned hard again.

"I still blame you and as far as I'm concerned you're the enemy."

"If that's what it takes for you to sleep at night, go for it. I'm a single mother with a nine-year-old and sixteen hundred dollars in the bank. Making my life more difficult isn't going to be much of a stretch, but sure. If you need to do that to feel important, I can't stop you."

Michelle's jaw tightened. "Then it's in your best interest to keep what I'm about to tell you to yourself."

"All right."

Michelle looked away. For a second it seemed that her shoulders slumped, that she was giving in to defeat. Carly waited, not sure if the weakness was real or a way to trick her. Before she could decide, the moment passed and she drew in a breath.

"The inn's financial state is desperate," Michelle began, then explained about the overdue mortgages and threat of foreclosure.

Because she needed one more thing to keep her up at night, Carly thought grimly, horrified and yet not even surprised by the news.

"She never said a word. Never hinted. Four months ago we were looking at catalogs of French linens."

"Tell me you didn't order any," Michelle said.

"We didn't. But we could have." Carly looked around at the gift shop. "How could she have done this? Don't bother answering. I'm just talking out loud. This is so her. So her."

Anger joined disbelief and resignation. Anger that Brenda, who had seemed to care about Gabby, would have put the child in harm's way.

Carly and Brenda had talked about the future so many times. How Carly would become a partner and then have financial security. The inn would never make her rich, but having money in the bank, a college fund for Gabby, the comfort of knowing she could afford a decent used car every six or seven years, would have been enough.

"I cared about her," Carly murmured, more to herself. "I was there for her when she got sick." She looked at Michelle. "I was there when she died."

As expected, Michelle's expression didn't change.

"She screwed us both. Do you want to keep your job?"

"Yes."

"I want to keep the inn. The bank has conditions. The loans have to be brought up-to-date. We have to maintain better than an eighty-five percent occupancy through the summer. That's twenty-six rooms at any given time."

Michelle hesitated. "There's one more thing. They want you to commit to stay on."

The words sank in slowly. "You can't fire me?"

"You sound smug."

"I've earned it."

"How the hell do you figure that? I'm gone thirty seconds and you weasel your way in here, taking advantage of my mother, sucking this place dry."

Carly glared at her. "That's crap and you know it. I didn't weasel my way into anything. I've worked my ass off here for practically no money. I work ten-or twelve-hour days, I take care of all the guests. Since I've been here, our repeat business is up sixty percent. Do you think they come back because your mother made them feel welcome? It was me."

"Aren't you a saint."

Carly angled toward her. "I'm someone who was here, which is more than I can say for you."

Color stained Michelle's cheeks. "I was away defending your country. Getting shot at."

"You were hiding. You didn't have the courage to come back. You stayed away because it was easier."

"What's your excuse?" Michelle asked, not denying the words. "If everything was so difficult, if you had to work so hard, why didn't you leave?"

"Because she told me I would get a piece of the inn. That I was earning my way into owning part of it."

Michelle stared at her for several seconds. "It wasn't hers to give," she said quietly.

"I found that out recently." That lie had been the hardest to handle.

"I told you the inn was mine. Before. When we were kids."

"I thought you were bragging."

"Maybe if you'd believed me, none of this would have happened."

"What does that mean?" Carly demanded. "That the inn being in trouble was my fault? You're not listening."

In the background a bell tinkled. She turned and saw that all the customers had fled the store. So much for selling anything else this morning.

"I want you to stay on," Michelle told her. "I'll draw up a contract. It will give you job security."

Something Carly could appreciate. "I want to stay in the owner's suite. It's the only home Gabby's ever known."

Michelle's mouth twisted. "Fine."

Carly desperately wanted to demand a raise, as well, but if the inn was in enough trouble that Michelle was willing to promise employment for a period of time, then there wasn't going to be any extra cash for her. Still, she would work harder at saving. She would come up with a plan, and when her contract ended, she would be prepared.

"Thank you for taking care of Brenda. At the end."

The words were as shocking as the news about the inn. Carly blinked. "You're welcome."

"I'm sure it was more meaningful for her than having me here. After all, you were the daughter of her heart, something she mentioned frequently in her emails."

Serve and point, Carly thought grimly. Michelle had learned to go for the throat.

"I'm not going to apologize for taking care of someone who was dying," she snapped. "Twist it however you want. I know what happened. But if it bugs you so much, maybe you should have come home. Or not left in the first place. Of course, you wouldn't have had to run off and join the army if you hadn't slept with my fiancé two days before the wedding. Considering you were my maid of honor, it was a bit of a shock for all of us."

"For you, most of all," Michelle said. "You knew what he was, what he'd done. Why did you marry him?"

"I was pregnant. I didn't think I had much of a choice. I wanted to avoid being a single mother." She gave a hollow laugh. "Not that it made a difference."

She walked to the counter, then turned back. The distance seemed necessary. "Here's the part I don't get. You're not even sorry you slept with him. You never once apologized. You were supposed to be my friend."

"So were you."

"What did I do?"

Michelle studied her for a long time. "Aside from having a convenient memory, nothing, I guess."

She was obviously bitter about something, but Carly couldn't figure what. She'd been the one betrayed by the two people she should have been able to trust. Talk about a convenient memory.

"I'm sorry my mother lied to you about the inn."

Carly opened her mouth, then closed it. "All right," she said cautiously, not sure she wasn't being set up.

"I mean it. It was never hers and she used that to keep you around. Neither of us is surprised by that, but it's still wrong."

"Thank you."

Michelle nodded.

"He left it to you in a trust?" Carly asked.

"Until I was twenty-five. Brenda kept running it after that. I would rather have had him than this," she said, raising her glance to the ceiling. "He didn't give me the option."

Carly thought about pointing out she'd lost her mother at the same time, with equally devastating consequences, but didn't want to spoil their very tenuous détente.

"I'll stay," Carly told her. "I'm happy to sign an employment agreement."

"For two years?"

Which was a whole lot longer than she'd expected. She wasn't sure they could work together for two years. But she was willing to try.

She nodded.

"I'm giving you a raise," Michelle told her. "It won't be much at first, but as soon as we're on better financial, footing, it will be more."

Like Carly believed that. "Okay."

"You don't sound convinced."

"I've heard it before."

"I'm not Brenda."

"I'm not a lot of things but that doesn't stop you from not trusting me."

Michelle surprised her by smiling. "Point taken. I'll put it in writing." The smile faded. "You're going to bite my head off, but I have to ask. Why don't you have your dad's house? Shouldn't you be living there rather than here?"

"I sold the house. It was Allen's idea." Her shiny new husband had convinced her they needed something bigger for their growing family. She'd foolishly agreed, accepting his plan for them to sell it first and then go looking for something else.

"He took off with all the money two days after we closed escrow. Every penny. It was in a joint account, making it community property. The cops patted me on the head and told me I was pretty enough to find another husband, but to be a little smarter next time."

She raised her chin slightly, waiting for the blow.

"I'm sorry."

"That's it? No emotional punch? No low blows?"

"I'm having an off day." Michelle pushed off the wall and limped toward her. The grayness was back, along with an air of weariness. "We have to talk about the inn. Who's going to work where. I'd like to do that tomorrow."

"Sure. Oh, I spoke with some people a couple of days ago. Psychologists. They have some kind of seminar in the area. A marriage retreat. They want to rent three rooms a week, Tuesday to Thursday, through the summer. I've checked the reservations and we have openings. I wanted to talk to you before I agreed."

"Tell them no problem. We need the money."

"I'll call this afternoon." She hesitated. "Do you need to take a pill or something?"

"I look that bad, huh? I'll be fine. Everything hurts. It's going to hurt for a long time."

"Do you want to talk about it?"

"Talk about what?"

"Anything."

"With you?" She laughed. "No."

"If you change your mind…"

"I won't. Even if you mean it, you couldn't handle it." The laughter faded. "I'm not a project, Carly. I'm your boss. If you remember that, we'll get along fine."

She turned and limped out.

Carly watched her go, torn between bitter anger and really annoying empathy. While she resented Michelle and the inherent unfairness of the situation, she could see her point. Michelle *was* her boss. The fact that they'd once been friends didn't seem to matter.

As for what Michelle had been through—she had a feeling it was worse than anything Carly could imagine. Maybe understanding wasn't possible, but a little compassion couldn't hurt.

She sighed. Who was she kidding—it would hurt a lot. But that didn't mean she wasn't going to try.

Eight

"**W**hy'd your mother name you Mango?" Michelle asked in a gasp, her breath coming in pants. "Was it a fruit thing? Do you have a sister named Nectarine?"

Jolts of agony ripped through her hip, up her side and down her leg. Mango, a tall, dangerous-looking, dark-haired guy with the heart and soul of the devil, grinned.

"It's a family name," he said easily, adding tension to the machine. "Five more."

Her sweat-slicked hands slipped on the grips.

"I can't," she said, knowing she'd reached the end—that place where she was close to begging for mercy.

"You can. You don't want to. There's a difference."

"I'm going to kill you."

Mango patted her shoulder. "If I had a nickel for every time someone threatened me, I'd be a rich man. Five more, Michelle. Don't make me use my physical-thera-pist voice. You won't like it."

If she could muster the strength, she would hit him. She knew how to punch in a way that left a bruise. One of the advantages of her military training. Not the official

kind, but still helpful. Of course, Mango was big enough
to snap her like a twig in return.

She wondered why a guy like him was working as
a physical therapist instead of—what was it Carly had
said?—working for some spy agency and killing people
with a matchbook cover.

"Quit stalling."

She swore at him, then moved her leg three more
times before her head went fuzzy and the edges began
to darken.

Faster than she would have thought possible, he had
her out of the machine, bent over, his hand forcing her
head down.

"Breathe," he instructed, his massive fingers gripping
her in such a way that she knew she wasn't going to be
allowed to sit upright until he released her. "I don't care
if you vomit, but you're not passing out."

"Is that information or are you giving me an order?"
she asked between breaths.

"Both."

She breathed deep and the room cleared. "I'm good."

He released her. "I'm better."

She leaned back against the equipment and tried to
smile. "I'm sure you are. Right now I don't give a rat."

"You will."

"Maybe."

"Cheerful. Guys like that in a woman. You're not
doing your exercises at home."

"Does anyone?"

"The ones who want to get better manage to find the
time. Who do I have to threaten to call to get you to co-
operate?"

"No one." She stood and turned her back, mostly to
avoid any pity he might accidentally show.

"There has to be someone. A friend. An enemy. I'm not picky."

"Okay, yeah. A friend." Damaris counted. If she included her nightly dance with the vodka bottle, she could say two friends. Practically a posse.

"Do the stretching, do the exercises. The more you listen to me, the faster you get to stop coming here."

"There's motivation."

She reached for her cane. Normally she ignored it but there was no way to walk out of here without help after a therapy session.

Mango patted her on the arm. "You're doing good. It'll get easier."

"You say that to all the girls."

He grinned. "You're a patient, not a girl. You don't get to hear what I say to them. Come on, I'll walk you out."

She trailed after him, stepping around equipment and other vets, mostly guys, working the program. Compared with a lot of the patients, she was lucky—barely injured. She still had her arms and legs, and any lingering trauma was carefully hidden on the inside where only she could see it.

Not wanting to go there, she allowed her gaze to drift to Mango's butt. It was impressive—high and tight. An athlete's butt. She would bet he looked good naked. Not that she could imagine caring about naked guys ever again.

"Next week," Mango told her. "Don't be late."

"Was I late today?"

"No, but I don't want to get my hopes up."

His easy grin was infectious. She found herself smiling right back, despite the steady throbbing in her hip.

She hobbled toward the exit, pausing to check out the bulletin board by the door. There were all kinds of postings. The usual assortment of items for sales, requests for car pooling and free kittens. She scanned them all, looking for a room to rent.

With the inn's financial trouble, she couldn't stay there and use one of the rooms they could be renting out every night. Plus, she didn't want to be that close to Carly. An apartment was more than she needed right now. She planned on working long hours for the next few months. A room was plenty. The trick would be getting one that wasn't too far away. She was willing to drive, but anything farther than forty minutes would be too much.

She'd nearly given up when she saw a small index card listing a room for rent on Blackberry Island. The address was only a couple of miles from the inn. The dirt-cheap price made her wonder if she would be sharing the space with anything that crawled, but she made the call, anyway, punching in the number on her cell phone.

"Tenly."

"Hi. I'm calling about the room for rent. I saw the card at the VA hospital."

The man on the other end paused. "Is the room for you?"

"Yes."

"It's a mother-in-law suite. No private entrance, but it's off the kitchen, at the other end of the house. You familiar with the island?"

"I grew up there. Michelle Sanderson."

"From the inn."

She wasn't surprised he knew. The island was small enough that most people knew one another. There was only one school—a K through 8—where all the kids went. After that, they were bused off island to the nearest high school.

"Jared Tenly."

She recognized the name but couldn't put a face to it. If she had to guess, she would say he was a few years older than her.

"When'd you get back?" he asked.

"A few months ago. I got to the island last week."

"You're at the VA hospital, so you were injured." He paused. "Okay, you can see the room when you want."

"How about now?"

"Now works."

"Give me half an hour to get there."

"I'll be waiting."

Michelle slung her backpack over her shoulder, then slid down from her truck, doing her best to take the brunt of her weight with her good leg. Even so, the jolt made her gasp and gag. Thinking about throwing up reminded her of Mango, which made her want to laugh. The combination had her choking and coughing, as if she'd swallowed wrong.

When she got control of herself, she eyed the walkway to the house. It was only about fifteen or twenty feet. She shook her head and reached for her cane. Dancing wasn't in her future anytime soon, she thought. At this point she would be thrilled to walk around without causing people to point and stare. At least the house was a single story. She couldn't imagine having to deal with stairs at the end of the day. Bad enough she would have to go up and down them at the inn.

Leaning heavily on the cane, she walked around the truck and went up the driveway rather than stepping on the curb. The house looked to have been built in the late forties, with a wide porch and decorative dormers. The paint—a soft blue—had faded with time to something closer to gray. The windows were clean enough not to be scary but not so bright that she had to worry that Jared Tenly was one of those weird men obsessed with washing everything in sight.

She'd made it halfway up the walk when the front door opened and a man stepped out. The sight of him brought her to a stop.

He was big—at least six-four, with shaggy blond hair and broad shoulders. She was five-eight, but he towered above her. Under regular circumstances, she probably wouldn't have cared, but with her hip and her current state of exhaustion, vulnerability threatened.

His face leaned toward interesting rather than pretty, although his blue eyes were nice. If she had to pick a single word to describe them, she would say *kind*. He wore the local guys' uniform of a faded plaid shirt tucked into worn jeans.

"Michelle?"

She nodded.

He looked her up and down, his gaze lingering on the cane. "We'll go around back."

He stepped off the porch easily, his stride long, chewing up ground. "The room's on the rear side of the house."

He led the way, holding open a gate for her. She saw a ramp leading up to the back door.

"Previous tenant," he said with a nod.

Lucky her. A ramp was easier than stairs. At least for now.

They went inside.

The kitchen had been updated about ten years ago. The cabinets were wood and plentiful, the stove looked as if it didn't get a whole lot of use. The vinyl floor had a few scratches but looked clean enough for her comfort level. She wasn't obsessive, but had no love for anything that skittered, crept or crawled.

"Living room and dining room are through there," he said, pointing to a doorway at the far end of the kitchen. "Want to see them?"

"Anything noteworthy?"

"No.

"Then I don't need to see them."

He led her in the other direction, down a short hall. He opened a door on the left, showing her a small utility room that contained a washer and dryer, then he stepped into the bedroom at the rear of the house.

It was a decent size, with a queen bed at one end and a TV on a dresser at the other. She checked out the closet, then the small three-quarter bath. The sight of the shower relieved her. At least she wouldn't have to step into a tub every day.

Last she walked through an archway to a small sun-room. Two chairs sat facing the big windows and the backyard behind. Grass led down to the steely-gray water lapping at the shore.

The space was big enough for her purposes. Clean, too. The neighborhood quiet.

She turned to him. "What do you do?"

"I have a couple of boats. Sports fishing and tours."

Seasonal, she thought, understanding how the winters could be long and financially lean. Renting out a room would give him a little more income each month. Everyone appreciated that.

"I'll take it," she said. "Do you have some kind of an application you want me to fill out?"

"No. Just give me a check. I rent by the month. Any idea how long you'll be staying?"

"Through the summer," she said, dropping her backpack to the bed and digging through it until she found her checkbook. Once business slowed at the inn, she could find a more permanent place.

She found a pen, then started to write.

When she was done, she looked at him.

"I don't cook," she told him.

"Neither do I. There's plenty of space in the refrigerator for whatever you want to keep there. I keep a couple of empty cupboards, too. I'll leave them open so you'll know which ones they are. No drugs, no loud parties."

"Not a problem. I won't have time for either."

"Good to know."

She held out the check. "I won't be sleeping with you."

One eyebrow rose as he looked her up and down. "You're not my type."

"Just so we're clear."

"I'm clear."

She handed over the money.

He took it from her and fished a key out of his pants pocket. "Here you go."

She closed her fingers around the cool metal.

"Moving in today?" he asked. "Just so I can get myself under control in time."

He was teasing her. She should have shot something back at him, but she couldn't think of anything appropriately cutting.

She knew what he was thinking. That she wasn't pretty enough, wasn't feminine. She'd never been especially girly, but living with a few thousand soldiers had made her even less inclined. Now she couldn't imagine ever caring about something like her clothes or nails. Her only goals in life were to save the inn and stop hurting. If she could even get one night of decent sleep, she would consider herself lucky.

"Either today or tomorrow," she said. "I have some other things to do."

"Need any help with your things?"

"No, thanks."

"All right. I'll see you around."

She nodded and turned.

Her foot caught on the carpet, locking her in place. Her weight shifted, landing on her bad hip and leg. The pain was a bullet of glass and fire, wrenching the last of her reserve from her and nearly bringing her to her knees. Only a strong grip on her upper arms kept her from falling.

She gulped in air, nearly weeping from the searing burn.

"I'm okay," she managed, shifted her weight and straightening.

Jared waited until she was steady before he released her.

She thought he would say something. Offer to help her to her truck or tell her she needed to go to the doctor. Instead, he remained silent. Maybe he didn't like to get involved. Maybe he knew she had to figure this out on her own.

She made it to the door, then glanced at him over her shoulder. "Thank you. I'll see you around."

"I'll be here."

She nodded and left.

Once in the truck, she glanced at the house. From the outside, it wasn't much. But to her it was everything she needed. A place to retreat and lick her wounds. Somewhere she didn't have to pretend. Sanctuary.

Nine

Carly had spent hours of her life sitting on the visitor's side of Brenda's desk. They'd discussed work, had talked about their plans, and sometimes Brenda had yelled at her.

The unhappy conversations had been long and difficult, with Brenda ranting and screaming, calling Carly names, threatening to fire her until her voice went hoarse. Sensing giving in to tears would mean the other woman had won, Carly had kept quiet, offering a few words of defense when she could, otherwise simply enduring.

Despite the fact that Brenda had been gone three months and Carly had a two-year employment agreement, she still felt a flutter of nerves as she walked into the familiar space.

She rarely used the room, preferring to do her paperwork from a much smaller office behind the linen storage closet. The sense of safety and privacy more than made up for the lack of windows and ancient furniture.

Michelle, still pale and thin, motioned for her to sit. Carly eyed the chair, wondering if she would ever be able to see it without remembering the screaming. Reminding herself that Michelle wasn't her mother and that she was needed would have to be enough for now.

"Thanks for getting me this," Michelle said, waving the papers Carly had given her. They listed everyone's duties, including her own, and approximate hours worked.

"I'm going to go through the books for the past couple of years and see where all the money went," Michelle continued. "From what I've been able to learn so far, there have been plenty of guests staying at the inn. I know the remodeling sucked up big chunks of cash."

Her gaze dropped to Carly's wrist, where one of Brenda's charm bracelets lay next to her watch.

Carly stiffened. Brenda had left her all her personal effects. It was in her will, the one Carly had taken to a local attorney to discuss. The one that made it clear the inn had never been Brenda's to offer.

Carly had packed up the other woman's personal belongings and put them in storage. Clothes, books, papers. A lifetime of intimate things. Even though Brenda had charged her with taking care of them, Carly hadn't been sure. Michelle was Brenda's daughter. The decisions should have been hers.

Brenda had also left Carly all her jewelry. The collection had grown over the years. Pretty rings and earrings. A few necklaces and the charm bracelets.

Carly had packed most of them away, as well, keeping a few pieces—the ones with good memories. Legally she could have kept it all. Brenda had been very specific in her will. But it hadn't seemed like the right thing to do.

Now she felt self-conscious about the bracelet, wanting to cover it with her free hand and explain.

"I need to follow the money," Michelle told her. "That

will take a few days. Maybe a week." She glanced at the list Carly had prepared. "You have a lot of responsibilities."

"I like to keep busy."

"You're scattered."

"I fill in where I'm needed."

"You're good with the guests."

Carly tilted her head, sure she couldn't have heard right. "What?"

"I've read a lot of the comment cards they leave behind and I've been talking to people."

"Not Damaris," she muttered before she could stop herself.

Michelle surprised her by smiling. "Not Damaris. But other people who work here. Everyone likes you."

Carly waited, but there was no slam that followed the comment. "I like what I do," she finally admitted. "Working with the guests is what I enjoy most."

"Then it all works out because I think you need to spend most of your day dealing with the guests. That's where the money is. We're rearranging the work schedule in the gift shop."

Carly thought about the store and sighed. "It's not making much money, is it?"

"I haven't looked into it in detail yet, but no. What the hell were you thinking?"

Vintage Michelle, she told herself. "I was thinking that your mother wanted to open a gift shop, and no, I couldn't talk her out of it and neither could you. I was thinking we could use a hotel-like gift shop off the lobby where we offered snacks, toiletries and a few local knick-knacks. She had Barty draw up the designs for what you see now."

"Barty?"

"The contractor."

"My mother slept with a guy named Barty?"

Carly grinned. "I think it was a family name."

"Like Mango? What is it with these family names?"

"Mango?"

"Never mind. So now we have Barty to thank for that monstrosity. I have no idea what we're going to do about it. Maybe fire-sale everything. I'll have to work up the numbers. I wonder what we can use the space for."

"The gift shop might be profitable if we had more focused inventory."

"We're competing with the stores in town."

"We have a captive audience with our guests. If they decide they want something, why go all that way when they can buy it here? With the gift shop as part of the hotel, our rent is cheaper. Maybe we could narrow the scope and sell it for a little less than everyone else."

"That could work."

"Excuse me while I fall over in my chair."

Michelle glanced at her. "You're allowed to have good ideas. You managed to work with my mother for nearly a decade. That means you're tough or really, really stubborn."

"Maybe both," Carly said, thinking she'd never thought of herself as tough, but she liked the sound of being that way.

"I'll run the numbers. It's all going to come down to math." She passed over a sheet of paper.

Carly leaned forward and took it.

A neat grid showed the various parts of the inn—the restaurant, front desk, housekeeping, the gift shop—and the hours of operation. Names had been placed in different boxes.

"It's a work schedule," Carly said, pleased to see it

was close to the one she used, with a few modifications. Mostly in her hours. They were substantially less.

"A lot easier to do on the computer," Michelle told her. "How can you survive without knowing how to use one?"

"I know how," Carly told her. "I've taken business classes at the community college. Brenda preferred to handle it all herself. When she got sick, I offered to help, but she refused."

"So it's not that you can't use the computer?"

"I know how."

"That's something. You'll let everyone know about the new schedule?"

"Sure."

"Then I guess we're done here."

Carly didn't stand.

As much as she hated to admit it, Michelle had been completely reasonable. Was that a temporary phenomenon or could she count on a boss who was even-tempered and rational? It was a heady thought.

"You have something else?" Michelle asked.

"A couple of things. They're related."

Michelle leaned back in her chair. "Go ahead."

"How are you feeling?"

"We're not talking about that."

The words came quickly, forcefully. Michelle's attention immediately went back to the computer screen. Carly wasn't sure if her work was that interesting or if was a defense mechanism. She would guess the latter.

"You're tired," Carly continued. "I know what I'm doing here. I can help."

"Do your job. That helps."

"That's it? You have nothing else to say?"

Michelle rolled her eyes. "What more do you want?

Should I tell you I'd be lost without you? That you complete me? That working together is great? I don't know what it's going to be."

"Meaning if the bank weren't forcing you to keep me, I'd be out on my ass?"

"I honestly don't know. I have no reason to trust you."

Carly wanted to point out that the truth was, in fact, the reverse. She shouldn't and couldn't trust Michelle.

"Whether you trust me or not, you need me. You've told me how things are here, so I'm going to do the same." She stood, partially to give herself a sense of power and partially to be able to bolt. "You need to dress better."

Michelle's expression hardened and a muscle under her left eye twitched. "Excuse me?"

"You heard me. This is a place of business where we deal with our guests on a personal basis. Your shirts are hanging on you and those cargo pants you wear are hideous. Dirty and stained and falling off. You need to dress more professionally."

Michelle slowly, painfully stood. She braced her hands on her desk and leaned forward. "Get out."

Carly stood her ground. "You're giving our guests the wrong impression."

"Get out."

"Get your hair cut and try a little makeup."

"Get out!"

The last two words were delivered at a volume that could shake windows.

"Fine. I'm leaving. But you know I'm right."

Still fuming from her run-in with Carly, Michelle stalked out into the warm afternoon. Okay, not stalked.

She walked slowly, limping, but she was moving purposefully in her heart.

She stepped into the watery sunlight and let the quiet peace of the outdoors calm her. Unfortunately, as she moved, she felt her cargo pants sliding down her hips, which reminded her of Carly, which made her want to scream. And she'd never been a screamer.

She wanted to blame Carly, but knew she was fighting a whole lot bigger battle than simply an annoying friend. Former friend, she reminded herself. And dammit all to hell, Carly was right about the clothes and her appearance. In truth, she was almost embarrassed about how she looked. She avoided mirrors—not a huge challenge these days. There was only a small one in her bathroom. But still, she knew she looked bad.

She eyed the grass on the expansive lawn, wondering if she had the strength to deal with the uneven ground. From there her gaze slid to all the daises. They were a cheerful flower and they also annoyed her.

The call of a crane caught her attention. Nature annoyed her, too, with her daisies and birds and—

Her gaze narrowed as she realized there were three or four cranes at the far end of the lawn, by the trees, their clawed feet stepping on the grass as they headed toward something she couldn't see.

Knowing walking on grass would count as exercise and make Mango happy, she set off to find out what they were doing. The afternoon was relatively warm—nearly the mid-sixties—and being outside was…nice.

She walked slowly, taking her time, being careful not to do anything stupid. When she was only a dozen or so feet from the trees she realized the cranes had their attention on Carly's daughter. Or at least on the small plate of cookies on the blanket next to her.

The girl was reading, her attention completely caught up in the book. Michelle took a second to study the blond hair, the slight body. She still had trouble believing Carly had a kid, but here was proof.

As she watched, she realized Gabby wasn't reading at all. That she was tense, her shoulders hunched, her head pulled close to her chest, her breathing rapid. Michelle recognized the symptoms of fear, but it took her a second to find the cause.

The cranes.

Like every other student on the island, Michelle had studied cranes in grade-school science classes. She knew the Puget Sound cranes were on the small side—maybe forty inches tall. They migrated every year, lived in pairs during breeding season and their dove-gray body feathers darkened to an almost blue-gray by the tail.

"Hey," Michelle said softly, before she could stop herself.

Gabby jumped, then looked up. The cranes hopped back.

"What are you doing here?" the girl demanded.

"I came outside because I couldn't stand being inside anymore. You ever get like that?"

Gabby studied her. "Maybe."

Michelle looked toward the chattering cranes. The boldest of the three started toward the cookies again. "When I was about your age, the cranes had it out for me. I spent the whole summer getting pooped on. It was disgusting."

"Really?"

Michelle nodded. "They're hard to avoid around here."

"I know. We have scientists who come and do research on them."

"Have they figured out how to stop them from pooping?"

Gabby smiled. "No."

"Figures. They're probably studying things like population and eggs and stuff."

The smile widened. "They are. You should talk to Leonard. He knows all about them. You can ask about the poop."

"There's a way to start a conversation. 'Hey, Leonard. About that crane poop.'"

Gabby giggled.

Michelle pointed to the cranes. "Are you afraid of them?" she asked bluntly.

The humor faded. "They always follow me."

"You have cookies. They want food."

"Not always. Sometimes I'm just out."

Michelle glanced at the blanket and thought about sitting down. The problem was she couldn't figure out how she would manage to get back on her feet. She didn't think the visual of her crawling back to the inn would help their guests feel more comfortable.

"I read this article once," Michelle said. "Puget Sound cranes can recognize human faces and somehow they tell other cranes about certain people. So if somebody is mean to a crane, the whole flock learns about it."

"I know," Gabby said, glancing at the nearby birds with more than a little fear in her eyes. "Scientists thought that only crows had facial recognition, but they've realized our cranes have it, too. They're special."

"Interesting. How do you know that?"

"I'm smart."

"And modest."

Gabby grinned.

"Okay, so one crane tells the other cranes and some-

how everyone in the flock knows about the latest gossip."
Michelle shrugged. "Obviously they associate you with
food, which is why they're hanging around, trying to in-
timidate you into giving up your cookies."

Gabby's eyes widened. "You're right. Because when I
read out here, I usually bring a snack. Do you think if I
stopped having food around, they'd stop bothering me?"

"Sure. They'd figure it out. You're not the only smart
one here."

Gabby tilted her head. "Does your leg hurt?"

"Pretty much all the time."

"You were injured in the war, right? That's what Mom
said. That you were protecting our country."

Michelle shifted, not sure what to say to that. Carly
being nice made her uncomfortable. Michelle was old-
school. Enemies should be clearly defined, like in car-
toons.

"I was serving, yes."

"That was really nice of you. Thank you."

Despite her resistance to the compliment, she found
herself touched by the girl's sincerity. "You're welcome."

"Next time I come out, I'll bring a chair so you can
sit down."

Michelle smiled, pleased by both the gesture and the
proof that Gabby wasn't afraid of her anymore. She had
enough demons to deal with. Especially ones that involved another little girl in a faraway place.

"I'll bring a book," she said, "and we'll read together."

Ten

"She's so annoying."

Carly made the pronouncement while stacking dishes in the sink and running water over them. Robert had joined them for dinner as he did at least once every couple of weeks. She appreciated the adult conversation and the chance to cook for someone with more adult sensibilities than Gabby, but there were times when she missed having a girlfriend to rant to. Robert was a typical guy. He had trouble simply listening and mostly wanted to fix the problem.

"Don't get me wrong. I'm happy to have a job."

"And job security," he said from a chair at the tiny kitchen table.

"That, too. That more than anything."

With her raise and careful planning, she could grow her nest egg. And if Michelle really did mean for her to work fewer hours, then she could get serious about getting her associate's degree in business.

"She's going to be different," Robert said. "It's been ten years and she's been through a lot."

"I know."

"She's wounded."

Carly sighed. "I should be more patient."

"You're not the only one figuring it all out."

She wasn't thrilled with him taking Michelle's side, but knew he was actually being reasonable.

"It is a lot to take in," she admitted, plunging her hands into the soapy water and scrubbing the first plate.

The rhythm of the familiar work relaxed her. There were too many evenings when she'd grabbed food from the kitchen and brought it back to have a quick dinner with her daughter before starting the evening ritual. Whatever else might be going on with her day, Carly was there at night.

The amount of love she felt for her child continued to surprise her. She hadn't been pleased to find herself pregnant—things with Allen had been difficult even before the wedding. She'd thought about breaking things off. But getting pregnant had made that impossible. She'd been terrified of being alone and had made what she thought was a deal with the devil to keep that from happening.

She would marry a man she knew wasn't good for her but in return she wouldn't be a single mother. Apparently she should have been clearer about the bargain.

Not that she would change anything now, she thought, rinsing plates and stacking them in the dish rack. The first couple of years had been harder than she'd believed possible. She'd been terrified all the time, overwhelmed with responsibility, barely able to afford diapers on the tiny paycheck she'd earned at the inn. Brenda had been there for her, both a blessing and a curse.

Brenda had seen them as similar. Abandoned by their husbands, single mothers. But Brenda had never had to worry about getting enough to eat or having to decide between gas for the car and getting her daughter vaccinated.

Over time the situation had improved. Carly had learned how to do nearly every job at the inn and slowly she'd made more money. Just when she'd decided she needed more financial stability, Brenda had started hinting she would allow Carly to earn her way into an ownership position.

"She lied to me," she said, staring down at the soap bubbles. "She stood there, looked me in the eye and lied to me."

"Michelle?"

Carly glanced at Robert and shook her head. "Brenda. All those years she told me I was part owner. I worked for practically nothing and I believed her."

He stood and crossed the two steps to the sink, then rested his large hand on her shoulder. "You couldn't have known."

"I should have. I should have asked for something in writing. I should have gone to see a lawyer."

"You trusted her."

"I was stupid."

The weight of his hand seemed to anchor her in place. She wanted to shrug out of the contact, but couldn't make her muscles move. Tension built between them. Not the good kind.

They'd been doing this too long, she told herself. Playing at being in a relationship. One without benefits. Maybe because they were too lazy to get into something meaningful with other people or because they were afraid to. Either way, they'd grown comfortable in a sort of half life.

"Things will be different now," he told her.

"I can't decide if that's good or bad."

"You don't have to worry about moving."

"That's something. I don't want to have to uproot Gabby more than necessary. She loves it here."

She ducked around him to wipe down the table. The tiny kitchen she'd always loved suddenly felt confining. She eyed the living room and wondered how to get him to go sit on the sofa. Or maybe leave.

"Give it time," he told her. "You and Michelle used to be friends. You'll get to know each other again."

"Friends? It's been years. We weren't exactly speaking when she left town."

"I'm sure her time in the army has changed her."

Carly rinsed out the dishcloth and hung it over the sink. "How do you know that? You barely knew her before."

"How could war not change someone?"

She wanted to point out that he had no clue what he was talking about. Watching *Band of Brothers* didn't make him an expert on the military. But she kept quiet because Robert had always been kind to her and there had been so many times when she'd needed that.

She studied his dark hair, his rugged face.

He'd gone to work in the family auto shop right out of high school. He'd dated the same girl for five years and would have married her if she hadn't been killed in a car accident two months before the wedding. He'd taken care of things when his father had died eight years ago and had gotten his mother settled in a nice condo in South Carolina.

He paid his bills on time, he liked to watch sports and he'd never deliberately hurt another person even once in his life.

Robert was the type of man who made a good husband and a better father. He could fix a faucet, explain fractions and sit through a foreign film with only minor grumbling.

She should have wanted to be with him. But she didn't. And it wasn't as if he was pushing *her* to settle down. Yet here they were, acting like husband and wife, talking about what was going on in their lives over dinner and kitchen cleanup.

No matter how she tried to talk herself into caring about him as something other than her former brother-in-law, she couldn't.

"Don't you want more than this?" she asked, blurting out the question. "Than what we have? Don't you want to fall in love, or at least find someone you're desperate to sleep with? We're both hiding, Robert. From the world or love or something. Don't you think we need more?"

"I like what we have."

"I do, too." She sighed. "It's easy. But easy isn't always right. I think maybe we should take a step back. Look for other options."

For a second he looked stricken, then he nodded once, grabbed his jacket and headed for the front door.

Carly groaned, hurrying after him. "Robert, wait. Don't be mad. Don't go."

He stopped, his hand on the knob. "You don't get to have it both ways," he said. And then he was gone.

Michelle could feel the daisies mocking her. They were everywhere. She could accept them in the garden— they were plants, after all, and it was easy enough not to look out the window. But they were other places, too. On the walls, both as paper and in a mural someone had painted. In vases and on pillows. There were books on daisies in the lobby, note cards with them in the gift shop. They were printed on fabric, woven into wreaths and worn as enameled pins, their colors brighter than nature intended. Blackberries were fine. At least you could eat them, but the damned daisies served no purpose.

When she'd served in the desert, she'd quickly learned what to watch out for. Camel spiders were poisonous and aggressive, moving toward anyone who approached rather than running away. Michelle knew if she turned her back, the daisies would act the same way, taking over more territory, eventually suffocating them all with petals and leaves.

An image of the inn buried in giant flowers was both humorous and slightly disturbing. Probably not something she should discuss with anyone.

A light rain fell. Despite the weather, the inn was busy. They'd been full the previous night and would be tonight. The blessing of weekends, she thought, moving through the lobby. A few families were in residence, along with several couples. The restaurant had been busy that morning, as well. She'd walked through on her way to the kitchen and her morning cup of coffee with Damaris.

Money flowing in would help, but it would take more than that to restore the business's financial footing. Michelle pulled the daisies from the small glass vase on her desk and dumped them in the trash, then returned her attention to her computer screen.

People were going to have to be let go. She'd been dancing around that reality for nearly a week, but couldn't escape the truth of it. The payroll was ridiculously large for an inn this size. Nearly every position was overstaffed.

Michelle had dealt with personnel issues before, but in the army, you got transferred rather than fired. Now she would be messing with people's lives in a way that didn't make her comfortable.

She'd been back nearly two weeks. She'd had a chance to review the books, the tax returns, the financial statements. Her mother had a lot to answer for. She wasn't going to have to explain herself to anyone in this world, but Michelle hoped there would be an accounting in the afterlife. Her mother's actions had been criminal at worst, and beyond selfish at best.

Nearly as distressing was the realization that Carly had been a voice of sanity, speaking out against the worst of Brenda's craziness. Michelle had heard it from several vendors and more than a few of the staff. Carly cared about the inn, did the right thing and made the guests love her.

Michelle stood and left her office. The ache in her hip was her constant companion. Sleep would probably help her heal faster, but she'd been unable to relax enough to let it happen. There were too many threats in the dark. Nightmares were sneaky, attacking where she least expected. Better to lie awake in the dark, safe.

She'd been in her rented room for several nights, enjoying the quiet and privacy. But liking the surroundings didn't make the past go away. She spent the hours of darkness waiting for an unknown, unnamed enemy to attack, and even though he never came, every morning she was as exhausted as if she'd fought him off by herself.

She limped toward the reception area, using the wall for support every few steps. She was going to have to talk to Carly about who should be let go. As much as Michelle didn't want to rely on her, she didn't have a choice. Carly knew the staff and she understood the inn. Just as helpful, she was willing to say things Michelle didn't want to hear. Like her crack about Michelle's clothes.

A quick trip to Wal-Mart had given her a selection of

black trousers and different shirts. Black athletic shoes replaced the lace-up boots she'd been wearing.

Although makeup was beyond her, she had an appointment to get her hair cut that afternoon at a local salon. She had to admit, looking better made her feel a little better. More here rather than in some kind of emotional limbo.

Carly wasn't at the front desk. The young woman there said she thought Carly had gone to check on her daughter.

"I'll catch her later," Michelle said, starting to return to her office, then thinking she would go to the kitchen and get more coffee before tackling her next task.

She paused by the display of brochures and advertisements for local businesses. A couple of maps showed where to eat and shop in town, while another offered a walking tour of historic Blackberry Island. The Mansion on the Hill, known as the Moth to locals, housed the island's only organic restaurant, along with a flower shop, yoga studio and Michelle wasn't sure what else. She only knew that much because of a flyer she'd seen. She straightened a few of the papers, then turned to head to the dining room, only to discover she wasn't alone.

A small child stood in front of her. A little girl of maybe three or four, with dark hair. She held a ratty stuffed cat in her arms. Most of the acrylic fur had been rubbed away, as if the poor creature had a skin condition. She would guess the toy had once been red. Now it was faded, and dirty in places.

But what got her attention were the girl's eyes. They were round and dark and frighteningly familiar.

She told herself this moment wasn't the same, wasn't real. That there was no danger. But the information didn't seem to make any sense, nor did it slow her thudding heart. She could feel herself starting to tremble.

"I'm learning to read," the kid said. "I already know my letters and I can read some words. The little ones."

The girl continued talking, but Michelle couldn't hear her anymore. Even as she told her body to move, to turn, to head for safety, she felt the coldness seeping through her. That's what came first for her. The cold.

It wasn't the result of a change in temperature. Instead, it came from within. It spiraled up and out, immobilizing her. First her legs wouldn't move and then her arms. The trembling stopped. Her breathing became shallow. As the edges of the world blurred and darkened, everything disappeared but a pinpoint of light.

From that pinpoint, disaster grew. The sounds were first. In the distance a deadly *clat-clat-clat* of gunfire was punctuated by explosions. The screams came next. The calls of the dying, the injured. Her sense of smell reacted last but it was the most powerful, dragging her back to that place. The smell of death. The distinct odor of spent ammunition, of blood, fire and smoke, burning oil. And then she was there. Back where she didn't want to be, weapon in her hands.

She was the last one left standing, the last one able to defend them all. Kill or be killed.

She heard the bullet that hit her a nanosecond before it screamed into her, sending her spinning back and causing the ground to race up and slam into her. Felt the bones shattering, the blood pumping down her leg.

She forced herself to keep moving, to roll onto her good side, to take aim.

She saw him then—the shooter. A lone man half-concealed by a burned-out Humvee. He raised his rifle and took aim.

She couldn't move fast enough. She knew that, knew this was the end. His hand moved and he pulled the trigger.

There was nothing. She didn't know if the gun jammed or if he was out of ammunition. Either way, she'd been given a second chance. She lined up the shot and then she saw it. Saw her.

The child holding on to his leg. The small girl with big eyes and long hair. The child who screamed when her father was killed with a single shot to the chest.

Michelle gasped, the pinpoint widened and she was released. She turned blindly, stumbled out of the room and down the hall, needing to be somewhere else. Anywhere else. She escaped to the bathroom and locked the door behind her. She barely made it to the toilet, before she had to bend over and vomit.

Minutes later, still shaking, still terrified of being pulled back into that other world, she unlocked the door. It immediately flung open.

"What do you think you're doing?" Carly demanded, standing in the restroom, glaring at her. "You just terrified one of our guests' children. She's screaming in her mother's arms about the scary lady who yelled at her. What the hell is wrong with you?"

"I didn't—"

"I don't want to hear excuses," Carly told her, anger brightening her eyes. "If you expect this inn to be a success, you need to get your act together and start behaving responsibly."

"I couldn't stop."

"Stop what? What are you talking about?"

"I killed a man. The one who shot me. I remembered. His daughter was with him. That's why—"

Carly went white.

Michelle swore. She hadn't meant to say any of it. She'd meant to shout back, to distract or accuse. Instead, there was the truth—a bare ugliness that caused her stomach to rise again.

She hurried back into the stall and threw up a second time. She straightened, gasping, then turned only to find that she was alone in the bathroom.

Barely able to drag her injured leg, she hobbled to the sink and splashed water on her face. A sergeant had once told her that dying was the easy part—it was living that was the real bitch. She knew now that he'd been telling the truth.

Eleven

Saturday mornings were often busy at the inn. Weekend guests needed direction to various points of interest, housekeeping waited impatiently for the late sleepers to vacate their rooms and plenty of locals came in for breakfast.

"This is the best area for antiquing," Carly said, circling stores on a street map. "If you take in the model-train museum, you'll be right by the Mansion on the Hill for lunch. I recommend the chowder and fresh corn bread. Seriously, it's delicious. Then you can walk north about two miles to the farthest winery and taste your way back to the inn."

She numbered the winery tasting rooms, then used a green highlighter to show a return route. "That will get you here about three-thirty. Just in time for a nap before dinner."

Mrs. Bernard laughed. "What a wonderful way to spend the day. Thank you."

Her husband took the map. "I think the museum is perfect payback for antiquing."

Mrs. Bernard linked arms with her husband. "You're right."

They thanked Carly again and strolled off together.

She watched them go. The Bernards had to be in their early sixties. They were a fit couple, with an ease about them. Their love was familiar. She wondered how long they'd been married and how many children they had together. If they had grandchildren.

She'd wanted that for herself, once. When she'd been younger and a lot more foolish. She wouldn't say innocent. The innocent part had died long ago. But finding the right guy, building a life—she'd wanted that.

"Along with a nice chunky lotto win," she murmured, putting away brochures and scanning the lobby for anyone else who needed her help.

Saturday mornings were all about making her guests happy. Usually people who made their way to Blackberry Island on Friday stayed through Sunday. Especially on a rare sunny spring weekend. All the rooms were booked—a happy occurrence.

With no one in sight, Carly found herself without a distraction. Which gave her time to think. Something she didn't want to do. Thinking was bad. Thinking meant remembering what Michelle had told her.

The starkness of the words had haunted her dreams. She'd slept fitfully the past couple of nights, troubled by Michelle's breakdown.

She'd known in her head that Michelle had traveled to a place of war, had seen terrible things. But killing someone was far beyond what she had ever imagined, let alone experienced. She'd never held a gun in her life, had only seen them in movies and on TV. In her life, guns weren't real and people died of things like car accidents or cancer or old age.

Michelle had been raised in the same sheltered place. How had she been able to adjust to the rigors of an overseas deployment? Carly didn't even truly understand what deployment meant. Sure, soldiers went to Afghanistan, and before that they went to Iraq. But how did they get there? Was there a collection point somewhere in the U.S., followed by a flight to Germany or something? What did the planes look like? Were they served meals?

Too many questions, Carly thought. And no answers.

She'd spent the past ten years resenting Michelle, hating her for sleeping with Allen and, ironically, missing her. They had been best friends until their senior year of high school. Then the actions of the adults in their lives had split them apart. Nearly a year later, they'd just barely started to come together again as friends when Allen had stepped between them.

For the first time since Michelle came back, Carly truly understood that everything about her former friend was different.

This morning Michelle had freaked out over a four-year-old little girl. A couple of days ago the same person had helped Gabby overcome her irrational fear of cranes. Gabby had told Carly all about it, had even proved her acceptance by walking onto the lawn and letting the cranes step as close as they wanted.

"As soon as they know I don't have any food with me, they'll go away," her daughter had said with a confidence that was both heartening and startling.

So which Michelle was real? Or did they both exist inside of her? Didn't everyone have sides?

Work, she told herself. Better to think about work.

She'd barely clicked on the reservation program when she saw Ellen Snow walk into the lobby.

Ellen, Carly and Michelle had been in school together from kindergarten through graduating high school. They'd never been more than casual friends, until Carly's senior year when everything had gone to hell. Carly knew she was to blame, accepted that, but honestly, she was tired of feeling guilty every time she saw the other woman. It had been over a decade. At what point did she get a pass?

"Good morning, Carly," Ellen said as she approached the reception desk.

"Ellen."

The other woman was dressed in cream-colored trousers and a pale blue silk blouse. Carly recognized the sheen on the fabric, knew the tailoring was expensive. Ellen had always had money.

She wore her blond hair back in a headband—an evil Alice in Wonderland, Carly thought. If only she would fall down some rabbit hole and never be seen again. Unfortunately, Carly's luck had never been that good.

"Did she tell you?" Ellen asked, looking smug.

Carly raised her eyebrows and pretended ignorance. Ellen had come to gloat, but Carly was going to make her work for it.

"Did who tell me what?"

"Did Michelle explain how close the inn is to foreclosure? How near you are to losing your job and being out on the street? Because when the bank takes over, that's what's going to happen. In case you were wondering."

Carly forced herself to keep on smiling, even as her body went numb. A consequence of a foreclosure she hadn't thought about, she admitted to herself. Because the passage of time didn't matter in Ellen's world. She still wanted revenge.

"I wasn't," Carly told her. "I'm not worried. Michelle and I have a lot of plans for the inn."

"Because the two of you work so well together."

Carly's smile faded. She was sure her eyes showed her shock, but she did her best to keep her mouth from falling open.

So that was it. Ellen's plan. That's why she'd insisted Carly be kept on. It had nothing to do with Carly's experience at running the inn. The other woman knew their past—everyone on the island did. She'd put them together deliberately and was waiting for them to implode.

"I want to see the reservations for the next two weeks." Ellen's tone was sharp.

"This is in an official capacity?" Carly asked.

"Yes. It is. I'm an officer of the bank, in case you've forgotten."

Carly hadn't.

She tapped the keys, then turned the screen toward Ellen.

"We're fully booked on weekends and nearly so mid-week. Don't worry. We'll keep our numbers up."

"Or so you hope," Ellen said, her gaze drifting from the screen. "I wonder what your happy guests would say if they knew the truth about you."

Despite the fact that it wasn't even noon, Carly felt weary. "At some point, most people move on. Maybe the reason you're still single is that you can't let go of the past."

Ellen's pleasant expression slipped, revealing a venomous stare. "You bitch. We all know. You can pretend all you want, play the good mother, but you're still the same slut you were back in high school. You'll sleep with the first guy who asks. You've always been that way. We know that's why your husband left. He found out what you are."

Carly took a step back, her face stinging as if she'd been slapped.

In the past few years she'd barely had any contact with Ellen and they hadn't spoken. She had no idea this much rage and resentment still burned inside of her. How many of Ellen's rules for the inn were about business and how many were about revenge?

"Does your board know that for you this is personal?" Carly asked.

The smooth, polite facade slipped back in place. "Don't threaten me. You don't have the skill set. I'm doing everything by the book. But make no mistake— I'll be thrilled when you're done with this town. In fact, I'll even give you a ride."

Michelle stood in the kitchen, listening to the rain. She was still damp with sweat from her physical-therapy appointment. Mango's name might be charming but he had a determination that left her gasping and weak—and not in a happy way.

According to Mango, she was getting better. The pain in her hips and trembling in her legs spoke otherwise, but she was willing to reserve judgment. If only she could sleep. But the nights remained long and the dreams ugly.

She reached for the bottle of vodka she'd bought on the way home. Her hands were slick and salty, her grip weak. The bottle slipped and she barely caught it. Heaven was just a sip away, she thought, bastardizing lyrics from an old country song she barely remembered her mother listening to years and years ago. If only she could get the damn bottle open.

"Need some help?" Jared walked into the kitchen and moved toward her.

She hadn't seen much of him since she'd moved in

the previous week. She considered that a positive aspect of their nonexistent relationship. Now she watched him warily as he took the bottle from her and easily opened the screw-top.

"Ice?" he asked.

"Sure."

"Mind if I join you?"

She raised her eyebrows. "You drink? I would have figured you to be one of those AA types. Abstaining from alcohol."

He collected two glasses, then got ice from the freezer door and poured them each about an inch of the clear liquid. He handed her a glass, then touched his to the side and took a swallow.

"Drinking was never one of my problems."

She took a sip, then another. The familiar icy burn slipped down her throat nice and easy.

"You have other problems?" she asked.

"Doesn't everyone?"

"God knows I do."

He eyed her over his glass, then took another drink. "You're not eating much."

"Are you my mother?"

She'd thought the question would piss him off, but Jared only smiled—a slow, easy grin that made her wonder why he lived alone in this big house. Why wasn't there some busty brunette in the kitchen and a couple of kids?

"Let me rephrase my statement. You need to eat."

She sighed. "I know."

"Look at that. Concession. And here I thought you were going to tell me you weren't hungry."

"I'm not."

"You are. You look like a skinny, abandoned dog, all bones and sad eyes."

His comment stung, but she kept her expression bland. "You sure know how to turn a girl's head."

"You said you didn't want your head turned. Your exact words were you weren't going to sleep with me."

"You only compliment a woman when you want sex?"

He shrugged. "I'm a guy."

At least he was honest. "Sometimes it's easier to drink."

"It's always easier to drink. That doesn't mean it's the right thing to do. If I get you something, will you eat?"

She wanted to say no but instead she nodded.

"Good. While I'm gone, you can take a shower."

"Are you implying I smell?"

"I'm more than implying."

He set down his drink and headed out the back door. She heard the crunch of his feet on gravel and peeked out the window over the kitchen sink. Jared was walking. At least she didn't have to feel responsible for him driving.

She finished her drink, then made her way back into her room. After closing the bedroom door, she collected fresh clothes, then locked herself in the bathroom and turned on the shower.

Twenty minutes later she was clean and feeling a little better about the state of her life. Her hip still screamed at her and when she moved it felt like the ends of broken bones rubbing together, but the rest of her wasn't too bad. She'd even used a little conditioner on her freshly trimmed hair and had used moisturizer after she'd dried off. At the rate she was going, in a matter of a year or two, she would practically be normal.

She avoided the work clothes she'd bought and tugged on a pair of sweats and a T-shirt. Drying her hair was beyond her so she quickly combed it off her face, then twisted it into a thick braid that hung down her back. Not exactly glamorous, but clean. That should be enough.

She returned to the kitchen to find Jared emptying the contents of a couple of greasy paper bags onto plates.

The smell wafted to her, generating memories—good ones, this time.

"You went to Arnie's?" she asked, her stomach growling for the first time in weeks, maybe months. Hunger replaced tension. "I haven't been there in years. We used to go there all the time in high school."

It was one of the few places she'd visited with her friends. Most of the time she'd been busy working at the inn, but every now and then she made an Arnie's run.

He dumped barbecue-pork sandwiches onto plates. The sauce had already stained the buns. He'd bought baked beans and coleslaw and thick steak-fries.

The table was built into an alcove. Bench seats lined both sides. She slid in, going slowly, trying not to pull her hip. Jared filled tall glasses with ice and water. She glanced toward the vodka bottle.

"Later," he told her, sitting opposite and handing her the water. "Eat."

She started to complain about his attitude, then figured it wasn't worth the trouble and reached for the sandwich.

The bread was warm and barbecue sauce oozed over her fingers. She took a bite, her teeth sinking into the thick slices of pork. The taste was better than she remembered—tangy and spicy. She chewed and swallowed, then took another bite. Hunger grew until she wanted to inhale every scrap of food in front of her.

Jared watched more than he ate, but she didn't care. Let him enjoy the show. While she devoured the sandwich, he scooped beans and coleslaw onto her plate and dumped out most of the fries in front of her.

She ate everything. Every scrap of cabbage, each bean, all the fries. She licked her fingers before wiping them on a napkin, then drank the glass of water in a single gulp.

It was more food than she'd eaten in the past week and at about two in the morning she would probably regret it, but right now she didn't care. She leaned back against the bench and sighed.

"That was good. Thank you."

"You're welcome."

He'd finished his sandwich and had a few fries, but left the rest for her.

"Did you get enough?" she asked. "Did I eat too much of it?"

"I don't want it back now."

She laughed. "Fair enough. What do I owe you?"

"It was a sandwich, Michelle. Not a new car. This one's on me."

"Okay. I appreciate it."

The rain started up again. She glanced toward the window and watched the water run down the glass. In mid-May the days were still cool, even if the sun was setting close to eight at night.

"How's life at the inn?" he asked.

"We're getting busy, which is good. I like being back." She glanced at him. "Mostly."

"What don't you like?"

"Working with Carly. She's someone I knew before."

"I know who Carly Williams is."

She raised her eyebrows. "Should I ask how?" Was there a story? Did he and Carly have a past? Before she could decide if she cared, he got up and collected the vodka bottle.

"We live on an island. I know everybody here."

"So you never…"

"Asking about my sex life?"

"One of us should have one."

"No. Not with her."

"Why not?"

"Why don't you like working with Carly?"

Michelle watched him pour them each a drink. She took her glass but only held it. "We used to be friends. A long time ago. It was complicated. Stuff happened and then we were friends again. Then we both met this guy. Allen."

She glanced at Jared, but he didn't say anything.

"I was crazy about him. He was charming and good-looking and I was so lonely. Then I found out he was dating Carly, too, and it broke my heart. I said he had to decide. I was so sure he was going to pick me, but he didn't. I found out later it was because she'd slept with him."

"Why didn't you, if he was so important to you?"

She took a sip. "I was still a virgin. Sleeping with a guy seemed like a big decision. Carly didn't have any worries on that front, so he dumped me for her and then they got engaged."

"Ouch."

"Yeah. It was tough. But the worst part wasn't losing Allen, which should have told me something about how I felt about him. It was losing her. She was still my friend, but every second of every day was about her and that damned wedding. It was like she was rubbing it in my face."

She was aware she was talking too much, sharing details that couldn't possibly interest Jared, but she couldn't seem to stop the flood of words. People said alcohol loosened inhibitions. Vodka had nothing on one of Arnie's pork sandwiches.

"My mother was all over the wedding, which made things harder for me. I had to be the maid of honor. That hurt."

She paused, knowing she didn't want to keep going. But somehow she found herself saying the rest.

"Two days before the wedding, Allen came to me. He said he'd made a mistake—that he'd really been in love with me and that he'd ended things with Carly. He seduced me and I let him and…" She looked out the window. "I was so stupid."

"You were young."

"Not that young. Carly found us and Allen told her it was my fault. That I'd tricked him into bed."

She could still remember him jumping up, still naked. He'd gone to Carly and actually started crying. He'd been so convincing, Michelle had nearly believed him herself. Only she'd known the truth. She had a feeling Carly had guessed it, as well, only she hadn't let on. Carly had blamed Michelle, as had Brenda.

"I took off that night, drove to Seattle and joined the army. I wanted to be anywhere but here and that seemed like my best option."

"Carly stole him from you and you stole him back. You're even."

She eyed him over her glass. "Not exactly how I would describe it."

"That doesn't change what happened."

"Maybe not, but now I have to work with her."

"It was a long time ago. You're different people."

"You got that right."

"At least you let yourself come home."

She took a drink. "What's that supposed to mean?"

"You didn't come back before. You were punishing yourself. If you're back now, you're done."

She glared at him. "Where the hell do you get off—?"

Her cell phone rang, interrupting her. She was so startled by the sound, she just stared at her phone. No one ever called her. She wasn't even sure why she kept the damn thing. She glanced at the screen and saw a Los Angeles number.

She pushed the ignore button and finished her drink. "Where was I?" she asked, more to herself than him.

"You were telling me to mind my own business."

"Were you listening?" she asked.

"No."

"Typical guy. You only hear what you want to hear."

"It keeps things simple. You miss your mom?"

"That wasn't a very subtle change of subject." She reached for the vodka bottle.

He poured more for her. "I wasn't trying to be subtle. She died while you were gone. It was recent, wasn't it?"

"A few months ago. Cancer. She went fast. I wasn't here."

"Should you have been?"

"It's considered polite."

"Do I look like I care about polite?"

"No."

"Should you have been here?" he asked again.

"I don't know," she said, admitting the truth. "I feel guilty for not being with her when she died."

"Where were you?"

"In a hospital in Germany, getting part of my hip replaced."

He didn't say anything.

She sighed. "I feel guilty because I'm glad I didn't have to make the decision. No one wants to be a bad person. I just can't figure out what I think about her."

"So don't. She's gone. Move on."

"You're not a very good psychologist."

"I own boats, Michelle. Ask me about the tide, the wind or the cost of diesel. I don't know much about anything, but I do know how to listen. So what's the real problem?"

Michelle held on tight to her drink. "I slept with my best friend's fiancé and I killed a man and I don't know which is worse."

He slid to the end of the bench and stood, then leaned over and kissed the top of her head. "You're going to have to be the one to figure that out, kid. Night."

He walked out of the kitchen, leaving her alone with the night and the bottle. She carefully stood. After tossing the paper bags, she rinsed the dishes and put them in the dishwasher and limped to her bedroom. She left the vodka bottle where it was. For tonight at least, she'd had enough.

Twelve

Carly circled the dining room with a pot of coffee. Isabella had called in sick and Carly was picking up her shift as hostess for breakfast. It was a little after nine on Monday morning. Most of their guests were already finished eating and the locals had long ago left for work. Three older ladies sat together, lingering over a map of the town, and Leonard was by the window, typing earnestly on his netbook.

She walked toward him, shaking her head when she saw the still-full plate of eggs in front of him. Leonard was the classic absentminded-professor type. She was amazed he managed to get through the day without walking in front of a car or absently tripping off the edge of a cliff.

"Morning, Leonard," she said, pausing by his table.

He glanced up at her, his eyes unfocused. "Oh, hi."

"Did you forget something?"

"What?"

She pointed to his plate. "Breakfast."

He stared at the plate for a second, before glancing back at her. "Right. Food. I need to eat. I was up late, watching the cranes. All the breeding pairs have nested. I have the numbers on nearly all the eggs. We're going to compare birthrates to eggs produced. I'll calculate how many chicks we expect, and then later, when they're hatched, we'll be able to refine our process."

She wondered how long he could talk about his cranes and their chicks, then decided she didn't want to know.

"Leonard? You're still not eating."

"What? Oh. Sorry." He picked up a fork. "Thanks for the reminder."

"You're welcome." She turned over an empty cup and poured in fresh coffee, then picked up the cold one he hadn't touched. "Have a good day."

"I will. I'm very excited to get those last eggs counted."

"Good luck with that."

"Thanks."

She walked away, thinking he was basically a sweet guy. Not for her, but maybe for someone who could appreciate his avian enthusiasm. There was someone for everyone—at least she hoped there was.

She returned the coffee carafe to the stand and surveyed the room. The ladies were gathering their things and getting ready to leave; soon she could head back to the inn.

Before she could make her way back to the kitchen to tell Damaris they were done for the morning, Michelle shuffled into the dining room.

Carly instinctively looked for a way to escape. Ducking out would be a whole lot easier than facing her. She still didn't know what to say to her. Their last encounter had been fraught with emotion. It was the only explanation for the other woman blurting out what had happened while she'd been in Afghanistan.

Michelle had given her information she didn't know what to do with. Compassion seemed the most reasonable reaction, but she was talking about someone who'd seriously screwed up her life, not to mention resented her. Life would be a whole lot easier if they could just go their separate ways.

Michelle settled at one of the clean tables and dumped several pages in front of her. Carly approached cautiously.

"Coffee?" she asked.

"No, thanks. We have to talk. I spent the weekend going over budgets and projections. Is this a good time?"

As there was only Leonard in the dining room and he was far more interested in his bird reports than anything they might say, she nodded and took the seat opposite.

Michelle passed her a couple of sheets of paper. "Here's how much we have in the inn's checking account and what is owed to the bank in the short term. We're okay with current payments, but there are six months in arrears and the penalties that go with that."

Carly stared at the numbers and immediately saw the problem. "We can't pay this and cover our expenses, payroll and stay current on the mortgages."

"Exactly. I have some savings. I can pay about half of it back, but we'll have to find the rest. Which means cutting expenses."

"I don't need my raise." She wanted to drag back the words the second she said them. She didn't own the inn—she was an employee. Michelle had made that very clear.

"While I appreciate the offer, it's not close to enough, so no. We have to look for other places to save money. Starting with cutting dinner here at the inn. We're in competition with some great restaurants in town. From what I can see, dinner is a financial sinkhole."

Carly thought about how quiet the dining room usually was and the evening staff had little to do. "I agree."

"Good. Because that's only a start. We need to let go of about a quarter of the current staff. A third would be better." Michelle paused. "I'd like your input on that. You know more about the day-to-day running of the inn."

Carly did her best to keep from looking surprised. "Of course. I'll go over the work schedules and look at how long various jobs are taking. Obviously some things can't be cut, regardless of how slow we get. Someone needs to be at the front desk from early until at least ten or eleven. But there might be ways to share responsibilities. The person on duty in the evening could clear email and send out reservation confirmations. That kind of thing."

"You've been thinking about this," Michelle said.

"I knew we had to start saving money. I've been making a list of ways to do that."

"I look forward to hearing your ideas."

"Does Wednesday work for you?"

"Sure." Michelle made a note on her papers.

The formal, professional conversation made Carly feel both better and worse. She liked it for work-related items. This way, everything was out in the open and there wouldn't be misunderstandings. But on a personal level, she felt strange. Because despite everything, Michelle was someone she had cared about deeply. Just her luck she couldn't wish those feelings away.

"The other area we need to look at is increasing the number of guests, especially midweek," Michelle said. "We're fine for weekends, at least through October. But that eighty-five-percent-occupancy number is going to be difficult to hit week after week."

"I have some ideas about inexpensive advertising," Carly told her. "There are plenty of regional websites with travel sections. The major TV stations, for starters. I've done research on advertising costs and they're reasonable. I can get you the report later this morning."

"When did you have time to check all that out?"

"I did it a few years ago," Carly admitted. "Brenda wasn't interested. There are also websites for business conferences. We couldn't take anything big, but a smaller group might enjoy being here and they're often midweek. Executive retreats are also an option."

"All good," Michelle said. "Get me what you have and I'll look it over. I know we can get through this if we stay focused. At least we have Ellen on our side. If it wasn't for her, I probably wouldn't still own the inn."

Carly glanced down at the table. She was less sure about Ellen's support. The banker's visit on Saturday had shown that she was far more interested in punishing than helping.

"What?" Michelle demanded.

"Be careful about Ellen," Carly said, trying to stay neutral while offering a warning. "I'm not sure she's as friendly as you think."

Michelle's gaze narrowed. "Why would you say that? She's helping me, standing between me and the damned committee that wants to shut down this place."

"Are you sure? Did you check?"

"Why would I check?"

"Because Ellen stopped by on Saturday. She wasn't exactly friendly."

"Her not liking you only makes me trust her more," Michelle snapped as she rose.

"Fine. Be angry at me, but don't let that blind you. I think Ellen has an agenda you're not aware of. I don't think she wants you to succeed. I'm saying you could check it out."

Carly told herself to stop talking. What did she care if Michelle failed? Except her future was on the line, too. Financially, she wasn't ready to leave.

"We're done here," Michelle said, turning to leave. As she shifted her weight, her leg gave out and she started to go down.

Carly rose and instinctively reached for her. Michelle caught herself on the edge of the table and straightened.

"Can I help?" Carly asked.

Michelle glanced at her over her shoulder. "You could go to hell. That would help a lot."

"Hello, beautiful."

Carly looked up from the registration-desk computer and blinked at the huge man standing in front of her. He was classically tall, dark and, while more muscular than handsome, fairly impressive in the "take me now and don't ask questions" department.

"Good morning," she said. "How can I help you?"

She hoped he wasn't a guest. With the exception of Leonard, single guys never stayed at the inn. Which meant if he was a guest, he was with a girl. Starting their stay by flirting with him wouldn't bode well.

"I'm looking for Michelle." The man smiled at Carly. "I'm Mango."

"Okay."

They were the only two syllables she could manage after the smile. The flash of white teeth shouldn't have unnerved her, but it did. Maybe it was because of the way his T-shirt stretched over huge muscles. Or the appreciation lurking in his eyes. She couldn't remember the last time a man had looked at her as something other than a piece of furniture.

Then the actual meaning of his words sank in and she deflated like a sad, sex-starved balloon.

"Michelle. Right. She's in her office." Carly pointed down the hall.

Instead of moving in that direction, Mango leaned toward her. "I'm her physical therapist. She offered to show me around the island. Nothing more. We're friends."

"Oh." That was nice to know. She hoped she didn't look too eager.

He rested his elbows on the desk. His dark eyes flashed with humor. "So is she here?"

"Uh-huh." She pointed down the hall. "In her office."

"Thanks, gorgeous."

He spoke absently, without even thinking. When he was safely out of earshot, she allowed herself to chuckle. Okay—that had been a nice break in an otherwise uneventful day. The takeaway was clear—her hormones had finished hibernating and were starting to get frisky.

She hadn't seriously considered dating in the past ten years. Not only wasn't there anyone who interested her, but Gabby had always been an issue. Now that her daughter was getting older and starting to have a life of her own, maybe the whole man-woman thing was something Carly should consider. Her entire body was one big tingle, and after a decade of living like a nun, it was nice to know that parts of her hadn't died. Or atrophied. After all, where there were tingles, there was hope.

Thirteen

The lingering effect of Mango continued long past when Carly would have thought it would fade. Gabby was having dinner with a friend, so Carly took advantage of the rare alone time to drive to Robert's garage. She hadn't seen him since he'd walked out of her place after breakfast. The fact that she thought they should both move on didn't mean she wanted him gone from her life. He would always be family. That was important to her and to Gabby.

She parked in front of the garage and walked in through the open pull-up door. Even though it was well after six, Robert was still working, bent over a car, doing his thing. Before she could figure out what to say, he straightened and saw her.

Nothing about his expression gave away what he was thinking. He studied her while she wrestled with the right opening, finally settling on a tried-and-true classic.

"Hello," she said.

He nodded.

The stiff movement told her he was still angry, or maybe hurt. So much for the truth setting her free.

"How's it going?" she asked.

"Fine. With you?"

"Okay. Good. Michelle and I are still finding our footing. She's pissed at me most of the time. When she's not, I'm pissed at her. It makes for colorful exchanges." There had been tension with Brenda, but this was different. Oddly better, she thought. With Michelle she could simply say, or yell, what she was thinking. Which made it more freeing, in a twisted kind of way.

"I'm busy." He turned away and walked toward the back of his garage.

She followed him. "No," she said loudly. "I won't be dismissed."

He spun back to her. "What do you expect from me?"

"Honesty. Real honesty. You're Gabby's uncle and the closest thing to a father she will ever have. I don't accept you simply disappearing. It's not what we want and I don't think it's what you want, either."

"You made it pretty clear what you didn't want."

"I'm sorry I was so blunt. I should have thought it through. But seriously, Robert, I'm not wrong. It's been a decade. Don't you think if we were going to fall madly in love it would have happened? We love each other, but not that way."

"You don't know what I feel."

"I know you've never once even tried to kiss me. While you are quite the gentleman, at some point, shouldn't passion have taken over?"

He twisted the shop rag he had in his hands. "I wanted to give you time."

"Ten years?"

Some of the tension seemed to fade away and he sighed. "Okay, yeah. That's a long time. For a while I thought we'd, you know, go that way, but then it never happened."

"For a reason. I think we're great friends. I want that. I want you around. But go on a date. Get laid. It's time."

The corner of his mouth turned up. "Interesting advice coming from you."

"The virgin slut? Yes, I know."

They stared at each other for another couple of seconds, then he jerked his head to the back of the garage. "Come on. I'll buy you a soda."

A few minutes later they were sitting in his break room, sipping from cold cans he'd pulled out of the ancient refrigerator.

"How's it really going with Michelle?" he asked.

"There are good days and bad days. She still looks awful. She's injured and adjusting."

"It takes time."

"Yes, I know. Give her a break." Carly didn't point out that for the past few years her life had been startlingly break-free. Instead, she brought him up-to-date on the various issues and events, leaving out Mango's hormone-inciting visit.

"Michelle is wrong about Ellen, and because she won't listen, it's going to come bite her in the butt. I can feel it. I just hope it doesn't take me down, too."

"You think Ellen is still mad about high school?"

"I would guarantee it. Apparently she doesn't share our same space-time continuum and what happened back then is as real as if it happened yesterday."

"Then she needs to move on."

"She needs a man."

He raised his eyebrows. "Not interested. She's scary."

Carly grinned. "Are you sure? I'm sure she would be

happy to fill the vault with cash and then you could roll around in all that money."

"I'll pass." He took a swallow of the soda. "Michelle will come around. She needs you."

"I need her, too."

Not just now, she thought sadly. They'd always needed each other, but when things had been their worst, they'd been torn apart.

Carly felt the tug of the past. She'd been seventeen when her mother had walked out. She still remembered the disbelief and devastation of coming home from school only to find her mother had abandoned her to the indifferent care of an alcoholic father. There'd been a brief note in which her mother had explained why she had to go.

She'd claimed to be in love, as if that explained and excused it all. She'd promised to stay in touch, which she hadn't, and had sworn she still loved Carly. That had been a lie, too. She'd never come back, had never sent for her daughter, spent a weekend with her. Birthdays had warranted a card and sometimes a phone call. There had been little else.

From the time Carly had found out she was pregnant, she'd vowed to do better. Her child would feel love every single day. Her child would live in a stable home. Having Allen as her daughter's father made those promises challenging, but so far she'd succeeded. Gabby was happy and healthy, full of life.

Maybe that was enough, she told herself. Maybe the proof of who she'd become could be found in the smiles of her daughter.

Michelle moved through the full dining room. Breakfast was always busy, even midweek. Plenty of locals came by before heading to work. The guests in the inn generally ate here, along with a few staying at the motel down the street. The smell of eggs and bacon and sausage mingled with the life-giving scent of coffee.

She greeted Isabella, then made her way around the tables. When she saw an empty coffee cup, she changed direction and grabbed a full pot.

"Good morning," she said, returning to a table of businessmen and pouring.

"Morning," one of them mumbled. The other three were bent over a laptop.

She smiled, not the least bit offended by being ignored. If they weren't looking, she didn't have to worry about them seeing her limp, didn't have to field questions about being hurt.

When she'd refilled all the coffees, she continued back toward the kitchen. It was still early, barely seven-thirty, and chaos reigned.

Damaris whipped a frothy bowl of eggs, adding a bit of cream, then salt, before pouring the mixture directly onto a hot griddle. Once they began to sizzle, she dropped cheese and vegetables in, then swirled and expertly flipped the omelet closed. After pulling down a clean plate, she slid the omelet into place. Blackberries followed, then the plate went next to three others.

"Order up," she announced.

A server jumped to grab it.

Damaris read the next order while she was stirring the scrambled eggs.

"Wheat toast," she yelled to her assistant, then glanced up and saw Michelle. "Good morning, little one. How are you feeling?"

The familiar words, the welcoming smile, all drew Michelle closer.

"Not bad, considering."

"You're limping less."

"It's early. I turn into a leg-dragging monster around three. Unless I have physical therapy—then it happens before noon."

"Pull up a stool. You can keep me company."

Michelle poured herself a cup of coffee, then did as requested. She knew where to sit so that she was close enough to talk, but still out of the way. She'd done it hundreds of times as a teenager. Hanging out with Damaris had always been safe. Unlike Brenda, whose emotions were as unpredictable as the shapes of the clouds racing across the sky, Damaris was constant.

"You sleeping?" Damaris asked, not looking up from the stove.

Michelle cradled her mug of coffee. "No."

"Shouldn't you be?"

"I should be doing a lot of things."

During their tour of the island, Mango had once again brought up the fact that he wanted Michelle to be in a support group. He'd reminded her that adjusting to civilian life was difficult after even a single tour in a war zone. She'd had three.

"Why aren't you?"

"Maybe I like being stubborn."

Damaris smiled. "One of your best qualities. I like that shirt. You're too skinny, but you look nice."

Michelle glanced down at the rayon blouse she'd bought for about fourteen dollars. Various shades of green swirled together. "You don't think it's too girly?"

"You *are* a girl and it makes your eyes darker."

"Maybe."

Damaris smiled, unmoved by her sulky tone. "Glad to be back at the inn?"

"Yeah. That's good." At least most of it. "I wish my mom hadn't been so stupid with the money. Sure, a new roof makes sense, but the rest of it? If she was going to remodel anything, why not put in new bathrooms for the guests? Did we really need a gift shop?"

"You're talking to the wrong person."

"I know. Ignore me."

"Never." Damaris handed her a plate. It held her favorite French toast with a side of bacon. "Eat."

"Yes, ma'am."

The other woman touched her cheek. "I'm glad to have you back, child. Let me know how I can help."

"Thanks, but I'm doing okay."

She took a couple of bites and chewed. Damaris continued to prepare eggs and pancakes, place sausages on plates and call that orders were up.

The room was warm, heat from the stove rising to join the steam from the dishwasher. Pans clattered, coffee perked, toast popped. A restaurant kitchen was far from quiet, but the sounds were easy. Safe. No explosions here.

By the time she'd eaten her way through the large serving, she felt better. Food and caffeine were a happy combination, she thought, setting her plate by the dishwasher and refilling her mug. The orders slowed enough that Damaris had time to pull up a stool for herself.

"You have something to tell me," the other woman said, holding a cup of coffee. "What is it?"

"We're going to have to stop serving dinner. It's too expensive."

Damaris raised her free hand. "Hallelujah. Finally."

"You're not upset?"

"I never wanted to add that meal. It was your mother's idea. She was going to get a liquor license, at least until she found out how much work it was. There's too much competition with the restaurants in town and keeping staff for a few customers is a waste."

"I thought you'd be upset."

"No. Easier for me, too. Even though I wasn't on, they'd call me a couple times a week with a question. Idiots." Her eyes danced behind her glasses. "You're making good choices."

"I appreciate the support. I'm letting everyone know today."

"There's a server, Cammie. See if she wants to work days. She's good."

Michelle made a note of the name. "Thanks."

"Anything for you."

They hugged briefly, then Michelle made her way back to the inn. As she walked toward the reception area, she glanced out toward the rear yard. The sun fought against the morning cloud cover and it wasn't clear who would win. Rain and light both danced across the grass. But what caught her attention was Gabby standing in the center of the lawn turning and turning, her arms outstretched, her face raised to the sky.

Her feet were bare, Michelle thought with a smile. The ultimate symbol of summer. Barefoot children—like she and Carly used to be.

She could remember the two of them running across the grass, carefree. So incredibly young, unaware of what life would hold and thrilled with the possibilities.

"I can feel the joy from here."

Michelle turned toward the speaker, not recognizing the tall, well-dressed woman. She had blond hair and an air of quiet confidence.

"Pauline Farley," the woman said, holding out her hand. "My husband, Seth, and I are the therapists who will be having the retreats here."

"Yes, of course. Michelle Sanderson."

They shook hands.

"We've been working with Carly on getting the rooms reserved and working out a schedule," Pauline said. "Everything has gone better than we'd dared hope. Thank you for that."

"You should be thanking Carly."

"I will, but as you own the inn, I wanted to tell you how much we appreciate her. It's never easy to be gone from home, so knowing someone competent was back here taking care of things must have been a comfort."

Michelle tilted her head. "That was very smooth."

Pauline looked more amused than chagrined. "The transition to subtle probing? I'm glad you liked it."

"Did someone ask you to talk to me or was my body language betraying me and you couldn't help yourself?"

"The latter," Pauline admitted. "My uncle was in Vietnam. When he came back, he got into drugs and was in and out of rehab for years. I was a kid, but it stayed with me."

"Is that why you became a therapist?"

"Some. I'm a good listener and I enjoy being around people. I have some specialized training in PTSD, if you're interested."

"I'm not."

Pauline's eyes crinkled with amusement. "As long as you're not ambivalent. For what it's worth, I'll be here. I'm not trying to be pushy."

"Yes, you are."

"All right. A little. I have this need to nurture."

Having someone take care of her was both the best and worst thing that could happen, Michelle thought. She wanted to surrender everything to someone else, and yet couldn't bring herself to trust another person that much.

Despite that, she found she liked Pauline. "If I change my mind, I'll let you know."

"Good."

They both turned back to Gabby, who had spun until she dropped. She lay on the grass, arms wide, the sound of her laughter drifting in through the open window.

"I envy her sense of self and freedom," Pauline admitted. "To be that uninhibited again."

"Me, too," Michelle admitted.

The road to normal had seemed shrouded and difficult to navigate. For the first time in what felt like years, she began to wonder if maybe there was a way back. Maybe not to the place where Gabby lived, but she would take getting within throwing distance, if that was possible.

Fourteen

Michelle knew she should probably apologize. Snapping at Carly, while excellent sport, wasn't fair. But the idea of forming the words, of then saying them, made her cringe.

At exactly ten, Carly stepped through her open door. She had a folder in her hands.

"Have a seat," Michelle said by way of greeting.

Carly settled opposite her.

Michelle tried to figure out how to get to the *S* word. Saying "I'm sorry" had never been her favorite, and these days, it was more difficult.

"The weather seems to be improving," she began.

Carly raised her eyebrows, obviously surprised by the small talk. "Yes. It's good for the daisies."

Michelle sank back in her chair and rolled her eyes. "Tell me the daisies were my mother's idea. They're everywhere. The garden is fine. I can accept that. But inside? The curtains, the cushions and those damned murals. Talk about ugly. Every time I see them, I wince."

Carly sat stiffly in her chair. Color stained her cheeks as her chin went up slightly. "I love the daisies and I picked out the daisy motif for the inn. I also painted the murals. Myself. By hand. It took weeks."

Shit. Shit and double shit.

Michelle held in a groan. "I'm sorry," she blurted. "I was trying to apologize and..." She paused. "You really like them?"

"Of course. They're cheerful."

"Aren't they a little excessive?"

"This is you apologizing?"

"What? Oh, right. Sorry. The daisies are great."

Carly relaxed a little. "That was sincere."

"I mean it. Love the daisies. Don't change a thing."

Carly smiled reluctantly. "I'm glad you agree."

They stared at each other. Michelle felt the beginnings of a truce. This was the Carly who had always known her better than anyone.

"Work," she said. "We should talk about work."

"I'm ready."

Michelle nodded. "I spoke with Damaris this morning and told her about the dinner service being canceled. I'll talk to the evening restaurant staff tonight and tell them Friday is their last day."

Carly opened her folder and pulled out a piece of paper. As she handed over the sheet, the light caught the movement of her charm bracelet. Make that Brenda's charm bracelet.

Michelle couldn't figure out how she could dislike her mother and still be annoyed that Carly had her charm bracelet. She ignored the tightness in her chest and took the paper Carly offered.

"What's this?" she asked.

"I've spoken to several of the restaurant managers in town and listed the openings they have. I explained why the staff was being let go and gave recommendations.

Obviously it will help the people being let go, but it helps the inn, too. With the unemployment insurance."

"Thank you," Michelle mumbled, realizing she should have thought of that herself. She really was having to re-learn her job. Not surprising after being gone for so long.

She studied the carefully handwritten names and num-bers. "Damaris mentioned we should ask Cammie if she wants to stay on."

"I thought so, too. Everyone says she's great to work with. Did you want to talk to her tonight?"

"Sure."

Carly had a list of the leased equipment that could be sent back and which would have to be kept for the terms of the lease.

"Here are my ideas for saving money," she said, hand-ing over three more sheets. "The first page talks about who we can let go and why, while the second two are different ideas for cutting our costs. I did a lot of brain-storming. Some of the ideas are a little out there, I know, but I put everything down, just in case one thing helps us brainstorm another."

Michelle stared at the neat writing. She could feel her-self moving from neutral to annoyed.

"How can you work here and not know how to use a computer?" she demanded before she could stop her-self. "For someone who claims to know how, you're sure avoiding showing me you can. Learn Excel. It's not that hard."

Carly stiffened. Her small fingers curled into her palms as she dropped her arms to her sides.

"I know how to use Excel," she said quietly, her chin coming up.

"Then what's with this?" Michelle waved the pages.

"Oliver Twist? 'Can I have some more, please?' Why did you do these by hand?"

"I don't have a computer."

Michelle felt the fight bleed out of her. "Sure you do. In your office."

"No, I don't. The computer at the registration desk doesn't have any other software on it. We were having problems with some of the summer help wasting time, so Brenda took off all the other programs. I used to use Brenda's computer, but she decided she wanted it password protected a few months ago. She never told me what the password was, so I couldn't get into anything."

Michelle hated being wrong in general and being wrong in front of Carly really bugged her.

"We'll get you a computer," she mumbled. "Some cheap thing with the software you need. Otherwise, you're no help to me."

"Thank you."

"Don't thank me. I'm doing it out of purely selfish reasons."

"That I believe."

Michelle stared at Carly. The other woman's expression didn't change. She still looked stoic if a little wary, but humor brightened her blue eyes.

Michelle felt her own mouth start to twitch.

"What's next?" she asked.

Carly motioned to the pages Michelle held. "My ideas for more savings."

Michelle scanned the papers. "You want to cut house-keeping?"

"They're not all working full days, even though they're paid for eight hours." She leaned forward. "I went through and reassigned rooms. The two bigger suites take longer, but the rest of the rooms go pretty quickly.

I can pick up the slack. It means me doing two of the smaller rooms, three days a week. Not a problem. In return for that, we can let two people go."

While the plan made sense, Michelle was looking for the catch. "You clean?"

Carly smiled. "I started as a maid. I know how, but feel free to check my work."

"I thought you were pregnant when you came to work here."

"I was. About eight months along."

"Brenda had you cleaning?"

Carly shrugged. "I needed the work. It wasn't that big a deal."

Michelle didn't know much about being pregnant, but scrubbing bathrooms all day seemed like a little more than someone that far along should be doing. She would have sworn there was no way she could ever feel bad for Carly. Leave it to Brenda to change that.

They went through the rest of Carly's suggestions. They were well considered and made a serious dent in the day-to-day expenses. Between losing the staff required for dinner and two maids, payroll would be cut by more than Michelle had even hoped.

"I appreciate you doing this," she said, feeling the pain in her hip crank up a notch. Sitting too long tended to aggravate it. So did standing and lying down.

"I want the inn to be a financial success. The alternative is it going to the bank and that doesn't help anyone." Carly paused as if realizing they were straying into dangerous territory. Talking about the bank meant talking about Ellen.

Michelle figured there had to be something between the two. Something in the past.

"Are you all right?" Carly asked. "I can tell you're in pain. Can I do anything?"

Michelle shook her head. "My hip hurts. It's healing, but it takes time."

"Didn't they give you something for the pain?"

"Sure. I don't take it much. I get fuzzy." Besides, she would rather drink when she got home. Even she knew painkillers and vodka didn't mix.

"Won't you heal better if you're not in pain?"

Michelle shot her a warning look. "Leave it alone."

"I don't remember you being this sensitive before you left."

"You go get shot and we'll see how sensitive you are." She held up a hand. "Sorry. I'm not at my most patient these days."

"It's okay."

Michelle risked the truth. "Sometimes it feels like you've taken over my life. At least the good parts. And I'm left with the rest of it."

"That's not true."

"It's a little true. You have the owner's apartment."

Carly's expression turned stricken. "We can move," she said quickly.

"No. That's not what I want. I'm happy where I'm renting. Distance is a good thing, right now. Besides, you've got Gabby." Michelle managed a smile. "She's great."

"Thank you. I think so." Carly hesitated, as if trying to make a decision. Then she nodded once and spoke. "I married Allen for all the wrong reasons. Believe me, I paid for that. He stole everything from me, because I was stupid. I had nothing. I was pregnant without a penny. I didn't have a job and I was so sick at first I couldn't keep one. I didn't have medical insurance or anything. Brenda hired me when I was eight months pregnant. She gave me a place to stay and didn't care that I waddled rather than walked. I wasn't taking your place, Michelle. I was desperate and I thought she was going to rescue me."

Michelle found herself feeling sorry for her. "Brenda wouldn't rescue anyone but herself."

Carly sighed. "I figured that out the hard way."

Of that, Michelle was sure. She had grown up with her mother's inconsistent rules and narcissistic worldviews. An action that made her mother laugh one day could be cause for a month's grounding the next. Everything was judged by how it related to her. They rarely went out to eat, but when they did, Brenda played her games. If she and Michelle ordered different things, Brenda wanted what her daughter ordered and would take her meal. If they ordered the same, Brenda claimed hers tasted funny. She would send it back and get something else. Brenda would tell her not to waste money on presents for holidays, then complain to all who would listen that her selfish daughter never bought her anything.

As much as Michelle didn't want to admit it, she knew Carly had truly been alone in the world. Alone and responsible for the child growing inside of her. Perhaps the most vulnerable a woman could be.

Brenda had taken advantage of that. She would have been unable to resist having someone beholden to her. Someone to twist and slowly destroy. Gabby's happy nature was a testament to Carly's determination and love.

"We were ambushed," she said, not sure why she was saying these words. Even as she told herself to stop, she couldn't seem to stop them from spilling out.

"There were several shooters and an IED. The Humvee went flying, then exploded. A few of us were tossed out. Not that it mattered if we survived that, because they were firing from everywhere."

She studied the pages in front of her as she spoke, looking at the neat handwriting, seeing the contrast of ink and paper rather than the history she re-created.

"We got all of them but one. I was the last man standing. Literally." Involuntarily, she looked at Carly. "He got me in the hip and I went down. I could still fire, but he was faster. Then his weapon jammed or his clip was empty."

She could feel the heat, the blood on her leg, hear the sounds of fire and screams. Dust filled the air and clogged her lungs.

She spoke of the small girl who had clung to her father. How her M16-A2 had felt heavy in her arms—probably the result of the blood loss. The moment when she knew she'd been given a chance to survive. A chance to take a shot.

"I killed him, with his daughter still clinging to him. I shot him and he died."

She stopped the telling there, mostly because the rest of it was a blur. The little girl had cried out, then run off. There had been a space of time when Michelle had tried to get to the others, to help where she could. It might have been a minute or two, it could have been hours.

The next thing she remembered was the medic bending over her, telling her she was damned lucky. As she was carried away, she'd glanced back at the fallen man. He was still there, his eyes open, his stare glassy.

"Is that why you can't sleep?" Carly asked.

"It's some of it. Trust me. When they say war is hell, they're not kidding."

"I'm sorry."

Michelle shrugged. "I'm the one who signed up. I'm the one who slept with Allen."

"You still blame me."

Michelle allowed herself a slight smile. "Crazy, huh? I slept with your fiancé and you're the bad guy. Even I don't get that one."

Carly fumbled with the bracelet, then unfastened it and dropped it onto the desk. "You should have this."

"No, thanks."

"She was your mother."

"She left her things to you for a reason."

"No." Carly stood. "I'll get you the rest of her jewelry later."

"Keep it. You had a better relationship with her than I ever did. I have the inn. That's enough."

"The inn was always yours."

"I know."

Carly nodded and left. Michelle was very aware that she carefully left the charm bracelet behind. She picked it up and studied the various charms, then dropped it in the top drawer of her desk.

Fifteen

Carly kept busy through the rest of the morning. She liked that she didn't have a whole lot of time to think about her conversation with Michelle—mostly because she couldn't decide what she felt about it. Talk about a complicated relationship.

On the one hand, her former friend had been nothing but bitchy since her arrival. Carly had busted her butt, working at the inn, doing her best, dealing with Brenda. On the other hand, Michelle had grown up with Brenda's difficult and emotionally abusive ways. She'd learned to thrive in impossible circumstances.

Michelle had slept with Allen—something that fell in the "inexcusable" category. But Carly was willing to admit that Allen had probably been as much to blame. And maybe she'd had a hand in it, too. After all, they'd both wanted to go out with him. She'd won him over by sleeping with him when Michelle wouldn't. Then, after the engagement, she'd flaunted her ring, her plans, all the while insisting Michelle be happy for her.

The latter had been more about the thrill of finally finding someone who would love her, but a little of it had been about rubbing Michelle's nose in it. Not her finest moment.

And now? Now they were grown-ups and she needed to decide what mattered and what didn't.

Carly finished checking the clean rooms—then returned to the front desk. Pauline and Seth had left welcome packages for the three couples who would be checking in that afternoon. She put them in a stack, along with their room keys.

Life would be easier if Michelle could just be mean all the time, she thought, walking to her office. Then she could cheerfully hate her and feel smug about doing her job. As it was, they were both stuck figuring out the present. Carly didn't even have righteous indignation on her side. After all, Michelle might have slept with Allen and then left town, but she'd kind of made up for it by joining the army and risking her life.

Carly stepped into the small space that was her office only to stop when she saw two boxes sitting on her desk. The first was for a laptop, the second, a printer.

She'd left her meeting with Michelle less than three hours ago. Had the other woman run right out and bought her a computer? She must have. It wasn't something Michelle would have hanging around in her back pocket.

On top of the computer box was a package of software for Microsoft Office, along with a note. "I hope you weren't lying about knowing Excel."

"I wasn't," Carly murmured, not sure if she should laugh or throw something.

She sat in her chair and stared at the packages. Why did she have to go and be nice?

She reached for the laptop box, prepared to open it. But before she could lift the top, she saw a business-size envelope with her name on the front.

She lifted the flap, then stared at the check inside.

Thank God she was sitting, she thought, staring at the writing. Otherwise, she would have passed out, fallen and hit her head. As it was, she couldn't breathe. Couldn't blink or speak or do anything but stare.

"I..."

Her body was numb, her brain spun, stopped, then lurched.

The check, drawn on a personal account belonging to Michelle Sanderson, was for ten thousand dollars.

Ten thousand.

Ten.

Thousand.

Carly started to stand, only to realize her legs were shaking too hard. She managed to suck in a breath, then another.

Was it real or a cruel trick? Because if it was real it gave her the kind of financial security she'd never had in her life. She could have a real emergency fund. If she got fired or left her job, she could afford to move and put down a deposit on an apartment in Seattle. She could take classes at the community college. She could afford the co-pays on her insurance.

Her eyes burned and it took her a second to realize she was fighting tears. What was this and why?

She managed to stand. Still clutching the check, she stumbled to Michelle's office and pushed open the door.

"I don't understand."

Michelle looked up from her computer. "It's all I can afford right now."

"I didn't ask for this."

"No, but you're owed it. My mother took advantage of you for the past ten years. Even with you living here, getting free housing and some meals, she barely paid you minimum wage. It was wrong. I'm sorry. This is to make up for your back pay. Like I said, it's all I can afford."

Carly let the words wash over her. Was it possible they were true?

"Just like that?" she asked.

Michelle shrugged. "Guilt is a powerful motivator. I don't like what she did to people."

What she did to you. She didn't say those words, but Carly heard them.

"Thank you," Carly whispered.

"You're welcome."

She started to leave. She turned back. "And for the computer." Now her lips curved. "I really do know how to use Excel."

"You'd better."

Per the new schedule, Tuesday afternoon Michelle was supposed to work the reception desk. Michelle leaned on the stool she'd dragged in from the kitchen and wondered if she was ready to face the public. After all, she wasn't feeling especially friendly these days.

Exhaustion didn't help. She still wasn't sleeping very much. When she did sleep, she found herself remembering things she would just as soon forget. While she was at it, she could also complain about the pain, but to what end? Eventually her hip would get better.

She saw a car pull up and nervously smoothed the front of her shirt. Since she'd been back, she'd avoided the guests in the inn. She'd forgotten what to say to them, how to interact. Carly should never have assigned her to front-desk duty. Only this was *her* inn, and if she expected to make it a success again, she was going to have to do a lot of things that made her uncomfortable.

She eyed the expensive sedan and the couple getting

out. The woman was in her late thirties, maybe early forties, with stylishly cropped blond hair. Michelle hadn't bothered to look at a fashion magazine in years, but she remembered enough to know the outfit alone would cost an easy four figures—not counting the shoes or the bag. The man had a sweater tied over his shoulders, which made her want to roll her eyes. Talk about an affectation.

She stifled a snort, then typed on the keyboard, pulling up the list of guests due to arrive that afternoon. The therapy group, she realized, reading the notes by the three sets of names.

Michelle glanced back out the window, seeing what she hadn't before. That the couple didn't speak or touch as they climbed the stairs. That the woman's back was stiff and the man looked both lost and unbearably sad. Suddenly their expensive clothes and fancy car didn't seem nearly as intimidating as they had before.

An SUV pulled in behind the sedan and another couple, about the same age, got out. Michelle braced herself and attempted a smile.

"Hello," she said as the first couple entered. "Welcome to the Blackberry Island Inn. I'm Michelle. Are you checking in?"

The man nodded. "Doug and Whitney Farmer."

Michelle found them on the list. "We've been expecting you."

She took the offered credit card and swiped it through the machine. Once it cleared, she handed them their room keys, along with the packages left for them. Then she detailed the hours of operation for the restaurant and the gift shop.

Doug and Whitney listened without speaking either to her or each other. Just watching them, she would say they didn't have a prayer of making their marriage work.

Not that she knew anything about relationship therapy. It must help some people, although she wasn't sure every marriage should be saved. Hers had been a disaster from the beginning, not to mention a huge mistake. They'd both been caught in the idea of being in love more than the reality of it. At least they hadn't had any kids to worry about. Less than four months after taking impulsive vows, they'd been signing divorce papers.

The second couple entered the lobby. The woman, a petite redhead, smiled broadly.

"Isn't this charming? I think it's charming. I love the daisies. Did you see the gardens? They're so beautiful. This is going to be wonderful."

Hers was a level of perky that made Michelle's teeth hurt. Good thing she wasn't in their therapy session, she thought. She would be forced to deck the woman. And wouldn't that be a springboard for discussion.

"Welcome," she said, starting her greeting again.

The Robbinses were from Bellevue, and *so* excited to be here. At least Fay was. Michelle checked them in.

Carly joined them then and offered to usher all the guests to their rooms.

"Each of your rooms has a fireplace," she said, leading the way to the stairs. "They're gas, so you only need to flip a switch. We have extra pillows and blankets in the armoire and anything you forgot is just a phone call away. I understand you'll be joining Pauline and Seth for dinner tonight. We've already printed out directions."

Carly's voice faded as she climbed the stairs.

Fay and her husband hung back a second. The petite redhead stared at the man beside her.

"What?" he asked, sounding defensive.

"You were staring at her boobs! How could you?"

With that, Fay flounced after Carly, her shoulders

shaking, as if she were in tears. Her husband stood there a second, head bowed, before he followed his wife.

They'd barely left before the third couple arrived. Michelle took care of them and sent them up the stairs to meet Carly.

A few minutes later, Carly walked into the foyer.

"That was strange," she murmured, glancing toward the stairs as if concerned about not being overheard. "Is it just me or were all those people sad?"

"Their marriages are in trouble."

"I know. I'm glad they're getting help, but it's…"

"Upsetting?" Michelle asked.

"Yes, and I can't figure out why."

Neither of them had grown up in especially happy homes, Michelle thought, but she wasn't sure if they were reacting to a broken marriage or the possibility of one being fixed.

"Maybe these few days will help them."

"I hope so," Carly murmured, staring at the stairs.

"They can come back every year to celebrate."

Carly laughed. "Okay, I like that ending. It seems happy. Marriage sure isn't easy."

Michelle would agree with that.

Carly's marriage had failed, as well, she realized. Only there'd been a child who'd been affected. A little girl who was growing up without a father. Something Michelle could relate to.

She drew in a breath. "I'm sorry I slept with Allen."

Carly swung back to face her, both eyebrows raised. "Okay," she said cautiously. "Thank you. For what it's worth, I know he had a part in it. A big part."

Something she hadn't been willing to admit at the time, Michelle thought, relieved Carly had taken a step toward middle ground.

"I was angry," Michelle said, settling on the stool to relieve pressure on her hip. "You had him and you were engaged and you wanted me to be a part of things. Maybe you meant it as a friend, but it seemed like you were rubbing my nose in it."

"I was," Carly admitted. "A little. Mostly, though, I was so happy. I thought I'd finally found someone to love me. I'd felt empty and broken for so long. If Allen loved me, then maybe I was okay. That's more what I was thinking. 'Look at me. I'm not a loser.'"

"You weren't a loser."

"Yeah, I was," Carly said. "He only picked me over you because I slept with him first. I really think he liked you better."

Michelle wasn't sure what to do with that information. "We were both reacting. But I want you to know I'm sorry."

"Me, too."

A moment of fragile peace, she thought, wondering how long it would be until it shattered like spun sugar.

She wanted to say more. She wanted to point out that she'd been a virgin and Allen had taken advantage of her, so she had even less blame, but to what end? The past existed. There was no going back. No undoing. There was only moving forward and hoping it all got better.

Sixteen

Carly stood on the shore, watching the gray water of the Sound. The rain had stopped but an angry wind buffeted the waves into swirling patterns. The cranes swept low, looking for food, or maybe playing a complicated game. Did birds play? Did they find life funny or annoying or familiar? Not questions she usually asked herself, but then she didn't often think about the Puget Sound cranes. Being around Leonard, however, meant thinking and talking about little else.

"We followed them out for miles," he was saying, his gaze trained on the sky. "They were searching for fish."

"Or messing with you," Carly said.

Leonard glanced at her, his eyes wide behind his glasses. "Why would they do that?"

"Because they can."

He flashed her a smile. "You're giving them too much credit. Culturally we like to anthropomorphize everything around us. Cranes don't have a sense of humor."

She hoped he was wrong. Laughing made life a lot more fun.

"You should come with me, sometime," he said. "Out on the boat."

She shook her head and took a step back. "No, thanks. I don't do boats. Or water."

"You live on an island."

"I get the irony of it, believe me, but no. I don't go in it or on it." She looked out at the Sound. "It's pretty from a safe distance, and I don't mind going on a bridge or a ferry. But anything smaller? No, thanks."

"What about when you go swimming?"

"I don't."

"Go or know how?"

"Both." She shuddered. She'd never been able to figure out why she was afraid of water, but that didn't make the fear go away. Just the thought of stepping into anything deeper than a bathtub made her nauseous.

"I could teach you."

It took a second for her to realize what he was saying, and the implication in the offer. Leonard had been at the inn for nearly three months. They'd become friends. Nothing more.

She angled toward him. He was tall and cute, with broad shoulders. He was a little skinny, but strong. A good man. A safe man. Like Robert, she thought. She was surrounded by nice guys and she wasn't interested in any of them. So far the only one who'd made her quiver had been Mango, whose flirtatious charm came too easily to him and, she suspected, too often.

"Leonard," she began, her voice gentle.

He pushed up his glasses and nodded. "Don't bother," he told her. "I know what you're going to say."

"How can you?"

He gave her a rueful smile. "I'm not the guy who gets the girl. Especially a girl like you."

"It's not you. I was married before and it didn't work and I just can't seem to want to get involved again."

"Do you still love him?"

"No. That's the strange part. I'm not sure I loved him back then." She hesitated, before adding the truth. "He cheated on me."

"With Michelle?"

"What? Why would you ask that?"

"She was gone and now she's back. There's tension between you." He flushed. "Damaris likes to talk."

"Great." She wondered what other secrets the cook was sharing with their guests. "It was a long time ago. Allen cheated with a lot of women."

"You married him, anyway?"

"I was stupid." In truth, she'd been pregnant, but Leonard had already heard enough about her sordid past.

"He's the stupid one for leaving."

She smiled. "Thank you. I appreciate the support. As much as I'd like to put all the blame on Allen, I have some responsibility in what went wrong."

"If you change your mind," he said, "about, you know…"

"You're very sweet."

"That means no." He shrugged. "I guess it could be worse. You could have said I was nice."

"The kiss of death?"

"You have no idea."

The heat was bad enough but the bugs were worse. The grasshoppers had arrived and they were everywhere. Crunching underfoot. Flying into her, getting tangled in her hair. Michelle hated the grasshoppers, hated the heat. The unbearable scorching air surrounded her like a thick, smoking blanket, sucking the air from her lungs. She turned, wanting to run but unable to. Her feet were tangled. She was hot, too hot. She couldn't breathe. Couldn't move. She screamed then. Screamed and screamed until the nightmare faded and she was in darkness.

Her breath came in gasps. She could feel her heart pounding in her chest, like thundering hooves. Sweat covered every part of her, and despite her burning skin, she shivered as the night air cooled her.

Confusion made it hard to think, to answer the basic questions like where was she and was she all right. Some of it was that she'd been deeply asleep—so deep she'd allowed the nightmares to surface. Some of it was she was still a little drunk. Which meant she couldn't have been asleep too long.

She automatically reached to her right and turned on a lamp. The clock on the nightstand said 12:34. She'd been in bed less than an hour.

As that thought registered, so did the room. She recognized the furniture, the shape, the murky shadow that was the sunroom. Something moved.

She spun toward the doorway and saw Jared standing there.

He had on jeans and nothing else. Golden hair covered his chest and angled down to the open waistband of his jeans. His feet were bare, his hair mussed. In other circumstances, she would have thought he looked sexy as hell. But his eyes were wary and he wasn't watching her the way a man watched a woman he wanted.

"What the hell are you doing here?" she demanded, pulling up the covers and glaring at him. "This is my room. If you can't respect my privacy, then I'm leaving."

"Don't get your panties in a bunch. I was checking on you."

"Why? Does it give you a thrill to watch women sleep?"

"Not especially. I wanted to make sure you were all right."

"Why wouldn't I be...?"

The nightmare, she thought grimly, remembering how it had ended. With her screaming. It hadn't all been in her sleep.

"Did I wake you?" she asked, less defensive now, but no more pleased with his presence.

He shrugged. "It happens."

The nurses at the hospital had told her she often screamed out in her sleep. The information had been delivered matter-of-factly. It wasn't as if she were the only one on the ward dealing with the aftermath of what she'd seen and done.

"How often?" she asked.

"A few times a week."

She winced. "Sorry."

"Don't be. You went through a lot over there."

"It would have been easier to come home with a rash. At least that's quiet."

"It'll get better."

"You know this how? Did one of the fish tell you?"

He shifted so he was leaning against the door frame. Involuntarily her gaze strayed to the open waistband of his jeans, then lower, to where he'd obviously hastily pulled up his zipper.

Something stirred low in her belly. What was he wearing underneath? Briefs? Boxers? Nothing?

"I served."

His words were at odds with her thoughts. It took her a second to remember what she'd asked, and when she did, she covered her face with her hands.

"Sorry. That's right. I knew you had. I'm a mess." She dropped her hands and looked up at him. "What did you do?"

"I was a sniper."

Sniper as in—

She swore silently. Talk about an unrelatable experience.

There was more. Bits and pieces drifted to her. Local gossip loved a juicy story and he'd had his local fifteen minutes of fame.

He'd returned to the island with a wife. She'd been young and pretty, from somewhere back east or the middle of the country. Maybe one of the vowel states. But she hadn't liked island life enough to stay. Or maybe it was being married to a guy who ran boats. Either way, she'd left. All that had happened just before Michelle had taken off.

"You have nightmares?" she asked. "From when you were in?"

"Not anymore. I got help. You need a group."

"I don't want a group."

"I didn't say you had to like it. You need to figure out how to make sense of it all. How to deal. You need someone, Michelle. Find a group."

His voice was low, the words insistent. Sexy.

Her gaze drifted across his bare chest. He was strong and powerful. A take-charge kind of guy, which could be both good and bad in bed, depending on his attitude. She had a feeling Jared was the good kind.

The sort of hot tickling deep in her belly stirred again.

What would he say if she invited him to join her? Yes would be her first choice, but she wasn't sure. For all she knew, he was involved with someone.

There were also other issues. For one, she had to pee.

For another, she would want to brush her teeth first and she couldn't figure out a way to do that casually.

"Think about it," he told her.

She had a bad feeling he wasn't talking about sex.

Even so, she nodded.

"I can get you a number," he added.

"You just happen to have information on veteran support groups lying around?"

"You're not my first rodeo, kid. You found the information on this room at the VA, right?"

"Uh-huh."

"I post it there on purpose. I keep this room for returning vets. To give them a safe place to get back into this world. After what I went through, I wanted to help."

She opened her mouth, then closed it. Great. She'd been thinking about sex and he considered her a mercy case. Wasn't that always the way it went?

"Get out," she growled.

He surprised her by grinning.

She reached behind her and grabbed a pillow. By the time she'd tossed it in his direction, he was already gone.

"Dickwad," she muttered as she sank back on the mattress and turned off the light.

But she was smiling, too, and for once the darkness seemed more friend than foe.

Carly straightened the bedspread, then stood back and studied the room.

The drapes were open, allowing the hint of sunlight to spill onto the hardwood floor. Lamps sat in the exact center of the two nightstands. The linens were fresh, the room dusted and vacuumed.

Against the wall, a narrow table held bottles of water, a coffeepot and bags of coffee, packages of cookies, a

few postcards and a map of the town. In the bathroom,
fluffy towels hung neatly; there were bathrobes on hooks
on the back of the door and a tray laden with soap and
bath salts and bubble bath stretched across the tub.

She'd forgotten the satisfaction of cleaning a room in
preparation for the next guest. She liked making sure
all the fixtures sparkled and that the bed was perfectly
made. She enjoyed putting out candles and setting the
radio on a classical station. She had a sense of pride in
her work.

These days all she got were lists of which snacks were
more popular and what coffee type got the most use.
Cleaning the rooms, she could see the package of cookies with only one missing, as if they'd been too awful to
finish. Either way, the inventory had to be replaced, but
better to know what people liked rather than what they
simply opened.

She made a few notes on her pad, then shoved it back
in her pocket. She'd taken on cleaning a couple of rooms
three afternoons a week as a way to help but was now
grateful for the chance to connect with their guests on a
more intimate basis.

She checked one last time to make sure she hadn't left
any cleaning supplies, then stripped off her gloves and
started out of the room. As she did, she heard uneven
steps in the hallway. Michelle came around the corner.

"I didn't know you could manage the stairs," she said
by way of greeting.

"It's a bitch, but I figured I'd better get up here."

Carly clenched her jaw and crushed the gloves in her
hand. She shouldn't even be surprised, she told herself,
stepping back to allow Michelle into the room she'd just
finished. Like mother, like daughter.

She knew what would happen next. The not-so-subtle

insults, the suggestions that were nothing more than a power play.

Michelle limped toward her, then came to stop and frowned.

"What?"

"Go ahead."

"Go ahead and do what? I came up here because I haven't managed the stairs since I've been back. You're cleaning rooms. The least I can do is haul my ass up here and look at the rooms. What if my mom turned this place into one of those theme places? With her crappy taste, God knows what could have happened."

The tension bled away, leaving her a little weak. "Oh."

"Oh? What's going on?"

"I thought you'd come upstairs to check out my work."

"You cleaned a room, Carly. You used to be a full-time housekeeper. What's to check?" Her brows drew together and she swore. "Let me guess. Yet another legacy from my charming mother. She used to do that to me, too. Offer suggestions."

Michelle cleared her throat. "'Perhaps if you cleaned the toilet counterclockwise.' That was my favorite. Because what? The rotational pull of the earth makes the scrubbing better if it's counterclockwise?"

Carly laughed. "She always told me I was putting the things on the bath tray wrong. One time I wrote down what she said, then kept the note with me and showed it to her the next time she complained, so she could see I was doing exactly what she said."

"Pretty ballsy of you. I doubt she was amused."

Carly remembered the icy stare, the cool way Brenda had said perhaps Carly would be happier working somewhere else. How she'd had to beg to keep her job.

"No, she wasn't pleased."

Michelle walked into the room and looked around. "It's nice," she said.

"You hate the bedding."

Michelle glanced at the daisy-covered fabric. "Yup. Every inch of it, but that's just me. I'm sure the guests love it."

"They don't complain about it."

"Practically the same thing." Michelle hobbled to the window and looked out. "I see our therapy people are busy."

Carly joined her. She could see the three couples at the far end of the lawn, near the beach. Seth and Pauline were talking to them.

"They haven't been a problem," she said. "They're up early and gone all day."

"And hey, probably not having sex in the beds. That's nice. I used to hate to find condoms in the trash. Yuck."

Carly laughed. "I'm with you there, but it's not as if we can ask them to take them home when they go."

"Why not? They brought them here in the first place. Pretend it's the beach. Take your bottles and cans with you when you go. Or in this case, used condoms."

"It doesn't work that way. They're our guests."

"You're romanticizing the business. That's never good."

They both laughed.

This was how it had been before, Carly thought. Easy. Back when they were friends, when life had made sense and she'd understood the rules. Before everything had changed.

She wanted that again. To be friends with Michelle. To have them trust each other.

Somewhere in the parking lot, a car backfired. Carly

glanced toward the noise, then back to the window where she saw a car pulling out.

"Someone needs to get his engine—"

Michelle had gone white. Sweat broke out on her face and a tremor rippled through her.

"Are you all right?" she asked, not sure what had happened.

Michelle glanced around as if she wasn't sure where she was. Carly reached for her.

"Don't touch me."

The words were more growl than speech, the tone guttural. Carly stepped back. Michelle sagged against the wall.

"Just go," she said. "I'll be fine."

Carly hesitated.

"Get out!"

The laughter was gone, as was the moment of connection. She collected her cleaning supplies and did as she was told.

Seventeen

Still shaking, Michelle escaped. She slipped more than walked down the stairs, every part of her on alert. The sound of the explosion—not an explosion, she told herself, something else—still ringing in her head.

She didn't remember walking through the lobby, although she must have because when she was next aware of her surroundings, she was in the empty dining room. She made her way to the kitchen and found Damaris prepping for lunch.

Her friend took one look at her and pulled out a stool.

"Sit," Damaris instructed. "Now."

Michelle stumbled forward, then sank heavily onto the stool, her hip screaming in protest.

"Don't tell Carly I have this," Damaris said as she walked into the pantry, then returned with a bottle of whiskey in her hand.

She poured an inch into a glass, glanced at Michelle, then added a little more.

"Drink," she instructed, handing it over.

Michelle swallowed a mouthful, letting the good burn erase the last of the fear.

"What happened?"

Michelle drew in a breath. "Nothing. It was so stupid. I was upstairs and a car backfired. But I thought…"

Damaris moved close and wrapped her arms around her. "Poor child. You've been through too much. It's not right. Women shouldn't be in the military."

That made Michelle laugh. "You're about seventy years behind the times."

"The times are wrong. Why'd you have to go off, anyway?"

Michelle raised her eyebrows.

"All right. Maybe you wanted to get away, but the army? For ten years?" Damaris released her. "And look at you now. All injured and jumpy. You're going to get better."

She wasn't sure if it was a question or a statement. "I'm trying." She finished the drink and set the glass on the counter. "What's the lunch special?"

"Grilled chicken and sun-dried tomatoes on focaccia bread. With extra cheese." Damaris wrinkled her nose. "Those psychologist people came to talk to me."

"Seth and Pauline?"

The cook nodded. "They asked me for more healthy choices on the lunch menu."

"This is your answer?"

"It's chicken."

Michelle didn't know if she should laugh or groan. "You couldn't come up with a salad?"

"Salad isn't a meal."

Not an argument Michelle was willing to take on.

She looked out the window and saw the psychologists in question leading their group through some kind of exercise. The women were standing, facing the men. Every time the women made a movement, the men copied them.

"Silliness," Damaris said with a sniff as she followed Michelle's gaze. "You're married, you stay married. That's the way it is. Being happy or not is up to you. A man can't make a woman happy. It's like asking a cat to grow wings. It's not in their nature. Happiness is in here."

She slapped her chest. "The quicker women accept men don't change, the happier they'll be. I married my husband on my eighteenth birthday. If I was expecting him to make me happy, I'd have died waiting. You have to make a life. Be a good wife, have children. That's happiness. Look at your father. Did he make your mother happy? Of course not."

"He left."

"Exactly. One day he was here, the next he was gone. She never got over it. I'm not saying he should have done what he did, but when he was gone, she had a choice."

The logic was twisted, but Michelle had to agree with the part about Brenda. Her mother could have gotten over what had happened. Instead, she'd chosen to be miserable.

"Mom took it hard," she murmured, wondering what her life would have been like if her mother had been a different person. Or was asking the question too much like wanting cats to grow wings?

"I don't care about her," Damaris said. "Not to speak ill of the dead, but you're the one I worry about. You had to take on too much, too soon. Your mother should have taken care of you. Instead, you took care of her."

Mostly out of guilt, Michelle thought. Because she'd known in her heart her father had loved her more than he'd loved his wife and even as a child she'd guessed that was wrong. Not that his love for his daughter had kept him from leaving.

She'd been sixteen when she'd walked in on her father

in bed with Carly's mother. The image had burned itself in her brain—two adults she'd loved and trusted betraying them all. She still remembered the sight of Lana's bare breasts bouncing and heaving as her body arched, Frank's head buried between her spread legs.

At first she hadn't realized what they were doing. She'd stood there, gaping, confused but with a growing sense of shame and horror. She must have made a sound, because they both suddenly turned and looked at her, their shocked expressions probably mirroring her own.

She'd run. Run down the stairs and out of the inn, making her way to the side of the road before throwing up. Then she'd kept on running until the cold and the rain had caused her to slow.

The tears had continued to pour down her cheeks. She'd been crying when her father had found her.

"I'm sorry you had to see that," he'd said.

That was as close as he'd come to apologizing. He'd never asked if she was all right or even said why he was betraying his wife with her best friend, the mother of Michelle's best friend. Instead, he'd talked about how important it was for Michelle to keep quiet.

"Your mother won't understand," he'd told her.

Michelle had wanted to scream that *she* didn't understand, either. That it wasn't right.

"You're my best girl. I need you to keep this a secret."

He'd explained why it was important, but she hadn't been able to hear much more. She'd agreed, more because she couldn't imagine talking about what she'd seen than because she agreed with his excuses.

She'd always been a daddy's girl. When she'd been little, he'd been the one to tuck her in, to read her stories. She'd felt safe. Protected.

All that disappeared the afternoon she'd found him in bed with Carly's mother.

Michelle had pretended to have the flu and had retreated to her bed for two days. She'd been unable to look at her father, to deal with her mother. Slowly, so slowly, life had resumed and she'd told herself to pretend it had never happened.

The following year when both Carly and Michelle were about to start their senior year of high school, her father and Lana had run off together. They'd disappeared into the night, leaving only notes behind. Their love had been too great to be denied, they'd written.

The second betrayal had forced the truth from Michelle. She'd admitted what she'd seen to both Brenda and Carly. She'd expected they would all grieve together. Instead, Brenda and Carly had banded together to blame Michelle. Her mother had insisted if Michelle had told the truth, Frank wouldn't have left. That somehow Brenda would have been able to stop him. Carly had agreed.

While her relationship with her mother had never been especially close, after Frank left, it had gotten worse. More devastating had been the loss of her best friend. Carly had disappeared from her life. Michelle had faced her last year of high school completely alone, having lost mother, father and best friend in a matter of hours.

Damaris pushed her glass toward her. "Drink," she instructed again. "We shouldn't be talking about this. You have enough on your mind. You don't need to be remembering the past."

"I agree," Michelle murmured, knowing it was too late for that. "He's been calling."

"Who? Your father?"

She nodded. "A couple of times. I don't know how he got my cell number."

"Don't look at me. I wouldn't give it to him."

"I know."

"Maybe Carly did."

Michelle was less sure. "Does she talk to her mother?"

"How would I know? She and I rarely speak."

"You work together."

Damaris sniffed. "We both work at the inn, but we've never been friendly. She's always in here, telling me what to do. I ignore her."

Something Michelle should put a stop to, she thought. Carly had earned her position at the inn. She thought about the handmade welcome cards and the care with which Carly had cleaned the rooms. Honestly, she was damned lucky Carly had taken a job here and stayed on as long as she did.

Damaris poured them both more whiskey. "You know her past. Once a whore, always a whore."

"No," Michelle said firmly. "I know she's not sleeping around. Carly loves her daughter too much to risk hurting her. She knows better than almost anyone what that can do to a family. Besides, she works long hours. When would she have time to sleep around?"

"Not now, but before. In high school. And that husband of hers. He was smart to leave."

Damaris had plenty of energy on the subject but not much in the way of facts.

"High school was a long time ago."

"Maybe, but she's no different. Trust me."

That was the problem, Michelle thought later that afternoon as she sat in her office. She did trust Damaris. But she trusted Carly, too, which left her in the awkward position of not knowing who to believe.

* * *

"We should shut the whole thing down," Michelle muttered, standing in the center of the gift shop, her hands on her hips.

"As long as you're keeping an open mind," Carly told her. "Come on, it doesn't make sense to simply shut the doors. For one thing, we have inventory to deal with. Some can be returned, but there's a restocking fee, so we'll lose money for sure. And until we figure out a way to use the space, we're giving up the rent money."

"What rent money?"

"Isn't the gift shop paying rent? That was the whole point. It was supposed to be a separate business, not associated with the inn. Brenda had the idea to get into retail."

Carly had been the one who had objected, saying it would be a distraction and a drain on finances. Of course, that had been back when she'd still thought she was earning her way into an ownership position. Brenda had sworn the gift shop was going to stand on its own.

Once it was in place, Carly found she enjoyed working in the store a few hours a week, but that didn't mean it was a good business decision.

Michelle leaned against the checkout table and sighed. "She lied. God, I'm getting so tired of saying that. Can I get it out of my system now? Whatever we talk about in the future, whatever happens, if it involved my mother, she lied. She lied and I'm sorry."

Carly blinked. "That was good. Sincere and honest, with a hint of whine. I think you're getting better."

Michelle narrowed her gaze. "Are you mocking my PTSD?"

"No. Just you. I have respect for your PTSD."

As Michelle studied her, Carly braced herself. The

moment could go either way. Michelle could laugh and they could take one more baby step toward being friends, or she could start throwing blackberry-covered stoneware.

"Kiss my ass," Michelle said with a grin.

"We were never that close." Carly let out the breath she'd been holding. "Okay. Gift-shop reality check. Based on the lack of rent paid by the gift shop, I'm guessing there aren't a separate set of books and it's not its own corporation?"

"No such luck."

"Any way to change that?" Carly held up her hand. "I guess the more important question is, would it help or hurt? Or maybe not be worth the trouble if we're going to shut it down. For what it's worth, I think we can make something here."

Michelle glanced around. "You're right—simply closing the doors is stupid. From what I can tell, we're making a little money off the place and I don't want to leave the square footage sitting empty. But there's a ton of inventory that isn't moving."

Carly shifted the printouts on the counter. "I've gone over the lists and marked what seems to be selling well and what's a disaster."

"Is there a column for what's ugly? Because there's plenty of ugly here."

"Let me guess. You hate everything with daisies on them."

"That's a start. At least the blackberries support the island."

"Daisies are pretty."

"You can eat a blackberry."

"Things only have value if they're edible? That puts a somewhat icky spin on the local baseball team."

Michelle laughed. "A couple of the players are cute enough to be delicious. Does that count?"

"It should." Carly turned her attention back to the printout. "The dolls are the first concern." She moved toward that part of the store and Michelle followed.

"They're a specialty item," Carly continued. "The average tourist isn't interested and the serious collectors don't know that they're here."

"You don't like them?"

"No. I think they're creepy. Those little hands. I worry they're going to come alive at night, get into my room and scoop out my brains."

Michelle tilted her head. "Really?"

"No, but I'm not a doll person. I've made a few calls and there's a doll store up in Bellingham. The owner is interested in our inventory. She would come and get them, paying us what we paid. We wouldn't make any money on the transaction, but we wouldn't lose any, either."

"I wish there was a way to make money on them."

"Me, too, but we haven't sold a single doll in two months. Most of the inventory is over a year old."

"They were a stupid purchase." Michelle sighed. "Let me guess... My mother's idea?"

"Yes, but I picked everything with daisies."

"Spreading the blame around?"

Carly fluttered her eyelids. "Some of the daisy items are our bestsellers."

Michelle pointed to the china collection in a daisy pattern. There were a few dishes, but most of the shelves held serving pieces, salt and pepper shakers, along with napkin holders and cake plates.

"Like those?"

"They sell really well, so yes, we could expand that. Carry even more."

"You're enjoying this, aren't you?"

"A little." Carly patted her arm. "Just tell yourself people are freaks. You'll feel better."

"It's going to take more than that."

Carly thought about pointing out she owned a few of the pieces herself, but she figured she'd teased Michelle enough. She liked that they were able to talk like colleagues instead of enemies and she appreciated that her boss had taken her advice with the clothes and was even wearing a little mascara. She was still painfully thin, but that would probably get better when her hip stopped hurting so much.

Michelle sighed. "Okay, fine. We'll keep the ugly dishes. What else?"

Carly pointed to the bolts of fabric. "Boston Flemming is a local textile artist. She hand paints fabric. Very exclusive, very pricey. Our store is the only place you can buy her work retail. When she's not creating directly for clients, she plays around with new ideas and we get to sell the results."

"Nice," Michelle said. "Looks expensive."

"About a hundred dollars a yard."

Michelle blinked. "I'm less interested in having a sofa re-covered right now."

They worked their way through the rest of the inventory list. They agreed on keeping the books and adding more local artists, and disagreed on the touristy items like magnets and pens. Michelle wanted them gone.

"We're a tourist destination. Grandma wants to take home something for the grandkids," Carly said. "They make money."

"Fine," Michelle grumbled. "You're right."

"Hearing that never gets old."

Michelle opened her mouth to respond, then her gaze shifted. Her eyes widened and her mouth curled into a surprised and happy smile.

Before Carly could figure out what had happened, Michelle went hurrying past, nearly running, her arms open.

Carly turned and saw her fling herself at a tall, dark-haired man who had just walked into the gift shop.

"I ignored the closed sign," he said, catching her as she flung herself at him.

"You're here!" Michelle said happily. "I can't believe you're here."

"I came to see you. Just like I promised."

They both laughed and the man spun Michelle in a circle. Carly could feel the affection between them, the pleasure at being back together.

So Michelle had a man in her life, she thought, turning and quietly walking out to give them privacy. A hunky man with smiling eyes. Some women had all the luck.

Eighteen

"I can't believe you're here," Michelle said, hugging Sam again. "Why didn't you tell me you were coming?"

"I just did."

His easy grin, the way his eyes crinkled when he smiled, were all familiar. "It's good to see you."

"You, too."

She led him out of the gift shop and down the hall to the restaurant. It wasn't open for lunch yet, but she motioned him to a table, then went to grab a warming carafe of coffee.

"You sit," he said, coming up behind her. "I can get the coffee."

"That bad, huh?"

"You're limping. I don't like to see you hurt."

Words designed to make her feel safe and protected. Emotions that were hard to find these days.

"When did you get here?" she asked when he returned. "On the morning ferry?"

"I've been here a couple of days," he said as he sat across from her.

"What? And you didn't call me?"

"I wanted to look around. Check things out." He pushed the sugar toward her. "You talked about this place so much, I needed to make sure infamous Blackberry Island was as great as you promised."

"And?"

"I like it."

"You couldn't come see me first? You had to approve of my hometown?"

"I'm applying for a job here. That's why I was checking it out. You okay with that?"

His dark blue eyes met hers as he waited for his answer. She knew he would leave the island if she told him to. That he wouldn't do anything to hurt or upset her. He'd always been one of the good guys.

"What kind of job?"

The grin returned. "You have to ask?"

"Sheriff."

"Deputy. I'll get to sheriff soon enough."

"They must have been thrilled by your résumé."

"They were impressed."

Sam had been in the army twenty years, and he'd spent nearly all of them in the military police. He had the training and experience any town sheriff could want.

"Need a character reference?" she asked.

"Not yet."

"You still could have told me you were here."

"I wanted to surprise you by saying I was applying for the job, so I waited until I was sure." He reached across the table and took her hand. "How are you?"

"Fine."

His dark eyes stared into hers and the smile faded.

"Ugh." She pulled her fingers free. "I mean it. I'm fine. How are you? You ready to be a full-time civilian?"

He rubbed his hair, still regulation. "Some things will take getting used to. You sleeping?"

"Why are we talking about me? I'm not that interesting."

"You are to me. Are you?"

"No. Sometimes." She cupped her hands around the mug. "I have nightmares. It sucks."

"You in a group?"

She groaned. "Not you, too."

"That's a no."

She glanced at him from under her lashes. "Did I say I was happy to see you? I spoke too soon."

"No, you didn't."

He was right. Sam was one of the few people she trusted absolutely. Having him around would mean someone had her back.

"If you don't want to talk about your emotional health—"

"I don't," she interrupted.

"How's the hip?"

"Better. It still hurts and I get tired, but I'm off the prescription painkillers. I use over-the-counter stuff now." And her new BFF in a bottle, but he didn't need to know that. "There are—"

She stopped and frowned at him. "Wait a minute. If you've been on the island for a couple of days, where have you been staying? Not here."

"They said you were full when I called."

"You should have asked for me. I could have thrown someone out for you."

He chuckled. "While the sentiment touches my heart, there's no need. I'm at the Tidewater Inn down the road."

"We have a better breakfast."

"I'll try it in the morning."

"You'd better. I'll check the reservations. We should have something."

"Not to worry. I'm fine where I am."

"I might insist."

"If it's important to you."

She smiled. "It's good to see you."

"It's because I'm so good-looking, right? I have that problem all the time. Women can't let go of me."

She leaned back in her chair and laughed. The sound came from deep in her belly, vibrating in her chest. It filled her, spilling out and making the constant pain in her hip fade. She laughed until she had to gasp and catch her breath.

"Thank you," she managed, wiping tears from her eyes.

"Part of my charm."

"You are charming."

She asked about his parents, who'd retired to Austin, and his sister. As they spoke, she noticed his attention drifting past her to something outside the window.

"What?" she asked, turning in her seat. "We have three couples here in some kind of therapy program. Are they out there doing those strange exercises?"

But none of her guests were in view. The only thing she could see was Carly and Gabby picking daisies.

Michelle looked back at Sam. "No."

"What? She's cute."

"Cute? What are we? In high school?"

"I didn't think you'd want me saying anything else in front of you."

"What do I care?"

"Then why are you glaring?"

She consciously relaxed her face. "I'm not glaring."

"Yeah, right. What's the problem? Is she married?"

"No. But as you can see, she has a child."

"I like kids."

"Since when? You stay away from her."

"I don't think I have to listen to you."

"You'll be sorry if you don't."

"Why?"

A question she couldn't answer. Even more disconcerting, she wasn't sure who she was trying to protect—Sam, Carly or herself.

"I know I'm a fool," the woman said, her voice shaking as tears spilled down her cheeks. "I tell myself to be strong. That I should leave him. That's what you're thinking, aren't you? That I'm an idiot?"

"No. Of course not."

Carly patted the other woman's shoulder sympathetically, hoping she looked more comfortable than she felt. She'd come into the lounge area to make sure there was fresh wood in the fireplace. Seth and Pauline wanted to use the space that evening and it was going to be cool. Carly had thought a crackling fire might both warm the guests and give them a little nudge in the romance department.

What she'd found in addition to plenty of wood was one of her guests curled up in the window seat, sobbing. Even worse, Carly couldn't remember her name. It was an *M* name. Mary? Marti? No, there were more syllables than that. Martina? Now Carly searched for a polite way to ask.

The woman, maybe in her mid-to-late thirties, dabbed at her face. "He cheats. That's why we're here. My mom says I need to pack up and go but I have two kids. They love him and I don't want to be a single mother. Besides, the rest of the relationship isn't so bad. I just keep hoping one day I'll be enough."

The tears began again. Carly sat there knowing she couldn't possibly ask the woman's name now. Nor did she have any advice to give.

"I'm such a loser," the other woman said.

"No, you're not. You're in a difficult situation. You have to make the right decision for you and your children. But it's your decision. Not anyone else's."

The woman nodded. "He loves me. I know he does."

"I'm sure he does."

The woman looked at her. "You think I'm fooling myself. That if he loved me, he wouldn't cheat."

"I didn't say that."

"You don't have to. I can see it in your eyes."

"Then you're seeing the wrong thing. Only you can know what's going on between you and your husband. No one else."

The woman covered her face with her hands. "I'm such a fool. Why can't I stop loving him? Why do I have to be stupid?"

"You're not stupid and you're not alone. We all do things that don't make sense to other people."

She dropped her hands and stared at Carly. "You don't look like you'd ever make a mistake like this."

"I've made dozens. More than that. My husband cheated on me two days before the wedding. With my best friend." She shrugged. "I married him, anyway."

Carly had felt trapped. She was pregnant. At the time she'd felt she didn't have a choice. That marrying Allen was better than being alone.

There'd been so much screaming, she thought, not wanting to remember but unable to stop herself. First she'd walked in on them. Allen had stood there, naked, swearing it wasn't his fault. That Michelle had seduced him. He'd been drunk and hadn't realized what he was doing.

Carly had accepted his story, even as she suspected he was lying. But confronting him and finding out the truth—well, she hadn't been sure she wanted that.

"Did he explain what had happened?" the woman asked.

"He had a story. I was pretty sure he was lying, but…"

"You had a wedding planned. You couldn't walk away from that."

"Isn't it more important to marry the right guy than one who cheats, though? Having to cancel a wedding would have been easier than getting divorced."

She would still have her father's house. If she hadn't married Allen, he wouldn't have had the chance to steal from her.

"It's done," she said. "Would I do it differently now? I'm not sure."

The woman bit her lower lip. "You finally left him?"

"Oh, no. He left me. He took everything." No point in going into details, she thought. She'd shared enough humiliation for one morning.

"John will never leave me," the woman said. "I know that. It's not his way."

Carly managed a smile. "Then you don't have to worry about that."

"I know. I guess I should be grateful for what I have and stop expecting him to be faithful."

Carly didn't think that should be the lesson learned, but wasn't sure she should say that.

"Pauline tells me that before I can make any decisions, I have to learn to respect myself," the woman admitted. "Like I know what that means."

Carly hadn't spent much time with Pauline, but her respect for the woman climbed a couple of notches. Self-respect was a hard one. Something she still wrestled with. Telling Robert they couldn't use each other to hide anymore had gone a long way to getting her closer to achieving what she wanted.

The woman looked at her. "Is it hard? Being alone?"

"Sometimes."

"Would you take him back?"

"No."

"That's the thing," the other woman admitted. "I don't want to lose him."

"Then don't."

She smiled. "I guess you're right. I'm not brave like you. I don't want to do it all alone. What I have is better than nothing. Thanks for listening."

She stood and walked back toward the inn.

Carly watched her go.

She'd never been overly successful in the relationship department but "better than nothing" didn't seem like a goal that would make anyone happy.

Saturday Michelle walked through the garden. The afternoon had turned sunny and the temperatures were in the low sixties. Practically a heat wave, she thought, eyeing the flowers swaying in the gentle breeze.

Was it her or were the daisies even brighter than usual? The reds and yellows, the pinks, practically glowed against the dark brown of the earth and the green lawn. No doubt the guests found them beautiful, but something about the damn daisies got on her nerves. She wanted to kick them all into submission or, at the very least, rip them up by the roots.

Not that she would. Doing something like that would

mean she would move from getting pressured to join a support group to being committed.

The back door to the inn opened and Gabby danced out. There was no other word to describe her happy movements as she turned and dipped and pranced barefoot across the patio, toward the lawn.

The girl held a thick book under one arm. Even from across the lawn, Michelle recognized the cover of a Harry Potter novel, although she couldn't say which one.

Gabby spotted her and waved, then hurried across the grass toward her.

Michelle watched her, envying the easy movements and remembering when she'd been about that age. Life had been a whole lot less complicated.

"Guess what?" Gabby called as she approached. The girl raced toward her, skidding to a stop on the grass. "I've been out three times reading and I haven't had food and the cranes aren't bothering me." She grinned. "They still come look, but then when they see I don't have a snack, they go away. I talked to Leonard about it." She wrinkled her nose. "He says they've somehow communicated I'm not a food source."

She giggled. "I guess that's like a bird grocery store. And then we talked about the cranes. Leonard knows a lot of interesting stuff, like how the birds have these lives with eggs and babies and he said I could go with him to see the chicks, only it's on this small boat and I'm scared of the water, but I used to be scared of the cranes, so maybe I don't have to be scared of the water."

She paused and drew in a breath.

Michelle stared at the girl, remembering the fearful child she'd met less than a month ago.

She wanted to say they were just cranes and not being afraid of them wasn't a big deal, but she was in no position to be critical of anyone's issues. Besides, she envied the child's ability to put aside terrors so quickly and easily. If only she could do the same.

Her gaze dropped to Gabby's bare feet. Or be that innocent again.

"I'm glad you're not scared of the cranes, and not being scared of the water is probably a good thing. We do live on an island."

Carly had always been terrified of the water. As a kid, she'd refused to put even a toe into the Sound. No matter how hot the day, she wouldn't go into a pool. Had Gabby learned that from her?

"Did you see it's sunny?" Gabby asked.

"I did."

"I like sunny days. And we're planning our summer movies. We go every week in the summer." She danced in place as she spoke.

She and Carly had gone to the movies weekly during summer, Michelle thought. They'd walked to the only movie theater in town and stood in line with the other kids. When the multiplex had been built, they'd thought it practically a theme park, it had been so thrilling. Ten choices at the same time.

She could see Carly in Gabby. The same shape and color of eyes, the smile. There were probably bits of Allen in her, too, but they seemed less important.

"The movies are great," Gabby was saying, "Mom says I get lip gloss when I turn ten."

"Good for you."

Gabby nodded. "I want a phone, but Mom says no to that. Most of my friends don't have phones, either." She paused. "I wanted to tell you that I'm sorry about Nana Brenda. That she died while you were away. You must be sad about it."

"Thank you," Michelle said, surprised Gabby would mention her mother. "Do you miss her?"

Gabby hesitated. "Sometimes she made Mom cry and I didn't like that. But she could be nice, too. We were friends, I think."

Michelle felt a combination of compassion and rage. Even from the grave, her mother was doing damage.

She put her hand on Gabby's small shoulder. "It's okay to be confused. You love your mom and want to protect her. Just like she protects you. You can remember the good stuff about Nana Brenda, too. People are complicated."

"I'm not supposed to talk about it," Gabby admitted in a whisper. "Mom said."

"I won't tell."

Gabby blessed her with a wide smile.

They headed back toward the inn, Gabby chatting about her friends and the summer camp she would attend. That she didn't like the outdoor stuff, but the computer programming was fun. Once they were inside, Gabby scampered off to find Carly. Michelle moved toward the front desk and saw Ellen Snow walking into the lobby.

"Hi," Ellen said with a smile when they'd spotted each other. "I'm running errands this morning and thought I'd stop by to see how things are going."

Michelle wasn't sure if this was a social call or more about business.

"We're doing great. Full for the weekend."

"I'm not surprised," the tall blonde said. "You have such a beautiful place. I love it here. I always have my friends from Seattle stay here if they want a fun get-away."

"I'll take the business."

They gravitated toward the sofas by the front window and took a seat across from each other. Ellen wore jeans and a light sweater over a tailored shirt. Her boots had three-inch heels. Michelle wasn't sure how she could walk in them but she was willing to admit they looked good.

"I've been meaning to come by sooner," Ellen admitted. "Time gets away from me. Maybe we can go to lunch or something."

"Sure," Michelle said, deciding it was better to be polite than admit the fact that she wasn't much for "going to lunch." She had work to do.

Ellen glanced around, then leaned forward. "Is everything all right with Carly?"

"Sure. Why?"

"I know the two of you don't get along. Who could blame you?"

Michelle shifted in her seat. "You're the one who insisted I work with her. That she stay on."

"No," Ellen said quickly, her gaze sympathetic. "It wasn't me. Our loan committee said it was important. I tried to talk them out of it. I couldn't make any headway and I didn't want to get into Carly's past, so we're both stuck."

Ellen crossed her legs and shrugged. "I know you're the one who really runs this place. Carly's great at smiling at the guests. As long as she doesn't make it obvious she's sleeping with them, I guess that works."

Michelle nearly fell off the sofa. "Excuse me? Carly's not sleeping with the guests."

Ellen laughed. "Well, sure. Not all of them. But she keeps her hand in, so to speak."

"I've been back a few weeks now and I can tell that Carly does a good job."

Ellen sighed. "You're amazingly loyal. I admire that. I would have cut her loose years ago. You remember what she was like in high school." There was another laugh, this one a little sharper around the edges. "She practically came to school with rug burn on her back. Is there even one guy she didn't sleep with?"

"That was a long time ago."

"People don't change." Ellen's expression sharpened. "Trust me on that. Carly is as she always was. My point is, I'm sorry you're stuck with her. I'll get that changed as soon as possible and then you'll have the satisfaction of firing her."

Michelle felt uncomfortable. Ellen was doing her best to bond and show she was on Michelle's side, but nothing about this conversation felt right.

"We have an employment contract," Michelle said, her voice quiet, her mind conflicted.

Ellen grinned. "And I have a lawyer. Don't worry—we're friends. I would never stick you with someone like that even a minute longer than necessary." She rose. "I have forty million things to do this morning. I just wanted to stop by and say hi. Let me know if I can do anything to help."

Michelle stood, nearly stumbling as pain jabbed her in the hip. Ellen gave a quick wave and walked out.

Michelle was left wondering what Carly had done to make the other woman dislike her so much and, oddly enough, trying to figure out how to make it all better.

Nineteen

Carly grabbed an armful of linens and backed out of the storage room. She couldn't see where she was going so when she bumped into something solid, she assumed she'd misjudged the path and had run into a wall. Then large, warm hands settled on her waist. Masculine hands.

The unexpected contact made her jump. She spun around to see who was touching her only to find Michelle's friend grinning down at her from the hallway.

"You looked like you were in trouble," he said, his blue eyes sparkling with humor, a slow, sexy smile curving his mouth. "It's my sworn duty to help a lady in distress."

She shoved the stack of linens at him. "Good to know. Want to carry these?"

"It's what I live for. Where are we going with them?"

"The end of the hall."

"I'm Sam," he said as he fell into step with her.

"Carly."

He was tall and lean, but with plenty of muscle. Good-looking enough to be interesting but not so handsome that a woman would have to worry he would want more bathroom-mirror time than her. What intrigued Carly the most, though, was his air of competence. He seemed like a man who knew how to take charge. After years of being on her own, that was pretty sexy to her.

They reached the supply room, where the housekeepers collected what they needed every day.

"You can put those on the counter," she said.

He lowered the linens, then stepped back while she sorted them.

"You're probably not sure what to ask next," he told her. "Let me help. I'm a friend of Michelle's and I'm in town for a job interview. I just got out of the army after serving twenty years, mostly as an MP. I call my momma every week, I prefer to hold doors open for women and believe on a first date the man should pay. So I guess that makes me old-fashioned."

Carly separated the sheets from the pillowcases and stacked them neatly. She made sure there were enough towels, little soaps and lotions. Finally she turned to Sam.

He stood confidently, aware of what he offered. She knew the type—he liked women and they liked him back. Which should have reminded her of Allen. Except her ex had been more interested in what he could get and she'd heard rumors not every guy was like that.

Funny how she'd gone nearly ten years without so much as a sexual twitch and in the space of a couple of weeks she'd met two guys who appealed to her. She wanted to do a little "my girl parts aren't dead" dance, but knew that would only be frightening for anyone watching.

"You think you're charming," she said.

"I've heard that a time or two."

"Married?"

"Divorced."

She crossed her arms over her chest and waited.

"Twice," he added with a shrug. "Okay, so sometimes I'm not the fastest learner. Both were impulses. I'm taking things slower, now. Settling into a new town. Speaking of which, I'd love to see more of it. What with you being a native and all, maybe you could show me around." The charming, seductive smile returned. "Just to be neighborly."

His voice held a hint of the South, as if he'd either been born there or spent a lot of time there. She had a feeling he was interested in more than a tour of Blackberry Island.

She hadn't been on a date since she'd first gone out with Allen. Her last sexual encounter had been when she was five months pregnant and had been with her husband. Since then there had been a long, barren desert when it came to men and sex.

Mango had reminded her of possibilities. Sam made her want to take a test drive. He made her aware of her body—especially the aforementioned girly parts. She wanted to shut the door, pull the fresh, clean towels onto the floor and invite him to a party. At the same time she knew there were a lot of reasons why she should resist. In the interest of not being stupid, she took a step back.

"What's a man like you doing settling down in a place like this?" she asked. "How'd you even find us?"

"Michelle talked about the island a lot. It sounded nice. I came and checked it out and decided to stay."

Michelle. Carly had nearly forgotten about her, about her reunion with Sam.

"You're with Michelle," Carly said, telling herself her job was more important than any man and having no trouble believing that. Unless she changed her form of employment, getting laid would not pay the bills. More important, she cared about Michelle.

"We're old friends." One eyebrow went up. "We're not together, if that's what you're thinking. We were, a long time ago. It was hot and heavy for about fifteen minutes. I wouldn't have asked you out if we were still involved. I'm not that guy."

He held up both hands. "We're just friends, I swear. You can ask her."

"That would be a little awkward," Carly murmured, wanting to believe him, but not completely convinced.

He dropped his hands to his side. "I'm one of the good guys. You can ask my mom."

"I don't know her."

He pulled out his cell phone. "We could give her call."

"I'd rather ask Michelle."

"You do that. Once she confirms what I said, you'll show me the town?"

"Sure."

He grinned. "I look forward to it."

Carly did, too, and she wasn't sure if that was good or very, very bad.

Michelle started every day the same way. She got to the inn early, parked her truck, then went into the restaurant and had breakfast with Damaris. The cook always had a plate ready and there was lots of coffee. Great food, great conversation and caffeine. She doubted there was any way to improve the morning.

Today, she paused in the dining room and looked around. Every table was full, she thought happily, practically hearing the sound of money falling into the register. Conversation competed with the clink of flatware and soft music playing in the background.

While it was currently cloudy, the weather guy swore the sun would be out later. More important, he'd promised a rain-free Memorial Day weekend.

Michelle wanted to believe him, but she'd grown up here. Rain loved to attend all the big summer weekends. Still, the thought of a full inn over a sunny weekend was enough to make her giddy.

She crossed toward the kitchen, smiling at customers as she went. Back when she'd been in high school there had only been twelve tables, she thought absently. Now there were at least double that. She reached the door for the kitchen, then turned and did a quick count.

More than double. There were thirty-two tables. Assuming at least half of them turned over, that was forty-eight checks for the morning. And it was only going to get busier over the weekend.

"Don't talk to me," Damaris said as she entered the kitchen. "What? Are we giving away breakfast? I'm getting too many orders."

Michelle laughed. "Don't forget, that's a good thing."

"For you. For me, it's more work." But the cook was grinning as she spoke. "You'll have to get your own breakfast this morning."

"I don't mind."

Michelle poured herself a mug of coffee, then used the tongs to grab a piece of bacon.

"We're booked through the weekend," she said. "Every room is full."

"I know." Damaris expertly flipped pancakes before adding a scoop of cheese and avocado to an omelet. "Carly was by yesterday to tell me. As if I couldn't figure out we'd be busy on a holiday weekend by myself."

She slid food onto plates, then yelled, "Order up," before glancing back at Michelle.

"She wanted to make sure I had enough supplies, that I'd remembered to order extra. What? Because the past twenty-five years of cooking don't count? Because I forget?"

"That's my fault," Michelle said, compelled to defend Carly. "I asked her to double-check everything in the inn."

"You're good to take her side," Damaris said. "But she doesn't deserve it. Do you know she talked to me about doing a brunch on Sundays. A brunch! She said it would be special and we'd take reservations. Can you imagine?"

"It's not a bad idea."

Damaris rolled her eyes. "You're the boss, not her. Why do you let her do these things?"

"She's doing her job. Damaris, you have to be okay with that."

Damaris grumbled something under her breath, then said, "Fine, but I don't have to like it."

Michelle popped bread into the toaster and remembered Ellen's visit. Ellen hated Carly, Damaris obviously wasn't a fan, but the staff loved her. So who was right?

"It won't kill you," Carly said, physically pushing Michelle toward the open door, wishing she had the strength to cause actual movement.

"It might."

"You're such a baby. It's a meeting of the Blackberry Island Women of Business. You're a woman with a business."

"Who lives on Blackberry Island," Michelle grumbled. "I get the connection. But I don't want to go."

"I'm not taking no for an answer."

"You're so bossy. It's not attractive. In case you wondered."

Carly sighed. "Gabby is more mature than you and she's nine."

"Almost ten. She's very excited about the lip gloss, by the way. She told me."

Carly stopped pushing and drew in a breath. "Did I thank you for helping her get over her fear of the cranes?"

Michelle faced her. "It's no big deal."

"It is to her and to me."

Michelle sighed. "Yeah, yeah, whatever."

"You still have trouble accepting a compliment, so don't blame this moment on the PTSD."

"What happened to respecting the condition?"

"I do. It's you I have trouble respecting."

Michelle responded with a groan. "Damned employment agreement. I should so fire your ass."

"You'd be lost without me."

"Maybe." She turned toward the women gathered in the inn's conference room. "Tell me again why we're here."

Carly laughed, then shoved her inside.

Every month the Blackberry Island Women of Business got together to talk about everything from potential opportunities to grow to problems any of them were having. Carly had joined about five years ago and had found the group both helpful and supportive. She provided the meeting place each month, and Yvette, who owned the Seaswept Bakery, brought goodies.

"Hi, everyone," Carly said as she and Michelle walked into the small conference room. "As you can see, our brave warrior has returned. You all know Michelle Sanderson owns the inn."

Michelle shot her a warning look that promised retribution for the "brave warrior" comment. Not the least bit worried, Carly gave a wink back.

"You remember Chelsea from high school. She owns Scoop and Stretch. It's the local Pilates and yoga studio. Yvette has the bakery. Ariel runs the Mansion on the Hill. Kim owns the flower shop there and Becky has Island Chic in town. Normally Boston Flemming, the textile artist, joins us, but she just had a baby."

Carly stayed close to Michelle as she made introductions. For all her teasing, she was aware that her boss was still dealing with a lot of issues. Her hip was the least of it. Too many things sent her back into combat, including loud noises. Meeting several new people was stressful for anyone. For Michelle, it seemed more difficult than ever.

So Carly stayed close. She handled the introductions, made the small talk and guided her friend to an empty chair before settling in the one next to it.

Yvette, their unofficial leader, started the meeting with a question about the summer tourism season.

"I'm ordering more inventory," Becky said. "Business is up."

She was a pretty redhead who dressed like a model in the pages of *Vogue*. Beside her Carly always felt a little frumpy and out of step. Becky could do more with a scarf than most women could with an entire wardrobe.

"There are more weddings planned on the island this summer," Kim announced. "There were twenty last summer and this summer there are thirty-six. I've hired two college students to help."

Conversation shifted to the new traffic signal by the bridge to the organic restaurant's fight with the zoning commission. They wanted the right to keep a pig to eat their consumable garbage.

Michelle listened, sipped coffee and nibbled on one of

the brownies Yvette had brought. After twenty minutes, she leaned toward Carly.

"Thanks," she murmured.

Carly wasn't sure if she was being thanked for bringing her or for sticking close, but it didn't matter. Either would do.

Twenty

Michelle parked in front of Jared's house and made her way to the back door. Her hip was feeling better. Less sore, less stiff. Her therapy sessions were starting to make a difference. If only there were the same kind of workout for her head. One where she could sweat her way out of nightmares and flashbacks. Lift weights and stop jumping at every loud noise. She wasn't a fan of pain but feeling emotionally on the edge was worse. Now that she didn't have the constant ache to distract her, she was more aware of her mental hiccups.

She went up the ramp to the door and let herself inside. Jared stood in the kitchen, filling a cooler with ice and beer.

She hadn't seen him since the night he'd come to her room to check on her. Typical guy, she thought, eyeing him. Get her all riled up and then disappear. Although technically she'd been the one avoiding him, but passing on blame was easier than accepting it.

"Hey," he said, glancing at her. "You're walking better."

"Yeah. I'm healing."

He wore a faded T-shirt over worn jeans. The man needed to go shopping, she thought, even as she appreciated how the fabric of his shirt clung to his shoulders and chest. Damn, he looked good. All strong and capable. Even better, he wasn't much of a talker. In her mind, conversation was highly overrated.

She was aware of him, aware of what she'd been thinking just a few nights before. Too bad she couldn't simply walk over and kiss him. Well, she could, but she doubted she would get the response she wanted. He'd made it clear he was running some kind of halfway house and she was merely the most current resident. He wasn't looking to get laid. Talk about sad.

"I'm going out on my boat," he said. "It's calm and the sunset will be nice. Want to come?"

She looked out the window. The clouds had faded, leaving behind blue skies. This time of year the days were long. Even if Jared didn't want to have his way with her, he was still good company. Being with him was safe—she didn't have to think before she spoke. She wasn't sure why she felt that way—or maybe she was. The fact that she was nothing more than a mercy case meant she was free to be herself. An argument could be made for sexual disinterest. She didn't have to like it, but she could take advantage of it.

"Sure," she said impulsively.

"I'm going to get some sandwiches for dinner. While I do that, you can change."

She glanced down at her black trousers and the knit shirt she'd pulled on that morning. Not exactly clothes for boating.

"I need ten minutes," she told him.

"Meet you back here."

She hurried to her bedroom. Most of her clothes and

personal things were still in boxes in storage at the inn. She hadn't bothered to pull out much. She didn't have room for her books or pictures, and the clothes were at least a size too big.

She weighed about twenty pounds less than she had when she'd first left Blackberry Island. She'd lost about seven pounds during boot camp. A regular exercise program had a way of doing that to a girl. The next eight had come off after she'd been shot. Since coming home she would guess she'd taken off another five. Most of the time she simply wasn't that interested in food. She would rather drink than eat.

A problem she was going to have to deal with at some point, she told herself. Just not today.

She stripped off her work clothes and applied sunscreen to her pale skin, then pulled open drawers to figure out what to wear.

There weren't a lot of choices. She settled on a pair of jeans, athletic shoes and a tank top. On her way out the door, she grabbed a chambray shirt because it would be cooler on the water.

Jared was back and waiting for her in the kitchen.

"You eat a lot of sandwiches," she said, taking the bag as he picked up the cooler of beer.

"They're easy, and if I change my mind, they'll keep a couple of days."

"You need a wife."

"Had one."

"Okay, you need another one."

"Not likely."

She followed him out to his truck, then stared at the cab and wondered how she was going to get inside. Her truck was small and she could just slide right in. Jared's was higher, with a rear seat. She couldn't step up high enough, and if she used the running board, she would be angled wrong.

He walked around the passenger side and took the sandwiches from her. After tossing the bag into the back, he grabbed her around the waist, lifted her and set her down in the seat.

"All right?" he asked.

She nodded. No way was she going to admit that she was all tingly from where he'd touched her. Talk about having it bad. Apparently her hip wasn't the only thing that was healing. It was time to get a shower massage installed and take care of business herself.

They drove to the Sunset Marina. She wasn't sure what to expect—if they would go out on one of his big charter boats. Instead, he led her to a thirty-foot cabin Bayliner. She groaned when she saw the name.

"Tell me you bought her used," she said.

"I did." He followed her gaze. "What?"

"*Daisy?* Your boat's name is *Daisy?* Let me guess. You believe it's bad luck to change a boat's name."

"No. I just haven't bothered. It's only a name."

"*Daisy?* I hate daisies."

"Who hates a flower?"

"Me."

"You don't complain like most women, but you're a whole lot more crabby."

"Part of my charm," she told him.

"Keep telling yourself that."

He took the sandwich bag from her and set it on top of the cooler, then reached for her hand.

She braced herself for the impact of warm fingers on hers, then told herself to snap out of it. She wasn't some prepubescent girl on a first date. She was a mature woman. So what if Jared turned her on? She could handle it.

What she couldn't handle was the dock.

The wooden structure moved with the lapping of the water, as did the boat. There were two steps up from the dock, then she had to swing her leg over and step down at the same time. She eyed the unexpected obstacle course and shook her head.

"I don't think I can do that."

Jared followed her gaze. "I don't think you can, either. Hang on, kid."

He reached for her. One second she was standing, feeling the pull in her hip as she braced herself against the motion. The next he'd swept her up in his arms.

He released her gently, letting her slide to her feet. When she was standing, she reached out an arm to punch him in the stomach. Hard. Only he grabbed her fist before she could make contact.

Humor brightened his eyes. "You're welcome."

"Give a girl a little warning before you manhandle her."

"How are you going to get off the boat?"

She ignored that and him, limped to a bench seat and sat down. After popping the top off a beer, she swallowed half the contents, then glared at him.

"And you liked it when I lifted you into the truck."

"I tolerated it. There's a difference."

Jared chuckled.

It only took him about three minutes to get the boat ready. Then he cast off and they were heading out of the marina.

Michelle did her best to ignore him. She turned her face into the wind and closed her eyes. Sea air and warm sun combined to relax her. She set the beer in a holder and reached up to unfasten her braid. There would be plenty of tangles later, but for now she wanted to feel free—as if she'd escaped whatever it was that bound her in place.

Jared took them out onto the Sound. When they were miles from shore, he cut the engine and let them drift.

"Keep an eye out," he told her. "We're not in the shipping lanes, but there are plenty of pleasure craft around. We don't want a close encounter."

"Who says I'm speaking to you?"

"You're not the type to hold a grudge."

"How do you know?"

"Am I wrong?"

"No. Well, not against you." Carly was another matter.

He handed her a sandwich, took a beer for himself and settled on the bench seat opposite.

She unwrapped her dinner and took a bite. "You could learn to cook," she said when she'd chewed and swallowed.

"I could but I won't."

"Typical guy."

"Do you cook?"

"Some. More than you."

"Low bar."

She looked at him from under her lashes. "Are you seeing someone?"

"Asking about my love life?"

"If you have one."

He sipped his beer. "I'm between entanglements."

"Because your ex broke your heart?"

"No. That was a long time ago. Neither of us knew what we were getting into. She hated everything about the island and then she started hating me. It's hard to move a business based in the ocean to Nebraska. Neither of us was willing to compromise. I hear she's married to a guy who sells insurance and they have a couple of kids. I'm sure she's happier with him."

She noticed he hadn't answered her question. Was he seeing someone? "Between entanglements" didn't mean there wasn't something casual going on. She told herself it wasn't important, but she was still curious.

They ate as the boat drifted in the current. A few cranes flew overhead. Michelle eyed them, not trusting them to keep their distance.

"How's the inn?" he asked. "Booked for the holiday weekend?"

"Every room. It's a happy time."

He chuckled. "We're busy, too. Charters on all the boats. Sunset cruises tomorrow and Saturday night. Hope it doesn't rain."

"It's not supposed to."

"I've heard that before."

They finished their sandwiches in silence. Michelle shifted in her seat so she could support her left leg and stared up at the sky.

The sun was still visible, but drifting toward the horizon. Cranes circled lazily over the water. She found herself more intrigued than hostile toward them. Probably the fact that she'd eaten, she thought. Or the beer. Either way she was feeling more mellow.

"You need to be in a group."

The quietly spoken statement shattered the relaxing mood. Michelle's body tensed and she instantly regretted the sandwich now sitting in her stomach.

"You're a broken record. Go to hell."

"Where I spend the night doesn't change the facts. You're still screaming."

Shame and embarrassment surged, leaving her face hot. "If it's a problem for you, I can move out."

"I didn't say it was a problem. I said you need to talk to someone about what happened."

"You volunteering?" She glanced over at him.

He shrugged. "I'm just a guy with a boat. You need someone who can lead you through the process."

"There's no process," she snapped. "There's getting on with my life, which is what I'm doing."

"It'll be easier if you talk about it."

"Why? How do you know that?"

"If you were doing so great on your own, you wouldn't be having nightmares."

Logic, she thought. Just like a man to use that against her.

"I'm fine."

"I'm not the one you have to convince."

She turned toward him and glared. "I suppose you got into some kind of support group when you got back?"

"No. That's one of the reasons my wife left me. I wasn't much fun to live with. Then my grandfather died and I had the business and I couldn't handle it. I went on a bender that lasted six months."

She eyed the beer he held. "But you still drink."

"Alcohol was the least of it, kid. I woke up in jail with absolutely no idea how I'd gotten there. It took me three hellish days to dry out and another six weeks to stop shaking from the withdrawal. I figured out I had a choice. I could deal with what I'd been through or I could turn into one of those guys living on the street." One corner of his mouth turned up. "Hard to fit a forty-foot fishing boat into a shopping cart."

"I'm not in danger of being homeless."

"Probably not, but you are on the road to screwing up

everything that matters to you. You were attacked. Your buddies were killed. You shot a man and it wasn't from a safe distance. You saw into his eyes when he died. In that moment, when it's you or him, it's an easy decision. It's only later you start to second-guess yourself."

He was right, she thought, taking another swallow of the beer. She did second-guess herself, even as she knew she hadn't had a choice. If only that girl hadn't been there.

"I'll think about it," she said, not wanting to talk about her feelings to anyone.

She waited for him to say she had to do more than think, but he didn't.

"You do this all the time," she said. "Take in some wounded war vet. Then what? Send him on his way? Are you going to kick me out as soon as I can sleep through the night?"

Jared regarded her steadily. His dark eyes were unreadable. Probably for the best. She wanted him thinking that he wanted to see her naked. What he was probably thinking instead was that she was too much trouble and way too broken.

"I don't kick anyone out," he told her. "When you're ready, you'll leave."

"That sounds almost spiritual."

"Okay by me."

Her cell phone rang. She grabbed it from her pocket and glanced around. "Where's the cell tower?"

"Over there." He pointed to a small rocky island north of them. She could see the metal structure reaching for the sky. "It's there for Coast Guard and Search and Rescue. The local fishermen take advantage of it to call and say they're on their way in."

Her phone continued to ring.

She glanced at the screen and saw the number. Her father. She pushed the ignore button.

"One day you're going to have to take that call," Jared told her.

"You don't know who it was."

"I know you're avoiding something. That never works. Eventually you have to face all your demons."

"Kill or be killed?" she asked, trying to keep her voice light but failing.

"If that's what it takes."

"I can't kill him."

"You don't have to. Sometimes staring a demon in the eye is enough."

She wanted sex and he wanted to discuss demons. Talk about a perfect match. "More advice? You're hardly my sensei and I'm not your little grasshopper."

Jared laughed. "But I have much to teach."

"Not to me you don't."

His humor faded. Something flashed through his eyes, something hot and hungry, but then it was gone so quickly, Michelle had a feeling she'd simply imagined it. Wishful thinking and all that.

"Maybe you're right," he said, coming to his feet. "Ready to head back?"

Not really. Being out here, away from everything, made her feel whole. As if the broken bits were merely an inconvenience and not a permanent state of being.

"Sure," she said. "Gonna let me drive?"

"No."

She grinned. "Chicken."

"When it comes to my boat? You bet."

Twenty-One

Memorial weekend was as busy as Carly had hoped. With every room full and the town overflowing with tourists, there wasn't a moment to breathe, let alone think. If she wasn't getting fresh towels, she was recommending restaurants, making reservations and organizing walking tours.

Gabby was spending the day with a friend and her family. Tomorrow she would hang with Robert in the morning, and Brittany, her favorite sitter, would come over for the afternoon. Monday there was a special all-day program through the city park department that Gabby was finally old enough to attend.

"This is perfect," Mrs. Mitchell said as she took the map Carly offered. "We just love coming here. Last year we stayed at a dreadful little motel down the road. Every time we walked past your inn we were so upset we hadn't made reservations here."

"We're happy to have you this weekend," Carly told her. "If there's anything we can do to make your stay more memorable, please let any of us know."

"We will." The couple turned away, then Mrs. Mitchell swung back. "Is there a plant nursery nearby? I just love your daisies. Can I buy some like them?"

"Sure." Carly gave her the name, then waved as the couple left.

Michelle walked up to the desk. "I heard that."

"Not everyone hates the daisies."

"There are also people who think wrestling is a real sport and not entertainment."

Carly held up both her hands, palms facing Michelle. "I don't care what you say—I'm having a great weekend. We're full, our guests are lovely and they're spending lots of money at both the restaurant and the gift shop. I'm in my Zen place and I'm staying there."

"Aren't you cheerful."

"I try."

"I'm sure the guests appreciate it. What are our reservations like for the next couple of weeks? I was thinking that Sam might prefer staying here."

Carly circled around the desk and went to the computer. "We're full on the weekend. Otherwise, we have at least one room open during the week."

Michelle drew in a breath. "Okay. I don't think I want to kick out a guest with a reservation."

Carly busied herself with the jar of pens on the counter. "So, um, Sam seems nice."

"He is. I met him four, maybe five years ago. There was a fight in a bar and he was breaking it up. Someone pulled me in and Sam got between me and the punch."

"Romantic," Carly said, studying her and hoping for clues as to their relationship now.

"Not exactly, but it showed he was a great guy. I trust him with my back."

"What about the rest of you?" Carly asked before she could stop herself.

"Not so much. We had a thing once. But we're better off friends. And as interesting as he is, I have something else to talk about."

"Sure. What?"

Michelle slapped several sheets of paper down next to the keyboard. "There's a problem with the restaurant."

"What do you mean? It's doing great. It's full every morning."

"Yeah, I know. That's the problem. We have thirty-two tables. So at the very least, there should be thirty-two receipts for breakfast. But some tables get used more than once. Guests come in early or late. So I'm thinking we should have about forty-five, maybe forty-eight receipts."

"That makes sense."

Michelle pointed to a list of receipt tickets. "Yesterday there were exactly thirty-two. The same with the day before."

Carly's restaurant experience consisted of acting as a hostess from time to time and refilling coffee cups. Brenda had been the one who had handled the restaurant. The few times Carly had tried to figure out what was going on, Damaris had made it clear she was overstepping her bounds.

"I've gone over a month's worth of receipts," Michelle said. "We never have more tickets than we have tables. I can't believe there's never any turnover."

"Who hands out the tickets to the servers? Or do they just grab them?"

"Isabella takes care of it."

"You should talk to her."

"I can't. She's Damaris's daughter-in-law. Damaris would never let anything bad happen at the restaurant. She cares about me and she cares about the inn."

Carly couldn't argue that Damaris cared about Michelle. That was obvious, but it looked as if someone was stealing.

"Maybe Damaris doesn't know. Maybe it's not Isabella. Even though she's supposed to hand out the tickets, maybe she doesn't. They could be in a stack somewhere. That would make it easy for one or more of the servers to be involved. Any server could be keeping the tickets when customers pay cash."

Michelle nodded. "I hadn't thought of that. I should—" She stared behind Carly. "I'll be right back."

Carly turned and saw Isabella walking across the front pathway. Michelle headed toward her. Carly glanced around and saw the lobby and front room were empty, so she followed Michelle outside.

Isabella had moved toward Michelle. Her dark hair gleamed in the sunlight and she was smiling.

"We're having a barbecue tonight and I'm marinating ribs. I need to run home and turn them." She laughed. "Ten minutes. I only need ten minutes."

"You're allowed to take a break," Michelle told her. "Don't worry about it. But before you go, I have a question."

"Sure."

"It's about the restaurant tickets."

"The ones the servers use for their orders?"

"Yes. Those. How does that work? Do you hand them out?"

Carly was watching Isabella. She would swear the other woman stiffened at the question, although her smile stayed in place.

"Yes. They're kept in the supply room off the kitchen. I get them every morning."

"Are they logged in? Do you know which server has which numbers?"

The smile faded. "No. I just leave them in a stack by my station. The servers take them as they need them. Why?"

"Just asking. The number of tables served every day. How much turnover is there?"

"Not much. Sometimes we're busy and we use a table more than once. More at breakfast than at lunch."

Isabella looked annoyed and Michelle seemed to be searching for the next question. Carly took a step forward.

"Do you keep track of the beginning and ending numbers on the tickets? Is there a log?"

Isabella frowned at her, then turned to Michelle, making it clear who she was willing to talk to. "There's no log. It's never been a problem. Why are you asking all this?"

"You ring up all the orders?" Carly asked. "You're the only one who has access to the cash register?"

Isabella pressed her lips together. Color blossomed on her cheeks. "What are you saying?" She glared at Michelle. "Is Carly my new boss? Can she talk to me like this? I thought I worked for you, not her."

Now it was Carly's turn to get offended. "There have been some irregularities with the receipts in the restaurant."

Isabella's eyes widened. "Are you accusing me of stealing? I would never do that. I close out the cash register the way I always have." Her mouth began to tremble. "I can't believe this. What has she been saying about me? I do a good job. Ask Damaris. We've been here, working for you, Michelle. Taking care of things."

Carly wanted to point out she'd been doing the same, but knew it was an irrelevant point. The issue at hand was the missing receipts.

"I know you have," Michelle said. "I'm sorry. I shouldn't have said anything."

"What?" Carly glared at her. "You're sorry? Someone might be stealing and you're apologizing?"

"It's not Isabella."

"How do you know?"

"Because I know Damaris." She patted the other woman's arm. "You need to go check your ribs."

Isabella nodded and hurried off.

Carly waited until she was out of earshot. "Are you crazy? She says it's not her, and you believe her? Just like that? What if she's lying?"

"She's not."

"Oh, I see. All your military training has made you an expert on liars? She admitted she's the only one with access to the cash register."

"It's not exactly a bank vault," Michelle snapped. "There's a key that you have to turn. That's it. Anyone could get into it."

"Maybe once in a while. But you're saying there's a pattern of missing receipts. If someone is doing that, wouldn't Isabella notice?"

"Not if the servers are destroying the receipts of the people who pay cash. If someone leaves money without needing change, there wouldn't be a trail. Once the order is filled in the kitchen, the copy of the ticket goes out with the plate."

"Then there needs to be a change in the system. You need a way to cross-check the receipts. They get signed in and out. Then we'll have a consecutive numbering system and it will be easy to figure out if tickets have been used without being paid for."

Michelle glanced out toward the water, then back at

the inn. "It's not Isabella. Damaris would never let her hurt me."

"Which means putting some checks and balances in place shouldn't hurt her feelings."

She knew the right answer was for Michelle to say this was business and hurting someone's feelings was immaterial. But the regular rules didn't apply to Damaris.

"Do you want me to take care of coming up with a system?" Carly asked.

"I'll do it," Michelle said, turning toward the inn. "It'll be better if it comes from me."

"It's not like you to wimp out," Carly said, wanting to stomp her foot. "You're tougher than this."

Michelle didn't bother to look back at her. "Everyone gets to have a bad day."

Twenty-Two

At two-thirty on Monday afternoon, the last of the guests drove away. Carly stood on the porch and watched the final car disappear down the road, then gave in to exhaustion and collapsed onto one of the wicker chairs.

So far today she'd organized a tour of town, suggested stops for a couple driving back to eastern Washington, checked out the guests who were leaving, had cleaned not one, not two but three rooms and had confirmed the linen order. Michelle had taken the afternoon shift in the gift shop, so it wasn't as if she was slacking off, either.

They'd been on the run since Friday morning, the inn overflowing with guests enjoying a rare sunny long weekend. One of the housekeepers had called in with car trouble the previous day, meaning in addition to her regular duties, Carly had cleaned ten rooms on Sunday. Her back ached, but her feet hurt more. All she wanted was a bath and about ten hours in her bed.

She would pick up Gabby at five and get to hear all about her daughter's day at camp. Hopefully the staff had tired her out and they could both be in bed by eight.

"I have to get moving," she murmured, hoping for inspiration. After all, sometime around four, more guests would be arriving. Instead, she leaned her head back against the cushions and sighed. No wonder the guests settled in out here for much of the evening. It was plenty comfortable.

She kicked off her shoes and propped her feet up on the ottoman. Her eyes drifted closed. She could hear the call of the cranes and distant laughter. Her muscles relaxed. She felt herself drifting, drifting.

Something soft and warm brushed across her mouth.

A kiss, she thought hazily. She inhaled the scent of mint and sunshine, knowing she didn't want to open her eyes. Dreams didn't get much better than this.

The kiss lingered, the pressure increased slightly. Just enough to make her realize she wasn't asleep and this wasn't a dream and what the hell?

She opened her eyes to find Sam leaning over her.

"Hey, Sleeping Beauty," he said with a grin. "You shouldn't tempt a man like that."

She opened her mouth, then closed it when she realized she was too stunned to speak. She scrambled backward, but the chair prevented her from getting away.

Sam immediately straightened, holding up both his hands. "Sorry. I didn't mean to startle you. You okay?"

She was tingling in places that hadn't seen action since before Gabby had been born. Did that qualify as okay?

"I'm fine," she managed.

He stood in front of her, as if wanting to make sure.

"Really," she said more firmly. "It was unexpected." She smiled. "But nice."

He shook his head. "I don't accept that. No guy wants to hear anything about him is 'nice.'"

Her smile deepened. "'Nice' is all I have."

"Damn." He took the chair next to her. "You're killing me. You know that, right?"

"Sorry."

"How was your weekend?" he asked.

"Busy. We were full. This is the start of our summer season. From now through Labor Day it's going to be crazy. But good crazy. We have to make enough to get through the leaner winter months."

Like squirrels storing nuts, she thought, not willing to say more about the financial situation at the inn. She didn't know how much Michelle had shared with her friend and she didn't want to tell secrets.

"What did you do?" she asked.

"I went out on a fishing boat yesterday. I haven't done that in years." He glanced at her, amusement brightening his eyes. "Too many landlocked assignments."

"You should have joined the navy."

"You didn't just say that."

"Sworn enemies?"

He leaned back in the chair. "Just not as good."

"Why do I think they'd say the same about you?"

"They probably would. Swabies are incapable of original thought."

"If you settle here, you can start going fishing regularly. Maybe get a boat."

"If I stay here, I can do a lot of things."

Was he flirting with her? She'd been single for so long, she wasn't sure. Between Gabby and work, there hadn't been time for a man, and it wasn't as if she was turning them away. Except for Robert and Leonard, most of the guys she met were with someone, away for the weekend. She was less enthused about dating local guys. She knew most of them from high school, which meant they had expectations she had no intentions of fulfilling.

Anyone eligible who moved to the island was quickly snapped up. Not that she'd been looking or was interested.

"What are you thinking?" he asked. "You're frowning."

"Nothing important." Mentioning her pathetic lack of a love life seemed foolish. "How are you liking our town?"

"It's nice. Friendly people. You still have to show me around."

"Sure, just not today." She wiggled her toes. "There's not a part of me that doesn't hurt."

"You've been on your feet for three days, haven't you?"

Longer, she thought, ignoring the insistent throb. "It's part of the job."

Sam shifted from the seat to her ottoman. He grabbed her feet before he sat and rested her heels on his thighs. Even as she told herself to pull back, he had her right foot in his large hands and was expertly rubbing the tender skin.

She wanted to tell him to stop, that they were in plain view of everyone and this was hardly professional behavior. Then his thumbs dug into the ball of her foot, finding the place that hurt the most and massaging it.

"You're good," she whispered, holding in a moan.

"I've had practice."

"Those two wives you mentioned?"

He laughed. "Among others. You'd be amazed what a good foot rub will get a guy."

"Seduction through massage?"

"Uh-huh."

He squeezed her toes, then pressed his thumbs into her heel.

"I can see how it would work," she murmured, closing her eyes and giving in to the treatment.

She would tell him to stop in a few minutes. She would pull herself together and be strong. But for now, she couldn't find it in herself to say no. Everyone had a vulnerability and apparently resisting foot rubs was hers.

She knew Sam's type—more from instinct than practice. He was charming and fun, in it for the moment. Not someone who would settle on one woman permanently. Not that she was looking for Mr. Right. But if she accepted what he was offering, she would have to remember that it was going to be fun while it lasted—nothing more.

He switched to her other foot, repeating the process and making her relax all over. Her eyelids got heavy and she found herself drifting again.

She was warm and comfortable, the sun playing peekaboo with the trees. A gentle breeze brushed against her skin. Soft laughter drew her back to the present.

She opened her eyes to find Sam standing.

"Come on," he said, holding out his hand.

"What?" She blinked, confused. Her shoes were back on. When had that happened?

"You're falling asleep. You need a nap."

"I can't. I have work to do."

"Not today."

She let him pull her to her feet. As she rose, she realized he wasn't that far away, which meant when she was standing, they were very, very close. Close enough for her to see the various colors of blue that made up his irises. Close enough to see the tiny scars on his eyebrow and chin. Close enough to feel the heat of his body. Heat that beckoned her, tempted her, made her want to walk a very dangerous path.

"Maybe I *should* lie down," she murmured, stepping away and trying to catch her breath.

This was crazy, she told herself. Sure, she hadn't been with a guy in a long time, but so what? She was used to doing without. Being around Sam wasn't a big deal. Only she found herself aware of every breath, of the slight brush of his arm against hers. Visions of being held by him, being touched by him, filled her brain. She wanted—no, *craved*—that skin-on-skin contact. A man over her, in her, taking her.

She shivered as the hunger became real. Talk about confusing. Despite her reputation, she'd never been very into sex. Well, not counting today.

"Cold?" he asked, putting his arm around her. "Where are your keys? You okay to drive home? Should I take you?"

"I live here," she said. "In back."

Probably not the smartest thing to say, given her condition, she thought as he led her inside.

"Point the way," he told her.

She did and they went down the hallway. At the door marked Private she fumbled with the lock, then managed to open the door.

Sam guided her inside, then stopped in the middle of the room.

"Given the circumstances," he said, "I'm going to stop here. Getting you ready for bed would test me in ways that I would definitely fail."

He shifted in front of her and put his hands on her waist. "But when you're feeling better, I sure would like to have you show me around."

She wasn't sure if he meant the town or something more. She knew which she wanted to believe, but wondered if that was wishful thinking on her part.

He stared into her eyes and swore. "Just once more," he whispered. "You can slap me if you want, but I have to—"

He lowered his mouth to hers. Carly saw the kiss coming and had plenty of time to back away. To resist. As if that was going to happen, she thought, raising her arms and wrapping them around his neck.

She had a feeling he only intended to repeat the kiss from before, but she wasn't sure how long it would be before she had a man in her arms again, and she planned to take advantage of the situation.

When his mouth settled on hers, she was ready. She tilted her head and eased forward until they were touching everywhere.

God, he felt good. All hard planes and muscles. She'd forgotten what it was like to be held by a man, to have strong arms supporting her and a firm mouth brushing against her own.

It didn't take him long to get the message and deepen the kiss. She parted when she felt his tongue touch her bottom lip and met him stroke for stroke.

Between her legs, blood rushed so hot and fast, she practically hurt. Her breasts swelled and her nipples were hard peaks of come-touch-me pain. Hunger exploded. Wanting grew, filling her, making her want to beg and claw. If she'd been able to consume him, she would have. As it was, she could only hold on and pray that kissing was going to be enough.

He drew back slightly and cupped her face in his hands. "Carly, are you—?"

Sure, ready, in the mood? She had no idea what he was going to say and she suddenly didn't give a damn. She needed him *now*. Naked, ready and taking her as fast as possible. In case he was confused by her intent, she pulled off her V-neck sweater, tossed it aside, then undid her bra. After grabbing his hands, she put them on her bare breasts.

"You're my kind of woman," he whispered, before claiming her with a kiss that made her toes curl.

It turned out he was her kind of man, as well. He got her naked in about sixteen seconds, then locked the door, stripped off his own clothes and led her to the sofa.

He kissed her all over, lingering between her legs. She arched toward him, feeling the perfect rhythm of his tongue, then lost herself in an orgasm that poured through her like liquid pleasure.

He moved to her breasts, sucking deeply, teasing the hard tips, at the same time rubbing her clitoris with his fingers. She came again, this time longer and louder. When he finally fumbled in his jeans pocket for a condom, she caught her breath long enough to push him onto his back next to the coffee table.

He slipped on the protection; she straddled him and rode him until they were both groaning and breathless.

Sweat coated her back and between her breasts. She had a feeling she was flushed and a little raw in places. A quick glance at the clock told her less than ten minutes had passed since she and Sam had walked in the room. She should probably be embarrassed. And she would be. Tomorrow. Right now she felt too good.

She slid off of him and sat on the carpet. Clothes were scattered everywhere. The empty condom wrapper was by her knee. She picked it up and held it toward him.

"Former Boy Scout?"

He sat next to her, bare legs stretched out. "Tradition. I've had one with me since I was a hopeful teenager."

"It's not the same one, is it?"

He gave her a very satisfied grin. "No. Not that same one."

She knew that there were a couple of stretch marks from her pregnancy and that her breasts weren't as perky as they had been a few years ago. That her tummy wasn't flat, and hey, like most women alive, she hated her thighs. But right now she didn't care. Besides, Sam's body was good enough for both of them.

She knew she should probably say something. Explain that she didn't usually have sex with strangers, nor was she usually so...orgasmic. But then she decided it didn't matter. They were both single adults who'd used protection. It wasn't anyone's business but theirs.

"I need to get back to work," she said.

"You going to dress first? I'm not saying the male guests wouldn't love the show, but I'm not sure how their wives would feel."

"Good point. Clothes, then work."

He stood and helped her to her feet, then pulled her close and kissed her again.

"Thanks," he told her.

"You're welcome. I needed that."

"Anytime you need it again, just let me know."

"You're a giver."

"That's me."

She appreciated his lighthearted attitude. Her mind was still in orgasm fog, so she wanted to say as little as possible. Sam was great and she was thrilled by the close encounter, but wasn't sure she wanted or needed anything more. Better to err on the side of caution.

They dressed, then he kissed her one last time before slipping out. She would follow in a few minutes.

As she waited, she leaned against the door and smiled. That had been perfect, she thought, her legs still a little weak. No matter what else happened, today was going to be a very good day.

Monday night, Michelle stayed late to go through the receivables for the weekend. Every aspect of the inn had done well. They'd put a lot of items in the gift shop on sale. Not huge discounts, but ten or fifteen percent. Those big sale signs had worked. They'd moved nearly three thousand dollars' worth of merchandise.

The restaurant had been jammed, with people in line for both breakfast and lunch. Carly had logged tickets in and out with the servers before every shift. From what Michelle could see, they matched up perfectly with the cash register, so that was a relief. The inn's bank balance would be a happy number come the morning, which meant bills could be paid and the extra put away for winter.

Carly walked into her office, a bottle of red wine in one hand and two glasses in the other. She held up both.

"Come on," she said. "I'll buy you a drink."

Michelle hesitated, then nodded and shut down her computer. She followed Carly out to the back patio.

It was nearly nine. The sun had just set and the sky was a blend of pinks and blues, with a bit of orange near the horizon. The air was still and not too cool.

A small table stood between two padded lounge chairs. On it were a wine opener and a plate of brownies.

"Nice," Michelle said, taking a seat and stretching out her leg. The dull ache faded to something better than manageable.

"I was going to go to bed early," Carly admitted as she went to work on the bottle. "Gabby and I made these after dinner. She was exhausted from camp and went to bed but suddenly I wasn't tired." She handed Michelle a glass of wine.

Carly settled into her lounger, then reached for a brownie. "No nuts," she said. "I remembered you don't like them."

"Thanks."

"You're welcome." Carly sipped her wine, then took a bite. "We had an amazing weekend."

"We did. The restaurant did great. I appreciate you following up on the tickets with the servers."

"All the money's accounted for?"

"Uh-huh."

"Good. I figured we'd have a big crowd. This was not the weekend to be losing money."

"I'm going to be taking in the mortgage payment tomorrow," Michelle said. "Along with what's owed for back payments. That will wipe me out but it'll be worth it."

Carly glanced at her. "I'm sorry Brenda screwed this all up. I mean that. I wish I could have stopped her."

Michelle nodded slowly. "I believe you. Part of me thinks she was just stupid and part of me wonders if she did it on purpose. The inn always mattered more to me than her. For me it was my future. I think she felt it was a trap."

"You worked your butt off here," Carly said. "I remember back in high school. You'd leave as soon as classes were over and come back here. It was like you had a full-time job."

"I felt like I didn't have a choice."

"Now you're back. It's going great. You'll pay off the mortgages and be able to relax."

Michelle nodded, then nibbled on the brownie, letting the moist, cakelike texture coat her tongue. She followed that with a sip of wine and knew she was about as close to heaven as she was going to get today.

"I knew my mom wouldn't take care of things," she admitted. "It turns out I was right." She sighed. "You were the smart one in high school. Hanging out with friends."

"I would rather have been with you," Carly told her.

"You came and helped me here."

"Until senior year."

When it had all gone to hell, Michelle thought.

Carly must have been thinking the same because she said, "We were both screwed up."

"I guess that happens when parents disappear."

"You should have told us."

Carly's statement, five simple words, hit Michelle like a sucker punch. She sat up and swung her feet to the ground, facing her.

"Don't even start," she said, her voice low, her good mood evaporating like fog in the sun.

"Why not?" Carly sat up, as well. "We might have been able to stop them."

"How? We were seventeen years old. What were we going to do? Chain ourselves to the car? They were the ones who cheated. They were the ones who snuck out in the night without telling anyone. It's not what I did."

"I know," Carly said. "I tell myself that. But with my mom gone, it was horrible."

"You think it was better for me?" Michelle demanded. "I was stuck here with Brenda."

"Who mostly ignored you."

"Your dad did the same. He was too drunk to know when you were around."

Michelle wanted to call the words back. Talking about the drinking was one of those taboo subjects. She'd been friends with Carly and knew the shame that came with having a drunk for a father.

Carly set down her glass and wiped her fingers on her jeans. Then she stood.

"He wasn't too drunk all the time. He started hitting me after she left. He screamed that it was my fault. That she hadn't loved me. He said that was why she left. Because of me. And he had never loved me." Carly stared up at the sky, then back at Michelle. "That's why I did it. That's why I went after all those boys. So I could make myself believe somebody cared about me."

Michelle started to say, "I cared," only she was distracted by what Carly had said. "You slept with everyone."

Carly's mouth twisted into something that was probably supposed to be a smile. "No," she said quietly. "I teased, I got close, but there was no sex. I never went 'all the way.'" The fake smile faded. "Allen was my first time. I gave him my virginity to win him from you. Talk about a shitty trade."

With that, she turned and walked back to the inn.

Michelle watched her go, feeling anger and frustration building inside of her. She wanted to scream that Carly wasn't telling the truth but knew the other woman had no reason to lie.

Allen had literally fucked them both. He was both their first times and he was a worthless bastard. They'd been so messed up, so confused about what their parents had done, how they'd acted. All their lives they'd depended on each other and yet in the crucial moment, when they'd needed each other the most, they'd gone their separate ways.

She sat there in the growing darkness and fought against feeling helpless. She could handle nearly anything but that. Restlessness drove her to her feet. She picked up the wine bottle, then threw it as hard as she could. It bounced onto the grass, lying there unshattered.

It wasn't enough. She needed to do more, to express the rage boiling inside of her. Nothing was right. She couldn't even define the problem, let alone fix it.

She turned frantically, looking for an enemy. Someone to blame, to hurt, to destroy. And then she saw them. The rows and rows of daisies, their happy faces turned toward the night sky.

She hurried toward the planter first and grabbed as many as she could reach, holding on close to the soil. She jerked upward—hard. They pulled out with a satisfying ripping sound and sensation. She went to the next plant and the next, then moved to the garden itself.

She flung stems and leaves and dirt over her shoulder. Her hip ached from her crouching position, but she didn't care. She dug and destroyed until they were all lying on the grass—dismembered flowers, like dying soldiers on a battlefield. And then she started to cry.

Twenty-Three

Carly woke up early. Her head hurt. She wanted to blame the wine, but she hadn't had enough to get really drunk, which was usually the first step in having a hangover. No, this pain came from a deeper source. From what had happened in her past and how she was unable to fully heal from old wounds.

She'd tossed and turned most of the night, unable to sleep. Her good mood and lingering pleasure from her encounter with Sam had been burned away by ugly reality and worse memories. She shouldn't have gotten into a conversation about the past with Michelle and, worse, blamed her for their parents leaving. She shouldn't have broken the beginnings of the relationship they were forging. To what end? To be right?

Carly sat up and brushed her hands against her face, wishing she could wipe away the memories as easily.

"Mom, Mom!"

Gabby raced into her room and flew into her bed. Carly pulled her into a hug.

"Morning," she said, wondering how many ibuprofen it would take to make her headache go away.

"How did you sleep?" Gabby asked, still warm from her bed. Her pj's had kittens on them, her feet were bare. "I slept good and it's sunny outside. Did you see? A sunny day."

Carly glanced toward the window. Light spilled in through the curtains. "I'm glad it's going to be nice today."

"I know. After school I'm going to help Leonard count baby chicks. We have to be careful because they're young and small."

Gabby bounced on the bed, her usual bundle of morning energy. Carly did her best not to wince as someone set up a jackhammer just behind her eyes and went to work.

Gabby scrambled off the bed. "Breakfast, breakfast." Her loud, singsong voice was torture.

"I'll be right there," Carly promised, doing her best to keep from wincing.

Gabby raced to the doorway, then turned back. "Mom, are you sick?"

So much for faking it. "I have a headache."

"Oh." Gabby dropped her voice to a whisper. "I'll be quiet."

"Thanks. I appreciate that."

Carly made her way to the kitchen. She turned on the coffee, then poured cereal into a bowl, followed by milk. Gabby put bread in the toaster and Carly collected fruit.

The familiar ritual soothed her. Sure, her past had sucked, but now she had Gabby. Her daughter was worth any price. Hardly a unique emotion. Isn't it what every parent felt about his or her child? Yet not all of them acted like it. Michelle's father had adored his daughter, telling anyone who would listen how important she was to him. Then he'd left her. Carly's mother had walked out without a word of warning. It had been three years before Carly had heard from her. Even now they only spoke a couple of times a year and exchanged cards at Christmas. Nothing more. Lana had only met her grand-daughter once.

Complications, Carly thought, taking her coffee to the window. Life was nothing but complications. She pulled back the curtain and nearly dropped her mug.

From her kitchen she could see the east side of the rear yard, along with part of the garden. Instead of rows and rows of colorful daisies, there was only mounded dirt and the remnants of the plants she'd lovingly cared for.

Still in a long T-shirt and bare feet, she walked to the back door and opened it.

"Mom, where are you going?" Gabby asked.

"Stay inside," Carly called, walking toward the de-struction.

She reached the corner of the inn and the whole back-yard lay before her.

Every daisy was gone, uprooted, ripped apart and left to die. Their stems and leaves and flowers covered the lawn, a carpet of green and white and red and yellow. The planters were empty, a few broken stalks standing tall. As if they didn't realize what had occurred.

She knew what had happened, knew who had done it. Michelle had wanted to hurt her and she'd done a hell of a job. Knowing she had to get back to her daughter, to keep Gabby from seeing all this, she turned around. It was only when she stumbled that she realized she was crying.

Michelle parked in the bank parking lot. She wasn't feeling chatty this morning, especially after a long, hard night. She'd barely been able to drag her butt out of bed.

Only the thought that she was going to pay off half the overdue part of the mortgage got her going. That and three cups of coffee.

Every time she thought about what had happened the previous night, she felt sick inside. Shame had a bitter taste and sat heavily in her stomach. Bad enough to act like a jerk. Worse to do it in such a way that the whole world could see.

There would be questions. A garden full of destroyed daisies wasn't going to go unnoticed. What would everyone think? No, not everyone, she thought. What would Damaris think? And Gabby? She already knew that Carly would get the message. Destruction of something she cared about. No psychology degree was needed to interpret that.

She collected the envelope with the checks and climbed out of her truck. Her hip hurt more today than it had in a while. Guilt, she thought. Or the time she'd spent kneeling on the grass, pulling out daisies.

She made her way into the bank and walked toward Ellen's office. The other woman was seated at her desk and looked up when Michelle entered.

"Good morning," Ellen said with a smile. "How are you? Did you have a great long weekend? I saw all the cars in the inn's parking lot. Good for you."

"Everything went well." She took the seat Ellen indicated, happy to get the weight off her hip. She put the envelopes on the desk and pushed them forward. "Here you go. June's payments and half of everything previously owed."

Ellen raised her eyebrows. "Impressive." She opened the envelope and pulled out the checks. "I'll get you receipts for these."

"Don't take this wrong, but I'll be happy to get the bank off my back."

"What do you mean?"

"All those rules. Once I'm current, they won't apply."

Ellen shook her head. "I'm afraid that's not true. The other terms and conditions will apply for the next two years." The smile returned. "Didn't I explain that? It was in the paperwork you signed when the loan originated. Oh, wait. Your mom signed that for you, didn't she?"

Michelle wanted to throw something—preferably Ellen—across the room. She was going to be stuck with the bank on her back for a couple of years? Even if she paid everything overdue?

"I'm sorry. I should have been more clear the last time we spoke. I thought you knew." Ellen sighed. "It's frustrating. There are so many new rules and regulations. The government makes everything so complicated." She leaned forward, her expression concerned. "Is it Carly? Are you having a tough time working with her? I say 'work,' but we both know it's not like she does any."

"Actually she does. We're cutting expenses and she's taking on more responsibilities. She's cleaning rooms a few afternoons a week, just to help out."

Ellen laughed. "I would pay money to see that."

"Why don't you like her?"

"We both know what she is. Carly is one of those women going through life taking what she wants and everyone who gets in her way be damned. You remember what she was like with Allen. She practically held a parade to show off the ring."

Michelle did remember, but she was surprised that would have appeared on Ellen's radar. "I hadn't realized you knew her that well."

"Carly's tough to avoid. But enough about her. Let's

talk about more pleasant things. Like how great you're doing at the inn. I'm thrilled. We had a board meeting just last week and I updated everyone on your status. That you're back and taking control." She picked up the cashier's checks and waved them. "So much for the big, bad bank winning."

"I appreciate you being on my side," Michelle said, even as she wondered if Ellen really was.

"Absolutely. My customers come first. And we have a past. Now that you're back, I hope we can be friends again."

Michelle didn't remember them being friends before. "Um, sure."

"Great. We can go to lunch. Maybe next week?"

Michelle nodded and made her escape. As she drove back to the inn, she decided the first thing she was going to do was find the paperwork for the mortgages and read them. She didn't want any more surprises when it came to her business.

As for Ellen, she still wasn't sure if the other woman really was a friend or if there was something else going on. Too bad there wasn't a contract that could explain the fine print in that relationship.

As for the rest of it…apologizing to Carly seemed impossible. But she was going to have to do something. And soon.

"Do you think it was teenagers?" Leonard asked as he loaded destroyed plants into the trash can.

"I don't know." Carly wasn't sure why she lied. Protecting Michelle was stupid. But she couldn't seem to bring herself to tell anyone the truth.

"They got them all, but only here in the back. I don't get it."

Carly supposed Michelle had run out of anger, or maybe her hip had hurt too much for her to rip out everything in front. Or it could just be that while she wanted to send a message to Carly, she wasn't willing to upset any guests arriving.

She scooped up another armful of the dead flowers and carried them to the can.

So much hard work for nothing, she thought, remembering the hours she'd spent looking at nurseries online, finding the exact daisies she wanted and ordering them. The garden had been a part of what she loved about her job. The flowers had brightened her mood every single day, providing color and pleasure. Now there was nothing but raw dirt and a sense that Michelle had attacked her personally.

"You okay?" Leonard asked, pushing up his glasses. "I'm sad this happened."

"I can help you plant some more. It won't be the same, but maybe it will still be pretty."

She forced herself to smile. "That's sweet. Thank you. I don't know when I'll get to replacing these, but when that happens, I'll let you know."

"What did Gabby say when she saw what had happened?"

"She didn't." Carly had gotten her off to school out the front of the inn. When her daughter got home, she would need some kind of an explanation, but had no idea what it should be.

"Whoever did this was seriously pissed. Or drunk." Leonard glanced around. "Or both."

Michelle hadn't been that drunk, Carly thought. But she was always angry. Carly knew she was the most obvious target, although given their past, shouldn't she be the one with the temper?

"You okay?" Leonard asked.

"I will be. I have a busy day and that helps."

He stood there, looking awkward, as if he wanted to say more or do more. Carly patted his arm.

"Thanks for helping me. You need to get to your cranes. Without you around to supervise, who knows what kind of trouble they could get up to?"

"I could stay."

She shook her head. "No. I'm okay." Or she would be. If nothing else, life had taught her how to survive tough times. This wasn't close to the worst she'd been through.

Leonard left. Carly wheeled the trash can back in place, then went inside and showered.

She spent the morning in the gift shop, helping customers and checking inventory. New merchandise would have to be ordered to replace that which had sold. It was a great time to shift focus.

She'd brought her laptop along and used the downtime to type up her thoughts, then emailed them to Michelle. After lunch, she went upstairs to check the cleaned rooms before new guests were checked in. As she entered the first one, she saw something outside in the yard. She crossed to the window and looked out.

Michelle knelt on the lawn, surrounded by flats of daisies. There were dozens of plants, maybe hundreds. Not the different types Carly had discovered over the years, but still bright and colorful. Michelle had a small shovel in one hand and was carefully setting each one in the ground.

Carly leaned against the window frame, watching. Her headache faded a little, as did the tension in her body. She'd been wondering if Michelle would apologize, but in some ways, this was better. Actions rather than words.

She didn't know why Michelle had ripped out the

daisies in the first place and maybe she didn't have to. Maybe replacing them was enough.

Michelle counted the receipts after breakfast and didn't like the result. Despite the fact that she'd told Isabella to log in server tickets, assigning them in sequential numbers, it hadn't happened. The numbers were randomly assigned, tickets were missing and there were fewer receipts than she thought there should be. Something was going on.

She remembered her work at the inn being easier than this, she thought as she walked through the now-empty dining room and headed for the kitchen. As a teenager, she hadn't had to deal with a gift shop and the restaurant had been tiny. It wasn't that there had been less to do; it's that everything had been more straightforward. Now there were complications. Personalities. Drama.

She walked into the kitchen. Damaris looked up from the garlic she was chopping and held up her hands.

"What?" the cook demanded, grinning as she spoke. "You're here to toss my pots and pans in the trash?"

"Very funny."

"I'm still impressed with what you did with the daisies. Too bad you put them back."

She hadn't exactly put them back. The ones she'd ripped out had been beyond saving. Instead, she'd bought new and had planted them. That had set her hip back a few days. Mango had yelled at her, telling her gardening wasn't helping her healing. She hadn't bothered explaining it had been a onetime event.

"Don't be impressed," Michelle told her. "I snapped. That's nothing to be proud of." She still wasn't sure why she'd done it.

If only she could sleep, she thought, wondering how

long it would take for the dreams to fade. Or get drunk enough to forget. Or stop jumping at loud noises or looking up from what she was doing and not being sure of where she was.

"Have a cinnamon roll," Damaris told her.

Despite everything, Michelle grinned. "Food doesn't solve all problems."

"It should."

She picked up a small plate and slid a blackberry cinnamon roll onto it. The icing was thick and gooey cinnamon-flavored glaze coated her fingers. She took a bite.

"They're amazing," she said.

"Secret recipe. Admit it. You'd be lost without me."

Her words echoed Michelle's joke with Carly. Carly, whom she'd hurt for no reason she could define and whose greatest sin was taking care of the inn.

"Receipts are missing from the restaurant," Michelle said. "I asked Isabella to keep the tickets in order and she didn't. She also didn't log them all in, so I have no way of knowing which server had what tickets."

Damaris went to work on a half-dozen onions. "So?"

"So, there's money missing."

Damaris kept her eyes on the cutting board. "Are you sure? Isabella's a good girl. I trust her. Maybe it's one of the servers. Or Carly. She's in and out of here."

"When? I never see her in the restaurant unless she's filling in for Isabella."

"She could do it." Damaris looked up. "You worry too much. We're making money, the customers are happy. Go run the inn and leave the restaurant to me. I'm on your side, Michelle."

"I know."

Michelle trusted Damaris, and Damaris trusted Isabella. Wasn't that some math thing? If A equals B, and B equals C, then A equals C. Which meant she should trust Isabella. Only she didn't.

Twenty-Four

Michelle watched Pauline and Seth shake hands with the last of the departing couples. The man and woman who had barely spoken a few days ago were smiling and laughing. They touched constantly. As Michelle watched, the man's free hand slipped over his wife's butt in one of those intimate, long-together-couple moves. There was intimacy in the moment, a connection, and watching them made her ache in ways that had nothing to do with her healing wounds and everything to do with a yearning much deeper than flesh and bone.

The couple got in their sports car and started down the drive. Seth said something to Pauline, then pulled out his cell phone and glanced at the screen. Although Michelle was too far away to hear what he was saying, she read his expression. The one that said he had to take the call.

Acting on impulse, Michelle stepped out of the inn and walked toward Pauline. The therapist saw her coming, smiled and waved, then met her on the porch.

"Another successful retreat?" Michelle asked.

"Yes. Very. Most couples who come to us really want

their relationship to work. Unfortunately, they're stuck in unproductive ruts and don't know how to get out. We have a few simple techniques that show them love is still there."

"And if it isn't?"

"Then they have to make some difficult choices." Pauline motioned to the chairs on the porch. "Seth will be a few minutes. If you have time to join me."

"I do."

They settled on the padded chairs. Michelle stretched out her legs and felt a comfortable pulling in her hip. One that spoke of healing rather than pain.

"You're walking more easily," Pauline observed.

"I'm getting better. At least physically."

"What about the rest of it?"

"I'm not looking for therapy."

"Of course not."

"I'm being social. Polite. Nothing more."

"I can see that."

Michelle studied the other woman, trying to figure out if she was being honest or slightly mocking. Pauline's gaze was steady, her blue eyes bright with interest but nothing else. Damned professional headshrinkers, Michelle thought glumly. A regular person didn't stand a chance.

"I dug out the daisies," she said, not expecting the words to pop out. "It was me."

"I'd wondered who'd massacred the garden."

"I was pissed and I hate the daisies."

"They can be annoying."

Michelle sighed. "This is where you tell me I'm crazy."

"You're not. Is that disappointing to hear?"

Michelle considered the question. "I can't decide."

Pauline smiled. "At least you're honest. Did your mother like the daisies?"

"She loved them. Not like Carly, but..." She paused, then swore. "How did you know about my mother?"

"I was fairly sure you weren't hatched." Pauline shrugged. "I sneak into the kitchen at off hours to steal Damaris's coffee cake. She likes to talk and I'm a good listener."

"What else did she tell you?"

"She thinks Isabella's baby isn't up to toilet training."

"You know what I mean."

"Yes, I do."

Michelle waited, but Pauline didn't say any more. She drew in a breath. "I wanted to hurt Carly, so I dug up the daisies. I guess I wanted to hurt my mother, too. Get back at her for all the shit she did to me."

She briefly outlined the financial disaster she'd come home to.

"There's no one left to blame," Michelle said, winding down from the story. "Carly did her best."

"Which you resent. It leaves you without an enemy you can defeat. That's frustrating. You have all this energy and nowhere to put it. Then one night, there are the daisies, mocking you."

Michelle grinned. "You've seen your share of mocking flowers, then?"

"I have, figuratively speaking." Pauline looked at her. "It's not wrong to have feelings. We all do. Where we start to cross the line is when we act inappropriately. You know that. You can feel it's not healthy or good for you. You're humiliated by the public display of what you see as the weakness of losing control. But look at it this way. You needed a wake-up call and you got it. So you'll figure out how to handle your emotions better. You replaced the daisies and you apologized. It's okay to screw up. It's what we do afterward that defines us."

For the first time since arriving back on Blackberry Island, Michelle felt her eyes fill with tears. "Thank you," she whispered.

Pauline reached out and squeezed her arm. "Please, Michelle, get some help. You're right on the edge. You can go either way. I think the world would be a better place if you found your way back. Don't become one of the lost souls. We already have too many."

Michelle paced the length of the backyard of the inn, eyeing the daisies but knowing that digging them up a second time would move her from the "quirky" category to something closer to "mentally deranged." She appreciated Pauline's advice and had even planned to take it. Until now.

She had proof. Not the kind she could take to the police, but enough for her to know who was stealing the money and how.

Total receipts were down on the days Isabella worked. Michelle had waited another week before coming to that conclusion. She'd checked the number of occupied tables every single day during breakfast. She knew how many got turned over and how many receipts there should be. Servers changed, the days of the weeks changed—the single constant was Isabella.

Firing her was the only option that made sense, but Michelle couldn't imagine doing that to Damaris. Isabella was a member of her family. Of course Damaris would believe in her. There was going to be a huge fight and accusations, and honestly, she would rather go out on patrol than deal with all that.

"You're looking fierce," Sam said, coming around the corner of the inn. "I like it."

"Don't be charming. I'm not in the mood."

"There's always room for charm. It's like Jell-O." He tugged on the end of a strand of hair. "Come on, Michelle. Tell Uncle Sam all about it."

"Ick," she said. "Don't say you're my uncle. It's creepy."

"Fair enough. Then tell an old friend who cares about you."

She drew in a breath. "Personnel issues. I don't want to talk about it." She looked at him. Sam was a good-looking guy. Too bad she didn't want to sleep with him. He would be happy to satisfy her for an afternoon or two and then be on his way. No promises, no questions. Only she couldn't seem to summon any interest.

"I've been ignoring you, haven't I?" she asked, wondering if the list of ways she was screwing up would ever get smaller. "You've been here for what? Two weeks? Longer? We haven't done anything together. I'm sorry."

"Don't be. I've managed to keep myself entertained."

"Do I want to know her name?"

Sam grinned. "It wasn't all about a woman. I got the job."

"What?" She flung herself at him, wrapping her arms around his neck. "That's great. Did you take it? Is it official? Can we celebrate?"

"I did take it, and yes, a celebration sounds like fun. I start next week, I've rented an apartment and my stuff is on its way from Texas."

He led her over to the chairs on the patio and motioned for her to sit. He settled across from her, then stretched out his long legs in front of him.

Sam had spent the past year at Fort Hood. Texas was a long way from the Pacific Northwest.

"You think you're going to be able to adjust to the rain?" she asked, her voice teasing.

"I can adjust to a lot of things. I'm ready to be a civilian again."

"It's been twenty years. How do you know you're going to like it?"

"I liked it before. Besides, I get to sleep in if I want."

"Do you?"

His gaze moved lazily to her face. "Sleep? Sure. Aren't you?"

"Not yet."

"Nightmares?"

She nodded. "I still jump at loud noises."

"I do, too, but I've gotten better at hiding the fact. It's not easy, going through what you did and then coming back here. You spent most of the past ten years in either Iraq or Afghanistan. Even doing a sissy job like you did, there were dangers."

She glared at him. "I didn't have a sissy job."

"You did and you know it."

"I wasn't in direct combat," she admitted. "Neither were you."

"I had my share of encounters."

She'd had the one, but he was talking about more than just the ambush. He was reminding her that there were ongoing rocket attacks, that it was never quiet.

She'd grown up here, on Blackberry Island, where life was regulated by the change of the seasons and tourists migrated like birds. She'd never expected to have to qualify on weapons every three months, deal with summers that were 128 degrees in the shade or watch out for camel spiders in her gear.

While her job had been more about keeping supplies flowing smoothly, she'd never been able to pretend she was anywhere else. The army had turned her into a soldier, but her heart and soul had stayed civilian. She'd thought that would make it easier for her to transition back to her regular world, but she'd been wrong.

"You did the right thing," Sam told her. "Killing him. You didn't have a choice."

"His daughter was with him. Holding on to him. She's going to grow up with that image, with that death, and it's my fault."

"Would you rather be dead?"

"No, but…"

"There's no but. Those are your two choices. You kill him or he kills you. That's why he was there that day. He wasn't going to the market or visiting his best friend. He was out to attack and destroy enemy soldiers. He's the one who chose to take his kid with him. What kind of father does that? Why didn't he leave her at home where she belonged? It wasn't about you, Michelle. Making it about you will only make it harder to move on."

She knew he was right about all of it, but hearing the words didn't seem to make a difference.

"You have to talk to someone," he told her.

"You're not the first one with that advice. I've been getting it a lot."

"You've always been stubborn. Most of the time that trait helps. This time it screws you up." For once he looked serious and determined. "You know I care about you, right?"

"Yes."

"Then listen to me. I've seen this happen. You start slipping in little ways, so you compensate. Maybe you drink a little more or do drugs or drive fast. Then you slip further. Before you know it, you're lost and now you've got a shitload of other problems. You using?"

"What? Drugs? No. I'm drinking." She grimaced. She hadn't meant to admit that.

"Get help. If you were going to be okay on your own, it would have happened already."

He had a point, just like Pauline had a point. Apparently someone somewhere was trying to send her a message. "I know. I'll find something."

"Let me guess. Soon. When you get around to it. You'll start Monday morning."

"Were you always this pushy?" she asked, hoping to distract him.

"No, but you've never been in this much trouble. You're cracking. It's not going to take much to push you over the edge."

She expected to feel a surge of anger. Being mad would give her strength. Instead, she was overwhelmed by a sudden wave of sadness. She half expected to see the dementors from the Harry Potter books. At least a scary, floating creature sucking happiness would be an explanation. One a whole lot easier than the truth.

"What if I don't get better?" she asked, fighting tears. "What if I can't?"

Sam rolled his eyes. "Because you're special? Get off your ass, do some work and you'll be fine."

Without thinking, she stood and crossed the small space between them. Her arm drew back and her hand closed in a fist. She wasn't sure how she was going to hurt him, but she knew pain would be involved.

He was on his feet faster than she thought possible, grabbing her fist and turning it easily, using her force against her. Less than a second later, she was locked against his body, completely immobilized, with an arm pressing across her rib cage.

Soft laughter filled her left ear. "You are in bad shape if you're trying to take me on."

"You pissed me off."

"I got that." He released her, then touched her cheek. "Get help."

"I will," she said grudgingly, wondering if she was telling the truth.

He hugged her and she hung on to him, absorbing his strength. When he released her, she looked up, prepared to thank him. Only his attention wasn't on her. He was looking at the inn.

No. Not looking. He was searching. She followed his gaze and saw a flash of movement. Carly was checking rooms.

"What are you—?" She stopped talking and stared.

She recognized the look, the slow, sexy grin, the expectation in his eyes. Damn him.

"You're interested in Carly?" she demanded.

"Sure. Why not? Have you seen her?"

"I can't escape her," Michelle muttered, knowing Carly was appealing. Tiny and blonde with plenty of curves and a girly air about her. She didn't have to be told to dress right or deal with things like waking up screaming or drinking too much. "I hate her."

"No, you don't."

"I should."

"She's your business partner and your friend."

"Don't confuse me with the facts. I can't believe you want to date her."

His expression shifted to something close to male satisfaction. Michelle felt her mouth drop open.

"You're sleeping with her?" Her voice was shrill with outrage. "When? How? Yuck."

"It's not a regular thing," he admitted.

"But you'd like it to be. She works here."

"And?"

"And, well, she does. And she has a kid."

"I like kids."

"When was the last time you were around one?"

"Is there a test?" he asked. "What's your problem?"

She wasn't sure, which made it hard to answer the question. She wanted to say it wasn't right, that he wasn't allowed to see Carly ever again—but if she said that, Sam would only laugh.

"Why are you upset?"

"I'm not."

He looked at her, not saying anything.

"I'm not," she repeated. "It's just weird. I don't like it."

"Then don't watch."

She shoved him. "Have I mentioned I don't like you very much?"

"You love me, and I love you. I always will. But that doesn't mean you get a say in my personal life."

She sighed. "I know."

Carly carefully sprinkled on the last edge of glitter, then waved the handmade card to let the glue dry. She was working ahead, getting the welcome cards ready in batches. The front wasn't quite as personalized, but she made sure the note inside was. In summer, with the inn full most of the time, she couldn't take the time to do much more.

Forty finished cards lay on her desk. She collected the

craft supplies and put them in their box, then slid the box onto the bottom shelf of the bookcase in her office.

The desk and bookcase were hers. The rest of the space served as a secondary storage room, with boxes of paper, printer cartridges and seasonal decorations.

At one time Carly had wanted a bigger office, something more professional, maybe with a window. But lately she'd decided she was okay with what she had. It might not be huge, but she had enough room for what she needed to be doing. In truth, she would rather be out with the guests than in here, dealing with numbers. The burning need to be in charge had faded.

Some of that was because working with Michelle was easier than working for Brenda. Michelle had her issues—the incident with the daisies proved that—but her outbursts weren't as unpredictable or vicious. With Brenda, Carly had been the target. With Michelle, she was just collateral damage.

She moved her laptop onto her desk and started it. As the machine whirred and hummed, she thought about Michelle ripping out all the daisies. She supposed she should still be upset by what had happened, but she'd let it go. Michelle hated the daisies. At that moment, she'd wanted to lash out, so she'd destroyed the flowers.

While that should be a big thing, it wasn't. She supposed because it was completely overt. Brenda had liked to sneak around, jabbing in unexpected ways. Michelle's blunt-force attacks weren't the least bit subtle. There was no wondering about intent or meaning.

Her computer finished booting up. The main screen appeared, icons scattered across a picture of Gabby holding daisies. Carly started to laugh. Okay, maybe she had gone a little flower mad with the decorating. Maybe she could tone things down a little.

Michelle stepped into the office, tapping lightly on the open door.

"Got a second?"

"Sure." Carly pointed to the narrow wooden chair across from her desk. "What's up?"

Michelle stared at her for a long moment. "I'm sorry about the daisies. I went a little crazy."

"It was impressive carnage."

"You're not pissed?"

"No. I can almost understand. Maybe there is too much of a daisy theme here. I'll tone things down."

Michelle's mouth twisted. "Don't say that. You should be furious with me."

"Sorry, no. I really do understand. At least as much as I can, under the circumstances."

Her dark eyes narrowed. "You're so damned annoying. Quit being nice. I'm not nice. I'm horrible and you're still here, still watching my back. Be a jerk, for God's sake."

Carly stood. "What is your problem?"

"Nothing. Everything. I can't..." She swore under her breath, then pulled something out of her back pocket. She dropped it on the desk, then turned and left.

Carly picked up the folded paper, opened it and realized it was a photo.

"Oh, no," she breathed, going both hot and cold. Her fingers trembled, causing the picture to shake.

The image was simple. It showed Michelle in a lace-covered dress, a bridal bouquet in her hand. She was standing next to a tall man in a suit.

A wedding picture, Carly thought in disbelief. And Sam was the groom.

Twenty-Five

Carly was able to escape the inn after lunch. Gabby wasn't due home for a couple of hours and the first new guests generally didn't check in until after three. She called Sam on his cell and asked him to meet her at the Coffee Shack, by the marina. He was waiting when she arrived.

After ordering an extra pump of mocha in her latte, she joined him outside on the deck. The afternoon was gray, but nearly seventy. Cranes circled overhead, calling out. She wondered if Leonard was nearby and wished she could have wanted to have sex with him. It would have made her life a lot less complicated.

Sam stood as she approached and held out a chair. "Finally," he said. "I was beginning to think you were sending me a message."

He'd called to ask her out. She'd agreed, but with all her responsibilities at work and with Gabby, she'd been unable to figure out a day and time. Mostly because she wasn't sure she wanted see him again. Being around him did things to her body that she didn't like. Or maybe she liked too much. Control was important to her. Being a responsible adult and mother. Unplanned sex on her sofa hadn't been her smartest move.

She passed over the folded picture. He opened it and grinned.

"I've seen this before," he told her.

"Not a surprise, considering you were there that day." She set down her coffee and leaned toward him. "You were married to Michelle."

"Is that a statement or a question?"

"A statement. You were married to her and you didn't tell me."

"So?"

"Don't you think that's information I would like to have?"

"Why aren't you yelling at Michelle? She didn't tell you, either."

"I'm not yelling." She consciously lowered her voice, then glanced around to make sure no one was close enough to hear the conversation. "Besides, I didn't sleep with Michelle. I slept with you. She's my boss. Can you see how knowing that might have been helpful?"

"I guess. Sorry. I wasn't keeping secrets. Michelle and I split three years ago. We've stayed friends. We're better that way. We never should have gotten married in the first place."

He sounded so casual, she thought grimly. While she wanted to shriek that he'd lied to her. Technically he hadn't, but there was a serious claim of omission here.

"Is she mad?" he asked.

"Let's just say she's not amused."

He frowned. "She usually doesn't care who I sleep with."

"Michelle and I have a past." There was the whole Allen issue. Did Michelle think Carly had slept with Sam to get even? The relationship wasn't the same—a divorced husband wasn't exactly a fiancé—but there was still a connection.

"You should have told me," she repeated.

"Would that have changed the outcome?"

"Yes."

"Then I'm glad I didn't. I like you, Carly. I want to spend time with you."

"I can't."

"Why? Because of Michelle? What does she have to do with anything?"

"I work for her."

"So?"

"She's my friend. It's too weird."

"She's not interested in me in that way. You can't go living your life based on something that happened years ago."

"I have to. I don't want to make her uncomfortable."

He stood and dropped the picture on the table. "You're making this bigger than it is. Trust me, she doesn't care."

"Maybe not, but I do."

He looked at her for a long moment. "All right, then. I guess I'll see you around."

He walked away without looking back. Carly watched him go. She knew she was making the right decision. Michelle might not appreciate it, but that was okay. Taking the moral high ground was important. Carly was tired of having to explain her actions, to justify a past she couldn't change. Better to do the right thing to begin with.

Wednesday morning Michelle stood by the rear doors of the inn and watched the three couples out on the lawn. One partner was blindfolded; the other was leading the first around. Pauline had explained that the "trust exercise" brought the couple together. Michelle wanted to doubt her but she'd seen the proof that the techniques worked.

Carly walked up to her. "What's going on?"

Michelle pointed to the couples. "Would you do that? Let some guy blindfold you and lead you around?"

"Sure. Why not?"

"I couldn't. Men are idiots."

Carly laughed. "Maybe, but a blindfold is nothing. If you're married, you're vulnerable all the time. Your partner could kill you in your sleep."

"Okay, that's twisted logic."

"Part of my sparkling personality. By the way, I'm not seeing Sam." She held out the photo. "I spoke to him and said I wasn't interested."

Michelle ignored the outstretched picture. "Why would you do that?"

"Because you were married to him."

"I never said you should break up with him."

"It was implied."

"No, it wasn't."

Carly drew in a breath. "Yeah, it was. I'm just telling you, we're not going to be dating."

"As long as it's not because of me."

Carly shoved the paper toward her. "Do you want this back or not?"

"You sound annoyed."

"That's because you're seriously pissing me off. You obviously do care whether or not I'm seeing him. If you didn't, you would have chosen another way to tell me the two of you had been married. You were going for shock value. It worked. Be happy."

Michelle couldn't remember the last time she'd felt

happy. These days she wasn't feeling much of anything. A little anxiety, maybe. A lot less pain. Mostly she was numb—as if the place that made her emotions had died. She wanted to tell herself not feeling anything was an improvement, but she had a feeling it was one more step on the road to the bad place.

"You can see him," Michelle said slowly, realizing she meant it. "You're right. I was going for shock value. But not because I was angry, exactly. It was a surprise. Finding out you were sleeping with him."

Carly flushed. "I didn't plan it."

"Sam's a sexy guy."

"Um, okay. But it's over."

"Your choice."

"I should punch you."

Michelle smiled. "You can try."

"Maybe not," Carly told her. "What with you being a trained professional and all."

"Exactly." She turned away from the window. "Sam and I were only together for a couple of months. We got married spontaneously. We quickly realized we were too much alike, which makes for a great friendship but not a good marriage."

"Thanks for sharing," Carly said stiffly.

Michelle glared at her for a second. "Fine. We'll talk work. I'm going to fire Isabella."

"What?"

"She's the one stealing." Michelle had done her best to hide from the truth as long as she could. "We make more money when she's not working than when she is. I've tried to figure out who else it is, but I can't. Damaris is going to be crushed."

"I'm sorry. When are you going to let her go?"

Michelle glanced at her watch. "Now. Before the lunch shift."

"I'll come with you. For moral support."

Michelle didn't tell her no. Maybe it would be good to have someone else there. Someone objective.

They walked to the dining room. Isabella was on her cell. She ended the call when she saw them and tucked her phone into her pocket.

"Damaris is in the kitchen," she said.

"We're not here to see her," Michelle told her. "We need to talk."

"All right."

Michelle didn't want to do this, didn't want to say the words, make the accusations, accept the consequences. She didn't want to be the bad guy. Why couldn't Isabella simply do her job and collect her paycheck?

"I'm going to let you go," Michelle said quietly. "I know you've been stealing money from the restaurant. I know you take the tickets of the customers who pay in cash and pocket their money. I've checked out everyone who works here and the common denominator is you."

Isabella's dark eyes flashed with anger, but she didn't speak. She turned and hurried to the kitchen. Seconds later she reappeared, pulling Damaris along with her.

"What?" the cook said, drying her hands on her apron. "I'm busy. I'm making soup."

"Tell her," Isabella said to Michelle, crossing her arms over her chest. "Say it to her."

Michelle looked between the two of them, not sure what was going on. "I'm firing Isabella for stealing."

"I told you she would figure it out," Isabella told her mother-in-law. "I said we should stop, but did you listen? No. You always know what's best." She glared at Michelle. "You're so stupid. It's not me. It's her. I do what she tells me to do. Everyone in the family does. Yes, I take the tickets when the customers pay with cash. It wasn't my idea."

Michelle didn't understand. Oh, sure, the words made sense and she could even believe Isabella was more of a follower than a mastermind, but Damaris? No. It wasn't possible.

"Be quiet," Damaris said. "Let me explain."

"Fine. I'm done here."

Isabella collected her purse from the hostess station and flounced out. Michelle stared back at the woman who had been her friend for well over a decade.

"How could you?"

Damaris pushed up her glasses, then held up her hands. "Just wait a second. Your mother took advantage of me for years. You know how little she paid me. I had a family to take care of. I'm the reason people come to this place. For the food. I told her that and she said if I wanted to leave, I could. But I didn't want to." Damaris touched Michelle's arm. "I stayed because of you."

Michelle felt the familiar sense of horror that accompanied every flashback. Only this time there wasn't gunfire or the oppressive heat. There were only lies. In some ways they were more deadly than a bullet.

"I gave you a raise," Michelle said, the words tumbling past numb lips. "I talked to you about what was going on."

"I know. I should have stopped taking so much. I didn't think you'd notice. That was my mistake."

Carly stepped closer. "No, Damaris, that wasn't your mistake. Your mistake was stealing from your employer. Both Brenda and Michelle trusted you. I'll accept you not giving a damn about Brenda, but you claim to care about

Michelle. You always said you were the one looking out for her interests. This is a funny way to show that."

"This has nothing to do with you," Damaris told her, fury blazing in her eyes. "I don't work for you."

"Well, that makes this easier, doesn't it?" Carly's voice was calm, as if she were in complete control.

Michelle was glad one of them was. She could barely keep breathing. She didn't want to be here, didn't want this happening.

"You'll go quietly," Carly said. "You'll tell people you decided you needed a change. You won't file for unemployment. You won't say anything bad about the inn or the restaurant and neither will Isabella. If you don't agree to these conditions, Michelle will go to the police and have you arrested."

Color stained Damaris's cheeks. "Don't you threaten me. Michelle would never do that." She swung her attention back to Michelle. "Tell her. Tell her I'm important to you. All right—I shouldn't have taken the money. I won't again. But I can't leave you. You need me."

If Michelle had made a list of people she could trust, she would have put Damaris near the top. Sam would probably be first, but Damaris would be second, maybe third. She couldn't say where she would put Carly. Until now.

The sudden shift, the change in reality, made her unsteady. She needed to hold on to something. To take a second and figure out what was happening.

"She doesn't need you," Carly said, still sounding reasonable. "She needs people she can depend on. Now it's time for you to leave."

Damaris put her hands on her hips. "Well?" she demanded.

Michelle shook her head, both hurt and unbelievably

sad. No, worse. "You can't stay. You did this and I don't want you around."

Damaris ripped off her apron and tossed it on the floor. "You'll never make it without me. The restaurant will fail."

"I'll have a letter drawn up by the morning," Carly said. "You'll be here at nine with Isabella to sign it. If you don't, I'll call the police."

"You can't do that."

"I can. Look into my eyes, Damaris. Do you have any doubts about my willingness to put your ass in jail?"

Damaris stepped toward Michelle. "You're going to let her do that? To me?"

Michelle's moment of bravado had faded, leaving her shaking. Her hip ached as it hadn't in weeks and her thighs trembled. She wasn't sure if she was going to faint or throw up.

"Get out."

Damaris swore again, then turned and stomped into the kitchen.

"I'm going to make sure she doesn't destroy any-thing," Carly said, moving after her. "Are you going to be all right?"

"Sure," Michelle managed.

She waited until Carly walked through the swinging door, then turned the other way and walked away as fast as she could. She went through the lobby, down the hall and into her office. Once she was inside, she closed the door, then crossed to her desk.

Her hands were shaking so hard, she could barely pull open the bottom desk drawer, but at last she managed it. A nearly full bottle of vodka lay on top of several fold-ers. She reached for it and unscrewed the top, then drank until the shaking stopped.

Twenty-Six

Carly stood in the center of the kitchen and told herself she could do this. She could manage lunch at the restaurant, even if they were missing a cook. And a hostess. At least there would be servers.

The dry-erase board on the wall listed the specials. Today there was quiche and chicken tortilla soup. A quick trip to the refrigerator told her the quiches were made and ready to go in the oven. The broth simmered on the stove, with most of the ingredients in various stages of prep. While Damaris never used a recipe, she had them on her computer. Carly was sure of it because she remembered Brenda badgering the cook to have a backup after she'd had to call in sick.

Carly walked to the ancient computer in the storeroom and found the recipes. She printed out the ones she would need and double-checked the time the quiche required in the oven.

"Hi."

She spun toward the voice and found Cammie standing in the doorway. The petite redhead was dressed for her lunch shift.

"I heard what happened and wondered if I could help."

"Word is traveling that fast?" Carly told herself not to be surprised.

"Isabella and I have a mutual friend. She called me to see if I knew anything. I came right here. I thought you'd need help."

"Thank you." Carly motioned to the kitchen. "We need to get lunch pulled together. I don't suppose you're secretly a master chef?"

"Sorry, no, but I can make a sandwich."

"Then we'll go with that."

They set to work together. Thankfully, the menu was fairly simple. A lot of sandwiches and salads, the specials and a few hot dishes. Carly knew there was no way she could deal with anything complicated, so made a note of what they wouldn't be serving. Cammie knew how to work the fryer, so that would help. With a little prayer and a lot of luck, they could manage the meal. But what about tomorrow and the next day?

Carly picked up the phone and called Michelle's office.

"What?"

"We'll need a temporary cook to—"

"Handle it," Michelle said, then hung up.

"Okay, then."

Carly put down the phone.

They were on an island. It wasn't as if she could call a local employment agency and get three candidates out by two. It was the height of tourist season. Mostly everyone who wanted to work already was and there was the added element of, hey, knowing how to cook. Even having Damaris go on vacation had been a nightmare. Except for last year.

Carly typed on the computer again. When she found what she was looking for, she picked up the phone.

"Hello?"

The voice was as brusque and strong as she remembered. "Helen?"

"Yes?"

"This is Carly Williams from the Blackberry Island Inn. You worked for us last fall when our cook was on vacation."

"I remember. I might be over the age of retirement, young lady, but I'm not senile. Is your cook going on vacation again?"

"Not exactly."

Carly explained that Damaris had left suddenly and they needed someone to fill in.

Helen was a retired schoolteacher who loved to cook. Brenda had found her through a mutual acquaintance.

"How long would you want me?" Helen asked.

Carly had no idea. "Um, a month?" That should give them plenty of time to find someone permanent.

There was a moment of silence. "I'd want a room at the inn. One with a nice view. And I'd have to bring my cat. I couldn't leave Mr. Whiskers with a sitter for that long."

Oh, God. They were fully booked on weekends, which meant disappointing someone by moving them to another hotel. And a cat in residence? How would that work? Logistics filed through her head as she calculated the greater loss—annoyed guests who would never come back versus the revenue generated by the restaurant. Math might not be her best subject, but even she knew the answer to that question.

"We can provide a room," she said. "For you and Mr. Whiskers."

Later, when Michelle threatened to kill her, she would remind her about the "handle it" conversation.

Carly and Helen settled on a salary and hours. Helen promised to arrive before lunch tomorrow, which was far better than they had the right to ask. Carly agreed to pick up a litter box and litter for Mr. Whiskers and hung up, hoping she'd made the right decision.

The next hour flew by. Carly watched the clock anxiously as the oven preheated for the quiche. By eleven-fifteen, they were as ready as they were going to get.

Michelle walked in then. She was pale and unsteady, her limp more noticeable than it had been in weeks.

"What are you doing?" she asked. "Why are you here?"

"We have to get ready for lunch."

"Just close the place." Defeat passed through her eyes. "What does it matter?"

"We have food that will spoil and people willing to pay for a meal," Carly told her. "That's what matters. Right now we can't afford to shut down."

She grabbed Michelle by the arm and dragged her into the storeroom. After closing the door, she faced her boss.

"I'm not shutting down the restaurant. We need the revenue and it adds value to the inn."

"But without Damaris…"

"She's not the only cook on the planet. I can handle lunch. Cammie's going to help me."

Michelle leaned against the built-in shelves and blinked, as if she wasn't understanding what was being said.

"You're going to cook lunch?"

"Yes. I just said that." Carly peered at her. "Are you drunk?"

"No. Maybe. Does it matter?"

Carly kind of thought it mattered a lot, but why have that conversation now?

"I'm sorry about Damaris, but we have to get through this. I know we can. I've hired a temporary cook. She's filled in for Damaris before. She's coming for a month." Carly swallowed, hating what she was going to say next. "She wants a room. A nice one with a view and she's bringing her cat."

She braced herself for the explosion, but Michelle only nodded. "Sure. Whatever."

"What's wrong with you?"

Instead of answering, Michelle walked into the kitchen. "Put me to work," she said when Carly followed.

"You can make sandwiches," Carly told her, thinking she would make sure everything was already cut. No way Michelle should be using a knife right now. Jeez. Talk about a mess.

She knew her friend was devastated, that Damaris's betrayal had rocked her, but she didn't understand the reaction. Michelle was more a "throw a chair through a window" kind of person. Like what had happened with the daisies. But then drunks were unpredictable. She'd had plenty of experience with her father to know that for sure.

A problem for another time, she thought, leading Michelle to the sink to wash her hands before putting on gloves, then handing her an apron.

Helen would arrive tomorrow. In less than twenty-four hours the crisis would be over. She would have her own personal breakdown then. One that included chocolate and wine.

Michelle was aware of the passage of time, of orders coming into the kitchen and food going out. She worked methodically, assembling sandwiches from the row of ingredients in front of her. The instructions were simple and she guessed on the amounts. As far as she knew, there weren't any complaints.

The vodka hadn't helped enough. She needed more because right now she could feel every exposed nerve and all the cuts to her heart. She couldn't seem to do anything but keep moving; she knew that she looked like an automaton, but on the inside she was screaming.

"This is the last order," one of the servers said, hurrying into the kitchen. "Quiche and soup. You did great. No one even noticed Damaris was gone. I kind of eavesdropped on a few conversations and no one said anything so I guess the news hasn't spread yet."

She might have said more—Michelle stopped listening. She'd heard enough to know that she could leave now.

After stripping off her gloves and tossing them on the counter, she unfastened the apron and let it fall to the floor. Then she started for the door.

Carly raced after her.

"Wait. What are you doing?"

"Leaving."

"But we have to talk about what happened. What we're going to do."

"Just handle it."

"I have to pick a room for Helen and cancel one of our guests, and Helen won't be here until after breakfast tomorrow. Which means we have to do this again."

Michelle stopped and looked at her. The pain was everywhere, which made it hard to think, let alone speak. She wanted to scream to the heavens, to demand an explanation. How could she have been so wrong? How could she have so misplaced her trust? If Damaris wasn't in her life, who did she have?

She'd been doing well, or so she thought. Healing. But Pauline had been right. She'd been on the edge, able to tip in either direction. Guess she'd just found out on which side she was going to fall.

"Michelle?"

Michelle turned away and kept walking. She got to her office and found her keys, then left. She drove slowly, carefully, parking in front of Jared's house before walking around back and stepping into the kitchen.

It was midafternoon. She expected to have the house to herself. Instead, she found him standing in front of the empty refrigerator.

"I have got to learn how to cook," he said, closing the door and grinning at her. "Or get married."

He was making a joke, she thought as she pushed past him and went to the cupboard. She should probably laugh. Show some kind of emotion. But it was too hard. All she wanted was relief from the ache and a promise that nothing would ever hurt this much again. Honest to God, she would rather be shot in the other hip than this.

"Michelle?"

She found an unopened bottle of vodka and quickly undid the screw-top. Not bothering with a glass, she took a swallow, then a second. The alcohol burned down her throat. When she went to raise her arm a third time, something warm and strong stopped her. She saw he'd taken hold of her arm, just above the elbow.

"Let go," she demanded.

"What happened?"

She put the bottle on the countertop and wondered if she could take him. Sam had taught her to fight dirty.

She'd rarely had to use the lessons, but she remembered most of them.

He released her arm. "Tell me."

The words were gentle, more a plea than a command. She shook her head, knowing she couldn't relive the moment. Not and stay in control.

"Something at the inn?"

She'd meant to walk away. To go to her room until he left her alone. Instead, her lips moved and then she couldn't stop.

"It's Damaris," she said, speaking quickly. "Our cook. I've known her since I was sixteen. I hired her and I trusted her. She wrote to me while I was gone. She sent me packages and told me what was going on. She worried about me and prayed for me. Not my mother. No one else bothered. Just Damaris."

Jared blurred and it took her a second to realize she was crying. Not delicately, not like a girl, but with deep, body-shaking sobs that ripped through her and stole her breath.

"I believed her," she said with a gasp. "I trusted her. All this time, I've depended on her. Every morning she makes me breakfast. I thought of her as the mother I always wanted. But it was a lie. All of it. She stole from me. She stole and she lied and then she walked out as if she doesn't care. As if I don't matter."

She bent over, trying to catch her breath, still sobbing and shaking. She knew she was going to collapse onto the kitchen floor and have to lie there like some wounded animal, broken.

Strong arms surrounded her, supporting her. Jared pulled her against him, then held her tight. She lashed out, fighting against the contact, the restraint. It was like kicking a wall. Nothing happened. Then she gave in and sagged against him.

She wasn't sure how long she cried. Even after the sobbing stopped, the tears continued. He rubbed her back and murmured soothingly, not really saying anything, just making sound. The tears slowed, as did her breathing. When she felt she was a little more under control, she pulled away.

"Sorry about that," she said, wiping her face on her sleeve. "I don't usually give in like that."

"Sure you do. You hide with this." He picked up the bottle of vodka. "But you're still losing it. You think getting drunk is easier, that it means you're winning. You're wrong. You're lost and everyone can see it but you."

She waited for the anger, for the righteous indignation, that would give her strength. Instead, there was only emptiness inside of her. A gaping hole that threatened to consume her soul and leave her nothing but a shell.

"I can't," she whispered, not sure if she meant she couldn't find herself or she couldn't stop her self-destructive behavior.

"Sure you can." His gaze was as hard as his voice, as unsympathetic. "Quit feeling sorry for yourself and do something."

Then he was gone. She was alone with her only friend. She grabbed the bottle and retreated to her room. With time, and a drink, she would be able to forget. At least for the night.

Twenty-Seven

Carly was in the restaurant at five-thirty in the morning. Despite the fact that it was so early even God shouldn't be up, the sun had already made an appearance. She told herself that the unusually cloudless sky was a sign that she was going to get through having to make breakfast for the hundred or so people who would show up hungry. She hoped she wasn't fooling herself.

The previous night she'd called Gabby's favorite sitter. Brittany had promised to be by a little before seven to get her ready for camp. Gabby had accepted the explanation that Damaris had left without asking a lot of questions. The two of them had never been especially close.

For a long time Carly had been unable to figure out why Damaris resented her so much. She'd assumed it had something to do with being loyal to Michelle. Now she wondered how much of the other woman's resentment had been because she was afraid Carly would figure out what she was doing.

A problem for another time, she told herself. Her more pressing problem was whether or not she could figure out how to make an omelet that both tasted good and looked halfway decent on a plate.

She entered the kitchen to find all the lights on and Cammie already at work.

"Bad news," she said. "Two of Damaris's assistants aren't coming in. They left voice mails saying they quit."

Carly glanced at the blinking light on the phone—the one indicating there were messages.

"Okay," she said, then licked her lips. "I guess this is up to us."

Cammie patted her on the shoulder. "We can do it. We've both been cooking for kids for years and they're pickier than any of our guests."

Carly nodded because she was afraid if she spoke, she would shriek. Panic and fear twisted through her chest, making it difficult to breathe.

"I'll get the recipes," Cammie told her. "We won't do a special this morning, which will help keep things simple. We're talking eggs, pancakes and cinnamon French toast. The cinnamon bread is made. Damaris did it in batches and defrosted it as she needed it. We have a couple more days' worth in the freezer."

Carly cleared her throat. "Good idea. I'll look over the menu to see if there's anything we shouldn't try without professional supervision."

The door to the kitchen swung open and Robert walked in.

Carly stared at him. "What are you doing here?"

"I heard what happened," he told her. "I can do something. Not cook," he added hastily, eyeing the stove. "Seat people. Pour coffee."

"I don't understand. How did you know what had happened?"

His gaze slid to Cammie, then away. "I heard from a

friend. This is your busy time. I can open the shop a little later for a couple of days."

Carly desperately wanted to sit down and hang her head between her legs. Maybe that would stop the world from spinning. At least Robert was here, possibly because he'd heard about what had happened from Cammie. But she didn't think he knew Cammie except in passing. Unless that had changed.

"Breathe," Cammie said. "You gotta breathe."

Personal issues later, she told herself. Breakfast first.

"Okay," she began. "Let's get organized."

Twenty minutes later she had the illusion of control if not the reality. Cammie had started cooking the first round of breakfast meats while Carly got everything they would need out onto the counters. They'd eliminated the four most complex items from the menu, leaving basics. Cammie had agreed to take on the omelets and Carly would cook everything else. They had enough servers, and with Robert handling seating and the cash register, they were okay in the front of the house, but they needed one more pair of hands in the back.

Just when Carly was about to call Brittany and ask if she felt up to the challenge, Michelle walked into the kitchen.

She looked worse than usual. Her clothes were fine, but her face was a Halloween color of gray. Dark, sunken circles hollowed the area under her eyes, and her lips were nearly as pale as her skin.

"Did you sleep at all?" Carly asked.

Michelle gave a quick shake of her head. "I don't want to talk about it. Just tell me what to do."

Carly decided to take her at her word and put her to work plating orders. A quick glance at the clock told her it was seven and time to get started. Just then one of the servers walked in with the first order of the morning.

The two hours of breakfast service passed in a blur. When it was over, Carly felt as if she'd run a marathon and didn't know how she was going to survive the rest of her day. Coffee, she thought, putting away the last of the butter and milk. Lots of coffee.

She walked into the dining room. Robert handed her the key to the cash register.

"Let me know if there are any problems when you reconcile the money," he told her.

"Are you expecting any?"

He smiled. "I can still do simple math, but I want to be sure."

"Thanks for coming in this morning. I appreciate your help."

"You're welcome." The smile faded. "You need someone to take care of you, Carly. You can't do everything on your own."

"Why not? Others do."

"You're special. I'll always believe that."

She didn't feel all that special right now, but she would accept the sentiment she knew was behind the statement.

"How long have you been seeing Cammie?" she asked.

He shifted his feet. "We've gone out a couple of times. She's nice. Her kids are great."

He paused, as if he were trying to decide what to say next. She broke in quickly.

"I hope you know how great she is. Cammie deserves a good guy in her life. You need someone, too, Robert. Someone who wants what you want."

Not exactly subtle, she told herself, but it was important to get the message across. She'd meant what she said—she wasn't going to depend on him anymore.

"I could still—" he began.

"No. You couldn't and I can't, either. Let's be friends, Robert."

"I worry about you."

"Don't do that, either."

He didn't look convinced, but he nodded. "You can be stubborn."

"Part of my charm."

Michelle wasn't in the mood to work the front desk. Bad enough she'd had to get up and help with breakfast. Now she had to smile and be pleasant to a bunch of people she didn't know and probably wouldn't like.

She needed to get out of here, she told herself. Go somewhere else. Only she loved the inn—or she had. Besides, where was there to go?

A white Toyota Corolla pulled up in front of the inn. It was barely ten in the morning and Michelle wasn't in the mood to check in anyone early. She would tell them to come back at three, like they were supposed to. Idiots.

A tall, thin woman with perfect posture and short iron-gray hair got out. She walked around and collected a pet carrier from the passenger's side.

Memories stirred. Carly had said something about hiring an interim cook. This must be her.

The woman walked inside, accompanied by feline cries of distress.

"Hello," she said as she approached the desk. "I'm Helen Swift." She set the carrier on the counter. "This is Mr. Whiskers. He doesn't travel well."

"Michelle Sanderson."

They shook hands.

Helen picked up the carrier. "I'll get Mr. Whiskers settled, then you can show me the kitchen. If I'm to take on lunch today, there isn't much time."

So much for pleasantries, Michelle thought, liking the older woman.

"You're retired?" Michelle asked. She handed Helen the key to her room and pointed to the stairs.

"Yes. I taught school for thirty-five years. Middle school." Her eyebrows rose as her brown eyes danced with humor. "Math, mostly. They gave me the difficult students. I preferred them to the smart ones, but then I've always enjoyed a challenge."

"Can I carry anything?" Michelle asked.

"I'm still capable," Helen said. "Lead on."

They went upstairs. Carly had reserved a west-facing room that overlooked the Sound. There was a small sitting room with a window seat, the bedroom and a large bath. A narrow desk had been pushed against a wall in the sitting room. A filled litter box sat under it, with a night-light next to it. In the bedroom, next to the closet, was a place mat with two empty dishes.

"Very nice," Helen said as she set the carrier on the bed and opened the door.

A sleek black-and-white cat stepped out, glaring as he went. Helen gave him a stroke on the back.

"There's a nice window seat for you, Mr. Whiskers," she said, her voice soft. "You situate yourself and I'll be back in a few hours."

She filled one of the bowls with water, then set it back in place.

"Show me the kitchen."

"Right this way."

They went downstairs and through the dining room. Helen paused to look around.

"I like how the windows allow in light," she said. "Very nice." Once in the kitchen, she made a quick tour. "Yes, I remember this. Well laid out."

She checked out the refrigerator, the pantry and the freezer. After studying the menu, she nodded once.

"Very well. I'll make you a list of immediate supplies. I can make do for lunch today, but I prefer to do better than simply making do on a regular basis. I'll also come up with ideas for specials after I go through what's been served in the past. I appreciate being asked to fill in. I prefer to think of myself as a useful sort of person. Retirement has been difficult."

She pressed her thin lips together. "It's been a year since I lost my husband. The days can be quite long without him."

"I'm sorry," Michelle said, feeling uncomfortable.

"Thank you. This will be good for me. A nice change of scene."

"You're going to have an assistant. I think it's Cammie. She was a server. Carly can let you know."

"That's fine. I can work with most anyone, as long as they're willing to do what I ask."

Michelle chuckled. "You remind me of several sergeants I've known."

Helen smiled, her whole face lighting up. "My husband was in the military. That's a very special compliment. Thank you."

Nothing about the middle ten days of June was noteworthy. Carly found herself both grateful for the reprieve and anxious about the next crisis. Because there would be one—of that she was sure.

Helen had settled in nicely. Her calm and organized personality meshed well with the servers. Damaris had signed the letter of resignation Carly had written for her, as had Isabella. A new hostess had been hired and Cammie had been moved permanently to the kitchen. So nearly everything was in order. Everything but Michelle.

Carly worried about her but didn't know what to do. Michelle mostly kept to her office and rarely spoke to anyone. Carly wasn't qualified to offer help, nor could she force Michelle to seek it elsewhere. Complications, she thought, straightening the brochures in the stand by the front doors.

Gabby had finished school the week before and had started her camp, which she adored. She also had found true love with Mr. Whiskers and her affection seemed returned. The cat let Gabby dress him in doll clothes and then push him around in her old play baby stroller.

She glanced outside and saw the sun had broken through the clouds. The temperature was finally in the seventies. The warm afternoon beckoned and she slipped outside to sit on the porch for a few minutes.

She was perched on the steps when a car from the sheriff's department pulled up. Sam climbed out.

He looked good in his khaki uniform and aviator sunglasses. He walked toward her, all confident male and powerful sexuality. If she'd been standing, she would have worried about her knees getting weak. As it was, she had to bite her lip to keep from begging him to take her, right there in front of God and everyone.

"Officer," she said, smiling.

"Ma'am."

She winced. "I don't consider myself of 'ma'am-ing' age just yet."

"It's a sign of respect." He pointed to the step, next to where she sat. "May I join you?"

She nodded.

He settled beside her. His shoulder brushed hers and she felt a jolt of heat that had nothing to do with it being summer.

"How's it going?" she asked. "Settling into your new job all right?"

"It's good. I like the island, the people. I'm starting to see why there are complaints about the tourists. This is exactly what I've been looking for."

"That's nice."

"I've missed you."

She angled toward him. He'd removed his sunglasses, which made him even more appealing. Temptation pulled at her. She told herself to be strong. Or at least sensible.

"We've hardly spent any time together," she said bluntly. "What's to miss?"

He grinned. "I like your sass. Let me rephrase that, then. I've been thinking about you a lot. I respect what you said about Michelle, but I don't agree with it. I'd like to see you, Carly. We can take it slow. What about you and me taking your daughter out on the duck boat?"

Going out on the water was about her least favorite thing in the world, but the duck boats were safe enough. They drove around town, then went down the boat ramp, directly into the water. The drive wasn't an issue—it was the on-the-water part she objected to. As long as she sat near where they kept the life jackets and looked at the horizon rather than the water, she would be okay.

"Sure," she said. "Gabby loves the duck boats." Robert had taken her last summer and she'd talked about the experience for days. Gabby's inherited fear of the water didn't extend to duck boats.

"Just like that?" he asked. "I thought I was going to have to convince you."

"Apparently Michelle doesn't care if we go out." Right now Michelle didn't care about anything.

"Good to know."

"I'm worried about her. She's not eating. I think she's drinking a lot. She looks horrible, like she hasn't slept in weeks."

"I know. But I've already said all I can about it to her."

Carly rolled her eyes. "Have you seen her lately?"

"No."

"She's getting worse. I've seen the news stories. I get that it's difficult for soldiers to adjust to being back home, but this is more than that. She needs help."

Sam drew his eyebrows together. "You make it sound serious."

"I think it is."

Sam looked out in the distance. "Some people need to hit rock bottom before they can move forward."

"Maybe," Carly said. "Look, don't tell her I said anything. It'll make her defensive and piss her off."

Sam stretched out his legs. "I've known some sisters in my time, but you two have the strangest relationship I've ever seen."

"We're not sisters."

"Your mother married her father, or do I have that wrong?"

"They're married."

They'd been married for years.

Sisters. Carly stared out at the garden as she turned the word over in her head. She and Michelle were sisters. Okay, stepsisters, but still. She'd never thought of their relationship like that. Had never considered their familial bond—if you could call it that.

She wondered if putting a name to it would change anything. Neither of them had any family they were close to. Which should mean having each other was important.

Twenty-Eight

Michelle sat on the edge of the dock, her tennis-shoe-clad feet dangling toward the water. It was late afternoon. She should still be at the inn what with this being a busy weekend, but she had escaped. These days she just couldn't handle all the responsibility. She knew she was leaving more and more in Carly's care, but she couldn't seem to summon any interest or concern.

Jared sat next to her. He'd just appeared and she didn't have the energy to tell him to go away. As long as he kept his mouth shut, they would be fine.

She hadn't seen much of him since her breakdown. Mostly because she'd been avoiding him. She'd been avoiding everyone.

"How's the inn?" Jared asked, breaking the silence.

"Fine." She started to tell him she didn't want to talk about it but instead found herself saying, "Everything's screwed up."

"No. Not everything. Just you."

She covered her face with her hands. "Don't start with me. I don't want to hear it."

"You're getting worse, not better. Your clothes are

hanging on you. You keep this up, you lose more weight, you're going to end up in the hospital."

Mango had given her the same lecture at her last physical-therapy appointment. It was the reason she hadn't been back to the VA hospital.

"I know you're not sleeping," he added.

She scrambled to her feet, then wished she'd been more careful as pain shot through her hip and down her leg.

"Stop it," she yelled. "Just stop it. You're not my mother. She wouldn't care about any of this and right now that sounds pretty good. If you want me to move out, just say it and I'll go."

Jared stared at her, his expression unreadable. "I don't want you to move out."

"Then leave me alone. You've ruined a perfectly good afternoon."

She picked up her shoes, turned and started walking back to the shore. Her legs felt weak, which happened a lot these day. She was also light-headed. Maybe she should eat something. Didn't Jared always have a damn sandwich in the refrigerator?

She'd nearly made it to the end of the dock when she heard him call out behind her, "What's the point in making it back if you only came home to die?"

His words followed her, but she didn't react. Didn't slow, didn't turn back. She just kept moving. That was all she could do.

Carly looked up to find Michelle standing in the doorway to her small office, glaring at her.

She took in the sallow skin with an undercoat of gray, the slightly bloodshot eyes, the gaunt cheekbones. Worry knotted in her stomach. Her father might have died from running his car into a tree, but that had simply been a detail. In truth the alcohol had killed him. And he'd looked a lot like Michelle did now.

"You need help."

"You're hardly qualified."

"You can't go on like this," Carly told her. "You have to know you're getting worse, not better. Please, Michelle. Get some help. Maybe Jared—"

"Leave him out of this," Michelle told her, her eyes flashing with feral rage. "Don't talk to him, don't look at him. Pretend he's not even alive. You got that?"

Carly felt the first whisper of fear. Michelle was worse than she'd first realized. Was it possible for a person to slip over the edge and not find her way back?

"I won't have anything to do with him," Carly said quickly. She pressed her hands against the top of her desk, searching her mind for answers. Was there someone she could get in touch with? She had to do something. Maybe Sam would know.

Michelle sucked in air. "Look, I know you're worried. It's not as bad as you think. I'm fine."

Michelle's cell phone rang. She pulled it from her pocket and stared at the screen. As she studied the number there, her face contorted, her eyes narrowing to slits, her mouth twisting.

"Stop calling me," she screamed, then threw the phone across the room. It bounced off a stack of boxes, the ring still sounding. "Stop it. Stop it!"

Carly got up and reached for the phone. She pushed the ignore button. The phone went silent.

They stood in the small room, looking at each other. Michelle turned away first.

"Sorry," she muttered. "That was my dad. I don't

know why he keeps phoning. I want him to leave me alone."

"You don't talk to him?"

"No. Why would I? You don't talk to your mom."

"Yeah, I do. Not often, but a couple of times a year. She came once, to visit. I wish she was more involved with Gabby, but that's not going to happen."

"How can you do that?" Michelle's voice was accusing. "They left us. They were horrible, selfish people. They don't deserve to be in our lives."

She grabbed the phone from Carly and dropped it to the floor, then stepped on it, as if trying to crush it.

"I want them to go away. Just go away."

The fear grew. Not for herself. Carly wasn't concerned that Michelle would physically hurt her. Instead, she worried for her.

"Michelle," she began.

"Don't. Don't say it. Just don't." Michelle turned in a circle, as if trapped and looking for a way out. Her eyes were wide, her face ashen. "I can't be here. I can't do this. Go away. Just go away."

And then she was running down the hallway. Carly hurried after her. Michelle moved quickly, her hip obviously better. She made it to her truck, then started the engine. She roared out of the parking lot, narrowly missing a tree at the entrance.

"Mom?"

Carly saw her daughter carrying Mr. Whiskers. "Yes, honey?"

"What's wrong with Michelle?"

"I don't know," Carly admitted, touching her daughter's hair and forcing herself to smile. "But she'll be better soon."

"Promise?"

Carly wondered how wrong it was to lie to her child. Not that she had a choice—Gabby was too young to deal with the truth.

"Yes. I promise."

Michelle sat in a chair in the back corner of the bar, shaking. She wasn't sure how long she'd been there or how much she'd had to drink. She half expected the bartender to refuse to serve her, but he didn't seem to notice how close she was to snapping. Apparently what mattered was that her credit card cleared.

She told herself she had to eat something, even if the thought of food made her stomach cramp in protest. She was sinking—she could feel it. Every day was harder. It wasn't even what had happened in Afghanistan, although that still haunted her. It was everything else. Being here, being anywhere, was too hard.

But she didn't have anywhere else to go. Which meant what? That it was time not to be anywhere? Was that the answer?

She closed her eyes, then opened them, nearly as afraid of the dark as she was of the light. She reached for her glass, but was shaking too hard to pick it up. Weakness invaded her. She wondered if she could simply die right there and no one would know why.

"Come on."

The voice came from in front of her. She blinked, then saw Jared standing by the table.

"What?"

"Come on. We're getting out of here."

He took hold of her arm and drew her to her feet, then half led, half carried her to the door.

He was going to make her do something, she thought. Make her face what was wrong, force her to get better.

He wasn't going to let her talk her way out of it. With the realization came both fear and relief. Maybe he could show her another way out.

"Where are we going?" she asked.

"Home."

Not to a hospital? Not to a rehab center or intervention?

"And then what? I'll just leave. I'll come back here." She wanted the words to sound defiant, but had a feeling her voice was too small.

"That's up to you."

The drive back to the house took less than five minutes. Jared helped her out of the front seat and onto the ground. He led her to the back door.

She knew there was going to be a lecture and a part of her hoped he was able to get through to her. She had her doubts, though. What could he possibly say that she hadn't already told herself? He wasn't magic. He was just a guy with a weak spot for those in need.

Despite the fact that it was after nine, it was still light out, so she could see everything clearly. Even the dog tied up by the door.

She came to a stop and stared. The dog was a good size—a mixed breed with a lot of Lab and maybe some shepherd. It had short hair, like a yellow Lab, with a dark muzzle and dark ears. When it saw them, it cowered, moving back as far as the rope around its neck would let it. The animal half turned.

Michelle gasped. She could see welts on the side of the dog and all its ribs. The animal radiated fear. It began to shake so hard it collapsed, then scrambled, trying to get into the corner of the small porch.

She felt sick. "What happened to him?"

"Who knows? A friend of mine works with animal

rescue. This little guy was picked up this morning. He'd been abused, then abandoned. I brought him here. He needs to be taken care of. Fed and rehabilitated."

She tore her gaze away from the dog and stared at Jared. "You're going to do that?"

"No. You are. He doesn't have anyone in the world, Michelle."

She took a step back. "I don't know anything about dogs."

"Then you're going to have to learn pretty fast. The vet says he's not sick. Just hurt and starving. Scared as hell. The people who were supposed to take care of him didn't. He might have been tortured. We're not sure." Jared fished his keys out of his pocket and started back toward the truck.

"There's some dog food in the house. You can figure the rest of it out as you go."

Twenty-Nine

Carly carried the tray of flatware, napkins, glasses and mugs to the next table. The weekend before the Fourth of July was crazy busy on the island. Between the cutback in people at the inn and dealing with the transition after Damaris had been fired, she was scrambling to get everything done. Michelle was supposed to be the one working the restaurant this Sunday morning, but since their encounter the previous afternoon, she hadn't been seen.

Carly wasn't sure what to do. Should she call Jared and ask if she was okay? Call the police? Keep her mouth shut? She reminded herself that if anything bad had happened, she would have heard. Sam would let her know. But worry was a constant companion, nibbling at the edge of her mind, making it tough to concentrate on anything else.

She set the first table, arranging the napkins, flatware, glasses and mugs automatically. At least the rest of the inn was going well. The restaurant business was as strong as ever. Helen was a godsend, providing great food and appealing specials. They'd sold out of her chicken salad on focaccia bread every time she'd made it. Carly wanted to talk to Michelle about making it part of the menu. Assuming Michelle was ever around for them to talk business.

She moved to the next table. The door to the restaurant opened. Carly turned to say they weren't serving lunch for another hour, but stopped when she saw Ellen.

The well-dressed blonde smiled as she approached. In her tailored suit and heels, she looked professional and attractive, but Carly saw the essence of shark in her smile. Bracing herself for the inevitable attack, she squared her shoulders and forced a pleasant expression.

"Hello, Ellen."

"Carly. You're still here. I'm surprised."

What? Here as in working at the restaurant or here as in still at the inn? "I don't understand."

"I would have thought Michelle would have fired you by now. You're hardly an asset to the business."

"Michelle can't fire me. You made sure of that. You told her the board insisted…" She stopped talking, finally understanding the game. "It wasn't the board, was it? There's no committee telling Michelle what she has to do or not do. With the loan being made current, there aren't any rules. Just whatever sick game you're playing."

Ellen's pleasant expression never changed. "I'd be careful, if I were you. You don't want to upset the one person who holds your destiny in her hands, do you? That would be very foolish. Especially considering you have a small child to take care of. If you didn't have a job here, where would you go? What would you do?" Her smile widened. "I've seen the books, Carly. Part of my due diligence. I know how very little you make. Considering you have to pay for a sitter to keep working, you must have a tough time making ends meet. There's not much of an emergency fund, is there? So losing your job, and subsequently your home, would be a disaster."

Three months ago it would have been, Carly thought bitterly. But Ellen didn't know about the ten thousand dollars. She didn't know Carly would hate to lose her job but that it wouldn't be as devastating as it could have been. She and Gabby would make it, thanks to Michelle.

"I'll take your silence as a yes," Ellen told her. "After all this time you have nothing. You are nothing. Payback's a bitch, isn't it?"

"Payback isn't the only one," she said calmly, refusing to let the other woman see that she was shaken.

"I want you to remember that every day," Ellen told her. "Remember how close you are to losing it all."

She gave a little wave, then left.

Carly waited until she was alone again, then allowed herself a brief second of fist-clenching before returning to setting the tables.

There was good news, she told herself firmly. Ellen's conditions about the inn might not be legal, which meant they weren't enforceable. On the downside, Michelle didn't have to keep Carly around, but maybe that was okay. She knew she'd more than proved herself. Why would Michelle want to get rid of her now?

Helen walked into the dining room. "Was someone just here? I thought I heard voices." She smiled. "Not in a way to alarm anyone."

Carly laughed and felt her tension ease a little. "Good to know."

"At my age, one needs to make the distinction. So, who was our visitor?"

"Ellen. Her bank had the loans on the inn. She stopped by to torture me a little. She does it for sport."

Helen sniffed. "I never could abide a bully. But you have nothing to worry about. She can't hurt you."

"She can influence Michelle."

"I don't think so. Michelle needs you. You're an integral part of the inn. She deals with the behind-the-scenes part of the business, but you're the face the customers see. And they like you. That's invaluable."

Carly hoped she was right. But even if she did lose her job, she and Gabby would still be all right.

"Why does Ellen dislike you?"

"Because of a few things that happened in high school. I stole her boyfriend."

"Some people love to live in the past," Helen said. "A waste of time, if you ask me. It can't be undone."

"Not Ellen's philosophy."

"That is going to be a problem for her, but not for you. Not if you don't let it. Now I'd better get back to work or people will go hungry at lunch."

Helen left and Carly returned to setting the tables. The realization that Ellen might be manipulating Michelle shouldn't be a surprise, but it was. Like Helen said, the past couldn't be changed. At some point Ellen had to figure that out or let it go. More easily said than done, Carly thought.

Still, she was going to have to share the latest revelation with Michelle. Based on their last conversation, it wasn't going to go well. But she wouldn't be keeping any secrets. No matter how ugly the telling.

Michelle sat on the floor in her bedroom. Afternoon light spilled into the room. The windows were open, letting the warm air drift inside, but the fact that the temperatures had finally warmed to close to eighty didn't help at all with the shaking.

She held up her hand and watched her fingers tremble. Not that she needed to look at them to confirm what she could feel in every cell in her body. She alternated between cold and hot, between wanting to throw up and a tightness in her chest that made it nearly impossible to breathe.

She'd been drinking so much lately, it had probably been weeks since her system had been free of alcohol. Vodka couldn't help her to forget, but it blurred the edges enough to make the flashbacks manageable. Letting it go meant dealing with reality. Not something she looked forward to.

She stretched out her legs, staring at her thin thighs and bony knees. She'd passed fashionably thin ten pounds ago. Now she looked like a refugee. There were bruises on her legs—probably more from a lack of nutrition than because she'd bumped anything. Her feet were dirty, her toenails too long. She hadn't shaved her legs in weeks. Which meant she should rethink shorts right now. Not that there was anyone to see.

A soft cry made her turn. The dog lay on the makeshift bed she'd created out of several blankets, finally asleep.

Neither of them had gotten much rest last night. She'd sat on the floor, waiting for the alcohol to slowly metabolize out of her system while the dog had cowered in the farthest corner from her. It had gulped the food she'd offered, lapped up some water, then had stood watching her. Obviously waiting for the next round of pain.

Sometime after midnight, she'd put the collar on him she'd found on the bed. The dog had nearly collapsed from fear as she'd approached, then shook as she fastened the strip of leather. She'd put on the leash and practically had to drag it outside to go to the bathroom. They'd repeated the process again this morning.

But sometime around noon the dog had crept to the stack of blankets and lain down. He'd watched her with his sad brown eyes until his lids had slowly closed and he'd gone to sleep. She'd been sitting as quietly as possible ever since.

Now she watched him twitch in his sleep, soft whines coming from his dreams. She didn't know much about dogs and less about what they thought, but she sensed his sleep had produced nightmares. Something she was all too familiar with.

Not sure what to do, she hummed quietly, hoping the sound would be calming. The dog came awake with a jerk.

"Hey," she whispered, staying in place. "It's okay. All right, it's not okay. It sucks, but you're safe now. I'm not going to hurt you." She watched him watch her. "This would be more helpful if you spoke English."

The dog's head was low, his body tense.

"It's been a while," she murmured. "You probably need to go to the bathroom and we both need to eat."

She stood and reached for the leash. The dog stood, as well, and backed into the corner.

"It's all right," she told him. "Shh. Shh. We're going outside. It's okay."

He trembled as she approached, but didn't run. She snapped on the leash and walked toward the door. He braced himself.

"Come on," she said, opening the door and patting her leg. "Let's go out."

His wounded eyes locked with hers, as if he were trying to figure out what threat she offered. Just when she was sure she was going to have to drag him again, he took a step toward her.

"Good boy. That's it. Let's go out."

He took another step.

They made it outside. She walked to the side of the yard he'd used before and waited while he did his business. When they were back in the house, she unfastened the leash and set it on the counter.

"Let's get you some lunch."

She'd had to guess on the amount of food he needed. The bag of dry food had listed measurements for different weights, but Michelle had no idea how big he was. She'd decided several small meals would probably be easier for him than one big one. He'd obviously been starving. Giving him too much might make him sick.

She set down the food, then walked to the refrigerator. Not that there was any point. She hadn't bothered keeping food around and Jared mostly ate out. But when she opened the door she was surprised to see the top shelf was nearly full. There were cartons of juice, bottles of ginger ale and Sprite. Three sandwiches nestled together, each clearly marked with the type, along with potato salad in a plastic container.

In her cupboard she found cookies and chips. Sugar and salt, she thought. Apparently Jared was a whole lot more interested in fattening her up than she'd thought.

She knew the drinks were to help her stay hydrated. The sugar in them would help with the shakes and withdrawal. Like the dog, she would have to take it slow.

She poured a large glass of juice. After collecting the turkey sandwich, the potato salad and a fork, she carried everything back into her room. The dog followed. She put the food on her nightstand and flipped on the TV.

As she turned to get into the bed, she bumped the

dog. They both jumped. He crouched and started for the corner.

"Wait," she called. "I'm sorry."

He stopped and looked at her.

He was still close enough for her to touch him. Slowly, she stretched out her arm. He took a step away. She slid toward him, murmuring she wasn't going to hurt him. He watched her, head low, tail tucked.

At last she was able to brush her fingers against his back. He shuddered but didn't move.

"Good boy," she whispered, touching him gently, avoiding the still-healing welts on his side. "That's better."

She petted his back, staying away from his head, although she did scratch the back of his neck. He raised his head a little and his long tail straightened a little.

"Oh, so you like that, do you? I'll remember for next time."

She returned to the bed. He walked over to his pile of blankets and settled down. She'd thought he might want a part of her lunch, but he ignored the fact that she was eating, closed his eyes and went to sleep.

Sometime after midnight, Michelle came awake with a start. She'd been dreaming that she was back in Afghanistan. Not the shooting, thank God, but reliving being there was enough to get her heart racing.

She sat up and realized she felt a little better. Not so shaky. Maybe the alcohol had left her system, or maybe it was the food. She'd had another sandwich for dinner, along with most of the chips. She'd found ice cream in the freezer and had decided that Jared deserved to be nominated for sainthood. Not that he'd been around to accept the offer. She hadn't seen him since he'd brought her home from the bar.

She glanced at the dog and saw he was watching her. He'd eaten and slept, as well. The last time she'd taken him out, he'd stood quietly while she'd attached the leash. It seemed they'd come to some kind of understanding.

"Let's go out," she said as she stood.

He rose and walked toward her. She reached down to pat him. He flinched, his skin rippling under her touch, but then he was still. He raised his head slightly, looking at her.

Slowly, she moved her hand to his cheek and rubbed gently. A trust exercise for both of them, she thought. She could hit him, but he could bite off her hand. Neither happened.

She dropped her hand and picked up the leash. He let her snap it in place without cowering. Progress, she thought.

Later, when he'd done his business and they were back in her room, she climbed back into bed. She left the light on, as much for herself as for him. She rolled onto her side and was about to close her eyes when she felt his steady gaze.

She shifted around to find him standing by the bed, looking at her.

"What?" she asked, raising herself onto her elbow. Was he hungry? Should she feed him again? "I need an instruction manual."

He continued to stare, then, with one giant leap, jumped onto the bed. He collapsed at the foot of it, curled up, his butt against her legs.

An unexpected development, she thought.

"I generally take a little longer to get into bed with a guy," she told him.

Instead of being impressed or the least bit chagrined, the dog closed his eyes and sighed.

"I know just how you feel," she said, dropping down to rest her head on her pillow.

The weight at the end of the mattress felt kind of good. At least neither of them was alone anymore. They would find a way to heal each other, which had probably been Jared's plan all along.

Thirty

Carly was working the front desk. They were fully booked for ten straight days, from the weekend before the Fourth through the weekend after. Having the holiday itself fall on a Wednesday this year was turning out to be good for business.

This Sunday morning she'd already recommended restaurants for brunch, including their own, had organized wine tasting and antiquing tours and had begged a local artist to open his gallery an hour early.

She'd been on the run since Friday, but if everything went well, she would get a couple of hours off that afternoon. No one was checking in and the cleaning staff was taking care of the rooms. A chance to relax with her daughter and maybe just breathe sounded pretty good.

She glanced at the phone and wondered if she would hear from Michelle. Not that her boss could use her cell. It was still in little pieces in a Baggie. Carly had collected them all after Michelle had gone crazy the other day. She wasn't sure what she was going to do with them, but at least she had them.

Sunlight spilled into the reception area. They were

promised a mostly sunny morning with clouds piling up in the afternoon. Rain tomorrow, which might send guests home early. It was probably wrong of her to be happy about that, but she wouldn't mind having the extra time to clean rooms before the next batch of visitors arrived. Tuesday would bring a new group for the therapy sessions. This time they would be working out their problems over the holiday, which should be interesting.

She heard a familiar engine and looked up to see Michelle pulling around the side of the building toward the employee parking lot. Concern twisted around apprehension. Was Michelle better or worse? Had she lost it completely or figured out a way to get help? There was only one way to tell.

She stayed in place at the front desk, trying to look busy. After a couple of minutes, she heard footsteps accompanied by an odd clicking sound. She looked up at Michelle walking toward her. At her side was a large, skinny dog with healing welts on its side and a terrified expression in its eyes.

"Hi," Michelle said.

She looked marginally better, Carly decided as she studied her. Less gray, but still pale. Her eyes were clearer and more focused, but her hands trembled as she held the leash.

"Hi."

"Sorry I disappeared. I had to deal with some stuff."

"Okay." Carly wasn't sure if she should ask if Michelle was still crazy or simply find out over time.

"I have a dog now."

"I can see that. I'm not sure Mr. Whiskers is going to approve. He's sort of settled into a place of authority around here."

A hint of a smile tugged at Michelle's mouth, then

faded. "He's a rescue dog. Somebody tortured him, then abandoned him. I'm pretty sure Mr. Whiskers would be able to kick his butt."

Carly moved out from behind the counter. "I've never understood why some people hurt animals."

She dropped to her knees by the dog. He trembled and sidestepped away. She stayed in place, offering her fingers for him to sniff. When he inched his muzzle toward her hand, she raised her other to his back and lightly stroked him.

"Hey, there," she murmured. "I know it's tough now, but things will get better. You've come to a good place. I think everyone here is going to spoil you, and what dog doesn't like that?"

He stared at her with sad eyes, but she thought he might look a little less afraid.

She rose. "Are you, um, here for the day?"

Michelle nodded. "Yes. But before I start work, I need you to do something for me."

She led the way to her office, the dog following on his leash. He glanced around, obviously terrified of what might jump out and hurt him.

As they went inside, Michelle passed over the leash. "Hold him for a second."

She started opening drawers and moving books around, pulling out bottles of vodka from various hiding places. When she was done, there were six bottles—some full, some nearly empty—on her desk.

"I need you to dump these," Michelle said, staring at the bottles rather than Carly. "Then check regularly. I don't plan to hide them anymore, but knowing you'll be looking will help."

Carly nodded. "Of course. Can I do anything else?"

"I don't know. I'm still figuring out what I'm supposed

to be doing. I'm sorry for disappearing like that and leaving you with everything. It's a busy weekend."

"We're full and that's good. Don't worry. We managed. Everyone pulled together. Helen is working out great. People love her food. We've had a run on her chicken salad on focaccia bread. You should try it."

Michelle smiled. "Is that a hint?"

"You've lost a lot of weight."

"I haven't been eating. I'm doing better. The dog and I both need to get our strength back."

"Are you keeping him?"

Michelle nodded slowly. "I am. I think we need each other. I never thought about getting a dog before, but I like having him around."

She drew in a breath. "I know this is a bad time to disappear again, but I need to go to a meeting this morning."

"It's Sunday."

"They have them."

Carly's gaze slid to the bottles. "Oh. That kind of meeting."

Michelle laughed. "No. I think the alcohol was a symptom, but not the real problem. I'm going to a support group for returning vets."

"Do you need me to babysit your dog?"

"I was going to take him with me. Then I can come back and work. Oh, do you know where there's a pet store? He needs food and a bed, maybe some toys. What do dogs like? Balls?"

"I can go," Carly offered. "I was going to duck out for a couple of hours this afternoon, anyway. I can take Gabby to the pet store with me. She'd love it."

"Are you sure? If you don't mind, I'll say yes, then stay here and look after things. I'll pay you back."

"It's not about the money." Carly drew in a breath. "I'm glad you're back. I was worried."

"I know. You were trying to help. I should have been more gracious."

"Why start now?"

Michelle grinned. "Good point." She picked up the Baggie containing the broken pieces of her phone. "I should probably get this fixed, too."

"I don't know. If you really don't want to get any calls, you've found the perfect solution."

"I think a phone could come in handy. I'll go first thing tomorrow."

There was a moment of silence, then Michelle said, "Thank you. For everything. I know I haven't been easy to deal with. Damaris pushed me over the edge. I thought I could trust her completely and it was all a lie. I didn't know how to handle that. You were there for me."

"You're welcome," Carly said, suddenly fighting tears. "I want to help and be someone you can depend on." She almost said that they were sisters and should be there for each other, but maybe it was too soon for that. She'd barely come to terms with that reality herself.

"At the risk of pissing you off," she said cautiously, "I do have to tell you one thing. It's not completely horrible," she added. "It's just strange."

Michelle drew in a breath. "Okay. What is it? Alien landings? The daisies have been sneaking out at night and killing people?"

"Ellen stopped by. She was her usual unpleasant self to me, which I'm used to. But she implied that the rules she put in place for you didn't come from any committee or the bank board. That she had done it herself, sort of as a power play."

"Can she do that?"

"I don't know. I have no experience with the banking world. I just wanted to tell you what happened."

"Nothing I'm dealing with today," Michelle admitted. "It's way above my pay grade right now. Anything else I should know about?"

"Mom, Mom, are you—?"

Gabby rounded the corner, then slid to a stop, her eyes huge.

"Mom, is that a dog?" Her voice was thick with reverence, as if she'd just been given the world.

"Yes. Michelle is taking care of him. Be careful, he's—"

There was no time to finish the statement, warning her daughter that the pathetic guy might not react well to a child's exuberance. Gabby barreled toward him, arms outstretched. The dog whimpered and started to back away, but his leash held him in place.

Then Gabby had reached him. She wrapped both arms around his body and leaned her head against his back.

Carly was already moving, prepared to get between Gabby and the teeth that were sure to follow.

But instead of attacking, the dog stood perfectly still, as if the stroking of little hands relaxed him. His long, skinny tail began a slow, tentative side-to-side movement.

Gabby straightened, her grin wide. "He's beautiful. Does he have a name? Can I take him for a walk? Do you think he'll like Mr. Whiskers? Can I dress him in clothes?"

Michelle laughed. "Impressive, kid. That's a list. Let's see. He doesn't have a name. I've been thinking of Chance."

"I like that," Gabby told her. She turned to the dog. "Hi, Chance. I'm Gabby. We're going to be best friends."

The tail wagged again.

"Chance needs to get used to his surroundings," Carly told her daughter. "He got in some trouble and that's why he's so skinny. He needs to get his strength back before he can play a lot. But I was thinking maybe we could go to the pet store this afternoon and buy him some food and a bed and stuff."

Gabby clapped her hands together. "Could we? Oh, yes, we'll get you good toys, Chance. Then you can get better and we'll play together."

"I'm sure he'd like that," Michelle told her. She looked up at Carly. "Thank you. For everything. I knew you'd take care of the inn."

Carly throat tightened. "I'm happy to help. Just ask for anything."

Michelle laughed. "I think I already have."

The meeting room was plain, with a couple of windows and chairs in rows. Michelle figured there were about twenty guys there. She was the only woman, but then she was also the only person who had brought a dog.

One guy talked about the nightmares he had and how he wasn't sleeping. Most of the group nodded, as if they, too, had the same problem. Another guy said that Ryan had been arrested for stealing a car. There were murmurs of sympathy. Michelle had no idea who Ryan was but guessed she wouldn't be meeting him anytime soon.

No one paid any attention to her, which was how she preferred things. She sat in the back, Chance stretching out next to her on the worn carpet. When the hour ended, the leader reminded them it was smarter to ask for help than to wait until there wasn't a choice.

Everyone stood. She half expected a group prayer, but they simply started walking toward the door, a few stopping to talk to each other. Michelle had nearly made it to freedom, when the leader tapped her on the shoulder.

"You're new," he said.

She nodded.

"We meet every day. You're welcome here."

"Thank you."

And that was it.

She walked to the parking lot feeling both relieved and maybe a little better. She was taking steps to heal. The process would be slow, but she would get there.

Her good mood lasted until she saw Jared leaning against her truck.

"What are you doing here?" she asked, angry more because she was embarrassed than because he'd done anything wrong.

"Loitering. How was the meeting?"

"Fine."

"You talk?"

"No."

He grinned. "You will."

"You think you're so smart."

"You're not my first rodeo."

Great. Because she wanted to be reminded she was nothing more than a project.

She opened her mouth to tell him to get the hell out of her life only to realize she was petting Chance on the head and he was letting her. She glanced down to find the dog leaning against her as she stroked his head and ears.

"Well, look at you," she said.

He looked up at her. Maybe it was her imagination, but she would swear his doggie eyes held something like hope.

She wished there was a way to tell him he could believe in her. That she would never betray him or hurt him. But he would have to learn that over time.

She turned her attention back to Jared. "You probably expect me to thank you."

He chuckled. "Not today, but sure. Eventually you will. You'll embarrass us both with your gratitude."

She hated the sound of that. "Don't expect me to sleep with you because of all this."

The chuckle turned to a laugh. "You're not ready," he said, pushing off her truck and straightening.

Not ready? What did that mean? And why did he get to say?

Before she could ask, he patted Chance and said, "I have a charter. I'll see you later."

She was left in the parking lot, watching him drive away, feeling as tongue-tied as she had back in high school.

"Men are stupid," Michelle muttered.

Chance looked at her, his eyebrows raised.

"Not you," she added.

His tail wagged.

Thirty-One

"Thanks for this," Carly said as Sam pulled into the pet-store parking lot.

"You're going to need a big, strong guy to help you carry everything," he said, catching Gabby's attention in the rearview mirror. "Isn't that right?"

Gabby giggled. "Uh-huh. We're going to get Chance the biggest bag of dog food they have. So he won't worry about being hungry anymore."

Sam had come by just as Carly and Gabby had been getting ready to leave. He'd offered to go with them and they'd both quickly accepted. Now, as Sam helped her daughter out of the truck, it occurred to her that she shouldn't have let Gabby meet him so quickly. If things didn't work out, Gabby could be hurt. She would have to make sure her daughter understood Sam was a friend and might not be much more than that ever.

Life was easier when it was man-free, she thought, following them into the pet store. *Note to self,* she thought humorously. *Now that you've started dating, stop.*

Sam grabbed a cart and they headed for the dog department. They stopped first at the beds. Gabby picked one that was red plaid with a soft pillow inside.

"I like the purple better," Gabby said as Sam angled it into the cart. "But Chance is a boy and sometimes boys don't like purple."

"That's true. But we like red."

They bought a second bed for Michelle's office at the inn, dog shampoo, flea treatment, bowls and the biggest bag of dog food Carly had ever seen. Nail clippers and a soft brush were added to the cart. Gabby found peanut-butter-flavored dog cookies and insisted they get some.

"Even dogs need cookies," she told her mother.

"If you say so."

They lingered over the toys. Gabby chose balls and a tugging rope and bone that was supposed to be good for a dog's teeth. Sam added a pooper-scooper, which made Gabby giggle.

When they'd purchased everything and loaded the car, Sam suggested they walk by the marina and have ice cream.

After getting their cones, they walked along the boardwalk. The clouds had come in, but there wasn't any rain and the air was warm. Tourists strolled, rode bikes and crowded the tour boats heading out onto the water.

"Still like it around here?" she asked.

"I do. It's a nice little town."

"Where did you grow up?"

"A small town you never heard of in Virginia. So I know the drill. Everybody keeps track of everybody else's business. Memories are long and if you screw up as a kid, it can haunt you for the rest of your life."

She glanced at him, then away, thinking about Ellen

and how very much she wanted to make sure Carly kept on paying for those mistakes.

"What?" he asked, keeping his voice low. Gabby was out in front of them, skipping along and occasionally hanging over the railing to stare down at the cranes on the rocks.

"You're right," she said. "It's just like that. We do get the tourists in every summer as a distraction, which helps. But for us locals…"

"A few things still making trouble?" he asked.

"Lately, yes." She glanced at him, wondering if she should tell him the truth. She probably should. In his line of work, he was bound to hear rumors.

"I had a reputation for being wild in high school," she admitted, speaking quietly so Gabby wouldn't hear. "Specifically my senior year. My mom left and my dad didn't much care what I did. I partied and got a reputation for sleeping around. I thought if I gave those guys what they wanted that I would feel special. Taken care of. It didn't work, of course."

She stopped talking and pressed her lips together. "The irony is I was a tease. I didn't have sex with anyone until I met the guy I married. But that's just details. The other story is more interesting to anyone."

"I'm sorry you're still hearing about it," Sam told her. "Scandal dies hard."

"Tell me about it. Since Gabby was born, you're the first guy I've dated. The first guy I've…" She cleared her throat. "You know."

He grinned. "I remember the 'you know.' I'm very fond of the 'you know.'"

She laughed. "I'd nearly forgotten I liked it, too." Her smile faded. "It's been years, but there are people around here who refuse to forget."

He put his arm around her. "Don't let them get to you, Carly. Their opinions don't matter."

They did when they could get her fired, she thought, remembering Ellen's threats. But she wasn't going to go into that with Sam.

Gabby rejoined them. When they'd finished their cones, they went back to the pet-store parking lot and drove to the inn. She directed him to drive around back so they could load everything into Michelle's office.

"Looks like you've got company," Sam said, pointing to the huge motor home parked behind the building.

Carly stared at it, confused. "Usually guests warn me when they're bringing a motor home. They want to make sure there's somewhere to park it."

As she watched, the side door opened and a tall man stepped out. He was in his fifties, fit, with dark hair and familiar eyes. When he reached the ground, he turned and helped out a petite blonde woman.

Gabby sucked in a breath. "Grandma?" she whispered.

Carly couldn't believe it. After all this time her mother and Michelle's father had returned to Blackberry Island.

Gabby stood next to Carly. It seemed that neither of them knew what to do, Carly thought. She and her mother talked maybe once a year. She never spoke to Frank. There had been no hint of their plans and now they were here.

Lana Sanderson smiled at her daughter and granddaughter. "You look surprised. Don't I get a hug?"

Gabby glanced up at her, as if looking for guidance. Carly drew in a breath and nodded. "Sure, Mom."

Carly hugged her briefly, then stepped back. Gabby hesitated before moving forward.

"Hello, dear," Lana said, lightly touching her granddaughter's hair. "You're so pretty. Just like your mom was at your age. I've missed you."

Carly wanted to ask if her mother had missed them, why did she never call or visit? Why did the holidays go by with little more than a postcard from some exotic location to celebrate the season?

Gabby returned to Carly's side and took her hand. Frank nodded at them both.

"Good to see you girls. How are things here at the inn?"

"We're busy."

Carly thought about Michelle's fragile state and wondered how she would react to the unexpected arrival.

Lana looked past her to Sam. "I don't believe we've met. I'm Carly's mother."

"Sam," he said, shifting the dog bed to the other arm and shaking hands with Lana and Frank. "A friend of Carly's."

And hey, Michelle's ex-husband, but why get into that?

Sam stepped back. "I'll, ah, put this in Michelle's office, then unload the truck."

"Good idea," Carly said, thinking escape sounded like a great idea. Too bad she couldn't.

He nodded and touched her shoulder. "You know how to get in touch with me if you need anything, right?"

"I promise." She sighed and lowered her voice. "Brace yourself. I mean that in a scary stalker way."

"I can handle it."

Sam ruffled Gabby's hair, then walked back around the inn. As Carly watched him go, she told herself at least she had something to look forward to. That she would get through the next few days and then her mother would be gone. Having Sam as a reward would certainly help.

* * *

Michelle arrived back at the inn to find Carly pacing back and forth on the front porch. She parked, then held the door open for Chance. He jumped down easily and stayed next to her as she walked toward the building.

Carly turned and Michelle saw the panic in her eyes.

"What happened?" Michelle demanded, not sure how much she could handle.

"Nobody's dead," Carly said. She hesitated, then swore. "I just don't understand. Don't they have a damn phone? Sure, they couldn't call you, but what about me? I'm here all the time. I'm easy to reach. But did they call? Of course not."

Michelle carefully regulated her breathing. She knew she was not at her best and any unexpected hiccup would be enough to put her back in danger.

"Okay," she said slowly. "Tell me."

"Your dad is here. Along with my mother. They showed up in a motor home." She twisted her hands together. "I don't get it. I talk to my mother maybe twice a year. It's not like we're close. She's met Gabby once. My daughter knows her grandmother from pictures. I've never spoken to your dad. And yet here they are. In the flesh."

Carly's near-hysteria was oddly calming, Michelle thought as she made her way up the stairs.

"It's okay," she told Carly. "We'll get through this."

"How do you figure? They're *here*."

Michelle probed her feelings. She knew she wasn't at her best, but somehow this new crisis wasn't so bad. Maybe because it wasn't important to her. Yes, her long-lost father had returned after eleven or twelve years. Yes, she had questions and even anger. But compared to what she'd been through, this was nothing.

"They're here and then they'll leave," she said, pleased by her sense of tranquility. By the knowledge that they couldn't touch her. Not where it mattered. Maybe that was the result of emotionally shutting down, but that was okay, too. She could resurrect her feelings after they were gone.

"How can you be so calm?" Carly demanded. "This is a nightmare."

"Now who's the drama queen?"

Carly stared at her. "You're really not upset."

"I'm really not. Probably because I don't have anything to spare. He's here. I'll deal. You have more to worry about."

"Gabby," Carly said with a sigh. "I hope my mom doesn't hurt her."

"You'll be there. You'll get her through whatever happens." Michelle patted Chance. "We both will."

Carly nodded, some of the panic fading from her eyes. "I like the new you."

"I'm withholding judgment, but I see potential."

Carly hesitated, then said, "Don't take this wrong."

She moved forward and wrapped her arms around Michelle.

Michelle stayed very still, accepting the embrace and the support that went with it. Slowly, carefully, she hugged Carly back, letting herself remember what it had been like when they'd been best friends. Just the two of them against the world.

Michelle walked into her office to find a stack of dog supplies in one corner, with a bed draped on top. A second bed lay by her desk.

She took Chance off his leash. He checked out the water dish—a cheerful yellow one with paw prints on the front—then walked over to the bed. His brow furrowed slightly as he glanced from it to her and back.

She smiled and crouched down, then patted the bed.

"Come on, Chance. This is for you."

He put one paw on the bed, then another. After turning around a couple of times, he collapsed with a sigh. She stroked his back and was rewarded with a thump of his tail.

"See," she told him. "This is how your life is going to be."

The issue of keeping him had not been a question, she realized. From the second Jared had shown her the skinny dog, she'd accepted him in her life. They were going to heal each other, she decided. The rescue agency had been in touch the morning before, making sure all was going well. She'd been given email access to the records they had on him, including a report from their veterinarian. According to the vet, Chance was about two years old, with no obvious health problems, except for those from his abuse.

She glanced at the time. He'd had a decent-size breakfast, but nothing since then. She got him a dog cookie from the ones Carly had left. His dark eyes perked up.

"Come here," she said, motioning for him to get out of the bed.

He stood and walked to stand in front of her.

"Chance, sit."

He sat.

She laughed. "Good boy. Look at you. We're going to have to figure out what else you can do."

She handed him the cookie. He took it gently and carried it back to his bed where he settled down, then chomped the cookie into dust and swallowed it. Contentment relaxed his doggie face as he gazed at her.

"You're welcome," she told him.

"That's not much of a dog."

The voice was familiar. There had been a time when the man behind the voice had been her world. Or at least the anchor in a swirling storm that was Brenda. She turned in her chair to study her father as he walked into her office.

"He's a rescue. I've only had him a few days. He'll get better."

She took in the graying hair, the lines around her father's eyes and mouth. He was a little thinner, a little older, but not much else had changed. If she had to point out a difference, she would say he looked happy. "Hello, Dad."

"Michelle." He hesitated, as if not sure if he should do something else, then settled in the chair by her desk. "I called a couple of times to tell you we were coming. I couldn't reach you."

She thought about the calls she'd ignored, followed by the breakdown that had included her destroying her phone. "I've been a little out of touch."

He studied her. "How are you?"

There was concern in the question. She'd only been sober and relatively sane for a couple of days. Her clothes were still too big, her skin pale. She looked like what she was—someone holding on by a thread.

"Better. Seriously, this is an improvement."

He swore softly. "Why didn't you call me, baby girl? I would have been here."

The familiar "baby girl" wormed through her defenses, making her feel small again. Like when she'd been little and had huddled in her bed, the covers pulled over her head as she tried desperately to shut out her parents' night fights.

She drew in a breath and looked at Chance. The sight of the sleeping dog centered her. She returned her attention to her father.

"You were gone. You left me, Dad. You walked out on me with no warning. It's been over a decade without a word. Why would I call you now?"

Her father shifted in his seat. "I know it looks bad, baby girl."

"I doesn't just look bad. It *is* bad."

"I know. It was so many things. Your mother. I never should have married her. But she was pregnant and I'd been raised to be responsible. You were the only good thing to come out of that marriage."

"I wasn't good enough to make you stay."

His expression turned pleading. "I waited until you were seventeen. I wanted you to be old enough to handle yourself. To take care of things." He leaned toward her. "I wanted to come back, but I knew Brenda would punish you if I did. So I stayed away, thinking when you were a little older, I'd swing by. But you left for the army and I didn't know how to get in touch with you."

It was all crap, she thought incredulously. Justifications. The man she'd loved and trusted, depended upon, had no real reason for what he'd done. He'd chosen his mistress over his child. For all his proclamations of love, he was more like her mother than she found comfortable.

The edges of the room didn't seem as focused. A sharp longing for oblivion ripped through her, making her ache for just a sip of vodka. One swallow. That's all she needed.

She grabbed the bottle of water on her desk and drank it instead. The cool liquid did nothing to make her feel better. The trembling began inside. It radiated out and she knew she only had a few minutes until she would be shaking all over.

"How long are you staying?" she asked.

"A couple of days. Lana's excited to see Carly and Gabby."

"I'll bet," she murmured, wondering if he would hear the sarcasm or accept the words at face value.

She drew herself up straighter in the chair, then sucked in a breath. "Dad, I have some work I need to do. Can we talk later?"

"Ah, sure." He gave her a quick smile. "I'll go round up Lana and we can find a place to have lunch. The island's grown while I've been gone."

She nodded, suddenly weary to the bone.

After her father had gone, she leaned back in her chair and closed her eyes. Slowly, too slowly, the need to drink faded and she was left with a hollow sensation. For all her Zen calm with Carly, she didn't have the skills to cope with this invasion. She had a feeling that telling her father and Lana to go away wouldn't solve the problem, which meant she needed help from another direction.

She got up and called to Chance, who immediately hurried to her side. They walked toward the registration desk, his nails clicking on the floor.

She found Carly at the computer, viciously jabbing on the keys.

"They went to lunch," Carly told her. "They don't want a room. That's something, I suppose. They have a reservation at the camping site at the north end of the island. I told them we were busy through the holiday, so I think we get a couple of days' reprieve." She paused. "You okay?"

"Less okay than I would like. You're right. Having them back is something to get upset about."

"This is one time I don't want to be right."

Michelle felt Chance standing next to her. When the dog leaned in slightly, she rubbed the top of his head. His presence comforted her.

"Thanks for getting all those supplies. I'll write you a check for the amount."

Carly nodded. "No problem. It was fun. Gabby's very excited to have both a dog and a cat at the inn."

"The pooper-scooper was a nice touch."

"Sam's idea."

Michelle raised her eyebrows. "You back together?"

"We're taking it slow. Is that okay?"

"I think taking it slow makes sense."

Carly wrinkled her nose. "You know what I mean. Does it bother you?"

Michelle thought about everything going on right now. "No," she said. "Honestly, it doesn't. Go for it. He's a pretty decent guy."

"I hope so."

A loud hissing sound interrupted them. Michelle turned to find Mr. Whiskers had strolled into the room. He stood about ten feet from Chance, his back arched, tail puffy and standing straight.

The hiss was impressive, Michelle thought, startled by the volume and intensity. More cobra than cat.

Apparently Chance thought so, too. He whimpered, then slid behind Michelle and began to tremble.

Mr. Whiskers stared at the dog for several more seconds, then slowly relaxed. His status as the superior pet established, he turned and walked to the far end of the room, jumped up onto the sunny windowsill and began grooming.

Michelle dropped to her knees and took Chance's face in her hands. "You have to stand up for yourself, big guy.

You outweigh that cat by a good forty pounds. Once we get some muscle on you, it will be more. You could take him. I'm sure of it."

Chance didn't look convinced.

"Maybe if you work on his sense of self," Carly offered.

Michelle laughed. "I'm open to suggestions on that one. Any ideas on improving doggie confidence?"

"Not really. I'm still trying to fix myself."

"Right there with you on that one." She hugged the dog. "Looks like you're going to have to figure it out yourself," she told him. "But whatever happens, I'll be here, taking care of you."

Thirty-Two

The Fourth of July dawned with clear skies and warm temperatures. Michelle and Chance arrived at the inn before seven and did a quick check of how things were going in the restaurant.

The smell of ribs and simmering barbecue beans hit her as they entered. The delicious scent mingled with the decadent aroma of chocolate-chip cookies being taken directly from the oven.

"Get that dog out of my kitchen," Helen said when she spotted them coming through the door.

Michelle paused. "Chance, sit."

The dog looked at her with worried eyes, but planted his butt right by the back door.

"Stay."

He whined, but didn't move.

"Impressive," Michelle murmured. Once the summer madness ended, she was going to talk to the dog trainer at the pet store about finding out what Chance could do. Maybe an obedience class or even agility would help his confidence. God knew she could use the distraction, as well.

She hadn't had a drink in ten days. She was finally sleeping reasonably well and eating more. Her clothes were hanging a little less loosely and she thought maybe her face didn't look so gaunt.

She knew she was still having the nightmares and screaming at night. For the most part Chance slept in his bed, but every now and then she woke up to find him pressing against her, his warm body giving comfort.

The best news of all was that she hadn't had to deal with her father or Lana since their arrival, but she was sure that reprieve would end sooner rather than later.

"You're coming to check on me?" Helen sounded more amused than concerned.

"Making sure you have what you need for today."

Instead of having a traditional lunch, they were offering lunches-to-go for their guests and anyone else who preordered. Picnic boxes and baskets were stacked on tables, waiting to be filled.

"I have it handled. Cammie's staying straight through until one, when we're closing. There were seven more orders for picnic lunches on the answering machine this morning. I'm making up a half-dozen extras for the idiots who can't figure out that preordering means *pre* and *order*."

Michelle grinned. "There's one in every crowd."

Helen looked past her to Chance. "How's he doing?"

"Better."

"I saved him a little something."

She handed Michelle a bowl with a couple of big rib bones. There was still meat on them, although not any sauce.

"Thank you." Michelle took the bowl. "I thought you were a cat person."

"I am, but he seems to be a decent sort of dog. I respect that." Her eyebrows drew together. "Just keep him out of my kitchen. Even Mr. Whiskers isn't allowed in here."

"Yes, ma'am."

Helen beamed. "You're a good girl, Michelle."

"I'm trying."

She went back to her office, Chance trailing along beside her. Once she'd booted her computer and checked to see if there were any messages, she took the dog out to the front lawn and handed him a bone.

He sniffed it first, then took it gently and carried it to a spot of sun. He collapsed on the grass with a contented sigh and started chewing.

"Chance!"

Gabby shot out the front door and went running toward the dog. Michelle started to intercept her, not sure how the once-starving dog would react to what could be seen as an attack while he was eating.

"Gabby, wait."

But she was too late. The ten-year-old flung herself at the dog. Chance released his bone and seemed to brace for impact. Gabby wrapped both her arms around the dog and they rolled together a couple of feet. Chance's tail thumped on the grass.

Michelle exhaled, relief causing her to sink to the grass. "I'm too old for this kind of stress," she muttered.

She watched the girl and the dog play, then Chance settled down with his bone, Gabby leaning against him, reading her latest book.

Michelle told herself to get to work, but she couldn't seem to move. Sitting here in the sun felt too good. A few minutes later, a shadow moved across her. She opened her eyes and saw Pauline standing beside her.

"You look relaxed," the other woman said. "And better."

"Thanks."

Pauline sank onto the grass. "Want to tell me about it?"

"Don't you ever go off duty?"

She grinned. "Occupational hazard. Technically, you can tell me to go pound sand."

"I'd probably put it another way."

Pauline laughed. "Which is why I like you. Now tell the good therapist what's going on."

Michelle stretched out her legs in front of her. "I'm not drinking. I'm going to meetings every day. The kind for vets, not AA."

"Whatever works."

"I'm still having trouble sleeping, but it's getting better." She pointed to Chance. "He helps."

"I'm sure he does." Pauline studied her. "And?"

"My dad's back in town. I haven't seen him since I was seventeen." She did a brief recap of the soap opera that was her life. "He has excuses, but no real reasons for what he did."

"People have trouble admitting when they act for purely selfish reasons. Telling the truth about something like that forces them to redefine their sense of self. So they make up a story. We all do it. Tell stories to explain the unexplainable. To get by. Sometimes the stories even help us survive that which would otherwise destroy us."

Michelle tore off a few pieces of grass. "You mean like Carly blaming me for her mother abandoning her to an alcoholic father?"

"Something like that. Sure."

"And me hating Carly for being here, while I was in the army, even though I volunteered."

Pauline nodded.

Michelle sat with the information for a few minutes, watching her dog gnaw on his bone and the girl who used him as a backrest.

Whatever mistakes Carly had made, she'd gotten it right with Gabby. Michelle didn't think she would have had either the character or the strength to raise a kid on her own. She was barely handling a dog.

"I don't want to let him back in my life," she murmured. "I want him to go away. Is that bad?"

Pauline touched her arm. "The idea that we have to unconditionally love our parents, no matter what they do to us, is a crock of shit." She grinned. "So to speak."

"Swearing. Good for you."

"You're not a patient. I get to be myself."

"I think I like you more now."

"I'm glad." The humor faded. "The last thing you need right now is your father opening old wounds. I agree with you. Get through the visit and then figure it out later."

"That's okay?"

"Are you asking my permission or do you want to know if that's a healthy decision?"

"Both."

"Go for it." Pauline stood and brushed off her jeans. "We have a session today. Seth and I decided anyone willing to give up their Fourth of July holiday to work on their marriage must be serious."

"Good luck."

"Thanks."

By eleven that morning, most of their guests had departed for holiday festivities. Michelle was well enough to add room cleaning to her list of activities. She finished the two she'd been assigned and headed back downstairs.

Carly was working the front desk, Chance tucked up under the bottom of the cabinet.

"How's it going?" she asked.

Carly shrugged. "Fine. They're at it earlier than usual."

Michelle glanced in the direction she pointed and saw their therapy couples out on the lawn, blindfolds in place. The trust exercise, she thought.

"Where's Gabby?"

"She's already down at the beach with friends."

"You want to join her?"

"No. I can work longer." Carly's nose wrinkled. "They're coming with us."

"The parents?"

"Yes. I never realized it before, but my mother is a lot like Brenda. Everything is about her. She came by last night and I asked her why she'd left. She completely changed the subject and when I pushed, she said some of it was about me. Implying it was my fault she ran off with the man married to her supposed best friend."

Michelle stared at her. "She didn't."

"There was more. I don't care."

Michelle knew that wasn't true. "You care a lot."

"Because I'm stupid. I want…" Carly shook her head slowly. "You know what? I don't want to deal with her. I want my daughter to have a good relationship with her grandmother, but I don't want my mom around very much. I don't like her. Is that awful?"

"No. It's normal. What happened to a good old-fashioned apology? All they have to do is say, 'Hey, we were selfish weasels. We're sorry.' But that's too much for them."

Carly nodded.

Michelle shook her head. "They'll be gone soon. Hang on to that."

"What? No hope for resolution?"

"Not every ending is tidy. I'm sober. You're a hell of a mother. That's enough of a win for me."

Carly's breath caught and tears filled her eyes.

"What?" Michelle demanded. She didn't think she'd said anything wrong.

"That was so nice," Carly whispered, her voice thick with emotion.

"Hell," Michelle muttered. "You are a good mother. And a good friend."

"You are, too."

"I'm a shitty friend, but I'm trying."

This time Michelle was the one to step forward, to hold out her arms. To risk first.

They embraced for several seconds, then stepped back.

Carly wiped the moisture from her cheeks. "Okay, new plan. We'll hang together until the folks leave. A united front. The next time they invade, we'll be braced."

"We'll lock them in the basement until they apologize."

Carly grinned. "We don't have a basement."

"Oh, right. Well, we're slow in the winter. We can build one."

They both laughed.

"Is Sam joining you at the beach?" Michelle asked.

"He's working."

"Too bad. He would enjoy the evening and be a good buffer."

"Maybe next time," Carly said. "When he's not the new guy."

Michelle nodded. "I'm going to head home for a

couple of hours, see if I can get some sleep." She would be on until the last guest arrived back, which could be after midnight. "I'll be back about four."

"I'll be here."

She called for Chance. The dog walked beside her to the truck, then jumped in the front passenger side and waited while she put the seat belt around him. She wasn't sure the harness would hold him, but figured he was safer that way. She flipped the switch to disable the air bag, then shut the door and walked to her own side.

As she started the engine, she felt more at ease than she had since the unexpected arrival of her father. Not that anything had changed, but now there was a plan. And she wasn't alone. The not being alone felt best of all.

One demon down, she thought. A dozen or so to go.

Michelle watched the sky from her position at the front desk of the inn. Once the last of twilight faded, she called for Chance and retreated to her office.

She knew what was coming. The fireworks display would last about ten minutes, but it would feel a lot longer for both of them. She shut the door. Earlier that evening she found an internet radio station playing rock music and now turned up the speakers. The sound would help.

Then she dropped to her knees and crawled under her desk, prepared to wait it out.

Chance look confused, but obligingly settled in beside her. She put her arm around him and waited.

A few minutes later, she heard the first of the explosions. While most people enjoyed the noise and the bursts of colorful lights in the sky, for her they were too close to recent reality.

"It's okay," she said, her voice nearly a chant. "Just

a few minutes and it will be done. We're not at war. No one will get hurt. It's fine. I'm fine."

Chance leaned against her, more seeming to comfort than because he was afraid. She felt herself starting to shake and didn't know what to do to stop it. Maybe this was just something she had to get through.

She wrapped both arms around the dog and hung on, burying her face in his shoulder. After a second, she felt something warm and wet on the side of her neck. She looked up and he swiped his tongue along her cheek.

Despite the fear and her desire for the fireworks to be over, she started to laugh.

"We've been sleeping together for over a week and you're just kissing me now? How like a guy."

Thirty-Three

Carly raised herself on tiptoe to get to the very top of the wall. It was Friday, and relatively quiet at the inn. The holiday crowd and therapy couples had left. The weekend guests had yet to arrive. The wall itself wasn't huge. She'd already put on a coat of primer, which had dried. The paint went on smoothly. She'd cut in by the ceiling and baseboards so the last bit with the roller would go quickly.

She'd just dipped the roller into the pan when Michelle walked up.

"What the hell are you doing?"

Carly didn't bother looking at her. "We need to work on your people skills."

"Fine. Hi. How are you? What the hell are you doing?"

Carly grinned. "Much better. I'm painting."

"I can see that."

"Then why did you ask?"

She felt more than saw Michelle stiffen. "You're annoying, you know that?"

"I think of myself as an easygoing person with a lot

of charm, but okay. Maybe I can be annoying. What specifically is bothering you?"

"There's a list," Michelle muttered. "Specifically, to quote you, why are you painting now? It's eleven-thirty in the morning. We have guests arriving this afternoon. Doesn't this seem like a badly timed project?"

"You hate the mural."

"I've hated it since I got back."

Carly continued to move the roller up and down, covering every inch of the wall. "Yes, but I didn't like you before or care that you hated it. Since you've been back I've accepted I might have gone a little overboard with the daisies."

She'd been trying to put her mark on the inn, back when she'd thought she would end up owning a portion of it.

"You didn't like me before?"

"You weren't very nice and you had a lot of attitude."

"I see."

"Don't pretend to be upset. You didn't like you, either."

"Have you been talking to Seth and Pauline? You're not trying to fix me, are you?"

Carly laughed. "Fixing you is well above my pay grade."

"You got that right."

"All done." Carly stepped back to study the wall. It was as if the mural had never been there.

"You didn't have to paint it over. It looked like it took a lot of work."

"It did, but I'm not a professional. A few of the daisies looked more like aliens than flowers. This is better."

"Thanks."

"You're welcome."

Michelle helped her collect her supplies. They took them to the utility room where Carly cleaned up the brush and roller. Gabby came running in.

"Frank and Grandma Lana want to go to lunch," she said, obviously bursting with excitement. "Here. They said everyone is talking about Helen's chicken salad and they want to spend time with us."

Carly smiled back at her daughter. "That sounds like fun. I'm available, but Michelle might be busy."

Gabby turned to her.

Michelle sighed. "I'd love to."

Gabby clapped her hands together and raced back to spread the good news.

"I was giving you an out," Carly said, setting the roller upright to drain in the sink.

"I appreciate that. But I'm the one who got her not to be afraid of the cranes. I'm practically a superhero. I don't want to let my best girl down."

Carly felt the jolt all the way down to the very bottom of her heart, but she was careful not to outwardly react, despite the truth she'd just realized. She hadn't simply regained what had been lost—she'd found someone who would love her daughter fully. Anyone crossing Gabby would have to answer to Michelle. She might not look that formidable now, but Carly knew exactly how worthy an opponent her friend could be.

They left the utility room and walked toward the front of the inn.

"Would it be rude to ask when they're leaving?" Michelle's voice was innocent enough.

"Yes, and you can't."

"Fine, but I hope it's soon."

"Me, too."

They passed by the still-drying paint.

"Nice wall," Michelle murmured.

"Bitch."

"You know it."

"Ms. Sanderson?"

Michelle looked up from her desk to find a thin, older man wearing glasses and carrying a computer tablet in his hand.

"Yes." She stood. "How can I help you?"

"I'm Gerald Vaughn from the Washington State Department of Health. I need to speak with you about your restaurant."

She didn't think she'd moved at all or made a sound, but Chance came awake and surged to her side. He didn't growl or even look at the health inspector. Instead, he leaned against her leg, making his presence known.

She stroked the dog, then nodded. "What's the problem?"

"We've had several complaints about the food being served. That the plates aren't clean, there are obvious rat droppings and foods not served at their correct temperatures. I'm here to inspect the premises. I would like you to accompany me."

The charges were so outrageous, she couldn't think of what to say. For all her faults, Damaris had kept a clean kitchen. Helen was even more demanding. A doctor could do emergency surgery on the counters and not risk infection. How on earth—?

Ellen, she thought furiously. Carly had warned her about Ellen and she hadn't listened.

She forced herself to smile. "Of course, Mr. Vaughn. I'm assuming you showing up on a Saturday is part of the surprise? No one expects a health inspector to work on the weekends."

"It is." He didn't smile back.

"I don't suppose we'll get the names of the people complaining."

"No. We keep that information confidential."

"Right. That makes sense. The reason I ask is because we have a problem with someone in town. There have been some personal disagreements and I think they might be making trouble."

Mr. Vaughn didn't look impressed by her statement. She was sure that he was used to hearing a ton of excuses. "We'll go look at the kitchen," she said, coming out from behind her desk. "But let me ask you this. If we pass perfectly, if there are no violations and you're impressed, will you at least make a note of what I said?"

"Ms. Sanderson, everyone has violations. Some are fairly minor, but no kitchen is perfect."

"As long as you're keeping an open mind."

She led him down the hall, Chance at her side. As they passed the entryway, she saw Ellen speaking with Carly. Carly looked distressed. Ellen looked over and winked.

Michelle remembered the terms of her supplemental-loan paperwork. If there were any violations against the inn, she was at risk of having the bank take over the property.

She felt her temper rise. No! This wasn't right. One person couldn't have that much control over her business, could they?

Nothing bad was going to happen, she promised herself. She hadn't come this far to lose everything. As soon as Mr. Vaughn finished his inspection, she would start a little digging of her own.

They walked into the kitchen where Helen was in the process of preparing for lunch. Chance stopped in his usual spot, just outside the door, lay down and prepared to wait.

"Helen, this is Mr. Vaughn from the Washington State Department of Health. There have been some complaints about the restaurant. Something about cleanliness and food temperature."

Michelle wasn't going to mention the rats. Helen wasn't a young woman and she didn't want shock causing a seizure of some kind.

Helen stared at the health inspector. She bristled visibly, but only said, "I'm unprepared for your visit, Mr. Vaughn, which is apparently how you planned it. Very well. Feel free to do what you must."

While the inspector put on gloves, Helen went back to dicing cooked chicken for her famous sandwiches. She looked cool and in control, which was damned impressive.

The next forty-five minutes passed painfully slowly. Michelle went into the hallway and sat on the floor next to Chance. He watched the inspector, as if prepared to defend her against the man.

Mr. Vaughn opened cupboards, used some kind of temperature gauge on food in the refrigerator and on the stove. He looked at the dishwasher, in the cupboards, checked their license and storage rooms. Finally he stripped off his gloves.

Michelle scrambled to her feet and rejoined him. "Well?"

"Impressive," Mr. Vaughn said, looking chagrined. "I've never seen a kitchen this clean before. At worst, everything is to state requirements, and in nearly every area, you exceed them. The complaint was received only a few days ago, and from what I can tell, these practices have been in place for some time."

Michelle wanted to stick out her tongue and remind the man she'd already told him this wasn't a legitimate complaint but didn't think that would be helpful.

"So we passed?"

"Yes, and I'll note in the records that this might have been some kind of nuisance call. We at the Department of Health take our work very seriously. People's health is at stake. We can't afford to have our limited resources wasted with this sort of prank."

Michelle smiled. "I think I know who did it. I'm going to have a little talk with her."

She shook hands with Mr. Vaughn, then made her way back to the front of the inn.

Ellen was still there, sitting on the sofa. She looked toward Michelle as she entered. Apparently Michelle's satisfaction showed on her face, because there wasn't any smiling and winking now.

Michelle walked up to Ellen.

"Hey," she said. "Thanks for calling in the complaint. Now the Department of Health loves us and thinks you're an idiot. I kind of like that."

Ellen stood, her blue eyes sharp with annoyance. "Be careful, Michelle. You don't want me against you."

"You already are. I nearly bought the whole 'let's be friends' thing. You're good—I'll give you credit for that. I don't know how much of this game is about what happened in high school and how much of it is you think you can get this prime waterfront property for cheap. Let me address both points."

She found it difficult not to smile. Yelling at people was fun.

"On the high-school front. Grow up. It was years ago. Get a life and move on. As to the property, that so isn't going to happen. I'm current with my loan. We're doing better than expected, so I can pay off even more of the principle. Maybe consolidate the loans. Probably not with your bank, though."

"There are other considerations," Ellen snarled.

"Those silly rules? I have it on good authority you can't do that."

"Says who?"

"Says me."

Ellen rolled her eyes. "Seriously, Michelle, don't get involved in things you don't understand."

"Like banking? Rules of disclosure and loan modification? You're right. I should stay out of that. But I think it's time I found a good lawyer to go over everything. Carly's in deep with the island's Women of Business association. At least one of them should be able to give me a recommendation. Maybe somebody tight with your bank's board."

"That's not going to change anything," Ellen told her, but Michelle had a feeling the other woman was more nervous than she let on.

"You should probably go now," Michelle said.

Ellen turned on her heel and left.

Michelle watched her go, then reached down to pat Chance. "We're a very weird species."

He leaned his head against her thigh, as if to say he wasn't one to judge.

Carly dug into the warm, rich soil of the inn's garden. With beautiful flowers came weeds, she thought, pulling one out by the roots and tossing it onto the growing pile on the lawn. Perhaps gardening could be a metaphor for life, she thought happily. Do a little digging and get rid of everything that's bothering you.

Chance lay next to her, stretched out on the grass. The

sun was warm, the morning quiet. It was going to be a good day.

"Carly!"

The call came from the other side of the inn, but the voice was distinctive. So much for a good day, Carly thought, sitting back on her heels and watching her mother approach.

So far they'd talked about everything unimportant. The weather, shopping, her mother and Frank's travel plans for the rest of the year. But except for Carly's attempt to find out what Lana had been thinking when she'd left, they'd avoided anything too personal.

Probably better that way, Carly told herself. Some things couldn't be fixed.

Her mother dropped to the grass beside her and patted Chance. "We're all packed up and ready to go. Frank's saying goodbye to Michelle right now. If it's all right with you, we'll swing by Gabby's day camp on the way out of town."

"Sure," Carly said, hoping her relief at the news didn't show. "I'll call them and let them know it's okay for you to see her."

"Thanks." Her mother sighed. "This has been wonderful. Reconnecting like this. Frank and I should have come back years ago. Of course, there would have been problems with Brenda. She's not one to forgive and forget."

"You two were so close," Carly said. "Did you miss her when you left?"

Lana shrugged. "I suppose. We were friends. Brenda was difficult, though. She only thought about herself. She never worried about hurting anyone around her. I was always the sensitive one, worrying about others." Lana smiled.

Yes, Carly thought. Abandoning one's only child to run off with a lover showed tremendous worry. "Yes, there was deep concern."

"I'm glad we got everything straightened out."

So much for sarcasm, Carly thought, not sure whether to laugh or surrender to the madness.

Lana leaned in and kissed her cheek. "We were thinking of coming back for Thanksgiving."

"Lucky us."

"I'll miss you," her mother said, hugging her. "Be good."

"The best."

Then Lana was gone.

Carly attacked a few more weeds, pulling them out by the roots, finding the task even more satisfying than before. She waited for a sense of regret or loss, but there was only the knowledge that she had everything she needed already. A relationship with her mom would be nice, but not necessary.

She reached the end of the bed and was about to head to the next one when a familiar car from the sheriff's office pulled in front of the inn.

Sam.

Carly turned to watch him approach, taking in the long, easy stride, the broad shoulders and sexy grace. She remembered that body from their lone but very powerful sexual encounter. Maybe she'd been a bit too hasty saying they should take things slowly. Maybe she could get a sitter for Gabby and have a fun-filled evening with the man in his new apartment. You know, take things to the next level.

"Hi," she called, shifting into a sitting position and shading her eyes against the sun.

"Carly."

Sam walked over, greeted Chance, then plopped down across from her on the grass.

"How's it going?" she asked. "You must be relieved the big holiday week is over. Now you can have it relatively easy until Labor Day."

"There's no easy with tourists in town." He dropped his hat to the grass and ran his hands through his hair. "I saw your folks pulling out."

"Yes, they're leaving."

"Are you okay with that?"

"Better than okay."

He grinned. "Good. I was thinking you and Gabby might want to go to the movies with me tomorrow night."

She laughed. "We just might."

"That's what I was hoping you'd say."

The movies would be fun, she thought. And later this week, she would look into the whole sitter idea and have her way with the handsome man in front of her.

The picnic tables in the park were well spaced and shaded. Evening sun drifted through the leaves and sparkled on the water. Boats bobbed in the marina. The main pier was home to benches for those who wanted to fish or just watch the activities and provided access to many of the tour boats. To the left of that was a shorter dock the intrepid used to dive into the chilly water of the Sound. Gabby and Chance strolled along the boardwalk, the dog keeping careful watch on the girl.

Michelle packed up the last of their trash and stuffed it in the picnic basket. She'd been the one to suggest the relaxing dinner away from the inn. They'd collected leftovers from Helen's kitchen and walked over.

"This is nice," Michelle said.

Carly nodded. "I agree. We should do this more. Get away from everything."

"Even Sam?"

Carly sighed. "No, but he's working."

"So I'm your second choice."

"I'm not fighting with you."

"Why not? It's fun."

Carly shook her head. "You're really twisted. You know that, right?"

"Trust me, I'm clear on my issues."

As Michelle spoke, Carly checked on her daughter's progress down the boardwalk. Gabby and Chance had stopped to talk to a couple of tourists. They were too far away for Carly to hear all the conversation, but a few words drifted to her on the marine breeze. The older couple laughed and patted Chance while Gabby danced in place. They looked up and saw Carly, then waved a greeting.

"Look at her," Carly said, letting the love for her daughter wash over her. "She's growing so fast and she's blossoming. You helped so much, showing her not to be afraid."

"That was nothing."

"It was a lot to her. She's starting to be more brave. I think watching you heal has been a big lesson."

Michelle grimaced. "I'm far from perfect."

"You don't have to be perfect to be a good parent."

"I'm not her parent."

"No. But you're a very nice second best."

Michelle laughed.

Carly glanced toward Gabby, then frowned when she saw her daughter and Chance had walked onto the shorter dock.

"Gabby," she yelled, moving toward her. Although the

wooden structure only jutted out about twenty feet into the Sound, there were no railings. Nothing to stop her daughter from falling in.

Michelle came after her. "Should she be out there? Why isn't there a railing? Can she swim?"

"No, she can't."

One of the cranes landed on the dock, just in front of Gabby. The girl stopped and stared at the bird. Even Chance was quiet beside her. Gabby stretched out her hand. The bird hopped away. Gabby laughed and turned to Chance, at the same time, taking a step back.

For Carly, it was one of those horrible moments when the inevitable became possible and time slowed. She knew exactly what was going to happen—lived it a thousand times before it really occurred.

Gabby was already too close to the edge of the dock. She shifted her weight to the foot hanging over nothing. Carly screamed, but like in a nightmare, the sound was captured and dissipated. Gabby's weight slowly shifted. Her arms came up as she tried to find her balance. Chance turned and lunged toward her. Carly ran faster, harder.

They were all too late. Gabby tipped to the side and plunged into the cold, dark water.

"No!" Carly screamed, her heart pounding against her ribs. She couldn't catch her breath but that didn't matter. Nothing mattered but her daughter.

Chance jumped right after Gabby fell, paddling toward the small head that bobbed to the surface. A distant cry for help cut through the quiet evening. Several people turned, not sure of what they'd heard.

Carly ignored it all. She ran across the boardwalk and onto the dock only to slam to a halt as she stared down at the swirling hell below.

Her heart still thundering, her lungs desperate for air, her whole body surging forward, she froze, unable to move. Water. She couldn't go in the water. Couldn't swim, couldn't defeat the numbing fear that grasped her and refused to let go.

She saw Gabby, arms flailing, crying out, coughing. Chance reached her and grabbed the back of her shirt in his teeth and started paddling for the shore some twenty feet away. But even as he dragged her, her face went underwater. Carly screamed.

There was a blur of movement beside her. Michelle dived into the water, surfacing seconds later close to Chance and Gabby. She reached for the girl.

Carly turned and ran back down the dock. She bumped into people as she went, strangers who had collected to watch. A few people were preparing to jump in. She made it onto the boardwalk, then down to the boat ramp where Michelle was headed, Gabby safely in her arms, Chance swimming beside them.

Carly felt the tears on her face, but they were nothing when compared with the shame and fear. Her daughter could have died because of her. Drowned and she couldn't have done anything to stop it.

She dropped to her knees, sobs shuddering through her. Then small, thin, wet arms grasped her so hard she couldn't breathe.

"Gabby."

"Mom, Mom, Mom."

They clung to each other, both shaking, both crying. Aware of how lucky she'd been, she hung on to her daughter and vowed she would never let go.

Thirty-Four

"I'm sorry," Carly whispered, her hands still trembling as she clutched the small glass of brandy she held.

"I'm officially bored now," Michelle told her from her place on the sofa in Carly's living room. "You've either thanked me or apologized about fifteen thousand times. Can we please change the subject?"

Carly nodded, knowing there weren't words to make herself feel better. She loved her daughter more than anyone in the world and still she'd failed her. When Gabby had needed her most, she'd been unable to be there.

"Stop it," Michelle said abruptly. "Beating yourself up over and over again isn't going to help either of you. Gabby is fine. She was barely coughing when I pulled her out, so she didn't swallow much water. She was a little wet and cold. She fell asleep in thirty seconds. She's fine."

"Because you saved her."

Michelle rolled her eyes. "You really are tiresome."

"I let her down. She could have died."

"She didn't. If I hadn't jumped in, someone else would

have. But if you're that shaken, then damn well learn to swim."

Carly thought about pointing out she was terrified of the water. That it had frightened her for as long as she could remember. But Michelle knew that already.

"You don't have to be an Olympic swimmer," her friend told her. "You just have to know how to doggie paddle around. Whether or not you learn, Gabby needs to. She lives a hundred yards from the Sound."

"You're right," Carly whispered. "About all of it."

"Being right." Michelle leaned back against the cushions and sighed. "That never gets old."

Despite everything, Carly smiled. Then she thought about getting into a pool and her stomach flipped over a couple of times. She put down the brandy glass.

Chance lay on the carpet at Michelle's feet. He'd been washed off, dried and then given an extra-big dog treat.

"He was amazing," Carly said.

"He has depths," Michelle said, rubbing his side with her bare foot. His tail thumped against the floor, but his eyes never opened. "I can't believe how far he's come in such a short period of time. I guess he was just waiting to find where he belongs."

"I'm glad you're keeping him."

"He's the best chance I have at a decent relationship with a guy."

"Maybe I should get a dog," Carly murmured. She looked at Michelle. "I—"

Michelle glared at her. "Don't."

Carly pressed her lips together. She had been about to thank her again. "I'm glad you're here," she said instead. "That you came back and we're working together." She realized Michelle was sipping brandy. "Wait a minute. Is it okay for you to drink?"

Michelle held up the glass. "I think so. I'm testing myself. My breakdown wasn't because of the alcohol. That was just a symptom of everything else that's wrong. Of course, if I start coming unglued again, we'll both know I'm wrong."

Carly thought about all they'd gone through since Michelle had come home. "If you start coming unglued again I'm having you committed."

"Nice. And I'm the one who saved your kid. Not much of a thank-you, if you ask me."

Carly laughed. "You didn't have to deal with yourself."

"I'll concede that point and little else." She put the glass down. There was still brandy in it. "I don't want any more. I think that's a good sign. You going to be okay?"

Carly wasn't sure but she nodded. "I'll be fine."

"Liar. Still, we're going to test the theory, too. I'm heading home. I'm beat."

Carly stood and walked her and Chance to the door. Michelle stepped out into the night, then stepped back and gave Carly a quick hug.

"You're a good mother and Gabby is lucky to have you."

Carly nodded. "Thanks."

She accepted the statement, even as she wondered if it could possibly be true.

Just then a white car pulled up and Sam jumped out.

"What happened? Somebody told me Gabby was hurt. Is she okay? Are you okay?"

Michelle smiled at them. "I'll let you deal with this one," she said and walked away.

Michelle drove home and climbed out of her truck. She was tired, her clothes were still damp despite some time in a dryer and she just wanted to go to sleep. While she was glad she'd been there to help Gabby, she didn't think it was the huge life-changing event Carly did.

"You would have saved her," she told the dog as she opened the passenger door and he jumped down. "Wouldn't you?"

Chance gave her a doggie grin and led the way to the house.

Michelle stepped into the kitchen and was surprised to find the lights were on and Jared was waiting for her at the table.

"I heard," he said by way of greeting. "You're a hero."

"Oh, please." She crossed to the refrigerator to check out the latest sandwich collection. "I didn't do anything that special."

"I doubt Carly would agree with you. Or Gabby, for that matter."

She patted Chance. "He's the real hero. He jumped in first, grabbed her and started swimming for shore."

"I always knew you were special," he told the dog. "Good boy."

Chance wagged his tail.

Jared walked across the kitchen, closed the refrigerator door, then drew Michelle against him. He cupped her face and slowly, deliberately, lowered his mouth to hers.

The contact was electric and seductive. The brush of his lips on hers, the heat of his touch, the feel of his long fingers touching her skin. She immediately lost all interest in food and found herself hungry only for this very special man.

She wrapped her arms around him, as much to hang on as to feel his strength. Their mouths clung to each other, then she parted and he slipped his tongue inside.

He kissed her deeply, arousing her, making her feel soft and feminine.

He straightened and stroked her hair. She stared into his eyes.

"So you finally think I'm ready?" she asked.

"No. I am."

She laughed. "You were never the problem."

He grinned, then kissed her again. His hands moved up and down her back before drifting around to the front of her waist and moving upward to cup her breasts.

Sometime later they managed to find their way to his bedroom. Chance had long since gone back into her room, maybe to give them privacy, maybe to dream about doggie heroics. Jared didn't bother with lights beyond the one in the hall. In the semidarkness, he took off her clothes, then his own and drew her to his bed.

He touched her everywhere, first with his fingers and then with his tongue. He loved her gently, carefully, mindful of her hip. When she was tense with need and shaking with arousal, he carefully kissed the very center of her, flinging her into an orgasm that shook her down to her soul. With aftershocks still rocking her world, he put on a condom, then slipped inside of her and took her for a second mind-blowing ride to paradise.

Later, still naked and breathing hard, they stretched out together. Jared continued to touch her, as if he couldn't get enough. A nice quality in a man, she thought lazily, her body drifting toward sleep.

The soft click of nails on hardwood drew her back to wakefulness. Chance walked around the room, walked over to her side of the mattress and jumped up. He settled against her bare legs, sighed once and closed his eyes.

Jared chuckled softly, shifting to give her more room. "We're going to need a bigger bed or a smaller dog."

"A bigger bed," she murmured.

"I'll get one in the morning.

Carly stepped into the pool telling herself she couldn't let fear win. Not only would having a panic attack frighten all the little kids in the class, but throwing up in the pool would really annoy the staff.

She felt ridiculous and self-conscious, the only adult in a pool full of nine- and ten-year-olds. Like the kids, she wore a life preserver around her neck, which didn't help her self-esteem at all. But she was determined. After only two days Gabby had recovered from her fall into the Sound, but Carly was still battling the memories. Every time she closed her eyes, she saw her daughter falling into the cold water, saw her going under and knew she couldn't save her.

The only solution was to grow a pair and learn to swim. Gabby was equally afraid at the thought of learning to swim but they'd agreed they were in this together. Holding hands, they stepped into the pool, shaking slightly, despite the warm water and seventy-degree air temperature. Telling herself the water was barely up to her thighs didn't make her feel any safer.

The instructor, a petite twentysomething with an easy smile and infinite patience, started the class with safety instructions. While the kids splashed around and shrieked, Carly paid careful attention, as if her life depended on her following the rules. She supposed if she wanted to avoid drowning, it did.

Every part of her screamed to get out of the water. That this was a bad idea, that she couldn't do it. She thought her heart might jump out of her chest and flop around on the side of the pool, mocking her as she died.

She wanted to run away, but she couldn't do it. Not with Gabby watching her every move.

"Make your way to the side," the instructor said.

Gabby scrambled to the side and hung on. Carly followed more slowly, every step through the water making her feel as if she was seconds from dying.

Another equally young instructor joined them in the water and demonstrated how they would hold the side and kick their legs and feet. Carly slowed her breathing, grabbed the cement and gamely pushed up her feet to try. Immediately, the sense of being out of control, of drowning, overwhelmed her.

She bit her lip so hard, she tasted blood. She had to get out of here before she sank. They were all going to die. Why couldn't anyone see that? What was wrong with them all?

Gabby's body stretched out, her legs drifted to the surface and she began to kick.

"I'm doing it, Mom! I'm doing it!"

"You are." The words came out like a croak, but Carly did her best to smile.

She wanted to give in to tears, to escape this watery hell, but knew she had to be here. Had to at least be able to swim well enough to not be so deathly afraid. She pushed off again and felt the panic. There was nothing between her and the bottom of the pool but her grip on the side and a life preserver she couldn't bring herself to trust.

The instructor moved next to her. "Just relax, Carly. It's not that hard." A hand pressed up against her stomach. "You can do it."

Carly felt herself rising a little in the water and began to kick. The hand drifted away but she stayed upright.

"You're doing it, too!" Gabby crowed.

"I am," Carly managed. The fear was still there, but determination was stronger. And so was she.

Michelle and Chance walked through town. The light drizzle seemed to bother the tourists, who huddled in stores and cafés, but Michelle liked the cool moisture after nearly a week of sunny skies. In deference to local laws and people nervous about dogs, she used a leash. Not that Chance strayed far from her side while they were out.

He'd come a long way, she thought, giving him a quick pat. He'd filled out, putting on plenty of muscle. He slept without nightmares, was getting more confident around strangers and showed an intuitive understanding of her moods. She was starting him in an obedience class in September. Once he mastered the basics, he would move into an advanced class right after. She hoped they would be learning the rules of agility training by spring.

Up ahead she saw Sam walking out of a local coffeehouse, travel mug in hand. She called his name. He looked up, saw her and grinned, then started toward her.

"Hey," he said, giving her a quick hug before squatting down and stroking Chance. "Hero dog. That's what everyone's saying, big guy." He glanced up at her. "They're talking about you, too, kid."

Michelle groaned as she stepped under an awning. "People need to find something else to occupy their time. Gabby's fine. She and Carly are taking swim classes so it will never be an issue again."

"I heard."

"Oh, that's right. You're spending a lot of time in the owner's suite, mister. Something you want to tell me?"

Sam straightened and gave her a slow, easy smile. "I like her. I like her a lot."

Michelle was pleased for him and, oddly enough, worried about Carly. "You know you have a lousy track record when it comes to women, right?"

"Yeah, which is why I'm taking it slow. I don't want to mess up." He touched her face. "You okay with me and Carly?"

"Yes, but if you hurt her, I'll take you out in ways that will make you cry like a little girl."

"Fair enough."

Thirty-Five

Michelle left her office and walked through the inn. They were having one of those brief lulls, when the guests were out and everything was quiet.

Mr. Whiskers strolled into the south-facing room and gave a plaintive meow. Chance followed. He walked toward the cat, who wound between his legs before rubbing the top of his feline head against Chance's chest. Together they strolled to the big window seat and jumped up. Chance stretched out first, then Mr. Whiskers moved next to him, half lying on the dog.

Michelle wasn't sure when the two of them had become friends, but they often spent sunny mornings together, basking. Occasionally she found Chance licking the cat, then enduring a kitty face wash of his own.

"Everyone in this place is weird," she murmured and headed toward the dining room.

"How's it going?" she asked Helen as she walked into the kitchen.

"The fruit tart is a hit. It doesn't seem to matter how many I bake, we sell out. I don't have any more time to devote to making them, so I've been teaching Cammie."

Cammie laughed. "I'm terrible with crust."

"It takes patience."

"It takes a skill I don't have, but I'll get there. I can do the rest of the tart with no problem." Cammie unfastened her apron. "I'm thinking of going to culinary school. Helen's been talking to me about it."

Michelle smiled. "That's great. There are several really good schools, some even in Seattle."

Cammie headed to the back. "See you later."

Helen waved, then turned to Michelle. "She has untapped talent, but I will hate to lose her help here. So what's new?"

"I heard from my lawyer." Michelle leaned against the counter and sighed with contentment. "I love it when a plan comes together."

"Good news, I take it?"

"The best. Ellen's bank is being investigated. There will be a formal report and we'll know the specifics when it's made public. The bottom line is the bank has made some personnel changes and some people we know are facing criminal charges."

Helen stared. "Seriously? Ellen broke the law?"

"Big-time."

"You probably won't approve of me admitting this, but I like the idea of her in prison. It comforts me."

"Me, too," Michelle told her. "I'm going to consolidate the loans into one, and if all goes well, I'll be paying them off in a few years."

"Excellent. Does Carly know?"

"Sure. I told her first."

Helen nodded approvingly. "I'm glad you two have figured out you belong together. Like sisters."

Which, Michelle thought, they sort of were.

She thought about how Helen was more than a sensible sort of person, as she called herself. She'd become the backbone of the inn.

"I'd like you to stay," she said impulsively. "Permanently. Is there any way you'd consider relocating to the island?"

As she asked the question, she realized she wasn't being impulsive at all. She and Carly had never bothered looking for Helen's replacement. Mostly because Helen fit so well.

The cook turned to the stove and stirred something on the pot. "Mr. Whiskers and I would like that very much," she said, her voice a little gruff. "I was thinking we could get a little house with a view of the water."

"That would be great. You could still bring him to the inn, if you wanted. To hang with Chance."

Helen looked at her, amusement dancing in her eyes. "A playdate for the pets?"

"Why not?"

"It sounds perfect."

Carly carried two plates to the guests and set them down. "Chicken salad on focaccia bread," she said with a smile. "This is a favorite around here. I hope you love your lunch."

"I'm sure we will," the woman said. She looked around, then lowered her voice. "My husband and I have heard so many wonderful things about the inn. We've wanted to stay here before, but you were booked. The best we could do was come for breakfast and lunch. We've been here three times already."

Carly's heart gave a little flutter. "I'm sorry there weren't any rooms. You should come back to stay with us another time."

The woman glanced at her husband, who nodded.

"We'll do that. Is there someone at the front desk? Can we check with them after lunch?"

"I'll be there. We'll pick a time and I'll make sure to reserve you a wonderful room."

"Thank you."

Carly nodded, then circled the room, checking to make sure everyone had drinks and seemed happy.

It was already the beginning of August. Only one more month until Labor Day and then the quiet of fall and winter. Based on how the past couple of months had gone, she was ready for a break. But happy. Times had been challenging, yet so much progress had been made.

The inn was doing great. Michelle had shared they had just enough money to see them through the quiet months, even with her paying down the mortgages. Most of their guests had already booked a weekend or two over the winter. Leonard's grant had been extended, meaning he would be staying four more months.

Helen was staying, Ellen was facing serious federal charges and Gabby was happy. Carly offered a little prayer of thanksgiving to whoever might be listening. Her life was good and she was grateful.

She seated two pairs of couples and got them their drinks. Working in the restaurant was a lot of fun. The fact that she only had to take a couple of lunch shifts a week kept it interesting rather than work. Okay, on her list of things to be happy about was her job. She couldn't imagine wanting to work anywhere else.

Michelle strolled in. "How's it going?"

"Great. We're full, as you can see. The customers are happy and yet another couple is talking about booking after the season. Yay, us."

Michelle nodded, but her attention seemed focused on something else.

"What?" Carly asked. "Is there a problem?"

"No. It's just… I've been thinking."

"Does it hurt?" Carly asked automatically, then waited for either the laugh or the rant. Either was fine. In truth, she enjoyed arguing with Michelle. They were well matched and honest. Sometimes the honesty was a little painful, but it was always welcome.

"I'm sorry," Michelle said abruptly.

Carly stared at her. "Excuse me?"

"I'm sorry. I'm sorry our parents left us and I'm sorry I didn't tell what I'd seen. I'm sorry we didn't stay friends, because that was exactly when we needed each other." Her green eyes filled with tears.

Carly blinked against unexpected emotion. "No, it's not your fault. I'm the one who rejected you after my mom left. It's my fault. I blamed you because I couldn't blame my mom. She's the one who did it. Not you. You were a kid. We both were."

"I know. But I slept with Allen. I shouldn't have. I was just so hurt."

"I was a bitch," Carly admitted. "Okay, sure, I was happy someone loved me. Or at least pretended to. But there was a part of me rubbing your nose in it. You had everything—the inn, purpose, Brenda. I know now she wasn't any great prize, but at the time, she was so much better than my dad. I was jealous of you."

"Me?" Michelle shook her head. "No. You were so sexy and popular."

"I was pretending to be a slut. That's not popular. It's stupid. Regardless, I should have believed in you."

"I should have believed in you, too," Michelle told her. "I'm sorry."

One second they were talking, then they were hugging. Carly was aware of everyone in the restaurant listening, of Helen coming out of the kitchen.

"We should charge extra for dinner theater," Carly said, her voice shaky.

Michelle laughed, then straightened. "You're my sister. I never got that before this summer. Isn't that weird?"

"I didn't get it, either."

"So we're both idiots?"

Carly laughed and wiped her face. "I guess."

Michelle grabbed her hand. "I want you to have half the inn. I want us to own this together. Partners. Then, no matter what, we'll have each other. Because we're family."

The tears came harder now. Carly tried to speak, but couldn't. To own part of the inn—to have something that was truly hers.

"Are you sure? I'd want to earn my way in."

"Don't you think you already have? I trust you, Carly. And I need you."

Carly nodded, then they were hugging again. Around them, people applauded. Michelle and Carly hung on to each other as if they would never let go.

Michelle and Chance walked out to the end of the dock, where Jared sat. There was a picnic basket beside him. He faced the setting sun, his bare feet dangling toward the water.

She joined him, sitting next to him. Chance sat between them, greeting Jared with enthusiastic whines and kisses.

"Hey, big boy," he said, putting his arm around the dog. He glanced at her. "Hey to you, too."

She smiled and pulled a soda out of the basket. "How was your day?"

"Not as exciting as yours."

She wrinkled her nose. "Tell me you did not hear about what happened in the restaurant."

"The tears, the declarations, the group hug. Oh, yeah. It's all over town."

"I need to move," she grumbled, but was smiling as she spoke. "What about privacy? What about respecting a person's right to have a life?"

"Sorry, kid. You're not going to get that here."

"I know."

Chance stretched out between them. Jared leaned in and kissed her on the mouth.

"You did a good thing," he said. "Giving Carly half the inn."

Michelle shifted uncomfortably. "She earned it and it's not like I don't need her help." She sighed. "Okay. I wanted to. I love her. I didn't mean to, but how can I help it? She was there for me. You were, too."

Which brought them to a place she didn't want to go.

"You're probably thinking I'm better now. That I should move on so you can open your house to some other vet in need."

She kept her voice light, as if she wouldn't be hurt by whatever he said.

"I do think you should move," he told her, looking at her. "But I was thinking more about down the hall. Into my room."

She clutched the cold can and did her best to process the statement. He was asking her to...

"I'm out of the healing business," he said. "I'm ready for something different." One corner of his mouth turned up. "I'm ready for you, Michelle. For us. For what the future brings. Stay with me. You and me and Chance."

She swallowed against a flood of emotion. "I'd like that."

"Good."

He put his arm around her. She shifted closer, leaning against both him and the dog. Chance sighed with contentment and closed his eyes.

"Maybe we could have a couple of kids," Jared added.

Kids? "You mean get married and start a family? Or something like that," she added, realizing he'd never said the *M* word.

The half smile turned into a grin. "Something exactly like that."

She did her best to keep from jumping up and screaming. It wouldn't be cool. But she did it on the inside and it felt just as wonderful. Then she bent down and pulled off her shoes, letting her bare feet dangle in the water.

Carly and Gabby walked down the road after their swimming lesson. The inn rose in front of them, all peaked roof and sparkling windows. She loved everything about the place, she thought contentedly. Especially the half that was hers.

She still couldn't believe Michelle had been so generous. But just last week they'd gone to a lawyer and started the paperwork. After all this time, she and Gabby would have security and a permanent home.

Gabby dragged her towel on the pavement, but Carly didn't care. Today was a good day.

"You did so great, Mom," Gabby said, dancing alongside her. "We both did."

Carly nodded. "You're fearless."

"I'm not afraid of swimming anymore. But you are

and you put your face in the water, anyway. The teacher said she was impressed."

Carly laughed. It was easier now, knowing she didn't have to face the dreaded pool for another week. "Thanks."

Up ahead Sam sat on the porch, waiting. Carly felt her heart jump a little when she spotted him. Gabby rushed ahead, eager to spend time with him.

When Gabby reached the porch, she said something to Sam, then turned and yelled, "Hurry! They're here!"

"Who's here?"

Gabby laughed. "Not who. Daisies. Michelle ordered you special daisies and they're here." The girl slapped both hands against her mouth as her eyes widened. "I wasn't supposed to tell," she mumbled.

Beside her, Sam laughed. "It's okay. She can pretend to be surprised."

Special daisies? Carly hurried to the porch. Not just to see the daisies, but because the best part of her world was waiting right there.

* * * * *

Visit www.BlackberryIsland.com for a **wealth** of bonus content about the quaint island and its inhabitants. You'll find a map of the island to print out for your book group, recipes, local news stories and more.

Suggested Lunch Menu

Helen's Chicken Salad sandwiches (recipe follows)
Italian Vegetable Soup (recipe follows)
Sugar cookies decorated to look like daisies for dessert

HELEN'S CHICKEN SALAD

4 cups cooked chicken, diced
1/2 cup diced celery
1/2 cup diced onion
1/2 cup diced apple
1/2 cup chopped pecans
1/2 cup shredded sharp cheddar cheese
1 cup mayonnaise
1 tablespoon mild vinegar (rice wine vinegar is great)
1/4 teaspoon salt
1/4 teaspoon pepper

Rotisserie chicken from the grocery store works great in this salad. Just take off the skin and finely dice the chicken. Or you can cook frozen chicken breasts. The best thing about these sandwiches is that they're easy to make. They can also be pretty healthy if you use fat-free cheese and fat-free mayonnaise.

Assemble the sandwiches on your favorite type of bread The Blackberry Island Inn uses focaccia bread, but Helen's fabulous chicken salad tastes great on every kind of bread.

ITALIAN VEGETABLE SOUP

2 tablespoons olive oil
1 onion, diced
4 cloves garlic, minced
1 cup carrots, sliced
1 cup green beans, chopped into 1/2-inch pieces
6 cups vegetable broth
1 can diced tomatoes with juice
1 zucchini, sliced
1 teaspoon dried basil
1/2 teaspoon dried oregano
1/2 teaspoon dried thyme
1/2 teaspoon salt
1/2 teaspoon pepper
1 bay leaf

Heat the olive oil in a heavy-bottomed soup pot. Add the onions and garlic and sauté until fragrant, about 30 seconds. Add the carrots, beans and vegetable broth. Heat to boiling. Lower the heat, cover and simmer for about 10 minutes. Add the remaining ingredients and simmer for 15 minutes more. (If you want a soupier soup, you can add more vegetable broth along with the remaining ingredients.)

For more free recipes, join the Members Only area at www.susanmallery.com!

Readers' Group Discussion Guide

1. What are the major themes of this story? How does the title support those themes? Explain your thoughts.

2. What story events caused the characters to change and grow? Who changed the most? Explain.

3. Author Susan Mallery is widely lauded for evoking strong reader emotions with her books. Which moments in *Barefoot Season* triggered the strongest emotions in you? Did the ending satisfy you, or do you wish the story would have had a different ending?

4. Did you relate most to Carly or Michelle? Why?

5. Why do you think Michelle was so angry with Carly when she first returned? According to Carly, *she* was the one who had the right to be angry. Do you agree? Why or why not?

6. Carly's past haunted her. Why do you think Carly stayed on Blackberry Island? Would you have moved to a different town? Why or why not? How have you changed since high school?

7. Michelle was damaged by the war, both physically and emotionally. Do you think her emotional damage would have been reduced if she hadn't also been injured physically? Why or why not? Do you think she would have healed faster? Why or why

not? Do you know someone who has been to war? Did he or she come back a different person?

8. What did you think of Damaris when she first appeared in *Barefoot Season?* How did your feelings about her change as the story progressed? How did you feel about Michelle's decision as to what to do about Damaris?

9. Have you ever stayed at a private inn or B and B? Did you like it more or less than staying at a hotel chain? Why?

10. What did you think of Chance and Mr. Whiskers? Have you ever known a dog and cat that became friends? Have you rescued an animal?